To know Bandy is to love him

D0550592

THREE CHEERS FOR ME

THE BANDY PAPERS, VOLUME ONE

Donald Jack

This edition published in 2017 by Farrago, an imprint
of Prelude Books Ltd
13 Carrington Road, Richmond, TW10 5AA, United Kingdom

www.farragobooks.com

By arrangement with Sybertooth Inc.

First published by Macmillan (New York) in 1962 and Heinemann
(London) in 1963. This edition follows the revised 1973 text, including
the author's changes and additions to make it the beginning of a series
rather than a standalone work.

ISBN: 978-1-911440-45-1

Have you read them all?

Treat yourself again to the first Bandy Papers novels –

Three Cheers for Me
Young Bandy doesn't seem cut out for life in the armed services, as we meet him at the start of the First World War.

That's Me in the Middle
Fortune's wheel is on the turn, leading to a series of edge-of-the-seat adventures for Bandy.

It's Me Again
The RAF top brass don't know what to do with maverick flying ace and well-known loose cannon Bart Bandy.

___

Turn to the end of this book for a full list of the series, plus – on the last page – **bonus access to a short radio play** by the author.

Part One

Part One

Beamington

ASTRIDE A DIRT road leading half-heartedly to Ottawa twenty miles away sprawled Beamington, Ontario, a town of sunbaked, frost cracked brick, splintering timber, and brown grass. It was a good town: there was no place where you could get a drink but there were nine churches.

As I walked down the main street, a dog with a long pink lolling tongue opened one glazed eye, then climbed to its feet with enormous effort. That dog had known me for fourteen years. It barked furiously.

I had a framed photograph under one arm and a rifle under the other. As I passed the hitch rack of the general store, one of the hired hands balanced on the rail pushed back his hat and said something derogatory. I gave no sign that I had overheard the remark, mainly because I hadn't. The farmers sitting in the shade of the store awning were all grinning. I nodded politely.

'Afternoon,' I said.

'Where you going with the gun, Lieutenant?' one of them said. 'Ain't no Germans hereabouts.'

I gave them my bland look, calculated to drive a man mad at forty paces.

'Lieutenant,' someone else remarked thoughtfully. 'I got a feeling the war's going to last a long time yet.'

Mr Hummock, who owned a farm close to the river, nodded wisely and prepared to speak. Everyone waited expectantly for the words of wisdom, for old Hummock was renowned in Beamington for his epigrams and his penetrating observations on the passing show. I slowed down to listen.

Old Hummock leaned over with infinite care until his belt creaked, and slavered neatly through a crack in the planking. He then spoke.

'I bet,' he said, decisively.

They all relaxed again in the shade.

Me, at Home

I CONTINUED ON out of town until I reached my private valley near the railway track. I put the rifle aside and broke the glass in the photograph against a fencepost.

As I picked out the remaining slivers I examined the photograph with care.

It was a group picture of about thirty young gentlemen, all staring glumly at the camera. There were eight of them in the front row, sitting on what looked like broken bottles. They looked anxious. The ten men behind them looked slightly less unhappy; they were sitting on a bench. In the centre of this row was an old man with side whiskers. He was actually smiling, although rather contemptuously. He had an armchair to sit in.

The eleven gentlemen in the back row were all standing. Behind them was an ivy-covered mansion. Through one of the upstairs windows an insane sheep seemed to be peering short-sightedly, but this may have been a trick of the light or a fault in the negative.

I jammed the photograph in the fork of a tree, then picked up the rifle and ammunition and walked back seventy-five feet, took aim, and put neat holes in five of the eight faces in the front row.

Quite pleased, but vowing to do better on the second row, I got down on my stomach and supported the barrel on a rock. Again the shots snapped and echoed through the railway cutting.

I walked back to the photo and saw that the last shot was fully two inches from the end face in the row.

As I fired at the last row a chipmunk scuttled along a fallen tree. A faint breeze rustled the leaves around me. I mention this because one of the leaves drifted down and spoiled my aim, and the bullet hit the frame and knocked the picture askew.

Apart from the last shot I was quite pleased to see that except for the second man from the left I had scored on all the faces. I hadn't fired at the second face because it belonged to my father, the Reverend Mr Bandy.

As I was looking at my father, a starling flew low overhead. Without thinking, I raised the rifle and fired at it. A single feather detached itself, and the starling dropped out of sight behind the railway embankment. I felt ashamed, killing that bird. I climbed over the fence on to the track, but it had fallen into the dense undergrowth near the river edge; so I turned back and, sitting on the grass, contemplated the riddled photograph again. I was faintly surprised to see that Father had once been young.

After a moment I threw away the two dozen faceless neophytes, lay back with my head cradled, and gazed over the river toward Quebec Province, feeling contented.

Not that I had much to be contented about. There was, for instance, my long face, which I knew to be smooth, bland, and maddening. Even at the age of fourteen its lack of expression had led me into many fights with other Beamington boys. I think the situation was that, just as they felt an urge to chalk slogans and fallacies on walls, so most of them felt impelled to express themselves on the blank wall of my face. I was always coming home with bruised lips or red marks on my cheeks. But the harder they hit me, the more determined I became that they should not affect my expression. I had got used to it. I liked it. I thought it looked aristocratic. It was an imperturbable face, and there was nothing they could do about it. After some years they began to give up, as if they had tried to make their mark on the world and had failed.

They grew bitter and cynical, volunteered for the army in droves, killed themselves or went to Regina, Saskatchewan.

I leaned upon my elbow, a little dizzy from the heat of the sun, and looked around, wondering idly but without much interest if I would ever see my native countryside again. I was leaving for the war in two days. It was July 1916.

I could see ten miles of the Ottawa River, and it reminded me of the time when I had been dared by several school friends to swim the river at this its widest point. I got across all right, and only then realized the catch: by the time I had recovered strength for the return journey it would be almost dark. They probably expected me to walk back by way of Ottawa, but that would have meant a journey of thirty miles. It was after midnight when I swam back to Ontario and three in the morning when I got home. My mother thrashed me, she had been so worried.

'How did you get on?' they asked next morning at school, tittering.

'Oh, all right. The water was a bit cold,' I had mumbled. Several of those boys had been over in France now for more than a year. I wondered if I would get across in time, before the war ended. News from the front was confusing, but several victories on the Somme had been claimed, and it was said that the Germans would be beaten by Christmas.

Of course, they had said that in 1914 and 1915; still... As I lay on my back with my hands behind my head, the sun warming my face, I sighed in contentment. I imagined myself charging a machine-gun nest single-handed. The King pinning a medal on my chest. 'Jolly good show, Bandy old man.' 'Thank you, your Majesty.' 'I'm having a cup of tea with the Archbishop of Canterbury later on. Would you care to join us?' Having tea with the Archbishop would make my father very proud. Fighting for King and Country and the Archbishop was a glorious thought. I felt full of patriotism and divine fervour, fighting for God and His victory against the barbaric Teutonic hordes who had been bayoneting Belgian babies steadily since 1914 according to the newspapers. I prayed, not for victory, for with God on our side that was assured, but that I might remain strong in my faith. I had had cause of late to reproach myself severely for slight waverings of devotion. These waverings, for some reason, almost invariably occurred in church. I arose, cleansed and with a new purity. The following evening, however, I was wavering disgracefully again when my father preached a sermon about Warriors going to the Wars in the cause of Truth and Freedom, with obscure and rather lame references to me. It was one thing to formulate these ideas to oneself, but it was a little embarrassing to be told them by someone else.

I was sitting in the family pew wearing a brand-new uniform and staring obliviously at my badges of rank. The single pip on each sleeve looked very lonely, and as I sat there, still as a mouse so as not to annoy my mother with the creaking of my Sam Browne, I found myself imagining these symbols to be not cloth stars but the crossed swords and batons of a general. General Bandy . . . General Bartholomew Bandy. It sounded quite good. General Sir Bartholomew Bandy, K.C.V.O. That sounded even better. Earl Bandy and Baron Bandy of Beamington. Hm.

But the truth, when you got right down to it, was that my *reveries heroiques* lacked conviction; I just could not see myself attaining a senior position in the army. It was an effort not to admit that I would probably have to struggle hard merely to maintain my present inferiority....

This would never do. I was wavering again. I forced myself to pay attention as my father thundered onward.

'... and the longer this war goes on, the clearer we understand the meaning of it, my friends ...' he was saying. The Reverend Mr Bandy had his long thin hands clasped tightly behind his gown as if each hand were trying to strangle the other, and as he rose and fell on his heels, his silvery hair rose and fell. I knew he was dying to pace up and down, but there was no room in the pulpit. 'It is the Great Adventure, not just against the barbaric legions of the heathen Hun, but against all revolutionaries, theorists, anarchists, and Charles Darwin.' My father had a spite against Darwin. *The Origin of Species* had been published more than half a century before, but the news had only recently filtered through to Beamington. 'This is the twentieth century crusade against the forces of evil and unrest abroad in the world that lie twisting and writhing in the bosoms of city dwellers, proletarians, and the godless theorists who have sprung up in the slime of modern civilization, while all about us, my dear friends, we see change, unrest, discontent, rebellion, new demands by the proletariat, critics of privilege, new and vile theories on everything from the nature of matter to the origin of man; while... while...'

Here my father paused, and I guessed that he had forgotten what he was going to say. This often happened, but such was the power of his personality that even a roomful of strong-minded and impatient farmers had been known to wait open-mouthed and spellbound, just as now the congregation was waiting in tense silence. He had even kept a bishop waiting once. The bishop had hung on to one of my father's sentences for so long that he had missed his train and had to be put up for the night in the spare bedroom, which he had to abandon hurriedly at three in the morning when the cat came in and made a mess in the corner. My father blamed that cat for his lack of advancement in the hierarchy.

As the Reverend Mr Bandy collected his thoughts and graduated to patriotism and duty, my eye strayed from the khaki sleeve to the bare arm in the lap beside me. It was a freckled forearm, with faint gold hairs. They were attached to Mabel, the doctor's daughter. I had been courting Mabel House for a long time; we were childhood sweethearts. She had once given me a black eye for pulling her pigtails. Everyone had expected us to marry as soon as I had obtained my degree in medicine from the University of Toronto, but I'd failed the fourth year, after shooting the Professor of Surgery in the back during some C.O.T.C. manoeuvres and then trying to pry out the bullet with a rusty penknife blade normally used for digging stones out of horses' hoofs. I'd subsequently gone

15

to Camp Niagara for infantry training. There had been the devil to pay at home when they found out.

Mabel's hand lay limply in her lap, palm upward. It looked inviting, and for a moment I wondered if she wanted to hold hands. But it would never do to hold hands in church.

I glanced at her curiously as she looked demurely at her lap. Was she sorry to see me go? It was hard to tell; she wasn't an emotional girl at all, very steady and serene, and she never fainted except on appropriate occasions, such as mice and scandalous suggestions.

To my right sat my mother in a voluminous dress that smelled of mothballs and old newspapers. Her clothes rustled like stealthy movements in the undergrowth. She had thin, bloodless lips.

My own lips were far from bloodless, and when I was twelve I had announced that I considered them sensuous. My father had been scandalized. I don't know why; I had inherited them from him.

Mother was devout and passionless. I had never seen her angry, even when she was thrashing me. On the other hand it was difficult to tell when she was pleased.

At last the sermon came to an end and a hymn was announced while at the same time the collection plates were brought out. My father always chose a rousing hymn during collection in the hope that the congregation might be spurred to recklessness with their dimes and quarters. By the third verse I became aware that both Mabel and Mother were half turned away from me as if I were doing something improper, but I was only singing.

As the organ thundered out the last verse in fortissimo, I raised my voice in an ecstasy of devotion, my mouth stretched to its limits for the final, bloodcurdling Amen. I really felt like singing that Sunday evening.

The service over, my father stalked solemnly from the pulpit. As the late July sunlight streamed through the stained-glass saints and the organist caressed a final murmur of music from the golden pipes, the congregation whispered and rustled, wallowed under the pews for lost handbags, coughed daintily into hand-crocheted lace, or tugged surreptitiously at undergarments that had tightened during the long service. As soon as he was out of sight, Mr Bandy fled through the side door, his gown streaming in the wind and dashed round to intercept his flock as it straggled out the front entrance. As he began shaking hands he clicked his lips as was his habit, pleased that none of his parishioners had managed to get away without the minister's usual words of condolence, encouragement, or guidance. Only on the grocer's son did he frown, strongly suspecting him of putting fly buttons in the collection plate.

Among the last to emerge were Dr and Mrs House, and Mabel.

'Good evening, Doctor, Mrs House,' Mr Bandy said, shaking hands. 'And Mabel. Well, well, well, we've grown up to be a very pretty young lady, haven't we?' he added gallantly, mistaking Mabel's embarrassment for modesty.

'She'll make some young fellow a fine wife,' Dr House said, looking around. I was just coming out with the tail end of the shuffling congregation. The Reverend Mr Bandy found himself shaking hands with an army officer in a spotless uniform.

'Well, young man, off to fight for King and Country, eh?' he said, nodding approvingly. Then he saw it was me. He tried to snatch his hand away but I was still shaking it.

'Let go,' Father hissed, gritting his teeth at my stupidity.

I let go and moved over to Mother and the doctor.

As Father commiserated for the fifth Sunday with a mother who had lost a son at the Front (advising her that his loss had been for the greater glory of God and informing her, as he strove to recall the boy's name, that his country would never forget him), the doctor turned to me.

'Well, Bartholomew, off tomorrow, aren't you?'

'Yes, sir.'

'Good, good. And I'm sure you'll be a credit to your parents.'

'Yes, sir.'

'Fight hard, live clean; then you won't go far wrong.'

'No, sir.'

The doctor looked at me severely for a moment, then took my arm and drew me aside, away from the ladies.

'Word of advice, Bartholomew,' he said, putting his hands behind his back and flapping his coattails vigorously, as if trying to get up airspeed for a quick flight around the church graveyard. It did not seem unlikely, for the doctor strongly resembled a bird, with his thin, scraggly neck, hooked nose and beady, searching eyes. What kind of bird, I wondered. A vulture? 'This liquor business,' he said. He paused and inclined his head towards me. (Yes, a vulture. Vegetarian, though.) 'Don't do it,' the doctor murmured.

'I wouldn't think of it, sir.'

'No good, you know, Bartholomew.'

'No, sir.'

House plucked at my lapel. 'Not even for warmth, my boy. That's the thin edge. Lot of men out there' – he jerked his head in the direction of the trenches, just beyond the churchyard gates –'they issue rum and stuff like that to keep them warm.' He shook his head slowly. 'No, my boy. It's not true warmth. Just the illusion of warmth. What happens is that the alcohol shrinks your veins and arteries, stimulates the nerve endings in the stomach, like acid, you see, giving you the illusion of warmth flowing through your body, while in actual fact... you see?'

'Yes, I see,' I whined. 'Mm, yes.'

The admonition was wasted anyway. I would never dream of drinking spirits, nor had any intention, if I may be so literary, of letting beer foam brush my lips with even the most Platonic of kisses.

'And also,' House went on, 'it destroys your brain. Every drink, every single dram, even the tiniest of tots destroys one more brain cell.' He stepped back and glared at me triumphantly. 'Three drinks – poof. Three brain cells gone. Ten drinks, ten cells. Before you know where you are – bang! A whole segment of your brain gone.'

'That's true, sir,' I said. The possibility of my taking a drink was so remote that I hardly bothered to formulate even to myself the knowledge that there were several billion brain cells and that liquor would eat away my kidneys long before it got even a foothold under my skull.

As I walked home in the mellow sunlight under a dappled canopy of leaves, Mabel also set about me.

'I suppose,' she said, pouting prettily, 'you'll soon forget me when you meet some of those beautiful European women.'

'Never,' I said, drawing the word out like an elastic band. We came slowly to a stop. There was no one in sight. I put my arm gently around her waist and was thrilled when she did not draw away.

'Even if you're gone for six whole months?'

'Even then.'

'Father says the war won't be over before Christmas.'

I leaned over but she drew away. 'Promise me you won't have anything to do with any other girls? They say the French girls are not so strong-willed as us.'

'If you'll give me a kiss, hm?'

Kissing had never really appealed to me very much, not that I had kissed anyone other than Mabel, a few aunts and Mother; but I thought perhaps that Mabel expected it

'Do you really love me, Bartholomew?'

This implied that I had already declared my love. I hadn't; but her lips were moist and her blonde hair gleamed in the filtered sun.

'I do, of course,' I said, trying to convert my treacherous voice to normal modulation. I pursed my lips and managed to bring them to within an inch of her dewy mouth before she withdrew again.

She stroked my cheek with one finger. 'You haven't promised yet,' she said with a slight and forlorn lisp.

Promised what? I hesitated, trying to remember what it was. I gave it up.

'I promise,' I said.

She let me kiss her; but drew away briskly after only two seconds.

'We'll be late for dinner,' she said.

My parents' idea of a send-off for me was a dinner of underdone mutton, gritty cabbage, and tinkling glasses of ice water with bouquets of chlorine; and their own friends. When coffee was served and everyone had finished praising Mother's cooking, the ladies retired to the front room and the men indulged in risqué tattle about livestock and the government. Nobody smoked; my father did not permit it.

Half an hour passed before Uncle Simon remembered with a start that the evening was supposed to belong to me. He looked at me, who at the age of twenty-three had been allowed to sit in with the men for the first time in my life and who had been glancing every two minutes at Mabel, just visible through the doorway, knitting. I had not spoken a word all evening. My father considered that minors (anyone under twenty-nine) should be seen but not heard. By half-past eight I was wishing that I could be neither seen nor heard.

'Well, Bartholomew, all ready to do your bit, eh, all packed, eh? I suppose by this time next month you'll be on the Field of Battle, performing Deeds of Derring-Do, eh?'

'He'll be in England for more training, I expect,' Coates the solicitor said. 'Forster's boy was stuck near Folkestone for months before he ever set foot in France.'

'How's he getting on?'

'Who, Forster's boy? He got trench foot'

'In the trenches?'

'In England.'

Uncle Simon cranked himself round toward me and took a wheezing breath. I looked at him with an expression of attentive respect born of long practice.

'Don't forget to keep your feet in good condition, my boy,' he said. 'A soldier's feet are his fortune.'

'Yes, Uncle.'

'I believe the casualties from trench foot are dreadful,' he went on.

'Plain carelessness,' said House. 'No excuse at all. It may be a little damp at the front, but to let your feet get that way is inexcusable. I see in the papers where the generals are thinking of punishing anyone who so abuses his extremities.'

'Quite right,' Mr Bandy said from the head of the table. Everyone turned to him, expecting him to go on; but apparently having nothing to add, he added nothing. I surmised that he was feeling uncomfortable after the mutton, and was wondering uneasily if some sheep parasite might not already be at work on his colon.

'So you remember, my boy,' Uncle Simon said, 'to keep a good supply of hot water always at hand.'

'And clean socks,' Coates said.

'Rub your feet thoroughly with oil,' Dr House said.

'Wash them at least once a month,' a farmer said.

'Don't forget to cut your toenails,' another farmer added. They all looked at him, and there was a moment's silence.

'What's that got to do with it?' House asked.

'Well, long toenails look kind of untidy,' the farmer said defensively. 'Especially when they start to curl underneath.'

There was another silence as they all sat, stupefied with mutton, and thought about my toenails. In the next room the ladies could be heard animatedly discussing knitting yarns and pickles. I heard Mabel joining in. Her tones were bright with interest.

'Don't fidget, Bartholomew,' the Reverend Mr Bandy said, belching devoutly.

At last, the ladies and gentlemen gathered in the front room and discussed subjects suitable to the Lord's Day and mixed company.

Even with three lamps burning, the front room was gloomy, with baleful shadows and starkly outlined faces. It rather reminded me of the dissecting room at the university, a very crowded dissecting room, for what space was left after the celebrants had tried to make themselves comfortable was taken up by several tons of greasy furniture. There were horsehair sofas, tottering tables, plant-pot stands, uneasy chairs, potted vegetation with dank, lifeless leaves, a vast black piano that I had been forced to play for fifteen solid years, mouldy drapes, a stack of sermons rotting on the windowsill and a picture of me in a sailor suit looking as if I needed to go to the bathroom.

I was grateful for the gloom, however, and for the bulk of Elward Coates, the solicitor, for he took up most of the sofa, forcing me close to Mabel. I was acutely conscious of the contact of her hip. For twenty minutes I had been trying to summon up courage to move even closer, perhaps even to hold her hand; but her fingers were in full view of the company and were busy with her knitting. I stared a little irritably at the anonymous garment she was purling and plaining, wondering what it would grow up to be. Judging by its present shape, it was to be a mitten for an octopus.

I took a deep breath preparatory to the convulsive and apparently motiveless move that would bring my hip even more firmly in contact with hers. Everyone had been sitting in profound silence for several minutes. All I needed was someone to speak and divert attention.

'You play the piano, don't you, Bartholomew?' Dr House said suddenly. 'Perhaps, as this is a special occasion, the Reverend might permit you to pick out some simple, wholesome melody suitable to a Sunday.'

Immediately everyone got up and began to babble excuses, glancing anxiously and repeatedly at their watches.

'Perhaps we'd better not keep Bartholomew up too late, don't you think?' Uncle Simon said.

Everyone agreed with alacrity, 'Bartholomew has to be especially wide awake tomorrow,' someone said, quite unnecessarily, I thought.

'What time are you leaving, Bartholomew?'

'Six,' I said.

'Hm, well, you'll need a good night's rest. I imagine it will be some time before you have a decent bed to lie in; the army, they say, is not noted for luxurious hostelry.'

Mabel smiled sweetly at me from the doorway. 'It will help him,' she said, 'to appreciate everything that has been done for him at home all these years.' She turned her smile on my mother, who twitched her nose. Mother was evidently pleased.

Meanwhile, everyone was trying to get through the doorway at the same time.

'They say the hammocks on board the troopships are comfortable enough, and the perfect answer to seasickness,' Uncle Simon said as he elbowed his way through, 'because the ship sways all around you but the hammock remains stationary.'

'A little adaptability under any circumstances should help him,' House said from the hallway. I followed them out. 'The main thing is to adapt quickly. You can sit comfortably even in mud if you use your head.'

'You mean, sit on my head in the mud?' I asked, my disappointment getting the better of me.

There was a surprised silence.

'Don't be foolish, Bartholomew,' Father said. 'I've noticed an increasing flippancy in him these last few days,' he went on. 'I sincerely hope the army is not going to coarsen you, Bartholomew.'

'Anyway, a little discomfort won't hurt you,' Mrs House said after a pause. 'You've been spoiled and pampered too long as it is.'

At the door the guests bade me an interminable goodbye. The doctor turned good-humouredly to me.

'Perhaps you would like to walk Mabel home, Bartholomew?'

'It's a little late,' Mrs House said with an expectant-motherly smile.

'Oh, I'm sure Bartholomew will deliver her safely, eh?' the doctor twinkled.

'Yes, sir,' I piped, wondering why House always made me feel ten years old. Father made me feel at least fifteen. Still, the doctor was a good sort, really – understanding. I was about to signify my gratitude when he added, 'All we ask is that Mabel be inside not later than ten o'clock.'

It was already half past nine, and it took fifteen minutes to walk to the doctor's house.

Mrs House giggled. 'Well, seeing as Bart is leaving tomorrow, I think we might let Mabel stay out an extra half-hour.' She smiled pointedly at me. 'I'm sure they have lots to discuss.'

There was a snicker. Mabel looked down with a faint blush. Everyone was staring at us. My father grunted moodily from the depths of the hall.

Mr Coates offered his hand. It felt like a legal document, and his large gold ring bit into my hand like a seal.

'Goodbye, young man,' he said, breathing heavily. He leaned forward. 'Don't forget you're a minister's son, my boy, and deport yourself accordingly.' The hair in his nostrils fluttered wildly. 'And kill a few Huns for me, won't you?'

He laughed abruptly, coughed in admiration of his own patriotism, and strode into the tepid twilight.

'Keep your feet dry,' the churchwarden said as he wrung my hand.

'Yes, sir.'

'And your musket,' a farmer added.

'Yes.'

'Goodbye, Bartholomew,' the farmer's wife said. 'Don't forget, you promised to write to us.'

'Yes, ma'am.' I glanced at the clock.

'What did you say, Bartholomew?' Father asked.

'Nothing, sir.'

'Oh. I could have sworn that you uttered a faint groan.'

One by one the guests, camphor-smelling in their Sunday best, wandered through the garden, stopped to exchange a few last words at the gate, then went home thankfully, no doubt contrasting the Reverend Mr Bandy's conversation and Mrs Bandy's cooking unfavourably with their own, and my lack of spirit with the healthy exuberance of their own offspring.

As we neared the doctor's house, I put my arm around Mabel. To my astonishment she burst into tears and pressed her face against my chest.

'Oh, Bart, what will I do when you're gone?' she wept. 'You may be away months!' She clung to me. It was quite pleasant. Nobody had ever clung to me before. I decided I liked being clung to.

'There, there,' I said, and patted her shoulder. This was better than I had anticipated. I tried to raise her face, but it refused to tilt. I felt my tunic becoming moist. The tears actually were genuine!

'I don't know why you had to volunteer for this rotten war anyway.'

Neither did I. 'They say the government of Sir Robert Borden intends to introduce conscription soon anyway,' I said. 'In my opinion, Sir Robert —'

'All the best boys are going to get themselves killed,' she sobbed. 'It's horrible.'

I felt very flattered. It was the nicest thing she had ever said to me. 'Don't you worry, dearest,' I murmured, 'I'll look after myself.'

'Oh, I'm not worried about you,' she said.

I started slightly.

'I know *you'll* be all right,' she said.

When I thought about it, nobody seemed in the least worried about my safety. 'What makes you so sure?' I asked.

'You're the kind of person who always survives,' she said, withdrawing and dabbing at her eyes with a lace handkerchief.

'Don't know why you should say that, Mabel. I've never been particularly lucky. How do you mean?'

'I don't know... I just can't see it, that's all. Everyone believes you'll come back all right.'

'Well then,' I said, feeling inexplicably gloomy, 'I don't see why you're crying.'

'You're horrible,' she said, and began crying again.

'I'm sorry, Mabel; I didn't mean it.' I tried to put my arm around her again, but her waist was stiff. I have always been tolerant about stiff manners, upper lips, tasks, and necks, but stiff waists I detest. They're so — stiff.

'You did mean it. You're always saying the wrong things.'

'What wrong things?'

'Always so – so calm.'

I stood there looking at her helplessly.

'So unromantic,' she added, sniffing.

'I'm trying to be romantic but you won't let me near you.'

'That's not what I mean.'

'Well, what do you mean then, Mabel?' I inquired. I wished she would sit down; my legs were beginning to ache.

'Oh, be quiet,' she said angrily. But then she suddenly threw her arms around me. 'Oh, Bart, do you really love me? Really and truly?' she said, looking up. Her lips were moist.

'Of course,' I said, tightening my arms around her. Her stays pressed against my ribs. I hesitated, then bent over to kiss her.

'And you'll always be mine?'

I kissed her. She kissed back with unexpected fire. I don't know what came over her. Her face was like a hot-water bottle. I was longing to sit down and rest my legs.

'Let's sit down,' I said.

She pulled away. 'We mustn't,' she said confusedly.

'Mustn't what?' I asked. 'I only want to sit down. My –'

'We're not even engaged,' she said. Her breathing was unsteady, and she looked as if she were going to swoon. What on earth was the matter with the girl?

'Come on,' I said, my eyes fixed on the garden seat.

She pulled away again. She was breathing hard, and I do believe she was trembling. 'Don't spoil it, dearest,' she murmured.

'Spoil what?' I asked.

'There you go again,' she said. She took a deep breath and seemed to recover. We were silent for a moment, looking at each other. 'I'd better go in,' she said coldly, holding on to a tree, 'or my father will be coming out.' She didn't move. 'It would be different,' she went on, 'if...'

'If what?'

She didn't answer but just looked at me.

It was all very confusing, but I think she was hinting at our engagement. Well, why not? I thought. I liked her. I – yes, loved her. I must love her. I had known her all my life. We had climbed trees together. She was just about the prettiest girl in Beamington. Everyone was sure we were going to announce our engagement. My father was not against it. Not that that had anything to do with it. I loved her. Everyone said so. She was beautiful in the moonlight

'Mabel.'

'Yes, Bartholomew?' she breathed.

'I – I –'

She waited almost thirty seconds. Dash it, why did we have to stand up and talk?

'I must go in,' she said. She held out her hand. 'Goodbye, Bartholomew.' She waited, half turned away, her hand outstretched, her virginal glove a phosphorescent yellow in the moonlight.

For no reason I suddenly recalled her hands as they knitted in our front parlour an hour ago, and remembered her voice raised in animated discussion on the merits of various knitting yarns and pickles. I knew what she was waiting for, what they were all waiting for, especially the Houses. They wanted Mabel to be comfortable, to have a professional man as a husband.

The pause lengthened. I had a sudden vision of the Houses just the other side of that wall. Both the doctor and Mrs House would be waiting inside for us; and when we came in hand in hand, pink with embarrassment and joie de vivre, they would rise and shake my hand and gloat over us, twitching and slavering a little with pleasure.

The thought suddenly terrified me. I held out my hand. 'Goodbye then, Mabel,' I blurted. 'I'll – m'yes, I'll see you when I come back or something. It shouldn't be long, I guess.'

She faced me, smiling brightly. 'Don't count on it, though, Bart.' She smiled.

'Don't count on what, Mabel?'

She smiled even more brightly. 'Who knows what might happen in the next six months? You never know. Not all the good-looking boys have gone to the war. There's no law that says that I have to wait for you, is there?'

I looked at her lovely face and the faint gleam that was now all I could see of her eyes, the gentle rise of her bosom, her calm beauty, and the glow of her hair like a halo against the canopy of trees behind her; and I got all choked up inside.

I remembered the good times we had had together, climbing the Gatineau Hills. I remembered the picnics we had had together, and paddling in the river, and reading Dickens and Shakespeare together; and I recalled her protectiveness toward me, looking after me, scolding me (but gently), and our sitting in church side by side, Sunday after Sunday, and how nice she had always been even during my most difficult years in school.

I decided that I detested her.

Of course it was a shock.

I'd known her all my life. We were considered inseparable. Our destinies had seemed intertwined as firmly as – two links in a lavatory chain.

Moreover, I had been brought up on the biblical pure white abstracts of truth, love, and charity. There had been no room for shades of emotional perversion such as this. But there it was. I'd had a sudden, hideous prescience: myself, sunk in an armchair with an Ottawa newspaper and slippers, trapped opposite Mabel twisting jumbo yarn into yet another tiny garment; and the pit-ter-patter of tiny Mabels all over the house, putting their sticky fingers in my ears.

'After all, Bartholomew, I'm a tiny bit older than you, as you know.'

'Yes,' I said in a panic. 'Three years older, yes.'

There was a silence, and I seemed to be hearing a faint grinding noise.

'I can't wait forever,' she answered. It sounded as if she were speaking through her teeth.

I shook her glove again. 'M'yes, you're quite right, Mabel,' I said. 'Yes, quite right.' I patted her on the shoulder. 'Well,' I cleared my throat, then waited for her to say something.

She said nothing, so I moved away toward the garden gate, tripping over a root.

At the gate I looked back. 'Well, bye-bye, Mabel. And, um, the best of luck, er... Mabel.' I closed the gate. 'My dear,' I added, laughing. I was perspiring.

I heard the front door slam from a quarter of a mile away. As soon as I reached the narrow lane that ran parallel to the river, I took off my tunic and mopped my face. My heart was just beginning to slow down to normal tempo.

I was astonished at myself, and more than a little distressed. Mabel was part of my life. My conduct had been deplorable. I had finally revealed myself in my true colours: grey and – and dark grey. I stood unmasked as an unfeeling, unromantic cad. I took a deep breath to ease the agitation of my limbs. Where were my tolerance, my chivalry, my reverence for women, my – everything? What kind of person was I? Beastly.

I had disappointed everyone. I would be frowned on from one end of the Ottawa Valley to the other. I knew how uncomfortable the disapproval of others could be in a place like Beamington. I was for it. At least, I would have been for it if I weren't going away.

I turned into the winding lane and found myself humming a popular song, but quickly stopped myself, ashamed. A popular song, too, not even a hymn. I was despicable.

I found myself walking on my hands. I threw my tunic in the air, walked on my hands, jumped to my feet, and caught the tunic just before it reached the ground. It was obvious that I was rapidly going to the dogs, but I felt so light – light-headed, I suppose.

A sound made me start. I turned and saw Denise Webster sitting on a gate, clapping her hands.

'Very good. Do it again.'

Embarrassed, I pulled on my tunic and began to fasten it. I had been behaving with a disgraceful lack of dignity. I felt very annoyed with Denise.

Denise was known as the Bad Girl of Beamington. We had been to school together. I had been hearing scandalous tales about her during the past year, including nefarious doings in the barley.

I looked at her disapprovingly. She was perched on the top bar of the gate, swinging her legs and not even having the decency to look arch or coy.

'You look happy, Bartholomew Bandy.'

I hesitated, wondering whether to walk on and ignore her.

'So you finally proposed to Mabel. Good for you.'

Denise was gripping the bar on each side. Her shoulders were thrown back, and in her white blouse with an open neck and long dark skirt she looked undeniably attractive, outlined against the moonlit river.

'I always knew you were the family-man type – in spite of that face of yours.'

Unwisely I answered, 'What's wrong with my face?'

'It has possibilities. You know what you remind me of?'

'What?' I asked huffily.

'A horse. A wicked horse.'

'I'm not wicked.'

'Didn't say you were,' she said, swinging a small foot back and forth. 'You're a nice, respectable, dutiful, churchgoing, 100 per cent Canadian boy. I bet you even say your prayers on the floor before getting into bed.'

'What's wrong with that?'

'Nothing. It's great. You don't even smoke, do you?'

I watched, scandalized as she calmly lit a cigarette. As the lucifer flamed, I saw her looking at me in amusement.

'Sinful, isn't it?' she remarked, blowing out the match and tossing it gracefully over her shoulder.

We were silent for a moment. I shuffled uneasily under her frank stare. I was afraid enough of virtuous women, but Denise... I wanted to move on, but I was curious.

'What did you mean, my face has possibilities?'

'Just that.'

'What are you doing here?'

She threw back her head. Her long black hair whispered in its own breeze and coiled sensuously about her ears. 'Oh, enjoying nature.'

Waiting for someone, I thought. I didn't want to find out who it was. It was likely to be a married man. She was rumoured to have been carrying on with more than one of them during the past year. Churchgoing men, too – although of course everyone went to church in Beamington, even Mr Byman, the haberdasher, who molested small boys.

'I saw you going home with Mabel. I was hoping you'd stop near here so I could hear what you said to her. I've never heard anyone propose before.'

'I'll bet you haven't,' I said. I was behaving very badly that evening.

'You're a smug, oily, priggish hypocrite, aren't you, Bartholomew?' she said, throwing away her cigarette with a sharp movement.

'I'm not a hypocrite.'

'Yes, you are.'

'How?'

'Taking a face like that to church. If that's not hypocrisy, I don't know what is.'

'Why do you carry on the way you do?'

'Why do you carry on the way *you* do?'

'It's the right way.'

'Who says so?'

'Everyone.'

'Bully for everyone.' She leaned over the gate and stared toward the river. Looking at her, I could understand the fascination she exerted.

The silence lengthened, and I was just about to say goodbye when she turned and leaned back against the gate.

'You're going away tomorrow?'

'Yes.'

'I hope you manage to keep yourself pure for your betrothed.' She smiled cynically for a moment; then her expression changed. 'I hope you come back safe, Bart.'

I had a strange sensation of gratitude. She was the first person who had shown even the slightest doubt about my safety. I coughed, and answered through my hand. Thank you, Denise.'

She turned away again. 'More than one boy won't come back.'

I suddenly remembered that one of the Beamington war casualties had been a boy friend of hers, someone she'd known for a long time. What was his name? He had been reported missing early in 1915. Perhaps Denise had loved him. Matthew Holte: that was the name. Holte had once pushed me over a bridge into a stream twenty-five feet below. I had been quite pleased when I heard he was missing; then in subsequent remorse I had prayed for him nightly for three weeks.

'Well, you'd better get back, or your mama will send you to bed without any supper.'

'Yes,' I said, preoccupied. 'Well, goodbye.'

'Goodbye,' she said, still looking at the river.

I started to move off.

'I suppose you'll be getting married when you come back?' she called after me.

'I'm not.'

'Not what?'

'Getting married.'

She turned incredulously. 'What?'

I don't know why I told her, but I did. 'I behaved very badly tonight.'

'You?'

'Everyone expected me to propose to her. But just as I was about to do so, a devil got in me, and all I did was shake hands. I feel very ashamed of myself.'

'Then go back and propose now.'

'Oh, no,' I said quickly. 'I'm not *that* ashamed.'

She stared at me, then said faintly. 'The poor girl will be heart-broken – don't you think?'

'Yes. I'm a heartless wretch.'

'But you're not going to do anything about it?' I didn't answer. 'It's just as well you're going away tomorrow,' she mused. 'You'd have had an awful time from her relatives and everybody... It's really true? Yes, I believe it is possible, now I think of it. Nobody with a face like yours could be that much of a ...'

'Yes,' I said. 'Well, I have to get up early.'

'You don't even care about her any more, do you?' Denise said.

'I'm utterly dismayed at my conduct.'

'I wonder if everyone's misjudged you, Bartholomew Bandy?' she said thoughtfully. 'Can it be that beneath that awful Gothic exterior there lurks a real terror?'

I was offended, and departed in silent dignity, somewhat marred by her laughter, which trailed after me like the scent she was wearing.

Father was waiting for me when I got home.

'Sit down, Bartholomew,' he said, pointing to an armchair that was cringing in one corner.

I sat down and looked at him dutifully.

'You'll be leaving home tomorrow, Bartholomew,' my father said, fixing his eyes on the frieze at the top of the wallpaper and starting to follow its intricate pattern to the next corner.

'Yes, Father.'

Mr Bandy halted his optical journey at the corner, adjusted his focus, then moved his gaze onward to the next corner.

'You will be going to Europe.'

'Yes, I know.'

'Don't interrupt. You will be going out into the world.'

'I've been living in Toronto for nearly three years –'

'I don't count Toronto,' he said. 'And again I shall be obliged if you will not interrupt. Where was I? Yes. Out into the world. It is a fast, nervous, cold, unsympathetic world.' The frieze was making him squint. He closed his eyes and massaged them, then focused them on me. 'It is also a sinful world.'

'Yes, Father. '

He stared at me searchingly for a moment, then apparently decided that the frieze was a more rewarding sight.

'You must promise me something, Bartholomew. '

'What?'

He turned, startled, then said irritably, 'I said you must promise me something.'

'Yes, sir, I promise.'

'I haven't told you what it is yet,' he snapped. He seemed very snappish tonight.

'Well, Father, I'm sure it's nothing dishonourable.'

'Of *course* it's nothing dishonourable,' he thundered. 'What's the matter with you, Bartholomew? Now you've made me lose my place.'

'Page thirty-five,' I said helpfully.

'Will you be quiet?' he shouted. It was a couple of minutes before he went on. 'Yes, a sinful world, full of temptation and innovation. I do not wish to slander Europe. It is, after all, our spiritual, or perhaps not spiritual – no, definitely not spiritual, I should have said *cultural* home. Well, perhaps – yes, it is our spiritual home, or I should say was; but even the most upright soul contains the horizontal decay of greed and – and passion ...' The Reverend Mr Bandy's voice faded just where the frieze ended near the window. He seemed to run out of inspiration, and went on in a down-to-earth voice: 'I want you to promise me that, in the time you will be away, you will studiously avoid the slightest temptation. I know I can rely on you not to succumb to habits such as smoking and indulging in vituperation, or looking at Parisian magazines. I know that you have, Bartholomew, too much sense for that. It is the major temptations that are the danger. I refer to the vices of intoxicants, gambling and – and the opposite sex. I want you to promise faithfully that during your sojourn in Europe you will spurn this triumvirate of evil.'

'I haven't the slightest inclination –'

'You haven't now. But when the temptation arises strongly...' Father's voice faded again and he stared with a shocked expression at the wall, as if a dreadful message had appeared on it in letters of ordure. I even glanced at the wall myself to make sure that it hadn't.

He sighed again, then continued wearily, 'And you will return pure in body and spirit for Miss House.' I rather felt this to be an anticlimax after the magnificent generalities that had preceded it.

I got up tentatively.

'Well, thank you, Father. I am always grateful for advice.'

'Good night, Bartholomew. I shall, of course, be up to see you off in the morning. Now go and say good night to your mother. She is waiting for you in the dining room.'

'Good night, Mother.'

'Good night, Bartholomew. I'll have breakfast ready at five.'

I leaned over carefully to kiss her cheek.

'You will take care of yourself, won't you?'

'Yes, Mother.'

'And you will write every single day?'

'Of course, Mother.'

'And keep yourself warm.'

'Yes.'

'Be respectful to your superiors at all times?'

'Certainly.'

'And' – she pressed my hand lightly –'stay away from women, won't you, Bartholomew?'

'Yes, Mother. I don't suppose there'll be many of them in the trenches.'

'Women are vessels of evil,' she said.

'M'yes.'

'Well?' she said, looking at me expectantly.

'Well what, Mother?'

'Haven't you any news for me, Bartholomew?'

'Hm?'

'About – Mabel?' she asked with a fond smile, or what I took to be a fond smile.

I had only a few hours to go, and it wasn't worth upsetting everyone.

'We – came to an understanding, Mother,' I said, and made an effort to look smug.

'I'm so glad,' she said, and embraced me.

It was with profound relief, glowing after a bath – a cold bath, thus combining a virtuous mortification of the flesh with a pleasant cooling of somewhat overheated skin – that I climbed into my narrow, uncomfortable Christian bed that night. After belabouring the pillow into reluctant submission to the shape of my head, I stared pleasurably at the whitewashed ceiling with the cracks that looked like the Tigris and Euphrates. From below I heard the front door close. That would be my father, who sometimes went out for a stroll before turning in. My mother was already in her own room.

I smirked pleasurably at myself as the cool silence of the house enveloped me, and wondered vaguely what the war would be like. In the newspapers it seemed to be reflected in small-scale maps in which advances of a hundred yards seemed like miles, and in the photographs of Canadian boys, smiling and triumphant with mementos and souvenirs, spiked helmets, Lugers, and pink garters....

I thought of Denise. Someone had once seen her bathing in the moonlight with Matt Holte. Mrs Learner, the butcher's wife, had told Mrs House, who had told Mabel, who had hinted at it to me. Everyone assumed that Denise had been in her birthday suit. The last of the bath water of my sleep drained scummily away over the dimpled cobbles of my imagination. I turned hastily back to purity. I thought of Mabel. She had always stuck by me. She had always been nice, sensible, and loyal. I was almost asleep when I remembered that I had not said my prayers, so I had to climb out of bed. When I got back in, I started thinking of Denise again. I was pretty tired next morning.

Me, Looking Miserable

I HAD OFTEN heard my grandfathers and grandmothers, who all came from England, describing it rather sentimentally, and through them I had come to imagine it as looking like an old pastoral landscape, slightly yellow with age. In fact, whenever I visualized an English scene I mentally included a gold frame, heavy and ornate.

So I wasn't surprised that it did look like an oil painting the day the convoy docked at Plymouth. Perhaps it was the contrast after the monotony of the sea, but the mellow colours of the hills at the approaches to the natural harbour seemed delectably unreal and soothing.

We pitched tents on Salisbury Plain, and even that featureless landscape looked romantic under the papyrus-coloured sunlight.

The enchantment ended next morning at Reveille. The winds came. Not the icy dry winds of the Ottawa Valley, but an onrush soaked in brine, like a wet sheet. It wrapped around us like a waistcoat fit for madmen. Within half a day my very ribs were clattering with cold, like someone drawing a stick along park railings. My nose ran, my teeth jittered, the backs of my hands became raw, red, and cracked. I wasn't a very pretty sight before; after days in that wind I looked like a tomcat, scarred and with tufts missing.

'So this,' I said to a sergeant, 'is summer in England.'

Training began, however, and every morning before breakfast, at the head of a squad of men, I walked and trotted two miles. I tried very hard to stop the disgraceful cursing of the men. I spoke quite sharply to them. It didn't do a bit of good.

I thought perhaps they would let up when they got used to the weather, but even when the sun glanced through for a full five minutes one day, they cursed harder than ever.

Then it started to rain. The wind itself had been so wet it was half an hour before I realized it was raining, especially as the deluge seemed to come from a blue sky.

'How can the natives stand it?' I asked the sergeant.

The rain continued. In three days the neat rows of tents were surrounded by rich gravy with sparking rivulets coursing through it and into the mess tents.

It rained for a week. Then at last there was a change in the weather. The rain didn't stop but the wind came back. It blew down half the tents. As soon as they were down, it hailed and sleeted. In the mornings soaking mists arose. A lumberjack shot himself.

The officers' tents were pitched in a triangle formed by high scrub and were better protected from the wind. Only one tent collapsed. I was soaked to my combinations before I got it up again.

Five days after the rain stopped, I was still wet. Then it started again.

'If it's like this in August,' I said to the sergeant, 'what must it be like in December?'

Not even sleep afforded relief. I went to bed before nine. By ten o'clock the steam was curling from my blankets in dense clouds. Huddled miserably at night under the rataplan of the rain, I must have looked for all the world like a heap of steaming dung.

It was so wet in September that training had to be halted for a time. The inaction made it harder to bear, and at first in twos and threes, then in dozens, the men began to go absent without leave, some of them even managing a couple of days in London before being picked up and returned in motor lorries.

I was on guard duty the night they brought in a record catch of 180 deserters, and I described it in a letter home.

'... and we are completing our training, as you see, on S--- P---!
[I wasn't sure whether Salisbury Plain was a military secret or not
– it ought to have been.] The weather has continued exceptionally
inclement and is having a rather poor moral effect on the men, a
good many of whom have taken to going absent to enjoy a few
days of spurious warmth and comfort in the shocking number of
taverns that dot the countryside.

'I myself have been out of the camp only once since we arrived, to a typical English market town, and could not help
contrasting it rather unfavourably with our own Beamington.
The place I went to, every second building seemed to be a 'public house', and I had to search quite diligently before I found a
church. I might explain that although I was quite wet and cold,
I did not for a moment consider entering one of these places, in
spite of the cheerful fires I could see burning in what I believe is
called the 'parlour'.

'However, I was talking about the men. I was on guard duty last
night and going my rounds of the sentries with the sergeant. One
of the men I inspected was an interesting old fellow named Squires.
I asked him if everything was all right, and he said everything was
fine, which made me a little suspicious, as he was soaking wet and
his feet had completely disappeared into the mud.

'However, I went on, and it seemed only a very short time before the first of the motors bringing back the absentees started to
arrive at the main gates. There seemed to be hundreds of them,
deserters, I mean. The peculiar thing was, they all looked quite
cheerful as they were marched off by the sergeant under guard,
almost as if they considered a few days in the fleshpots ample com-
pensation for the punishment that was about to befall them. Well,
on the fourth or fifth lorry who should be one of the deserters
but this Private Squires! I was frankly astonished, and drawing
him aside, questioned him as to what on earth he thought he was
doing. Hopping it, he said.

'One of the guards told me that they had seen him loping along
about half a mile down the road.

'He had even deposited his rifle under a bush! Just imagine it!

'Well, in the circumstances, he being on guard at the time of his defection, all would not have gone well with him, especially as he was on active service. I have to confess that in a moment of weakness I let him off, on condition that he promise not to abandon his post again that night.

'Fortunately, the corporal in charge of that particular lorry did not report Squires.

'I let Squires off because he assured me that he had hidden his rifle in a dry spot so that no harm would come to it. A rifle is terribly important in the army, you see. Later on I had doubts about its being kept dry, the countryside being in the condition it was in, dripping.

'I am your obedient and loving son, Bartholomew W. Bandy, Lt.'

My father wrote back reproving me for what he called an incipient levity. I could not for the life of me imagine what had prompted him to make this observation.

After that, I stopped writing every day, contenting myself with a weekly letter, because it was rather difficult to maintain communication without mentioning the army and things like that, and so risking a rather low moral tone.

One day on the grenade range I had a narrow escape. I was in charge of a small party of bombers. One of them was a thin, sallow man from Toronto called Soapes. I had been a bit uneasy about him from the start, since he had been showing signs of fright at the thought of hurling a live bomb.

We were in a small sandbagged enclosure five or so feet below ground level, and well protected from the blasts by a parapet of more sandbags. I gave everyone careful instructions, repeated them three times slowly, and threw the first bomb myself before handing the second bomb to Squires.

Squires, in spite of a bad habit of clattering his false teeth together like a riveting gun, had shown himself to be reliable. He got rid of the grenade with creditable alacrity.

The next soldier, Private Barbara, began badly by releasing the spring clip in the pit before throwing the bomb. Unfortunately, of all persons it had to fly at, it chose Private Soapes; and in trying to catch it he somehow managed to entangle it in his trouser pocket. For some reason Soapes immediately got the idea that the spring arm was the bomb itself. He gave a terrified scream and tried to tear the piece of metal out of his pocket. It caught in the lining of his trousers, and although it tore a large hole it remained stuck. Whereupon, still screaming at the top of his voice, he started to remove his trousers. Under different circumstances I would probably have congratulated him on his quick thinking.

Meanwhile, unnerved by the shrieks of Soapes, the rest of the men had made a concerted rush for the narrow, double-sand-bagged entrance. But there they had wedged themselves so firmly that not one of them was able to get through. By now they were all shouting, as well as kicking, biting, scratching, and elbowing in their frenzy to get away from the trousers.

In the middle of all this, I suddenly noticed Private Barbara staring stupidly at the antics of Private Soapes, who indeed presented an absurd sight, hopping around on one leg with his trousers half off and screaming like a stuck pig. Private Barbara had not moved a muscle since the spring arm had flown at Soapes. There was a distinctly unpleasant sensation in my stomach when I realized that Barbara was still holding the Mills bomb, and that it was smoking. When it smokes, it's due to go off.

I opened my mouth to shout a warning to Barbara, but discovered to my surprise that it was already open and that I was already shouting. Now Barbara noticed the smoking grenade still in his hand. His expression changed; he could not have looked more surprised had he found himself holding a haddock.

I snatched the grenade from him. Luckily his fingers were slack – I could not see myself spending half a minute prying the thing loose otherwise – and heaved it over the parapet. Simultaneously, another object flew up and followed it over the sandbags. It was Private Soapes' trousers.

Gradually order was restored. Numerous voices from outside the pit were calling us, asking what had happened. I was informed later that Soapes' screams had been heard for miles. But as no one cared to enter the pit until they had found out what was wrong, and as my own men were still incoherent, I had ample time to sort things out before some senior officer approached close enough to make a mental note of my face, a fate I had striven to avoid throughout primary and advanced training.

After all that, the grenade failed to explode, which meant I had to go out there and destroy it. I also had to retrieve Soapes' trousers for him. He refused to get them himself. I handed them over with what I hoped was an expression of contempt.

'I think it's been a very poor show, Soapes,' I said.

I mentioned senior officers a moment ago: my relations with them had not been entirely satisfactory to date. I had done my best to make myself inconspicuous during initial training at Niagara, but with a face like mine it was not easy. I worked hard and tried to give them as little grounds for complaint as possible. I was always most respectful and carried out their orders with dispatch. Yet somehow I never seemed to please them. It was almost as if they suspected my willingness and alacrity of having insubordinate undertones.

I tried harder than ever. I carried out every order efficiently, moved fast, concentrated hard, made copious notes during lectures, and trained with single-minded devotion. The result was that I was given a lot of extra duties. By now I could hardly open my mouth without a look of suspicion appearing on their faces. I began to get a bit tired of it all.

It was most unfair because one of my brother officers, Bob Hill, who was frequently quite disrespectful in a lazy, charming way, and never did any more than he was forced to, whose salute was the sloppiest in the entire army, and whose uniform looked as if it had been pressed by an irresponsible orangutan – he got on marvellously with our superior officers. The adjutant even treated him to dinner.

I couldn't understand it. Sometimes it almost seemed as if the army considered real soldierly qualities to be slightly dishonourable.

At any rate, about the Salisbury Plain period I finally made up my mind to act more naturally. All my life I had been listening to people with a look of dutiful respect that I'm afraid I didn't always feel. Denise was right: I was a hypocrite.

Some High-Up Friends

I T WAS OCTOBER before I got to France. After those miserable weeks on Salisbury Plain I was quite looking forward to the trenches and a little excitement. At last I was on my way to join the Victorian Light Infantry Regiment of the Tenth Canadian Division in reserve in the Albert Region. I was travelling with an acquaintance called Rupert Randle. Out of a group of fifteen or so officers, we were the only ones who went up by train. The remainder somehow managed to arrange transport by motorcar.

I had thought the troop train from Montreal to Halifax was crowded, but it did not compare with the train from Le Havre. It took us fifteen minutes to negotiate only ten feet of corridor, wrenching our way through a solid wall of soldiers, some of whom were three deep on the floor. It was all very sordid.

We peered in one compartment after another, but they were jammed.

'Give it up, mon,' a Scottish lieutenant whose leg we had trodden on advised us. 'There's not a single seat left in the whole bloody train.'

But I went on searching. I had had to stand at the ship's rail during the entire crossing of the Channel on a small, filthy steamer, and I had heard that French trains were like snails. I was determined to get a seat.

My pertinacity was rewarded. I saw a space in the middle of a seat in the end compartment. It was an upholstered seat, too. I was just about to open the door when Rupert clutched my arm.

'It's reserved for senior officers,' he shouted above the clatter of the wheels, as the train rushed headlong into the night at five miles an hour.

It was then I saw that the compartment was flushed with red tabs. At least two of the occupants were generals. My heart sank as I pressed my nose against the glass and peered longingly in at the luxurious, smoke-filled interior. But I could see no sticker on the window indicating that the compartment was reserved.

They were all talking and laughing. They seemed to be having a good time. I gazed wistfully at the space in the middle of one of the seats. The officers on each side were taking up a lot of room, but the space was still many inches wide, and it was upholstered. After all, I thought, why not?

'Why don't you take that seat, Rupert?' I said. 'The compartment isn't officially reserved.'

Rupert gazed inside for a moment, then shuddered slightly. 'Not me,' he said.

'Then I'm going to.'

He seized my arm. 'You're not!'

'Why not? They're not ogres. Look, see? They're laughing.'

'In with *them?*'

'Why not?'

'You can't! They're generals!'

'I don't see why I should stand when there's a seat'

'Don't be a fool. Bandy!'

'Yes,' a voice said. '*Do* be a fool. Go on in. Don't let a bunch of rotten brass hats get the better of you.'

The voice had a peculiar wheeze to it. I looked around to see who was speaking, but couldn't see him anywhere.

'Go ahead,' the voice wheezed again. 'Are you a man or a mouse?'

I put my hand on the door handle.

'That's the stuff,' the voice said painfully. 'I'd go in myself if I was in a position to.'

The voice seemed to be coming from below. I looked down and saw that it was a corporal who was speaking. I was standing on him.

I tried to get off his chest, but there was no room. 'I'm very sorry,' I apologized.

'That's quite all right,' the corporal said, drawing in a deep shuddering breath that caused me to rise perceptibly. 'I like people standing on me. All my life I've been stood on.' There was a pause while he took another breath and went on thoughtfully, 'I suppose it's an innate need of discipline, of being sat on, squashed, you know.'

I managed to get one foot on the floor. 'All the same,' I said apologetically, 'it can't be very comfortable.'

'That's all right,' he said 'You're not so heavy. The heavier the better, anyway.'

'What weight are you, Lieutenant?' a large sergeant asked me.

'About 170 pounds.'

'How about me?' the sergeant asked the corporal. 'I'm nearly 200. Will I do?'

'Sure,' the corporal said. 'The more, the merrier, that's what I say.' He laughed bitterly. His laughter caused me to lose balance, and I clutched the door for support. The door slid open and I half fell into the compartment.

Five pairs of eyes stared at me. I turned to go out again, but someone had already closed the door. I was trapped. After a momentary panic I decided there was nothing else for it but to stay. It would have been impossible to get back to the corridor anyway, the doorway was so jammed with bodies. I turned and nodded politely; then on an afterthought I tried to salute but succeeded only in rapping my knuckles painfully on a wooden panel.

They had all stopped talking, all staring hard. There was a pair of legs stretched across the compartment belonging to a major.

He made no effort to move them. I stepped over them carefully. I flung my valise on to the baggage rack and threw my trench coat on top of it. It fell off. I just managed to catch it, stumbling a little over another outstretched pair of legs.

'Sorry,' I said.

The dead silence continued. There was not even the sound of breathing.

With infinite care I lowered myself into the upholstered space between the two gentlemen on the right.

Opposite I saw a lieutenant-colonel and two brigadiers. I glanced quickly toward my right. In the window position I met a gaze so frigid that I shuddered visibly. It belonged to a lieutenant-general. On my left was a staff major. He had an ice-cold aristocratic face and two buck teeth.

Every one of them continued to stare at me.

'Good evening,' I said. The brigadiers seated opposite started.

I must admit I was acutely uncomfortable. The general and the major on each side of me were generously spread out on the seat, leaving me practically no room. I realized that my buttocks were barely touching the seat

These officers were making not the slightest effort to move over, although they had plenty of room. The major in particular was leaning at an angle so that there was a good six inches between him and the end of the seat. I felt a little annoyed about that. I started to wiggle, and gradually felt myself sinking between them until finally I was in contact with the upholstery. It was a tight fit but a great improvement.

The silence continued for another minute. There was still not even the sound of breathing. They hadn't taken their eyes off me since my abrupt arrival.

'That's better,' I said conversationally.

The brigadier opposite started again.

'Facing the engine, I mean,' I went on. 'I always like to face the engine.'

The brigadier opposite gave this some thought, for the glassy look left his eye. He blinked. It was the first movement I had seen. I was very grateful for that blink.

But the deathly silence continued. I began to wonder if I might not have been more comfortable on the corporal. I cleared my throat.

One of them started to hum, and I was pleased to note that it was a hymn tune. I recognized it immediately. It was 'Rock of Ages'. I looked around approvingly to see who was humming it when I met the gaze of the general. The tune died away immediately, and it was only then that I realized it was I who had been humming. I cleared my throat again and looked out the window. It wasn't quite dark, and the countryside seemed grey and flat. It was almost as bleak out there as it was inside.

I looked down at my hands. There was dirt under my left thumbnail. I tried to dig it out.

The merciless silence continued. They had all been talking loudly before I came in. Perhaps, I thought, they had been discussing military secrets.

After three more bloodcurdling minutes, during which the others not only did not speak but did not even blink again, I reached up for my valise, took it down, opened it, and took out my large, heavy Bible, replaced the valise, and discreetly crushed myself back between the major and the general. I tried very hard to avoid digging them in the ribs as I opened the Good Book. Wetting my left thumb and forefinger, I turned over the pages until I came to an interesting part, and began to read.

Turning the second page, I happened to glance up, and could not repress a start, because whereas before, the surrounding faces had seemed to express an outraged reserve, they now mirrored a stupefied astonishment. They kept looking from me to the, I must admit, rather large volume, then from the volume back to me, as if they had never seen a Bible before.

I tried to read on, but that glimpse of their faces had disconcerted me.

I thought of putting my head back and trying to sleep. I had not had a decent night's sleep since leaving Beamington. The army, I had discovered, distrusted sleep, and was always doing its best to discourage it.

But the thought of those ten eyes on me as I lay defenceless against the cushions changed my mind.

To make matters worse, I now needed to go to the lavatory.

For the first time I began to doubt whether I had been wise to leave home. I had just begun to think regretfully of Mabel, and moved to settle back more comfortably in the seat, when I felt the Bible sliding off my knees. I could easily have caught it had I not been wedged in so firmly between the major and the general, but as it was it fell on the foot of the brigadier opposite.

A most peculiar phenomenon occurred: his eyes dilated and inch by inch his head started to tilt to one side. He was also holding his breath and his nostrils were expanding and contracting like gills.

He seemed to be holding his breath an unnaturally long time. I became so tense, waiting for him to expel it, that I forgot to reach down and heave the book off his foot. I had never seen anyone hold his breath for so long.

At last a thin, keening sound began to emerge from his twisted lips; and slowly he sank back in his seat, his eyes becoming bloodshot. Pulling myself together I leaned over and lifting the Bible, wrenched it on to my lap again with an involuntary grunt.

'Terribly sorry,' I said. 'It slipped off.'

The brigadier took two or three deep breaths that were evidently highly satisfying.

He spoke. 'How,' he said. He cleared his throat and started again. 'How far are you going on this train?'

'To the railhead, sir,' I said.

He nodded slowly. Then he looked out the window.

Well, at least I had managed to break the ice.

For a moment I felt slightly resentful at their attitude; then I reminded myself that they were, after all, high officers and had many cares and worries on their minds. The whole conduct of the war, I told myself firmly, depended on these intellects. So I forgave the unpleasant silence.

By now I needed quite badly to relieve myself. But I was determined not to leave, knowing full well that I'd never get back in again.

Still, it would have been nice to have heard a little of their conversation. Among persons of such exalted rank it could hardly fail to be full of scintillating talk, full of worldly and military subtlety.

And finally they did speak. It was round about Etapes, I think.

'I hear old Farthing-Prebble's got XXX, sir,' the brigadier in the window seat mumbled to the general next to me.

'Old Farthing-Prebble of G.2 (D)?'

'Yerser, G.2(D)D2, sir.'

'G.2(D)D2, X D.A.Q.M.G., dig-dig got XXX?'

'My word, top hole! XXX, A?' someone else added.

'Taff Div. H.Q. Promul. G.2(D) last wik, eh? Yes.'

'By gad! What about Grunty C.B.R.E. X D.A.D.O.S. um?'

'Gonesir, GSO.3 ups G.H.Q. Reserve CCN, bai gad.'

'My word . . . member ole G. with his penchant for 0.3 Umbleton, eh, eh? Ha!'

'Ha!'

The general and the brigadier-general laughed briefly. I was looking from one to the other with a pleasant smile, trying to make out what they meant. The general had his mouth open and was about to add something when he saw me grinning. His mouth closed and he glared. Everyone subsided, and the silence settled in again more thickly than ever.

I don't know what it was that prompted me to contribute a few words myself. Perhaps it was through a belief that even generals might like to discuss ordinary, common or garden subjects as a relief from the intellectual altitude of high strategy. Or maybe it was because I was trying to take my mind off my own physical distress.

Anyway, I said, 'What's it like at the front, sir?' to the B.G. in the corner. I chose him because he seemed to own the least un-friendly face.

They all looked at me again, startled. The B.G. seemed to have difficulty taking in the fact that I had actually addressed him.

After a moment he said, 'What?'

'The front, sir. You see, I've never been there. I'm straight out from Canada.'

'Canada?' he said, blinking.

'Yes, sir. You know. Dominion of Canada. Across the Atlantic.'

'Atlantic?' the B.G. said blankly.

'Atlantic Ocean, sir. Took us two weeks to get across. Came over on the *S.S. Dismalia.*'

'*Dismalia?*' the brigadier said incredulously.

'A large passenger boat it was. We all slept in hammocks.'

'Hamm –' the B.G. began. Then he shook himself, blinked sev-eral times, and looked at the brigadier beside him. 'What's the feller talkin' about, Cecil?' he asked.

There was a pause while the B.G. thought for a moment. Then he said gruffly, 'Hammocks.'

The other brigadier stared at him for a longish spell. 'Oh,' he said.

There was a sudden convulsive movement beside me. It was the general, turning his head.

'Hammocks?' he said loudly. 'Who's talking about hammocks? What's that to do with old Farthing-Prebble?'

They all looked at me. The major on my left suddenly barked, 'Well? Speak up, man!'

I stared at him, then at the others. I thought perhaps they had not properly adjusted themselves from some lofty military contemplation on tactical analysis. 'I wasn't actually referring to Farthing-Prebble,' I said. 'In fact I don't even know where it is.'

'Where what is?'

'Farthing-Prebble, sir.'

They all looked at each other. The corner brigadier turned to the brigadier opposite me. 'What's he talkin' about now?' he asked testily.

'I want to get to the bottom of this,' the lieutenant general said angrily. 'Where do hammocks come in?'

'They don't actually come in, sir,' the major said respectfully, 'they're already there, in a manner of speaking. They usually hang from the ceiling.'

The general's eyes bulged. 'Farthing-Prebble – hanging from the ceiling?' he shouted. 'What's he doing there?'

'No, sir,' the major said very respectfully, 'one sleeps in them.'

'I'll get to the bottom of this if it's the last thing I do!' the general shouted, thumping his knee with his fist. His face was becoming purple. I began to feel alarmed. 'What I want to know is what the devil Farthing-Prebble is doing in a hammock! He's supposed to be taking over Thirty Corps!'

'If that's the kind of man he is,' the brigadier in the corner said, 'he ought to be sent back to Div.'

'He certainly will be!' the general thundered. 'Never heard anything like it in me life! Links!'

The colonel in the corner who had been asleep started violently and straightened up. 'Yessir,' he said, stretching his mouth and dilating his eyes to get them open properly.

'Take a note, Links!' the general shouted. 'Farthing-Prebble! Thirty Corps! Out!'

'Right, sir,' the colonel said, scribbling furiously in a tiny notebook.

'I'll not have my officers sleeping on the job,' the general went on. 'Hammocks, indeed! Keenness, alertness, discipline!' He subsided and muttered for a bit. He saw me staring at him, wide-eyed. He leaned forward and patted me on the knee.

'Good work,' he said, nodding, 'I'll remember that.'

He lay back and closed his eyes. Then he opened them and looked fiercely around until he found me again.

'What's your name?'

'Bandy, sir. B. W., sir.'

'Good work, Bandy,' he said, and appeared to go to sleep instantaneously.

I looked at the colonel. I looked at the brigadiers. I looked at the major. They were all nodding approvingly at me.

After all, I thought to myself, it's just that I haven't been in the army long enough to grasp the nuances of these things. Probably I had misunderstood the entire conversation.

Yes, that must be it, I thought, and settled back with a sigh of contentment. Obviously the whole thing was something entirely beyond the comprehension of a lowly subaltern. I was half asleep before I realized that I had hardly any need to go to the bathroom any more. I sighed again, pleasurably, and drifted into slumber, surrounded by a major, a lieutenant-colonel and three generals – my friends.

Settling Down in the Mud

IT WAS SEVERAL days before Rupert and I got to Battalion, not because of the tardiness of the train – French trains weren't as slow as all that – but because we had to loiter at a base camp. I never did find out exactly where it was. I remember that there was a straight row of cypress trees. Why they were in a straight row I couldn't make out. Like the camp, they seemed to serve no useful purpose.

My friend Rupert Randle was also destined for the Second Battalion, V.L.I. I had noticed him vaguely on the ship coming over, but had not spoken to him until Salisbury Plain. He was a thin youth with a stoop and eyes like glasses of ginger beer, and was always reading the Bible. He saw me similarly occupied one day and from then on attached himself to me.

Although he was a gentle soul and pious, he made me uneasy because he was always following me around; also, he had a habit of placing his face only an inch from mine whenever he addressed me. I found myself constantly backing away, it being distasteful to have one's horizon entirely filled with face. During our longer conversations I sometimes covered as much as a hundred yards backward. This was rather perilous, as there were many gravel pits in the area. He reminded me of Sammy, the village idiot of Beamington, who had trailed me like a dog throughout the summer of '14. And there was also an ugly female student at the University of Toronto who had sometimes gone to extreme lengths to sit next to me during lectures; on one occasion she actually scrambled over the back of the bench when she saw a place beside me, totally indifferent to the resultant exposure of her blue cotton knickers.

Besides, people were beginning to look at me strangely. I was used to this, but when the medical officer started to take a professional interest in us both I became uneasy. With Rupert's face thrust forward to within an inch of mine, and mine thrust backward almost between my shoulders, he advancing step by step and I retreating step by step, the M.O. might have been excused a suspicion that we were engaged in some obscurely unpleasant Indian ritual leading up to an orgy. To get away from Rupert I took up machine-gun practice. Rupert hated machine guns. I became an expert Lewis gunner.

Rupert intended to go into the Church after the war. He was genuinely convinced that this was his vocation, and that *ipso facto* God was watching over him.

At last our posting came through, and once again we entrained for the railhead, both reading the Good Book steadily throughout the journey.

Battalion headquarters was in a place called Villiers-Aiglon in the Somme region, and was a farm building. The livestock of the farm consisted, as far as I could make out, in nothing but pedigree field mice.

It was six at night when we staggered up to the orderly room, laden with our kit; we had not found anyone else to carry it. We were both starving, too.

The adjutant and the colonel were talking when we were shown in by a clerk. We stood to attention but they didn't seem to notice us. I was so tired that it was a minute before their conversation began to make an impression on me.

The colonel was twirling his swagger stick and saying: 'I've had a sneaking suspicion for some time that they don't know what they're doing. Nothing much, you know. Just little signs, you know, here and there – like court-martialling a man who's been dead a month, and ordering a gas attack with the wind blowing the wrong way, and sending the tanks into six feet of mud, and asking us to send in returns on how many men in the battalion have been suffering lately from leprosy. That kind of thing. Nothing you can really put your finger on. But making Sir Boisenberry Vandel a corps commander! That's really something.'

'Yes,' the adjutant said, 'it's the kind of thing begins to make you think.' They both thought for a moment. 'What's old Farthing-Prebble supposed to have done, anyway?'

'Hm? Oh – I don't think I got it right,' the colonel said. 'They said it was something about his being found asleep on the job, in a hammock. Though how they could tell with old F-P whether he was asleep or otherwise beats me.'

'Farthing-Prebble, did you say?' I asked, haltingly.

At the sound of my voice they both turned and looked me up and down.

The colonel, I now saw, was a big man with the largest face I had ever met, with a small black moustache in the middle. 'Who are you?' he said.

'Bandy, B. W., sir,' I said. I tried to salute, but my arm got caught in my respirator strap. 'Just been posted. And this is ...' But for the life of me I couldn't remember Rupert's surname. It might have been the colonel's stare that put me off. I could see Rupert looking at me reproachfully, as if he thought I were trying to disown him.

An expectant silence fell. I realized that they were hanging on to my sentence. Surely I wasn't taking after my father? 'Rupert,' I finished lamely. What on earth was that second name? Alliterative with Rupert, I knew that.

'Rupert?' the colonel said.

Then I remembered it, but by that time it was too late: they might think that I was in the habit of thinking of my companion simply as Rupert. It was hideously unmilitary. The colonel would almost certainly find it curious. 'Yes, sir,' I said. 'Lieutenant Rupert. Randle Rupert,' I added, inspired.

'I see,' the colonel said. He looked at me carefully, then quickly averted his eyes and massaged them between thumb and forefinger.

'It's not,' Rupert said, 'it's Randle, Rupert Randle.'

'Randle Rupert Randle?' the colonel asked.

'Rupert Randle,' Rupert said. He sounded offended.

'I see,' the colonel said. He looked back at me. He held out his hand, but then seemed to change his mind and withdrew it quickly. He turned to the adjutant. 'Do you know about them?'

'No, sir. Never heard of them.'

The colonel turned back to us. 'He's never heard of you,' he said.

'We were posted here,' I said.

'My adjutant's never heard of you,' the colonel said decisively, throwing his swagger stick in the air and catching it neatly. He was obviously proud of his dexterity with the little cane. 'And my adjutant's always right. You don't belong here.' He sounded glad.

'Where were you supposed to go?' the adjutant asked.

'We were posted here,' Rupert said dismally.

'Then we'll have to send you back marked 'Not at this address,' ' the colonel said.

'Returned to sender,' the adjutant added.

'They do look like a couple of stray parcels, don't they?' the colonel mused. 'I wonder what's in them?'

'Eggshells, tea, and stale cake,' the adjutant said.

'We're certainly not food parcels,' I said. 'We've had hardly anything to eat for twenty-four hours.'

I handed over our orders. The adjutant perused them.

'Well,' he sighed, 'I'm afraid they do belong to us, sir.'

'Never mind. They'll soon be dead,' the colonel said brightly. He and the adjutant then stared at each other in surprise, then broke into loud guffaws.

'Soon be dead,' the adjutant snorted. 'That's rich; that really is a good one, sir.' He had to hang on to the desk for support.

The colonel stopped laughing abruptly. He waved an arm wearily. 'Send them on,' he said. 'Perhaps B Company could use them.'

The adjutant studied us, and strummed his lower lip. 'This your first time out?'

We nodded.

'Where you from?' the colonel asked. Randle said, 'London, Ontario, sir.'

'Beamington, sir.'

'Beamington? You ever heard of Beamington, Fred?' The adjutant shook his head. The colonel looked at me gravely, as if all were lost.

'My adjutant's never heard of Beamington,' he said.

'It's near Ottawa, sir,' I said.

He shook his head. He had made up his mind. 'Sorry,' he said. 'My adjutant's never wrong.'

'Perhaps I'm mistaken,' I said.

The colonel looked at me. 'Don't you usually stand at attention when you're talking to a colonel?'

'I *am* standing at attention, sir.'

'Oh, I see. It's your uniform that's standing at ease; is that it?'

'I guess so, sir.'

'Well, you'd better speak to your uniform pretty sharply, old boy,' the colonel said. 'I don't care what my men do, but I won't have slackness in my uniforms.'

The adjutant snickered and the colonel's mouth twitched. 'However, I won't press the matter any further,' he said. 'But *you* press it, see? Understand?' The adjutant was holding on to the desk again. I began to wonder what kind of a battalion I had got myself into.

'Yes, I understand, sir,' I said with quiet dignity; but this seemed to increase their merriment. They had to hold on to each other for support.

The colonel again recovered abruptly. 'All right, gentlemen. B Company it is.' He put his hands on his hips and looked happy. 'You'll be glad to know you've arrived at a very good time indeed.

A full-scale attack, no less. Isn't that splendid? It's against Beaumont-Hamel, and it's in three days. I'm telling you all this because as usual everyone knows about it, including the enemy. Aren't you thrilled?'

'To bits, sir,' I said.

The colonel didn't like that 'Yes,' he scowled. 'That's just what you will be. Thrilled to bits. We're just recovering from our last thrill.'

'I can see that, Colonel.'

He put his hands on his hips again and looked at me. Too late I saw that I had gone too far.

'Yes,' he said softly. 'I've a feeling that if you're still with us after Beaumont-Hamel, you'll be very useful in trench raids and suicide missions and things like that. Eh, Fred?'

'Yes, sir,' the adjutant said. 'It's obvious he has the offensive spirit.'

I felt like getting down on my hands and knees and licking the mud off the colonel's field boots.

We had been travelling for twenty-four hours, and catering arrangements at the scheduled railway halts had been poor to non-existent, so we were hungry and drooping even before the three-mile walk to the company billets outside the town.

As we trudged along, a thunderstorm came up. That was all we needed, a good soaking. I had only recently dried out after Salisbury Plain. But, surprisingly, the rain did not come. It was several minutes before we realized that it was not a thunderstorm at all. It was the Front.

But when we finally got to the billets, we found a scene of intense activity. The men were falling in hurriedly. Horses snorted and jingled; N.C.O.s bawled instructions; lamps swung and flickered over a bedlam of distraught confusion. I stopped a second lieutenant. 'What's happening? Is there an attack?'

'We're moving off.'

Rupert and I looked at each other through leaden eyelids.

'Where to?'

'Where the hell do you think?' the lieutenant asked angrily. He turned and shouted at a dim group of men. 'Fall in, for God's sake!' he blazed. A horse reared, and there was a crash as a lantern shattered. A distant flare shed a faint, sick light over the chaos. The sound of the guns seemed to increase.

It was some minutes before we found our company commander, Captain Karley. He shook hands hurriedly.

'Glad to have you with us,' he shouted. 'Is there only two of you?'

'Yes.'

'Damn, I told them I needed three! Oh, well. Bandy, you have the sixth platoon, you the seventh. I'm sorry you have to go up straightaway, but it can't be helped. Throw your kit on the G.S. wagon there – good God, what've you got? Brought your entire possessions with you, man? We're not house movers, you know. Oh, well, too late now, but you're both carrying far too much. Berry!' he yelled at a passing sergeant. This is Lieutenant Randle. Show him your platoon, will you?' Randle and the sergeant moved off into the melee. I looked after him, bewildered. 'Your sergeant is Sergeant Pink – shut up, there!' the company commander shouted at a group of men chattering around a pack pony. They paid no attention. 'Sorry I haven't time to talk, Bandy; hope you'll be happy with us.'

'Thank you, Capt –'

Karley started to move off. 'Captain, we've had nothing to eat for nearly –'

'Sorry,' he shouted over his shoulder, 'you'll have to wait 'til we get up,' and he was gone.

So instead of a nice comfortable bed in a private house surrounded by happy French peasants, we were faced with a route march into the dead of night. I had hardly slung my baggage on to the mess wagon when shouts of command echoed down the road and the company marched off. I had to run up and down the column twice before I found Number Six Platoon.

The pace was killing and uneven. As we had orders to keep closed up, one moment we were trotting to close ranks and the next shuffling to avoid treading on the men in front. There was a chill wind but I was sweating. My head ached. I was starving.

The guns grew louder, and the sky became vivid with pretty pink flashes. At two in the morning we got tangled up with a supply column. The march then became a nightmare with the neighing of frightened horses and rasping of axles, men floundering in a road that had become so rutted and muddy it was hard to distinguish it from the ditches and fields to either side. I had on a brand-new trench coat; it soon looked like Sir Walter Raleigh's celebrated garment after Elizabeth had tramped on it. I stepped into a puddle that turned out to be a small crater. I was nearly run down by an officer on a charger who cursed me roundly. The groaning of limbers and fieldpieces, yells, thuds, drums, and curses made the night hideous with sound.

As, somehow, we managed to separate ourselves from the column, to my dull astonishment I heard a train. I had not expected a train so close to the front. It sounded like an express. The next thing I knew, men all around were lying down in the mire.

'Get down, you idiot!' That was the lieutenant I had addressed before. I lay down, too exhausted to wonder why, and the next moment the express came into the station and burst with a crash just the other side of the road. It was my first 5.9. My tin hat fell off, got filled with water, and when I fumbled it on again I got a deluge down my neck. It was just like Salisbury Plain.

Soon we were passing through the field batteries, which were firing continuously. At four in the morning we rested beside a wall – all that was left of a row of houses. We were supposed to be in the line by daybreak, but the sun was up before we straggled into the last communications trench. It was a foot deep in water. Three times in ten yards I tripped over a loose telephone wire that was supposed to be stapled to the side of the trench. It started to rain, but I was already so wet and muddy that it made no difference.

I was carrying my valise with the vast Bible in it, a heavy burden.

As we staggered, slipped, and fell along the uneven trench, we had frequently to press against the clay walls to allow stretcher bearers and walking wounded to pass, going the other way.

Shells were screaming overhead, each type making a different sound. I hardly noticed them.

It was after seven, I think, when I finally half fell down the steps to an extremely smelly dugout adjoining company headquarters and was assigned a bed made of eight sandbags and some skipping rope. The first thing I saw were two rats fighting.

I collapsed slowly on to the bed and was in the act of raising one leg into reclining position when Karley bustled in.

'Well, Bandy, getting yourself settled in, eh? That's fine; make yourself comfortable. I can see you're going to settle in quickly, eh? Yes, well now, I'm putting you in charge of a work party; you'll find Corporal Swelter outside waiting for you. Go on up to the firing line; the traverses need seeing to. Get them fixed up, will you? Did I tell you your platoon will be in support trench here first before the big day, did I?'

'Food,' I said. 'Food.'

'Of course, of course,' Karley said sympathetically, 'just as soon as they get the kitchens up we'll all have a nice hot breakfast. It may take a little time, though, so you'll be able to work undisturbed, I should think, for at least three hours. How are you enjoying the bombardment?'

'What bar-bar 'bardment?' I said.

'That's the spirit,' Karley said. 'I can see you're a veteran already. Well, off you go, old chappie, as the English say, and don't forget to give a hand yourself; in this company the officers work too, of course.' And he was gone, skipping as nimbly as a wild goat from Banff, in spite of his vast bulk.

It was ten before we had breakfast. The bread had been dropped repeatedly in the mud, and tasted of mustard gas and sweaty extremities. I forced myself to eat standing up so that I wouldn't fall asleep. Officers were not allowed to sleep during the day. The men were almost as fatigued as I was. I found one man asleep on his feet and hadn't the heart to wake him. Besides, I wasn't sure he was in my platoon. The only face I knew was Sergeant Pink's, which was not a pleasant one. He was lazy, too. He went round chivvying the men but not doing anything himself. I was helping a man to do a buttressing job when Captain Karley trotted up.

'That's fine, Bandy; doing a good job there. When you've finished that, will you detail a couple of men to dig out the listening tunnel? It's collapsed a few yards out. These trenches are in a lousy state, aren't they? Very slack people before us, I must say; still, we'll do the best we can, won't you, Bandy? Carry on, then.' and he waltzed out of sight. He looked quite happy, as if he enjoyed war.

I called Sergeant Pink. 'Take a couple of shovels, select a man, and dig out the listening tunnel, Sergeant.'

'Listening tunnel, sir?' Pink asked. I was six foot tall, but Pink looked down on me. He had the nastiest pair of eyes I'd ever seen, and his breath smelled like a graveyard. 'What is a listening tunnel?'

'I haven't the slightest idea, but go and dig it out anyway.'

'If I don't know what it is, how'm I going to know what to dig out, Lieutenant?'

There then ensued a longish argument. I was staggering with fatigue, and there seemed to be three Sergeant Pinks, and they were the meanest-looking bunch; I'm afraid I lost my temper with all three of them and forced them into doing something about the listening tunnel, which turned out to be a trench pushed into no man's land a few yards for the purpose of eavesdropping on the enemy to hear what he was up to, if anything. I assumed that Pink was toying with me to maintain ascendancy over the platoon. I made a mental note to keep a wary eye on him.

At noon I got my second wind, all fatigue dropping away like a cloak, and I felt fine. The Germans were not shelling our trench, but there was a lot of machine-gun fire. The bullets flying over took some getting used to. They sounded like a whip being cracked. Occasionally one would strike the wire and turn over and over with an unpleasant gargling sound. The noise of our own shells ranging on the German lines was almost continuous. I hoped there would be none of the enemy left to oppose us when we attacked.

It was five in the afternoon before I met the other officers officially. When I went down into the H.Q. dugout, they were sitting round a homemade table, drinking whisky.

'Ah, Bandy,' Karley said, 'come and sit in. You've met the others, I guess. No? Well, this is Ben Spanner, second in command of the company, and the lice tell me he's the best-tasting officer in the division.'

'Do you have lice?'

They looked at me in astonishment.

'Do you mean to say you've been here a full day and you haven't got them yet? Well, my boy, that must be a record.'

Lieutenant Spanner was a tall thin man with a mournful brown face and a grave manner. Although he was possibly only thirty-five, his face was deeply lined. He had a sepulchral voice and had been a schoolteacher in Winnipeg.

'You know Randle, of course. This is Sanderson; he's from the Maritimes somewhere. Not been with us very long but a good lad; he brought us this bottle of whisky.'

Sanderson was the second lieutenant I'd already spoken to. He looked about nineteen, and was handsome and angry-looking. He nodded curtly.

'Here.' Karley handed me a mug. 'For some incredible reason Mr Randle doesn't drink, so you'd better –'

'I don't drink either, Captain.'

He and Spanner looked at me open-mouthed, then at Rupert, then back to me, then at each other. Sanderson looked contemptuous.

'Am I hearing things?' Karley said faintly. He stuck a finger in his ear and wiggled it around, then slapped the side of his head. 'Spanner, surely I need an ear specialist. That's twice in five minutes I've heard the same macabre words. This dugout must be haunted by the wretched spirits of former subalterns who died in dreadful agony brought on by sobriety. Surely, Bandy, you're joking?'

'My father's a minister of the Church.'

'You're not offering that as a reason? My old dad had false teeth, but I never felt any urge to knock out my own teeth in filial sympathy.'

'I was always a dutiful son,' I murmured, sitting on an S.A.A. box with a sigh. 'Whenever Father broke his leg I felt impelled to break mine, too. It runs in the family, you see. My grandfather, for example, had a habit of belching, so my father was forced to emulate him. Mind you, his belches are always extremely pious.'

'Oh, of course,' Spanner said.

'With the two of them burping away, must have sounded like a frog farm,' Karley said.

'Indeed yes. Frogs used to come from miles around to join in; hence the name of our house, Toad Hall, Belchington.'

'Well,' Karley said, clasping his hands round his knees and rocking back and forth, 'I don't know what you fellows are going to drink. The water is so full of chlorine you don't even need a mug to put it in. It's undrinkable except when it's beaten to death first, with whisky.'

'Of course, there's always tea,' Spanner said doubtfully. The sacking covering the entrance to the dugout fluttered wildly and there was a dull, heavy explosion. A mist of dust swirled down from the ceiling, and as if it were a reflex Karley and Spanner placed their hands over their mugs before the dust could fall in, and continued talking without a pause.

'Well, to business,' Karley said. 'You fellows have picked a poor time to join the battalion, I'm afraid, just before an attack. We like to introduce you to the mud, blood, et cetera in easy stages, gradually working forward to the firing line. But we're so short of men, you see – still one officer short, and none of the platoons up to strength, quite. Sergeant Pink has been commanding sixth platoon by himself for quite a while, so I'm glad you've come.'

'Nobody ever seems to last in B Company,' Spanner said morosely, 'except Pink. Can't help feeling there's a moral there, somewhere.'

'We've had some tough fighting lately,' Karley said in a pleased tone. 'We came out of a show near Albert with 60 per cent casualties.'

'Good gracious,' I said.

'Yes. I lost three officers out of five. You were in that show, weren't you, Jimmy?'

Sanderson nodded without looking up, and finished his drink.

'Yes.' Karley laughed. 'It's funny, the high proportion of officers killed.'

'I don't think it's funny at all,' Rupert said.

'Good for promotion, anyway,' I offered.

'Not really, Bandy old boy, as the English say. You see, it's always the second lieutenants who get it. The Heinies now, they look after their officers better; you hardly ever see a dead German officer on the field of battle, whereas our side is positively littered with second loots.'

'Knee-deep,' Spanner said with a faint spark of animation.

'That's very encouraging,' I said. 'Thanks very much.'

They giggled. 'Anyway,' Karley went on, 'the position now is we're involved in this attack on Beaumont-Hamel in two days from now –'

'November 13th,' Spanner said darkly.

'The 13th, yes, at six-thirty. We'll go into the details later, but it's an all-out effort. We simply have to take Beaumont-Hamel. It's enormously important.'

'Why?' Spanner asked.

'Haven't the faintest idea, Spanner, my dear, but that's what they say. It's an eight-division job, by the way.'

Sanderson winced.

'Naturally the Heinies know all about it, and they'll be ready for us. But we –'

Rupert leaned forward, alarmed. 'I thought the colonel was joking,' he said. 'Do they really know?'

'They always know,' said Spanner.

'For one thing, they can see our preparations, and even if they couldn't see them they could hear them, and if they could neither see nor hear them the barrage would tell them. A barrage like this is a sure sign of an attack.'

We listened to the barrage. It sounded quite faint, but then we were twenty feet below ground.

'Fortunately, our objective is limited. We have to take only their first and second lines opposite here –'

'Only,' Spanner said.

'And then the Seventh will leap through up to Misery Wood five hundred yards beyond. Then – but, we'll go into the details later, as I said. It'll be a squeeze in the line before the attack – four companies in four hundred yards. However, the main thing will be to get across quickly.'

'How far is it?'

'Three, four hundred feet on the average.'

'It should take only a minute,' I said.

They looked at me. 'Shouldn't it?' I asked.

Karley plucked at his lower lip as if it were a guitar. 'It may take a smidgen longer than that,' he said.

Sanderson said sharply, 'Haven't you looked over the top yet?'

'Haven't had time.'

'If I were you, I'd take time.'

'It's a bit uneven out there,' Karley explained. 'And then, of course, there's the barbed wire.'

It was already too dark to see much that night. The Germans were putting up flares that illuminated no man's land with a harsh glare, but the light exaggerated the slightest hillock and cast jagged shadows. It made the land look ghastly.

But when I peered through a periscope next morning during a lull in the bombardment, I saw that the flares had not been exaggerating and that 'a bit uneven' was an understatement. It was a travesty of honest earth, cratered like the moon and savagely upheaved. The wire on our side was torn and there were numerous gaps in it. I couldn't see the German wire. In fact, I couldn't even see the German line, but there was a thin curl of smoke going up from one of their dugouts. Cooking breakfast, presumably. Blood pudding and sauerkraut, or whatever they ate. The smoke was outlined against the rising sun.

The barrage started up again, and I watched the shells bursting on the enemy side. The smoke was black and yellow. Surely nothing could live through a bombardment like that? An airplane was droning high overhead, surrounded by black puffs of smoke.

I realized with a start that I had forgotten to say my prayers that morning, and went back into the dugout to do so.

I now had a servant allocated to me, a small, fairly alert man called Daughters; but he had little time to do anything for me, everyone being busy shoring up collapsed sections of the line. He did find time to bring me one or two extra cups of tea, however. The tea tasted nasty but there was nothing else to drink, and as I was beginning to feel dehydrated, I forced it down.

I had given my rum ration that morning to Spanner. He offered me a handful of cigarettes in exchange, but of course I didn't smoke. This seemed to make him gloomier than ever.

I had hoped to get to know my platoon during the afternoon while I was in command of the line, but Pink kept getting in the way, and then the enemy began to shell us with shrapnel, and after that I was too busy keeping alive to indulge in casual conversation.

The air bursts seemed to be right over the trenches, and within two minutes a corporal in another platoon was struck in the back and his tunic turned dark with blood. He looked very surprised as he sat at the bottom of the trench. When they lifted him on to a stretcher, I saw tears in his eyes. I really think it was at that moment that my disillusionment with the infantry began.

The shells were bursting in the air all along the line, and it was raining lumps of metal. A member of my platoon was struck in the hand. He was overjoyed and went off down the C.T. singing. He had a 'blighty', which meant that he would be shipped home.

There was nothing we could do about the shrapnel, and after a couple of hours of it I began to have a feeling of helplessness that increased alarmingly when my helmet was struck a glancing blow.

The German counter-barrage increased in intensity throughout the afternoon, and for the first time I began to have doubts about the following morning. After all, we had been shelling their guns and positions for days, but it didn't seem to have had the slightest effect. By six that night we were being plastered not only with air bursts but also with 5.9s, *Minenwurfers*, howitzers, canisters, and several other kinds of nastiness. It seemed incredible that only one direct hit was made. All the same, by stand-to we'd had twenty-eight casualties, and I was in a kind of drab despair at our helplessness to do anything about it. Our own guns kept on firing streams of shells, and though the enemy lines were erupting in smoke and flame, the counter-barrage steadily increased, and they kept it up far into the night. Even Karley lost some of his cheerfulness.

'It's obvious they know,' he said. He stared into the rum I'd just given him, and sighed. 'Oh, well, one thing to be thankful for. This is likely to be the last offensive of the year.'

I had the ten to midnight watch, then slept fitfully until four. When I came up, loaded with wire cutters, periscope, revolver, field glasses, compass, map case, gas respirator, whistle, Mills bombs, ammunition, and a tin flute – where the flute came from I couldn't remember – the barrage was at its height. We checked the synchronization of our watches again, then waited for the dawn.

I stood next to Pink during the last few minutes, with the rest of the men huddled, shivering with cold, on either side. The sky was already lightening. I felt as if some small frightened animal were skittering around inside me. It was an effort to stop my teeth from clattering.

'Well, Sergeant,' I screeched, 'in a few minutes I guess we'll all be bayoneting the enemy in his trenches.' The thought made me sick.

'There won't be any.'

'Any what?'

'Heinies.'

'How do you mean?'

'They don't hold their front line like we do.'

'Do you mean to say we'll be charging empty trenches?'

'If there are any there, they'll double back to their second lines,' he bawled, his mouth close to my ear. 'Then when you're dead, Lieutenant, and everyone else 'cept me, they'll walk back and start playing cards again, like nothing's happened, see?'

The minutes dragged on. The barrage increased until it was a continuous roar of sound. Everyone looked grey.

The barrage stopped.

An awful, dread silence fell over the battlefield.

It was two minutes to six-thirty. I gripped my revolver excitedly.

I wasn't in the least afraid. It was just the skittering animal inside me that was in a panic, but I wasn't responsible for the state of *its* nerves. It felt like a chipmunk, and seemed to be nibbling my liver.

The chipmunk made me think of my private valley in Beamington. Not far from it, Pete Penner would already be in the barn, seeing to his cow. I wished I were Peter Penner. I wished I were his cow.

On second thoughts I decided it would be no fun, being a cow. I remembered a vet groping around inside one once, his arm buried up to the shoulders, searching, I should think, for the afterbirth. The cow had expressed indignation by relieving itself over the vet. I hadn't blamed the beast one bit.

It was one minute to six-thirty. The trench parapet seemed to be higher than ever. The fire step was crowded with crouching men. I heard someone being sick. The men of my platoon were silent, blank. I wanted to say something inspiring to them, but all I could think about was cows. I caught Pink's eye. He had been watching me with a sly grin. I realized that I had been looking blindly at my watch every ten seconds. Must stop that. Mustn't let him think I was afraid. I wasn't. It was only the chipmunk that was terrified. This was what I was here for, after all – to kill the enemy. I must remember that.

It was six-thirty.

The barrage started up again with a tremendous crash. The shells were exploding only a few feet over. Everyone stirred and shuffled. Somebody yawned repeatedly. On a level with my eyes I could see a pair of legs, tense and ready for the spring into no man's land. I looked up. A terrible long way to the parapet.

The barrage now started to creep toward the enemy. Still the whistle had not shrilled. Horrified, I realized that my legs had turned to foam. I knew I would never get over the parapet. I was in a panic. I seemed to have no strength left. I had a vision of four men, each holding an arm or leg, trying to haul me over the top.

'Is it true that you were so petrified with cowardice that you had to be pulled over the top by your own men?' they were asking at the court-martial.

'It was the chipmunk's fault,' I was whining. 'It was a Prussian chipmunk and it was eating a hole in my liver, not to mention the bites it was taking out of my long peroneal.'

They were just calling me a rotten cow-ward when the whistle blew and I leaped into the air and found myself lying crosswise on the bags. I had made it. I lay there congratulating myself until someone trod on my head.

'Come on, men!' I shouted, charged forward, and promptly fell into a crump hole. Dripping with filth, I sucked myself out, skirted two more shell craters that overlapped, and reached a fairly level piece of ground just beyond the tattered wire. Some of my men were still clambering over the bags. Already scores of soldiers were ahead of me, wreathed in smoke, faces set and twitching. I charged onward, shouting in the approved bloodthirsty manner.

There were hundreds of men all over the landscape. It was a peculiar feeling to be out in the open again after two days underground. One felt exposed. The barrage, which was supposed to creep just ahead of us was already too far ahead, already past the enemy front line. German bullets were starting to snap past. Then their artillery started up, ranging accurately on their own wire. A shell burst with a dull bang only a few yards away, and bits of it hissed. Someone near me fell on his knees slowly, as if to pray. Machine-gun bullets were lashing overhead. I started to slither into another crump hole but the smell of it drove me out.

The men ahead of me were in dense groups. They were supposed to spread out. A lot of them seemed to be falling. I had to leap over one man who was flailing about and holding his stomach.

The German wire was now only forty or so feet off, but there was a great deal of machine-gun fire. I stopped, turned to wave on my men, but found them passing me on either side, not paying the slightest attention. I was surprised to see how few of them there were. Indeed, the attack seemed to have thinned us out considerably, and there was no more bunching up.

A shell burst in a wet hole beside me and drenched me with stinking yellow water. I saw Karley just as he stumbled and fell. I staggered over.

'I'm all right; get on, get on,' he yelled.

The wire had been cut up by the bombardment, but it was still dense and I spent I don't know how long running up and down, trying to find a way through. I saw Pink get through it, and followed him. The next moment we were in the trenches. I fell on top of one of our men.

'Sorry,' I said, but then saw he was dead.

The trench was full of Canadians but no Germans, dead or alive. We had attained our first objective. I was just preening myself on my remarkable leadership when Sanderson appeared on the parapet, waving his arms.

'Come on, come on!'

I scrambled out of the battered trench and waved the others on valiantly, giving Private Daughters a hand. He was so light in spite of his equipment that in hauling him up I made him fly through the air. He didn't look too grateful.

As we started off toward our objective, we were greeted by a hail of fire so intense that we stopped, fell back a pace, and started to sink slowly and gracefully to the protection of the earth. Bullets and shell fragments were whipping and buzzing by the million. Sanderson pressed on and fell dead.

'Come on, come on!' someone yelled.

The men started up and forward again, but two or three immediately fell, one being struck with such force that he was pitched headfirst back into the trench. I felt my face fanned by the breeze from a stream of lead, and something plucked at my coat. I waved the others on frantically. Another bullet grazed the side of my knee. The men hesitated. It was impossible to go on, ridiculous. I dropped, and crawled forward into a crump hole. I found myself next to Pink and asked him if he was all right.

He was. 'This is as far as I go,' he announced. 'No sense in taking unnecessary risks. Safety first, that's my motto.'

The hole was shallow, and the bullets were passing unpleasantly close overhead. Our faces were pressed in the mud with our noses almost touching.

'What happens now?' I asked. Our eyes were so close we were squinting. 'Couldn't we go up their communications trench instead?' I was asking too many questions. Decisions, I told myself. 'Yes, that's what we'll do. Come on.' I gave him no time to reply, but turned and wriggled up the other side of the crump hole, then chanced an upright dash to the trench. Again I fell on a soldier, a live one this time. It was Karley.

'What the hell do you think you're doing?' he shouted. He started to get up again; then Pink fell on him. Karley made an excellent cushion.

'Follow me,' I shouted to some men. I began to trot along, searching for the communications trench.

I found a trench going more or less in the right direction and was about to start along it, revolver in hand, when I noticed that nobody was following. I went back to the men. 'Aren't you coming?' I shouted above the uproar.

'Where to?' Karley shouted.

'Couldn't we attack up the communications trench?'

Karley looked at me curiously for a moment, then nodded. 'All right.'

There were about forty men crammed in the trench. I grabbed Pink. 'Get some men and follow me!' I shouted.

Pink glanced at Karley, then began to shout names. The din of battle was so loud it was five minutes before he could make himself understood. Everyone else was frantically at work fortifying the rear wall of the line. There was no sign of Spanner or Randle.

We got back to the C.T., Pink just behind me, and started along it. After a few yards we slowed to a shuffle. I slipped the safety catch off my revolver and ordered the others to fix bayonets. This seemed to alarm them considerably. Around the third bend I came face to face with a German. It was a fine, youthful face with dazzling blue eyes. He had blond hair under his cloth cap. He looked like a very pleasant boy, hardly more than eighteen or nineteen. He was holding a piece of dark brown bread in his hand with dripping or something on it

We stared at each other, then both let out a yell at the same moment, and both turned and vanished round our respective corners. I could get only five yards down the trench because Pink was blocking the way.

'Germans!' I panted.

Pink was already pulling out a grenade. He flung it over my head, and it landed not far beyond me. Naturally it failed to roll round the corner.

I yelled again and tried to get past him, but Pink was in the way. I never met such a slow person. It was all right for him; if the grenade went off it would be me who would get it, not him. I was pounding his shoulder.

'Darn you, get on, get on!' I yelled. He had only three feet to go to the next bend but he was hardly moving. Meanwhile the grenade was smoking. I seemed to be having no luck with Mills bombs. I was pushing Pink frantically. He completely blocked the trench, with his legs astride.

It was hopeless. Pink was a big man. I couldn't get past him. I did the only thing possible. I dived between his legs and in a second had hurled myself past the bend just as the bomb went off.

I waited for Pink to follow me, rehearsing what I was going to say to him. But he did not appear. I looked cautiously round the corner and saw him sitting staring at me angrily. I went up to him.

'You clumsy idiot, what do you think you were doing?' I shouted furiously. 'You nearly got me killed! Just damned well whose side are you –' I stopped short when I realized I was actually swearing. It was especially grave since I had reproved Pink only yesterday for using bad language. But I *was* upset

I was about to go on when one of the men who was crowding around, Private Markis, touched my arm.

'No use talking to him, sir.'

It was only then that I noticed the back of Pink's head. He had been hit by his own grenade.

We gathered around to look at him, forgetting the Germans. The ground trembled under a heavy explosion, and damp air smote us, making us teeter.

'So old Pink got it at last,' Markis said. I liked the look of Markis. He was older than the others, with a small black moustache and big hands.

'What happened?' someone asked.

'There's Germans up the trench,' I said. I couldn't take my eyes off Pink. He looked so angry, as if it were all my fault, which of course it was.

The men glanced at one another and shifted about 'What you going to do, Lieutenant?' Private Rolo asked with a trace of anxiety.

'I guess it's our duty to fight our way up the trench,' I said. They all nodded dutifully. No one moved. 'After all, that's what we're here for,' I said. They nodded again, silently. 'To kill the enemy,' I added.

Rolo stuck his little finger in his rifle barrel and wiggled it around morosely. Someone else tried to scratch his head, but found his helmet in the way. His nails rasped on the steel 'How many of us are there?' I asked.

We all looked at each other and counted. 'Only six,' someone said.

There was a pause.

'There's likely to be a couple of hundred Heinies further up,' I said.

'That's right,' Rolo said. Rolo was a little fat man with four or five bags under each eye.

There was a whiz, then a tremendous bang down the trench. We all ducked. I thought hard. 'Six men,' I mused. 'That's not too good.'

They shook their heads.

'After all,' I said, 'we've taken the first line. That's not a bad day's work.'

They agreed.

'Besides,' I said, 'the trench here is so narrow we could only fight one at a time.'

'You've got something there, Lieutenant,' Markis said.

'We did pretty well just getting this far,' I went on.

Markis said, 'When someone like Pink gets it, it makes you think.'

'Poor Sergeant Pink,' Rolo said sadly. 'After two years. . . The lousy son of a bitch,' he added.

'That's not in very good taste,' I said stiffly.

'Neither was Pink,' Markis said.

'All the same, I'm a swine, talking that way about the dead,' Rolo said contentedly. 'How could I be so mean?'

Someone patted him on the arm.

'It's unforgivable of me,' Rolo insisted. 'All the same, he was a lousy son of a bitch.'

We all looked at Pink reflectively.

'Well,' I said, 'we're not doing much good here, are we?'

'No.'

'We might as well be getting back, then.'

'What about Pink?' Poole said. 'Oughtn't we to take him back?'

'I don't think so,' Markis said. 'We've had him for two years. Let the Heinies have him for a change.'

'We'd better get going, then,' Rolo said. 'For all we know, the others may have abandoned the position by now.'

We stumbled back as fast as we could, but Karley and the others were still there. They seemed surprised to see us.

'How did you get on?' Karley shouted in my ear.

'Ran into enemy. Lost Pink,' I shouted back cryptically.

'It's a terrible war,' Karley shouted pleasantly. 'Sanderson's kaput, Spanner and your pal are missing, we've lost two-thirds of the company, the attack's bogged down, the Heinies will probably counterattack in an hour or so, the leapfrogging battalion's pinned down by artillery fire, the C.O. of A Company's been blown to bits, this position is untenable, and we've nothing to eat. Apart from that the attack's going splendidly.'

'We'll become spoiled if we're not careful,' I shouted.

Karley slapped me on the back, then trotted off down the trench.

The Germans didn't counterattack within an hour, as Karley had surmised, but put down a barrage that killed one man about every five minutes. At noon we got frantic orders from Battalion to press on; the units on the left had taken their objective but were being enfiladed. We didn't have many men left to make the attack, but because Battalion insisted, at one o'clock we tried to go over the top.

I was almost out of the trench when someone was shot and fell back. By the time I had got out from under him and squelched ten yards forward, I found myself making the attack single-handed. There was not a soul in sight.

Well, I couldn't see myself waging the war entirely by myself, so I dived into the nearest hole just as a shell exploded so close that I was caught by the blast and knocked unconscious.

When I came to I found Markis beside me.

'Thought you'd got it that time, Lieutenant,' he remarked. He was lying on his hands, trying to keep his face dry. In the water behind us a body sprawled, half submerged. My hearing was apparently affected. I could hear Markis quite clearly, but the barrage seemed a long way off. I had lost half my uniform, my revolver, and my helmet.

'What time is it?' I muttered, trying to raise my arm. But I must have been lying on it, for it had gone quite dead. It felt like someone else's arm. Then I realized that it was someone else's arm.

'Just after one,' Markis said.

'Do you mean I've been unconscious for twenty-four hours? Fantastic.'

'No, about a minute.'

'Oh.'

Machine-gun fire was repeatedly traversing the crump hole. Every now and then shrapnel plopped into the water behind us. The man in the water was still wearing his helmet, and, overcoming my squeamishness, I took it off him.

Is this what the war is like? I thought to myself. Going forward into a solid wall of lead, men dying for a few yards of shattered trench, fighting an enemy one never saw except by accident? The whole thing was so – so inglorious, so-

An airplane like a dragonfly flew overhead, and even though it was about a mile up I could see the occupant, or one of the occupants, looking over the side. He must have felt contemptuous.

It made me think.

Something slithered headfirst into the hole, and I'd have got a fright if there had been any feeling left in me. But the thing was Captain Karley, who had mud, blood, and a smile on his face.

'Well,' he said, 'I think this is as far as we go. Get back to the trench with all haste, my friends, before the whiz-bangs get you.' To underline his wisdom, a shell dropped to earth not far away. The enemy was ranging on the captured trench, and as the shells habitually fell just short or just over, we were not in a very good position, ten yards out from it.

'I bet you'd accept a tot of rum now, eh, Bandy?' Karley shouted jovially.

I even thought about it for a few seconds before shaking my head.

'Ten million men have already discovered that alcohol is a necessity in this war!' Karley shouted. 'Sooner or later you'll realize it for yourself.'

'Alcoholic warmth is just an illusion of warmth,' I yelled.

'What the hell – as long as you *think* you're warm, that's good enough, isn't it?'

I considered this. Karley started to laugh, perhaps just a little hysterically, stopped, took a swig from a whisky flask, and held it out

'Like to try it?'

'No, no thanks.' I saw Markis looking. 'Markis could do with some, though.'

'No, that's O.K., Captain,' Markis said unconvincingly. Karley handed him the flask. Reluctantly, Markis swallowed nearly half of it.

'Let's go!' Karley shouted. He stood up. He actually *stood up* and *walked* back to the trench. It was reckless, brave, superhuman; and yet Karley seemed to be the only really human person I had met in the army.

I gestured for Markis to go, then slithered after him, hugging the mud lovingly. I had to crawl round a headless body.

It was incredible that anyone was still alive. But the trench was quite full when I sprawled into it, gasping and spitting dirt. I was glad to see that the company sergeant-major had survived, too. He was as beefy as Karley and a foot taller. His name was

Higginbottom, and he was always tremendously busy. After my first introduction to him, I had caught only brief glimpses of him as he stumped purposefully along the line, cursing at people.

That was why it was such a shock to see him squatting at the bottom of the trench, doing absolutely nothing.

But of course there was nothing to be done.

Karley was asking Higginbottom about Spanner. Nobody knew anything about him; and for the first time I saw Karley looking as grim as the rest of us. Someone said they had seen Randle a bit farther along the line, unhurt. I went to see him. The enemy was putting down a murderous fire as I picked my way down the shattered line, but I was thinking about the German I had bumped into. He had looked not the least malevolent, and he had been holding a piece of brown bread. It was difficult to hate someone with brown bread in his hand, with or without dripping on it. I made a mental note to ask Karley if he believed that bayoneting-Belgian-babies business.

I found Rupert in an evil-smelling dugout. There was a wounded man just inside the door with a field dressing on his bared chest. His face was blue. It looked like a lung wound. There were several soldiers huddled in the semidarkness.

Rupert lay in a corner.

'How long have you been here?'

'Since about seven, I suppose. I got stuck in the wire. It was dreadful. I was nearly killed.'

'You're not hurt at all?'

'I can't get up.'

I felt his legs. 'Nothing wrong with them. Try and stand.'

'It's no use, Bartholomew. I'll never get up again.'

I looked around at the others. They were lying about, staring vacantly. The wounded man bubbled and rolled his head from side to side. He ought not to be sitting up. I went over.

'Move away,' I said to a couple of lightly wounded.

I laid the wounded man in the space vacated and cleaned his wound, using my water bottle. It was a lung wound all right. I put on a clean dressing and bound it up tightly. The man had a chance if nobody moved him. He could hardly be left here, but getting him on to a stretcher was likely to kill him. I tried to comfort him, but he couldn't hear me, so I went back to Rupert.

'Get up, Randle. There's nothing wrong with you.'

He shook his head listlessly.

'Please get up,' I said. 'You're not showing much Christian strength.'

'I was nearly killed,' he muttered.

'But you weren't, so come on.' But he made no effort.

I talked to one of the soldiers about the lung case, and went back and sat in the dirt next to Karley.

'I don't think this is my kind of war after all,' I said. 'I've always been a bit squeamish about filth and squalor.'

'What's wrong? It's a lovely war. Just one big laugh,' Karley said. 'I once worked out how long it would take to get just to the frontiers of Germany at the present rate of progress, assuming no retreats. It worked out at December 6, 1958. Jesus, I laugh whenever I think about it.'

'I don't know how you can use that word,' I said.

'What? Laugh?'

'Taking the name of our Lord in vain.'

He was silent for a moment. 'I used to believe in that kind of thing, believe it or not.'

'Why not now?'

He glanced sideways at a body huddled up against the trench wall.

I bellowed a short sermon, ending with something to the effect that God was on our side.

'What makes you think that? From everything I've seen he's on the other side.'

'Of course he's on our side.'

'How do you know?'

'I just know, that's all.'

'Suppose I said I knew the world was flat.'

'But it's round. Everyone says it is. Anyway, it's been proved.'

'Exactly.'

I stared at him, offended. 'You shouldn't talk that way.'

'I've earned the right to talk that way,' Karley said. 'I've heard your bishops talking about God and Right and a Just Cause, but all I've seen is my company getting decimated regularly every three months.'

'That's a terrible way to talk.'

'Good luck to you. Bandy,' Karley said, smiling faintly.

I stared at him. Once, in the dissecting room at the University of Toronto, I had been going on, perhaps at inordinate length, about matters religious and the shocking degree of agnosticism prevalent among medical students; and the boy next to me had started to probe here and there in the cadaver as if searching for something. I'd asked him what he was looking for. 'For that soul you keep talking about,' he had said. 'I can't find it any where.' Another student joined in. 'Say, I wonder if it's in this thing here,' he had said, making a longitudinal incision in a certain leathery appendage.

That had not troubled me; I'd ignored it as being an eristic and rather adolescent jibe. But Karley was different, somehow.

He slapped me on the shoulder comfortingly.

'What happens now?' I asked, glad to change the subject.

'Unless we get support quick, we just wait here until there's nothing left of us, and then our ghosts drift back to the graves called dugouts. That's what always happens.'

'This infantry business. There doesn't seem to be much future in it.'

'You haven't taken long finding that out.'

We listened to the bombardment for a moment

'What's your first name again?'

'Bartholomew.'

'It would be.'

'What's yours?'

'Karley. It's the only name I have left. The other got shot away near Neuve-Chapelle.'

The sergeant-major crawled up. 'Mr Spanner is here, sir,' he said hoarsely.

'Is he all right?' Karley asked quickly.

'Rambling, sir, but not too bad. Got knocked on the head; been lying just the other side of the wire.'

Karley went off quickly.

'Bit of a mess, sir.'

'Yes,' I said.

'Still, could be worse.'

We ducked as a shell exploded just over the parapet and showered us with dirt.

We were counterattacked at about four in the afternoon, and they very nearly made it.

Shortly afterward we received orders to pull out. I went back with a soldier called Dorset, who had been hit in the trapezius muscle. I had to carry him. It was an interminable journey. I began to despair after two hours of trying to cross that few feet of filthy, stinking ground. I became convinced that in the darkness I was walking parallel to the trenches and was doomed to crawl and stagger until finally I reached the North Sea – or the Alps, for I didn't even know if I was proceeding east or west, having lost my compass.

At last I heard voices, and called out for help. Two or three pairs of hands pulled us in, and Dorset was put on a stretcher and carted away without delay. I told one of the Red Cross people about the soldier with the lung wound, but there was nothing that could be done about him. I went to H.Q. dugout, but there was no sign of Karley.

When I got back to my own dugout, there was Randle, fast asleep. He had even taken off his boots, which was against orders.

For a moment I had a feeling that I had dreamed the whole thing, that neither of us had been out of the dugout all day.

Karley got back, and when we made the roll call there were only four survivors in my platoon: Poole, Markis, Rolo, and Templeton. Out of the original company of 141 men, nineteen returned unwounded. The incredible thing was that Beaumont-Hamel was actually taken a few days later, all nineteen houses of it.

Resisting Temptation

AFTER THAT, THEY withdrew the four companies of the second battalion for rebuilding near Amiens. As Amiens was only twenty miles away, naturally we went on foot. I must have presented a proud sight, marching at the head of my platoon of four men.

After a few miles we had a real road to walk on. Its camber was slight, but the feeling of it underfoot was so unfamiliar after the days of soft ground and mud that we kept staggering sideways like crabs.

We were in rest near Amiens for some weeks. Gradually the reinforcements from Canada got the battalion back to full strength.

Presumably they also re-formed the other battalions of the Victorian Light Infantry Regiment, but one never knew what was happening elsewhere. The company was our entire horizon. Similarly, we never knew what the division as a whole was doing, what the corps was up to, what the army was achieving, the Allies accomplishing, or how the war was going. All we knew was that the colonel's adjutant had been informed by the brigade major who had heard it from a GSO2 who had it on good authority from a reparations officer that the war was going splendidly.

The men were delighted to be within deserting distance of a city that, after the battered towns of the front line, seemed to be a teeming metropolis. Not even Amiens' prices could damp their enthusiasm for its relative gaiety.

As for myself, I went into town twice and was pleased to see the stained glass in the cathedral almost unharmed. I got lost the first time I went, and was accosted by a woman. The second time, I drove in with Captain Karley (his friend Spanner was on leave) and we had an expensive dinner. Karley grew gay on red wine and champagne and finally vanished with the restaurateur's daughter into the gloomy, cockroach-infested depths of the back rooms, leaving me to get back to camp on foot. I got lost again.

Mostly, though, I stayed in my tent to catch up on sleep, write letters, and read the Good Book intensely.

Rupert refused to enter Amiens but talked to me at all hours of the day and night. Once he sat up on his elbow at three in the morning. 'Are you awake?' he asked in a penetrating whisper. He went on without waiting for a reply. 'You know, I'm beginning to have doubts.'

This was so intriguing that I said, 'Doubts? You mean, religion?'

'Certainly not,' he said in a shocked tone. 'Whatever gave you that idea?'

What indeed.

'I mean about coming through this thing alive.'

'Oh,' I said. Then, 'Why?'

'Well, look what happened to all those others. Some of them were quite devout men. A corporal in my platoon was almost as, well, religious as I, but he was – He always began his letters home, 'Dear sister in Christ,' you know. But they got him the second he went over the top.'

We were silent for a moment.

'Bartholomew?'

'Yes?'

'Do you know I've never – well, been with a –' The last word was drowned by a cough.

'A what?'

'A woman,' he said angrily.

It took a moment to adjust to this new topic.

'How do you mean?'

'You know.'

'You mean – ?'

'Yes. Someone I knew back home had been, well, with a woman when he was only nineteen.' Rupert was silent for a moment 'I'm twenty-three,' he said.

We both contemplated this in such profound silence that I was able to get back to sleep.

I was awakened again at five.

'Bartholomew?'

'Mmm?'

'Have you?'

'What?'

'Been with –'

'You mean –'

'Yes.'

'No.'

Rupert sighed and went back to sleep. He seemed annoyed with me.

Spanner came back from leave, very disgruntled. He brought some smoked salmon from Fortnum and Mason's with him. Bringing back smoked salmon from Fortnum and Mason's seemed to be a tradition in the army.

The days passed in orderly officer duties, lectures on gas, Boer War tactics, bugle calls, and a lot of other things I'd learned months before. I took a lot of church parades, shouted 'at the halt on the left, form platoon,' and managed to get rid of most of my lice.

We dined for a time in Battalion Mess, presided over by the lieutenant-colonel, who told a good many dirty stories, skilfully twirling his swagger stick between his fingers the while. Having earned his displeasure, I tried to make myself as inconspicuous as possible, but failed the first day when he noticed I wasn't laughing.

'What's the matter, Bandy, are my little pleasantries too much for your pristine ears?'

Everyone chortled.

'I don't approve of foul stories, sir,' I said.

Everyone groaned.

'You don't approve, eh? Frankly, Bandy, you terrify me.'

I thought it better to keep quiet.

'But you're inspiring at the same time. Inspiring in your purity. The chaplain tolerates my poor, tired efforts, but you don't.'

It was with a shock that I saw the padre was indeed in the mess. He had been sitting there all along with a set smile on his face.

The colonel said a good many more cutting things, but in so inimitable a fashion that everyone was vastly amused.

After that he told disgusting stories every day, looking at me pointedly, as if interested solely in my reaction.

Gradually I saw that he would never leave me alone. Silent dignity having failed, I decided to return to my natural behaviour.

On Boxing Day he told a particularly revolting story. By now, everyone had joined in the game of turning pointedly to me at the end of each story, my expression apparently adding to their enjoyment

'What, Bandy, still not appreciating my little drolleries?' the colonel remarked, tap-tapping the table with his stick.

'No, sir.'

'Perhaps he doesn't understand them?' the adjutant suggested.

'By heavens, Fred, I think you've got something there! That must be the explanation. Admit it now, Bandy; you don't really understand them. Well, let's see. I'll tell another little story, and we'll examine Lieutenant Bandy afterward to see if he understands it. Perhaps, why, perhaps we'll even have him laughing. Well, here goes:

'A farmer was taking his prize cow to market to be inseminated – I won't use the simpler, Saxon word in consideration of Bandy's feelings – and of course also the chaplain's. Eh, Padre?'

The padre smiled and shifted uncomfortably.

'Well, as I said, the farmer was taking the cow to be bulled, and as he was going down a country lane, Giles was sitting on a fence – this is an English joke, Bandy.

' "Where be you taking cow, George?" Giles asked.

' "Oi be taking it to market to be bulled."

'Giles nodded, and George went on his way, but when he got to market the bull wasn't there, so he had to go home. The next day he passed Giles again.

' "Where be you taking cow, George?" Giles asked.

' "Oi be taking it to market to be bulled."

'Giles nodded, and George went on; but again the bull had failed to turn up, so George had to go home again.

'The third day he passed Giles again.

' "Where be you taking cow, George?"

' "Oi be taking it to market to be bulled."

' "Oi don't like to seem to be interfering, like," Giles said, "but seems to me you be making a regular whore out of that cow." '

The colonel waited expectantly.

'No, Bandy? No smile? Does Bandy not see the joke?'

'I don't think he knows what inseminated *or* bulled means, sir,' the adjutant said.

'Well, let's see. What does it mean, Bandy? '

I told him.

'Excellent! Full marks! A round of applause, please, for Subaltern Bandy.'

Everyone clapped heartily, looking at me with gleaming red faces, including, I was saddened to note, Rupert.

'Now, next. Do you know what a market is, Bandy?'

'Yes, sir, where they sell vegetables.'

'Fine. Finally, do you know what a whore is? Do you know, Bandy?'

'Yes, sir.'

'What is it?'

'An immoral woman, sir.'

'Very, very good. So will you now kindly explain to the company the joke. Will you. Bandy?'

'Yes, sir.' I thought for a moment. 'This farmer George was taking his cow to market to be inseminated by a bull, but the bull wasn't there, which was hardly surprising because they don't allow that kind of thing in the middle of a market. It's not good for the children. George was therefore wasting his time. The usual procedure is for the bull to be brought to the cow. George obviously was an incompetent gentleman farmer devoted to raising hordes of gentlemen, with or without pedigrees.

'Also, sir, as you admitted that it was a market devoted to selling vegetables, George was not merely incompetent but absurd if he expected to find a bull there. Why, he'd be looking in a china shop next –'

'But this is an English market, Bandy. All sorts of nasty, immoral things go on at English markets,' the colonel said, rapping the table angrily.

'Yes, sir, but I happen to know that there weren't any bulls at this particular market; they'd long since slaughtered them off to make swagger sticks out of their pizzles. Did you know that's what swagger sticks were made of, sir?'

'I –' the colonel said.

'It's a fact, sir, so that when you're striding along twirling your swagger stick you are in effect making obscene gestures hardly in keeping with the military proprieties. I don't think the brigadier would like that, sir.'

The colonel was in the middle of twirling his stick He looked at it with a slight start, then put it on the table.

'We're not discussing swagger sticks,' he said. 'We're discussing markets, and I say there was a bull in that market, do you hear?'

'If you insist, sir.'

'I do insist'

'In that case why did George have to take his cow there three times?'

'Because the bull wasn't feeling well,' the colonel said. He was about to pick up his stick to rap the table but changed his mind.

Captain Karley murmured: 'Personally I think the bull recognized the cow as his cousin. That would explain everything, sir.'

' 'That's right,' the colonel said gratefully.

'If they were cousins,' Spanner said, 'wouldn't that be incest?' He sounded disapproving.

'That would be the end of the world as we know it,' I remarked.

'Don't listen to them, sir,' the adjutant said, glaring. 'This incest business is red herrings.'

'Whoever heard of red herrings committing incest?' I said. 'Incidentally, are herrings red? I always thought they were brown.'

'Certainly they're red,' Karley said, 'with shame, because they're always committing incest'

The colonel wasn't allowing the initiative to be seized from him. He scratched his face angrily. 'It's not the herrings that were guilty of incest,' he said. 'It's the bull.'

'Don't you think the cow was more to blame?' a subaltern asked, timidly. 'After all, it was she who made the advances, *Cherchez la femme*, you know,' he added as an afterthought.

'Certainly,' Karley said spiritedly. 'She advanced all the way to market, under fire from Giles.'

'So it was really Giles to blame for the whole sorry business,' Spanner said. 'Holding up the cow's advance. I wouldn't be surprised if he was really a German spy in disguise.'

There then ensued a heated discussion about Giles. Becoming bored in the middle of it, I wandered out just as the colonel, in a fit of pique, threw his stick at the phonograph, which was playing a popular song called, 'You're the Apple of My Eye, Although You're Rotten to the Core'.

My days were now fully occupied in instructing my platoon from the infantry training manual and lecturing on a variety of subjects ranging from gas to the Care and Maintenance of One's Weapon. I let Markis, now a corporal, give the lecture on prophylaxis because he seemed to know more about it than me. I became quite fluent during these lecture sessions, although I rarely knew what I was talking about.

Meanwhile, as the time drew near for our next tour in the trenches, Rupert became more and more morose. On New Year's Eve he disappeared and didn't come back until four in the morning. Shortly after the first of January we went back up, and were ten days in support and five days in the line.

This time it was quite different. The war seemed to have worn itself out. During our support days the guns thumped only intermittently. We spent the time improving the trenches and dugouts. The weather was foul. I caught a cold. For the others, the arrival of the gallon demijohns of rum became the event of the day. I shared mine equally between Karley, Spanner, Barayan, and Selby. The latter two were our new company officers. Barayan was from Edmonton, tall, handsome, and charming; Selby had been with another battalion and was usually half to nine-tenths inebriated.

Day after day after day we shivered in the line or huddled in the evil-smelling, rat-infested dugouts. I tried to busy myself looking after the men, but they were resourceful enough, especially Corporal Markis, who was once caught trying to bring in a four-poster from a newly wrecked house. Foiled in this endeavour he made do with a magnificent spring mattress supported on barbed wire. My new sergeant, called Bunser, was a strange character. He was small and had a dark, blue face, and went around with his shoulders hunched under a cape so that he looked like a bundle of old rags wrapped in waterproofing. For some reason every single member of my platoon was under average height. I felt like Snow White among the seven dwarfs, except that there were more than seven of them.

Every time I went into their dugout, they were playing cards. Everyone in the army seemed to play cards, devotedly, fanatically. I learned how to play poker, just by watching them. Once, Markis, who always won, gave me an interesting lecture on the subject. He also told me that I ought to try it myself; I'd be a natural.

'Why?'

'You got the best poker face I ever saw.'

Nothing much happened during that tour; The snipers picked off their usual daily quota.

We had five days of rest, billeted at a farmhouse whose owners, an old French couple, had stayed on even though they had lost all their stock and their fields had been trampled and furrowed into quagmires by boots and gun carriages. I spent my time on work parties, sleeping and watching the airplanes wander back and forth over the lines, and began to envy the pilots. We received a large batch of mail while at rest. I had five letters from home and a brochure from a medical-supply firm in the States offering me a year's supply of pessary rings at an unheard-of discount. The letters from Mother informed me that everyone still disapproved of me strongly and that I ought to write to Mabel; that Dr House had said that his daughter was well out of it; that Gerry Ince had come home from the front minus an arm; that the barley crop had been exceptionally good. Mother also hoped I was keeping up my piano lessons.

I almost did write to Mabel; but when I poised the pen over paper I found that I could not remember her face, so I made a paper dart instead.

The entire Somme front having gone to sleep, we were moved to the Flanders section of the line. The division rattled on rails and stumbled on *pavé* for four days, then to everyone's disgust went straight into the front line.

I had thought the conditions were poor enough in the Somme. They were a bed of roses compared with Ypres. I never saw such an abominable desolation, even though two or three inches of snow obscured the harsher wounds. The furrows of the front and support trenches were like poisonous scars. No man's land was a cesspool, without even the merciful covering of snow, for the snow had been dissipated by the crumps.

The dugout I shared with Randle and Barayan was carved out of clay, and the walls trickled.

We were perpetually soaked and trembling with cold. The daily half-pint of rum was the one bright spot, and watching the others drink it with obvious relish, it became an increasing effort to resist the temptation. My teeth clattered audibly, but

I was stubborn. My servant made me numerous cups of coffee, but it was almost always half cold before it was delivered, and didn't make me any warmer. Finally, Karley became annoyed with me.

'Man, you'll never get warm unless you start drinking the stuff.'

'But you told me it only keeps you warm for half an hour.'

'Half an hour's better than no loaf, isn't it? Do you think, you stubborn idiot, that they'd include it with the rations and the ammo if it wasn't a necessity? Drink it, man!'

'I promised my fa –'

'Promised! What does *he* know what it's like out here?'

'We're not prejudiced, you know,' Spanner murmured from the depths of the blanket he was huddled in. 'We're quite happy to go on drinking your ration. It's for your own good.'

'For my own good,' I repeated. 'M'yes, the thin edge of the wedge.'

'Randle is drinking his.'

I turned, startled, to Barayan. He was looking at me with his black eyes gleaming. 'What?' I looked at Rupert incredulously.

'Sure,' Karley said. 'Haven't you noticed he hasn't been selling it to us lately?'

I stared at Rupert for a moment, then back to Karley, holding my hands over the candle to warm them. 'Anyway, that's nothing to do with me. I promised, and I always keep my promises.'

They all snorted disgustedly. 'You're a bumpkin,' Selby snapped.

'What do promises matter?' Barayan said.

'They matter to me.'

'Oh, God. A man of principle.'

'Look, Bandy,' Spanner said. 'Don't look at it as demon rum. It's medicine, pure and simple. Now, drink it up like a good boy, and release us from the suspense.'

'I can stand the cold.'

Karley glared. 'Well, we can't stand you standing the cold,' he snapped. 'Look at your great blank face, man: it's purple. Do you want to go around looking like a baboon's behind? Drink it!'

'No, thanks. I already feel myself going downhill rapidly enough without that. If I started on rum I'd graduate to whisky. Before I knew where I was, I'd be reading novels.'

'Once and for all, are you going to drink it?' Karley shouted.

'No.'

'Oh, yes you are,' Karley said. He stood up. 'I order you formally, as your company commander, to drink that rum.'

'Go to hell.'

There was a dead silence, broken only by the crump of shells, the chatter of machine guns, the droning of a plane, and the squeal of rats. Karley was wide-eyed. Even Spanner had emerged from his blanket, his lean blue jaw slack with astonishment. Rupert was popeyed.

'Did you hear what I heard?' Karley asked faintly.

'I did,' Spanner said grimly.

'He swore. He actually used bad language.' Karley put his hand to his head and staggered, then sat down weakly, still staring at me. 'He actually said 'hell'.'

'Gentlemen.' Spanner got up in slow dignity and raised his mug. 'A toast.'

They all arose.

'To Second Lieutenant Bandy, Bartholomew W., who, on this nineteenth day of January in the year of our Lord nineteen hundred and seventeen, spoke for the first time like a true soldier.'

They drank solemnly.

'Gentlemen,' Spanner said, 'I don't think we need press our Mr Bandy any further. The thin edge is in; the die is cast. You can lead a horse to water, or rather rum – and this is not entirely irrelevant, for Bandy does resemble a horse – and sooner or later it will drink. It's just a matter of time, now. And time, as everyone knows, is on our side.'

That night when Barayan was on duty I asked Rupert if it was true.

'Why not?' There was silence for a moment, then: 'You know, Bandy, you have to adjust. You can't be a stick-in-the-mud all your life.'

'I can't?'

'No,' Rupert said. 'After all, this is France, not Canada.'

'That's true,' I said.

'Life is to be lived.'

'Thank you for reminding me.'

'But you – you're not getting anything out of it.'

'How?'

'Well. . .' Rupert leaned over. 'We are in a dangerous situation,' he announced.

'Oh?'

'It calls for an adjustment to one's standards, one's – behaviour. Take for example...' He hesitated. 'Well, you don't even know anything, well, about women, for example. Do you?'

'No.'

'There you are,' he said.

'There who are, where?' I asked curiously. I had an idea this was leading somewhere.

'You haven't lived.'

'Have you?' I asked.

He wriggled in his sleeping bag. 'Certainly,' he said.

'Just because you've been drinking rum?'

'Of course not,' he said. 'I mean the other.'

I thought about it. It was true. I hadn't lived, not even in Toronto, at the university.

'You know, Bandy – you won't mind if I say this, I hope – but you're a terrible prig. Personally, I suspect anyone who goes round parading his piety and moral superiority. It's not superiority at all; it's lack of experience.'

'What are you talking about, Rupert?'

'That's another thing. Must you call me Rupert? Everyone else addresses each other by their surnames. We're not at school, you know.'

'I'll try to remember. Now will you tell me what you're talking about?'

'I'm not talking about anything,' he said crossly.

'What do you mean by experience?'

Rupert, or rather Randle, clicked his tongue and gave an impatient sigh. 'You *are* a fool, Bandy. I don't know what I ever saw in you.' He plucked morosely at his flea bag. 'You know, they're still laughing at you over the beer vats.'

He was referring to my reaction when on taking the men for their ablutions one day at rest I found they were using huge beer vats in an abandoned brewery as bathtubs. Only the lice that were building cities in my armpits had overcome my reluctance to dip myself in the officers' vat; I had complained of smelling of beer for two days afterward.

There was a long silence. Rupert started to speak two or three times, but didn't. Finally he said, 'And I suppose when you were in Amiens you just went to look at the cathedral.'

'Yes, why?'

'One can't spend all one's life looking round churches.'

'I only spent a couple of hours. Now, if you'll excuse me, I'm going back to sleep.'

I was almost asleep when he said, 'I went with a woman.'

I sat up. 'What woman?'

'How should I know?' he said. He clicked his tongue impatiently. 'I wasn't interested in her *name*.'

'So that's what you meant by experience. When was this?'

'On New Year's Day.'

'Oh.' I remembered.

Randle lay back with a sigh. 'She called me *Cheri*,' he said. 'She was very affectionate.'

'Well, I hope you looked after yourself,' I said, and lay down again.

'How do you mean? She didn't steal my money, if that's what you mean.'

'You know what I mean.'

'Oh, that. Certainly,' he said, loftily.

There was another pause. Then he said with a half snigger, 'Though I must admit I was alarmed later when I got a ...' He coughed. 'But it went away.'

I sat up again. 'You mean a sore?'

'Yes,' he almost shouted. 'Do you have to be so – so –' He struggled for the word, couldn't find it, and snuggled down into his bag.

'And it went away? How long did it last?'

He sighed noisily. 'I didn't mark it on a calendar,' he said acidly. 'I didn't have my stop watch with me. Now are you satisfied? You know, I'm becoming rather shocked at you, Bandy. This curiosity seems to me definitely unhealthy. A couple of weeks,' he added scornfully.

I was forced to sound knowledgeable. 'I guess you know the incubation period for the *Spirochaeta pallida* is about two to three weeks.'

'You're talking nonsense as usual.'

'If I were you I'd go to the M.O. tomorrow. '

'But I tell you it's gone.'

'All the more reason. It's entrenching itself in your bloodstream. You'd better counterattack.'

'Oh, Lord, another amateur strategist.'

'Good night,' I said.

'Are you sure?'

'Yes.'

'How?'

'I picked it up,' I said.

'*You've* got it, too?'

'Certainly not. I mean, I picked up the information. At medical school.' I heard him lie down slowly. It was a long time before he answered.

'I think you're bluffing.'

I didn't say anything.

'I definitely won't. Never.'

I remained silent.

'I'll never go. What would he think? What would everyone think?'

'What does that matter?' I said.

'I'll never,' he said, in tones of finality.

But he did and it was and he went, and I never saw him again at the Front, because something happened that set me on the downward path, plunging me into the abyss, into a bottomless pit of iniquity, immorality, and the grossest excesses.

A Peculiar Patrol

I DIDN'T KNOW the lieutenant-colonel had arrived until I clattered down into the H.Q. dugout. He was delighted to see me. His eyes lighted up.

'The very man!' he exclaimed. 'Come in, Bandy. We've some excellent news for you. '

'Yes, sir?'

'We've been combing the entire army for a man of resource, cunning, energy, and initiative. And guess who is the only man to fit these exacting qualifications?'

'Me?'

'You, Bandy.'

'That's very gratifying, sir.'

'Isn't it?'

Karley murmured, 'We were thinking more of Lieutenant Randle, sir.'

'Is Randle a man of resource, cunning, et cetera?'

'Well, not exactly, sir, but –'

'And I know that Bandy is. I recognized it right from the beginning, didn't I, Fred? A man of singularly independent spirit.'

'At the moment,' I said, 'a definite feeling of incompetence is stealing over me.'

I noticed the colonel was no longer carrying his swagger stick, and looked lost without it.

'I've been very lenient with you until now, Bandy,' he said fairly calmly, 'in spite of your unique lack of deference in the presence of senior officers, not to mention your face. I've court-martialled men for less than that face. But never mind your face – though it's very hard not to. No, it's your way of speaking. Any ordinary mortal trembles when confronted by a colonel. Why don't you? I ask purely out of curiosity. Does the military hierarchy mean so little to you? Tell me. I'm most interested to find out what makes a freak.'

I was about to answer, when I saw Karley gazing at me fixedly. He moved his head a quarter of an inch to the left, then a quarter-inch to the right

'They mean a lot to me, sir.'

'They do, do they?'

He stared at me coldly for another minute; then went on more calmly: 'All right. I'm tired of the conversation. How would you like to capture a prisoner for us?'

'All right, sir.'

'Oh? You think you can do it? You're feeling competent again?'

'Yes, sir.'

'I'm so relieved. Very well. We want to know who's opposite us. Tonight, just after dark, while the Heinies are cooking their sausages, you are to take two or three men and make a raid on their trenches.'

'Can I go too, sir?' Karley asked.

'No, you can't, Captain, and that's final. Don't you trust Bandy?'

'I only thought –'

'Don't think. Leave that to the brigadier; it's his show. And you'd better make it a good one, Bandy. Because I'll be here to welcome you back.'

After stand-to I had a last word with Karley, who seemed to be in an irritable mood. I told him I was taking Markis, Rolo, and another man, called Briggs.

'You all set?'

'Yes, thank you, Karley.'

'Are you sure you won't have a drink before you go? You'll be cold out there –'

'No, thanks.'

'All right, you're an idiot, a stubborn –' He sighed. 'Got the wire cutters?' Spanner whispered something in his ear. Karley brightened. 'Yes.'

'You'll have to hack your way through our own wire. You've seen where the gap is on their side; about a hundred yards to the left from here. You'll have an awkward crawl across, and it'll be pitch black; the moon isn't due until ten. You'll have to rely on Heinie light. And listen, Bandy,' Karley added fiercely, 'get in, grab the first man you see, and get out – fast! If he struggles, kill him. His badges will tell us what we want to know.'

'Kill him?' I seemed to be having trouble with my breathing.

'Don't you understand plain English?'

'Yes.'

He looked at me, his hands on his hips. 'Perhaps you'd prefer to have a short debate in his trenches?'

'No, Captain.'

'All right, then.' Karley looked peevishly at his watch. 'You're off in five. Naturally –'

Spanner interrupted. 'They're throwing up a lot of light,' he said, looking at the sky.

'All the better to see you with, my dear,' Karley said. 'You'd better get up to the trench.'

Markis, Rolo, Briggs, and I crouched on the fire step. Markis carried a blackjack and a revolver, Briggs and Rolo had knives and grenades; and I had a revolver and grenades. It was Markis' fiftieth patrol, Rolo's twentieth, my third, and Briggs's third.

Things were fairly calm. The field guns were silent. Now and again a howitzer tossed a shell into the German back areas. Every three minutes or so the other side sent up star shells that illuminated the battlefield in a harsh glare. In their light the sporadic flakes of snow were like fireflies.

'Don't forget,' Karley rasped in my ear, 'in and out quick.'

'Good luck,' Spanner said mournfully.

We crawled up and over, and, as planned, Markis and I went first, clipping the wire until our wrists ached. The cutters, as usual, were inefficient. After three years of war you'd have thought they'd be able to produce decent wire cutters. It took a long time to get through.

We were ten feet beyond the wire when we got caught in the light of a star shell. We buried our faces in the frozen ground and waited until the shadows lengthened before crawling on. The others drank thirstily from their water bottles. For a peculiar moment I thought I caught a whiff of rum in the air, but as this was hardly likely in the midst of no man's land I dismissed the idea.

After another fifteen minutes of crawling obliquely toward the gap in the enemy wire (which took us only ten yards in a forward direction), we wriggled into a large crump hole to rest. In the light of a new star shell we saw it was half filled with frozen water, with a human hand sticking out of it. It seemed to be waving at us cheerfully. Rolo shook hands with it.

'How do you do,' he whispered.

We were about to crawl from the far side of the hole when a machine gun opened up and began methodically to traverse just over the ground. We ducked down again and waited until the bullets had finished spitting over the top before pressing onward.

It was at this point that the other side stopped sending up star shells. We found ourselves in complete darkness. A quarter of an hour later I was completely lost. I felt quite angry at the Germans.

'Are we sure we're going in the right direction?' Markis whispered.

'How the hell we going to find the gap in this darkness?' Rolo complained.

'Sh-hh,' I ordered.

Markis, Rolo, and Briggs sucked at their water bottles again.

We stopped and thought. Not that it was much use thinking. There were no landmarks to guide us even if we had dared raise our heads to study them. I half wished the machine gun would open up again, to give us some sense of direction. But there was an ominous calm.

'What a lousy war!' Rolo grumbled disgustedly. 'I musta crawled a hundred miles since I joined. My tits are just about wore smooth.'

Briggs started to guffaw. 'Shut up,' I whispered. 'And don't be so disgusting, Rolo.'

'Which way do we go now?' Markis asked.

I had my compass in my hand and tried to read it, but the fluorescence wasn't clear enough. I fumbled for Markis' head, then pushed the compass under his nose. 'Can you see what it says?'

'What what says?'

'The compass I'm holding under your nose.'

There was a pause. 'Can't see a thing,' he said.

I took it back and looked again. I almost had it in my eye like a monocle, but it was unreadable.

'I've gone round so many crump holes I don't know where I am,' Markis whispered. He hiccupped. Briggs laughed again.

'P'raps – p'raps –' Rolo began. We waited.

'Perhaps what?' I whispered.

'I've forgotten what I was going to say,' Rolo said loudly.

'Sh-hh.'

Rolo giggled.

'What's wrong with you all?' I muttered. 'This is no laughing matter.'

There was a gurgling sound that gave me a fright 'What's that?' I whispered.

'Wha's what?'

'That gurgling sound.'

There was silence for a moment.

'It's the water from – the water in our water bottles, sir, Lieutenant. 'S pretty strong.'

All three of them laughed.

'For heaven's sake, men,' I whispered hoarsely. I was feeling hot and dry-mouthed from the smell of the earth, the exertion of crawling, and the embarrassment of our position.

'I've remembered,' Rolo said loudly.

'Sh-hh!'

'But I've remembered.'

'Remembered what?' I asked, exasperated.

'What I was going to say.'

'When?' Markis asked.

'When what?'

There was another gurgling sound. 'When,' Rolo said.

'Don't drink all your water, Markis; you may need it later,' I said.

'I need it now, Lieutenant,' he said. His voice sounded odd.

Rolo said, 'Doesn't anyone want to know what I remembered?' He sounded sulky.

'What?'

'What what?' Rolo asked, interested.

'What you remembered, ya clown,' Markis said.

'Keep your voices down,' I said desperately.

'Hey,' Briggs said excitedly. 'That rhymes! "What you remembered, you clown, keep your voices down." How about that?'

'It doesn't scan,' Markis said with an air of finality.

What on earth was wrong with them? I wondered. I was about to reprove them; but my throat was too parched. I reached for my water bottle, and with elaborate care, in order to avoid raising my elbow too high, removed the stopper, tipped it up, and drank.

I had taken several mouthfuls before I became aware of a burning sensation in my throat. I put the bottle down, coughing and spluttering. Tears poured from my eyes like twin fountains. I strangled some air into my lungs. The sides of my throat seemed to have fused together.

'Are you O.K., sir?' Markis asked.

It was another half-minute before I could answer.

The water,' I gasped. 'There's something wrong with it.'

I could feel Markis fumbling around for the bottle. As he did so I caught a strong whiff of rum on his breath.

'Markis!'

'Sir?'

'Markis,' I whispered hoarsely, 'are you – is that rum you've been drinking?' And then an awful thought struck me. I seized my own water bottle, and sniffed.

'My God!' I said.

'What, sir?'

'They've emptied out my water and put rum in it.'

'Dirty dogsh,' Rolo said.

I lay there with my cheek on the earth, thinking angrily. It must have been Karley – or Spanner. What a thing to do, what a rotten trick! What a nasty, underhanded trick! I fumed. I sniffed the water bottle again. There was no doubt about it.

I became aware of a great heat spreading inside me. My forehead felt like a hot plate. I felt as if my head ended just above my eyes. I put my hand up to make sure it didn't. It did.

'Markis.'

'Yessir?'

'The top of my head's been blown off. You'll have to take over.'

'Are you sure, sir?'

'Quite sure.' I lifted the water bottle. 'I'd better have another drink to ease the pain, when it comes.' I drank, and my eyes filled with tears again, but this time at the thought of dying so young. I spluttered sadly.

I felt Markis pawing my head. 'Your helmet's still on, Lieutenant.'

'I know, Markis, but's down over m'ears. Can't see.'

'Maybe's because's dark.'

After a minute I managed to get the stopper back in the bottle and hung the strap over my shoulder. My head still felt flat, but I had lost interest in it. So had the others.

'What do we do now?' I asked.

'You're the boss,' Markis said.

'Yes, that's right,' I agreed sadly. 'Enough of this dillydallying. Forward, men.' I started to crawl away, but, detecting no movement, came back. 'Aren't you coming?'

'Where to?' Rolo asked.

I had to think hard. What was it we were supposed to do?

'To attack?'

'There's no bombardment,' Markis said 'We can't attack without a bombardment.'

'Who cares about a bombardment?' Briggs said recklessly. 'We don't need any lousy bombardment.'

'We can't attack without a bombardment,' Markis said. He sounded quite definite. 'It's unheard of.'

'Oh, I don't know,' Rolo said.

'We *got* to have a bombardment,' Markis said, 'and that's final. Ain't it, Lieutenant?'

'Yes,' I said, 'so let's not have any more argument.'

'Maybe we ought to go back,' Rolo suggested.

'Where is "back"?'

'What?'

'I said, where is "back"?' Markis said. 'For that matter,' he added, 'where is forward? Not to mention sideways, upwards, and downwise.'

'Forward is the direction your head is pointing,' Rolo said. 'And backward is where your feet are.'

'Suppose you're sitting up backward?' Markis asked loudly.

'Sh-hh,' we all said.

'In that case forward would be upward and backward would be forward. What then?'

'We would need a ladder in order to advance,' I said authoritatively. It was wonderful how warm I was feeling. I un-stoppered the water bottle again. 'All this talking is making me thirsty,' I remarked.

'Yes, let's all have a drink,' Briggs said. So we all had a drink.

'Well,' I said, 'we can't lay, er, lie here all night, can we? Doesn't *anyone* remember what we're supposed to do?'

'Maybe we're just out for a walk. You know, stretch our legs?' Rolo suggested.

'No,' I said, 'there's more to it than that, I'm sure.' Then I remembered. I tried to snap my fingers. 'I've got it,' I said. 'Prisoners. We have to take a prisoner. Come on, let's go.'

So we started off again. The Germans sent up a single star shell, and we made quite good progress while it burned in the sky. I saw some barbed wire ahead.

'We've made it,' I whispered. 'There's even a gap in it, though not as big as, big as the gap as we saw from the – what?'

There was no answer. I looked around. I was alone.

I lay down to brood about this development. I didn't dare call out, being so close to the enemy wire. This was terrible. Well, I would just have to take a prisoner on my own.

I finished off the rest of the rum. There seemed to be a terrible lot of it. Rum didn't seem much good as a thirst quencher. I felt rather disappointed in it. But there was no doubt that it tasted no worse than the water from the water wagons.

I felt very hot indeed.

I crawled through the gap in the wire and up to the parapet of sandbags. I could hear a thin mutter of voices from the other side and the faint clump of boots on duckboard.

I lay for several seconds or minutes, waiting for silence.

Then, cautiously, I looked over the parapet.

Their trench was about the same depth as ours. Someone was just coming round a bend in the line. He was alone as far as I could see, which wasn't far. He wasn't even wearing a helmet, just some kind of cloth cap. I took out my revolver, and as he passed underneath I leaned over and hit him on the head. He fell in a heap.

I climbed over and dropped on to the fire step. Just as I had heaved the body on to the parapet, I heard someone coming. With commendable initiative I plucked a grenade and heaved it round the bend. There was a shout, then more shouts, then running feet. For good measure I emptied my revolver more or less in the right direction, heaved myself up and started off, dragging my prisoner through the wire. I had gone a good twenty yards before I realized I was standing upright. There were shouts from the trench behind, and a moment later they started shooting. A withering fire burst around me.

Still standing, I began to heave grenades back at them as fast as I could pull the pins. Bullets were snapping all around me. It was good fun. All this time we've been fighting the war all scrunched up underground, I thought to myself, and there was no need. I've made a great discovery. It's easy to stand up. I felt very pleased with myself. However, when our own side began to reply with machine guns from behind me, I decided not to hang around any longer. I heaved the still unconscious body of my prisoner on my back and started to run, still upright, toward the middle of no man's land. He was very heavy. We fell into a crump hole.

The fire grew heavier, and a few moments later the field artillery joined in. Soon the air above the hole was alive with lead, the night hellish with noise. Both sides were firing. Flares and star shells soared skyward by the hundred. I lay at the bottom of the hole watching it, giggling and waving my arms.

'Mine!' I was shouting, meaning the barrage. 'Mine, all mine!'

It went on like that for half an hour. The other side was putting down a murderous fire, a dense blanket of shells. In the middle of it my prisoner started to groan, and I reached for my revolver again, but seemed to have lost it. The German – a big fellow as far as I could see – was now making efforts to sit up. What could I hit him with? He would start making all kinds of trouble. I tried to take off my boots, intending to hit him with one, but couldn't get them off. Then I had a brain wave, reached for my tin hat, which fortunately was still in place, held it in both hands, carefully measured the distance in the intermittent light from the shell explosions, and brought it down on his head with a crack. He fell over without a word.

It took two hours before the barrage died down. During that time, as I grew rapidly cooler, I also lost a lot of my courage. I could hardly believe it was I who had been behaving so absurdly. When I hit my prisoner on the head for the fourth time, I did so with some distaste. I felt sorry for him. He would have a nasty headache in the morning.

As I lay face down beside him, I wondered what had happened to the other three.

As abruptly as it had started up, the exchange of fire died away. It was then I saw that the moon was halfway up in the sky. That made it past midnight

It was incredible, but it seemed that I had been in no man's land for over six hours.

The enemy was still putting up plenty of light. Nervous people, the Germans. Funny, though. His star shells seemed to be coming from in front rather than behind.

I waited a further half-hour. Every now and then a machine gun spattered across the battlefield. It was not going to be a very safe journey back. I wondered how I was going to drag the prisoner. When I remembered the way I had carried him thus far, I shuddered.

The single machine gun had still not given up for the night. I was now starving and covered with the mud that had melted under me. However, I couldn't stay out all night. I turned the body over and was about to heave it over my shoulder when a star shell burst directly overhead and I saw the red tabs.

I sank back, staring. Could it be that I had captured a senior officer? A second later I saw that I had. Only, it was one of ours. In the dazzling light I even recognized him.

It was the colonel.

If it was possible to grow colder, I did. I couldn't believe my eyes. It wasn't possible. Surely it was a trick of the light? It wasn't. He lay there, covered in filth and three medal ribbons, a belt with a holster in front, and knee-length boots that shone through the mud covering them. Even unconscious he looked bitter. I realized then the ghastly truth: in the darkness I must have turned back on my own lines – and thrown grenades, too. I put my head down and groaned.

It was five minutes before I could think what to do. I considered shooting myself. I thought of remaining in the crump hole until the end of the war. I seriously considered crawling onward and surrendering.

But in the end I decided there was only one thing to do. I had to take him back. I had to take my medicine and face the music.

At that moment of truth his eyelids started to flicker, and he groaned. Without thinking, I took off my helmet and whacked him with it again. He made no further protest.

I had to act quickly. The moon would soon be overhead, and it was bright; it would illuminate the battlefield far more efficiently than any flare. I was so weak with shock it took me ten minutes just to drag him out of the crump hole. Just as I did so I was hit – in the behind.

What did it I never knew, I hadn't heard any shots. But there was no doubt that I was hit. A bullet in the buttocks is quite painful.

I remember little from that point until I got back through our wire, tearing the colonel's pants in the process.

I called out faintly, 'Hello, there.'

There was an immediate click of a rifle bolt.

'Don't shoot It's me.'

There was a moment of silence. A machine gun popped in the distance, then stopped.

'What's the password?' a voice said.

I opened my mouth, then closed it again. I couldn't remember it. I couldn't even remember if I had been given one.

'I've forgotten.'

Bang. A bullet snapped only inches above my head.

'Listen, I'm Bandy, Bandy!'

'Don't care what your condition is,' the voice said reasonably. 'No password, no pass.' There was another bang that deafened me, and a bullet whacked into the ground and filled my left ear with dirt.

'All right, damn you, I'm a German, I surrender,' I shouted.

'That's better,' the voice said. 'Come on in, then.'

I scrambled over, gasping as my gluteus maximus tautened. I started to pull the colonel after me.

'Jeez, it's Bandy right enough. Captain!'

Karley hurtled up, followed by Barayan.

'Bandy!'

'I've got the colonel,' I said. 'I brought him back. Sorry,' I added.

They stared incredulously at the colonel sprawled on the duckboards in a filthy state. He was groaning and coming to. I nearly hit him with my tin hat again from sheer force of habit.

The adjutant pushed through and bent over the form.

'He seems to be unhurt.' There was a sob in the adjutant's voice. He seemed to love the colonel very much. He stood up and grasped my hand. 'Good work, Bandy. You'll get a medal for this.'

I fell down. Willing hands laid me gently on the fire step.

'No,' I said, 'the other way round, please.'

They laid me on my face. 'Stretcher!' someone shouted.

Everyone was pressing around. Barayan knelt beside me. 'That was brilliant, Bart. How did you do it?'

'Do what?'

'Recapture the colonel?'

I didn't seem to understand what he was saying. Recapture the colonel? What did that mean? 'Oh, that,' I said. 'It was nothing.'

'There was a hell of a flap when they found he'd been snatched,' Karley said.

'Who?'

'The colonel. He'd just finished kicking up hell in A Company —'

'Do you mean to say I was 'way over in A Company sector?' I asked incredulously.

'They were raided by about forty Germans,' Barayan said excitedly. 'Real crazy guys. Bombs were flying all over the place.'

'Forty?'

'That's what they said. With bombs, pistols, bayonets, everything.'

'Was – Was anyone hurt?'

'Well, no, as a matter of fact. But when they managed to fight their way back through the bombs and so on, they found the colonel had been snatched. Brigade's been having babies all over the place. They threatened to court-martial A Company commander and shoot the adjutant here.'

The adjutant knelt beside me and looked emotional. 'Brilliant work, Bandy,' he choked. 'I'll send off a message to Brigade, telling about your action. You intercepted the German raiding party; that's right, isn't it?'

'I'm afraid you've got it all wrong,' I said.

'What did he say?' the adjutant asked Karley.

'He's delirious, I guess,' Karley said doubtfully.

'It was a tremendous piece of work,' the adjutant went on enthusiastically. 'You fought forty Germans. You were severely wounded but still you fought on. All your men were killed. It was magnificent.'

'What happened then?' I asked.

'You routed the enemy,' the adjutant continued. 'And in spite of your wounds you stuck by the colonel. You brought him back safely. Wrested him from the jaws of death, or at least shameful captivity.'

Stretcher-bearers came up, and I was gently lifted aboard – face down.

'Markis and the others – they didn't return?' I asked.

'No.'

'What heroism!' the adjutant said. 'His first thoughts for his brave men...' He bit his lip and turned away.

I learned later that Markis, Rolo, and Briggs had been taken prisoner. They had done better than I. At least they had *found* the enemy trenches.

As the stretcher-bearers picked me up, I saw the colonel sitting on the fire step, groaning and holding his head. I looked away quickly. Captain Karley took off my water bottle, uncorked it, and held it upside down. A single drop ran out.

He winked.

Part Two

Part Two

In the Uniform
of the R.F.C.

I WAS AT something less than 3,000 feet, gazing placidly across at a small town somewhere to the west of London when, for no apparent reason, the engine of the Maurice Farman Shorthorn spluttered, gulped, belched, then stopped dead.

I had done a full five and a half hours in the air, and this was the first time anything untoward had happened to me, not counting the first trip after soloing, when the machine had stood on its nose on landing. But that hadn't been my fault; one of the wheels had tripped over a mechanic, or perhaps it was an anthill.

A forced landing. Sweat started under my eyes in spite of the icy wind, and if there was anything I detested it was sweat under one's eyes. It gave one such an unwashed feeling. And if there was anything I detested it was an unwashed feeling.

With commendable aplomb, sangfroid, and level-headedness in this my first emergency, I put on bank, intending to return to the airdrome three miles behind. The machine promptly went into a sickening spin. By the time I had pulled the crate together – no mean achievement, I might add – we were at less than 1,000 and my bones had dissolved into splinters and porridge.

I brought the stick back shakily until the plane was gliding into wind at a safe fifty, and fiddled around a bit. But the engine was quite dead, so I closed the throttle and switched off, praying that next time I wouldn't act with quite so much resolution. Any more cool, decisive actions like that last one, and I'd be a dead duck.

I kept telling myself there was nothing to worry about. Every pilot had to face this situation some time or other. The thing to do was to keep straight on and not to lose flying speed.

That was the trouble: I spent so much time convincing myself that all was well with the world that the world became distinctly more dangerous; I was down to 500 feet before it occurred to me to look over the side for a possible landing place.

I was doing everything wrong. It was one of the golden rules that in an emergency such as this, one should immediately look for somewhere safe to land. I'd already left it too late. A searching look around revealed that I had selected the only perilous terrain for miles around, a dense wood. A half mile to port was a large white house complete with large flat lawn. I hoped the owner was watching, so he'd know where to send the ambulance.

I brought the stick back another inch or so, which reduced speed to just over forty. The wood was passing lazily underneath. My heart leaped: the wood ended not too far ahead, and beyond its fringe was a field. I was going to reach it! No, there was a wire fence in the way. I was going to hit the fence. I didn't fancy missing the trees only to somersault on the wire and have this chicken coop wrapped around me.

It was all especially irritating because this would have been just about my last trip on Shorthorns before going on to advanced training.

Oh, heavens. The field was no good even if I did reach it. Seeming flat from 500 feet, at 50 it turned out to be soggy marshland, holed and ridged by at least five thousand cows. I felt extremely annoyed with whoever had allowed them to make such a disgusting mess of my landing ground, some irresponsible agrarian dolt –

This was it. A wheel whispered through the top of a tree. Twenty-five feet – a branch slashed at the nacelle. The plane lurched like a drunken dragonfly. I clenched my teeth as it shuddered, and hauled back on the stick.

There was a delicious sensation in my bowels, and the peculiar arrangement of wires, boat-like nacelle, pusher engine, and fluttering tail sailed just over the fence and dropped daintily on to the field. I let go the controls and clung to the sides. The Shorthorn bounced wildly like a ballet dancer with fleas in his tights, then tripped forward a few paces, lurched, paused as if wondering whether or not to end it all, then settled back jarringly on its tail. There was dead silence.

I sat up there for a few minutes, enjoying life, then climbed down, weak-kneed but happy. 'Very nice,' I said aloud. 'M'yes, very nice indeed.' It was, too. The Rumpety had managed to get itself down on to a hopeless landing ground without even breaking the undercart. It was quite an achievement.

'Very nice,' I said again, and patted the beast. Then I had to climb hurriedly over the fence and disappear into the woods as another emergency occurred.

Thoroughly relieved (at my escape) I looked at the Farman sitting fastidiously at the edge of the field. The Shorthorn was a peculiar beast. I was never tired of looking at it and finding fresh things to admire in the perverse complexity of its design. It looked like two boys' kites tangled in a runaway engine. It was a pusher aircraft: the Renault motor shoved it through the air from somewhere behind a laminated wooden boat where one sat, high up and vulnerable to every sneering gaze. There were wires everywhere. It was only after several trips that I was able to thread myself through the maze to the nacelle without getting hopelessly lost. The Shorthorn had been used in the early stages of the war as a Scout with a machine gun up front; now it was strictly a trainer, and not a very satisfactory one. The only thing that could be said in its favour was that it landed like a feather. Provided one knew how to land a feather.

I took off my crash helmet and let the cold wind fan my sodden locks, and looked around vaguely, wondering whether to stay by the aircraft until help came or to set out for the white house. Deciding to stay, I sat on a log under a tree and lit a cigarette. I held out my hand with the cigarette between the long and index fingers and noted smugly that there was scarcely a tremor from it. I was either an intrepid birdman or else had a faulty nervous system.

It was peaceful in the wood. I hacked at the ground with my heel, and puffed amateurishly.

Even after two months I was still feeling surprised at the speed with which things had happened since being punctured by a bullet in Flanders.

I was fortunate in having been wounded during a period of little activity, so that I received the very best and most personal attention from a medical organization geared to the reception of thousands of casualties simultaneously. I was rapidly shuffled from casualty clearing station to Red Cross hospital and finally to the general hospital on the Channel coast. There my behind had mended rapidly and I had been all set to return to the infantry when I found myself in an entirely different branch of the service.

Three things helped me make the decision. First, I had been deciding for four months that trench warfare did not really suit me. Second, I met a pilot who suggested I should join the Royal Flying Corps. Third, the colonel told me to. I must admit it was this third argument that carried the most weight

My unsuitability for trench warfare had already been demonstrated.

As for the pilot: when I first moved into the ward in the general hospital there were only two other occupants, and as they were acquaintances and spent most of their time together, sampling the amusements of the hospital, which consisted mainly in gambling and flirtation, I was able to catch up with my correspondence and try to understand the jokes in *Punch* ('Well, goodbye, Old Chap, and Good Luck! I'm going in here to Do my Bit, the best way I can. The more everybody scrapes together for the War Loan, the sooner you'll be Back from the Trenches') or just stare out the window at the mist-shrouded trees and lawns of ice. It was the coldest February in a thousand years, they said. I thought often of Karley, and in abandoning him later felt rather like a traitor, I don't know why.

Then the pilot in question moved into the ward. After surviving more than eight months of warfare in reconnaissance machines when casualties had been extremely heavy, he had broken his leg by getting drunk and falling down a couple of steps. He got to yarning for hours on end about the air war, and the more he told me, the more interested I became. While the fighting itself sounded a little alarming, at least when the patrol was finished the pilots could come home to comfortable billets, hot meals, hot showers, and clean socks. This was a consideration that could not easily be dismissed after the trenches, where one was never warm, never clean, and never entirely out of danger, and where even in reserve one was rarely comfortable. Even if it had not been for the colonel, I might have been persuaded.

He came to see me two days before I was due to leave hospital, and we had a nice chat in an empty ward with me standing at attention and him lounging in a comfortable armchair.

'I was on my way to London on leave and I heard you were here, Bandy, so I just thought I'd drop in and see you.'

'That's very good of you, sir, but you shouldn't have bothered.'

'Oh, but I wanted to, Bandy. I wanted to make sure you were comfy and happy. I also wanted to bring you a present'

'Oh, goody, sir.'

He took out a Smith and Wesson revolver, and for a moment I thought he was going to shoot me then and there; but he contained himself and merely pointed it at me in an offhanded manner.

'It is yours, isn't it?'

'Where did you find it, sir?'

'It was found in A Company sector – round about where those forty Germans raided the line and took me prisoner.'

'Oh,' I said.

'Yes,' he said pleasantly, his large face coming a little closer. 'It is your revolver, isn't it? Well, enough of the gun – take it, take it, Bandy. Yes,' he went on, tilting backward in his chair near the window. 'I've thought about that little contretemps quite a lot during the past week, and I dimly seem to remember waking up in a large, filthy hole in no man's land, but strangely enough, in the few seconds of consciousness vouchsafed to me, becoming dimly aware, not of forty nasty Germans but just one shadowy, hiccupping form.

'The next moment there was a metallic clang as if I had been hit by a bucket, and I was off in the Arms of Morpheus again. Funny, wasn't it? I mean, one moment I'm walking along the old duckboards, humming to myself, perhaps doing a little musing, when I'm bashed on the head, wake up in a crump hole, am bashed again and come to, to find myself kindly returned to my own trenches. If that's not funny,' he went on bitterly, 'I'm Daisy Dublin, Queen of the May.'

'Come on,' he coaxed, 'just tell me. I can't do anything about it now. Admit it.'

'These are terrible suspicions to harbour, Colonel,' I murmured. 'Whatever the suspicions are,' I added cautiously.

'Yes, aren't they?' There was a pause. 'All right,' he said, rubbing his forehead tiredly, 'don't answer. I'm not really strong enough yet for the truth, anyway.'

He got up and stared out the window at the bleak grey countryside. An R.A.M.C. captain, crouched against the icy wind, was just scurrying into a wing of the hospital. 'I suppose you know you were recommended for the M.C.?' the colonel said thoughtfully.

'Good heavens.'

'Yes. But I soon put a stop to that. Though it took a lot of peculiar logic to dissuade the brigadier. Fortunately he is susceptible to peculiar logic.'

'You didn't confide your suspicions, sir?' I faltered.

'I did not, Bandy. Do you think I'm an idiot? However, he did insist on promoting you.' He glanced at me, then turned away hurriedly. 'Yes,' he murmured, 'you hit your battalion commander on the head, and the next thing you know they've promoted you for it. Next time, Bandy, you might try hitting the brigadier – he'd probably make you a major or something. Why, there's no end to the possibilities it opens up, not to mention people's skulls. Yes, I can see it quite clearly – Brigadier Bandy, surrounded by the top army commanders, all with bandages round their heads. Recruiting posters showing a colonel with a bloodstained head pointing at the civvies and saying, THERE'S A CAREER FOR YOU IN THE MODERN ARMY; then, in little letters: *If You Know How To Slug the Right People*. Of course,' the colonel went on, starting to slaver, 'that's the reason for the general's baton they say is in every soldier's knapsack – it's there to – to ...'

'Steady, sir,' I murmured.

The colonel sat down quickly and passed limp fingers over his forehead. 'I'll be all right in a minute,' he said.

He took a deep breath. 'However, the point is, what are we going to do now, Bandy?'

'Transfer me, Colonel?'

'I've thought of that. But it would look – ungrateful, wouldn't it?'

I saw what he meant.

'No,' he went on. 'That's not the answer. But I feel it could be something along those lines.' He paused, got up again and looked at the violent sky. 'Good flying weather,' he remarked conversationally.

'I have it,' I said. 'I could transfer to the Royal Flying Corps.'

'Why, I never thought of that,' he said, rising slowly on to his toes, then slowly lowering himself to the floor. 'That's brilliant, Bandy. That would solve everything. I hear the life expectancy in the R.F.C. is now at least six weeks – which,' he remarked pleasantly, 'is somewhat longer than a subaltern, even of your exceptional ability, would be likely to attain – especially on my front. I refer of course,' he added unnecessarily, 'to the coming spring offensive, which is likely to be exceptionally severe. Now, it just

125

so happens that I chance, by accident, purely fortuitously, to have some official forms here in my pocket. Amazing coincidence. If you would care to fill them out I could get them stamped and everything, and have them at the War Office by tomorrow morning. It's all right, don't try to thank me, I'm going to London anyway. I would even be glad to include a special note of recommendation; I happen to know the staff captain in charge of these things. Why,' he said enthusiastically, 'I could have you up there so damned quick –' He broke off and looked at me. 'After all,' he said anxiously, 'think of all those wonderful months in training, Bandy. Near London, too, most likely.'

'Yes, sir,' I said, writing.

'I don't want to force you into anything,' he said, snatching up the documents before I had a chance to dry the ink. He waved them briefly in the air, made sure I'd signed, and hurried to the door.

'Goodbye,' he said. He hurried off, humming an air from *Chu-Chin-Chow*. A minute later he came back for his pen.

Eight days later I was at Number 2 School of Military Aeronautics at Oxford for theoretical and practical instruction in the theory of flight, navigation, map and compass reading, engines, rigging, bad language, and Morse, and by the end of March I had soloed in this very Shorthorn that now lay trapped in a field in Berkshire, after two and a half hours dual instruction. It appeared that although I might not always get on so well on terra firma, in the air I was in my element: a born flyer.

I had long since finished the cigarette. I walked into the middle of the field to make myself clearly visible in case another Rumpety should happen to clatter overhead looking for me, but the only sounds were the barking of a dog from some distant sylvan glade and the merry cheeping of our little feathered pests. But the sun was warm, the sky cloudless, and it was good to be alive.

However, I couldn't hang around a soggy field all day. I was on the point of setting off in the direction of the white house I had seen a half mile to the west when a movement among the trees caught my eye. A moment later a girl in a black riding habit, mounted on a brown horse, emerged and stopped at the fence.

She was studying the airplane when I came up, and it was with some reluctance that she turned her gaze to the less rewarding sight of me. She had fine dark eyes, long black eyelashes, and a pale face.

'Good morning,' she said in a soft, reserved tone as if coming across a flying machine in the woods were a normal part of her daily life. I found out a minute later that it was.

'Good morning,' I said, emulating her discreet tone.

We looked at each other in silence for a few seconds; then she shifted her eyes back to Rumpety. Well, the horse at least was interested in me. It was staring at me in a puzzled fashion, as if it had seen me somewhere before but couldn't quite remember where. We eyed each other curiously. Then, because I was feeling good, I said good morning to the horse as well. It nodded, a little distantly I thought. All the same, there was a spark between us.

I turned to the girl. 'Do you know,' I asked, 'of anywhere I could telephone from, Miss?' The sound of my voice seemed to startle the horse, for it backed away nervously and the girl had trouble bringing it near me again.

'You're from the elementary training squadron, I suppose?' she said in an abrupt voice. I must have looked slightly surprised, for she explained: 'Their machines have a habit of crashing all over the countryside round here.' She glanced at me, frowning. 'You haven't got concussion or anything, have you?'

I knew what she meant. 'No, Miss,' I said. 'This is my normal expression.'

'Oh. Well, if you'd like to follow me I'll take you up to the house. You can telephone from there.'

'Fine,' I said, and vaulted nimbly over the fence as she turned to go. I actually made it.

The horse wasn't impressed, however. He showed the whites of his eyes and drew back his lips, exposing nicotine-stained teeth. There was something about that horse, definitely some bond between us; but I had the feeling now that he felt for me a strange equine antipathy.

'I hope you didn't hurt yourself,' the girl said gravely. 'Perhaps you should ride back.'

'No, it's all right,' I mumbled.

The house was the white one I'd seen from the air. It had an elegantly proportioned facade in the Georgian style and there must have been nearly two hundred acres of well-bred lawn in front of the simple, dignified entrance. The house itself was raised on a shallow, grassy plateau. I couldn't help stopping to look at it, and had a funny feeling that might possibly have been love at first sight. It was beautiful.

'Burma Park,' the girl said. These were the only words spoken during the twenty minutes it took us to reach the stables at the back of the house.

The girl handed the horse over to the groom, a sad, persecuted-looking man with very short legs, who tugged at his forelock in the immemorial tradition. As the animal was led away, something made me glance back at it. And damned if the horse didn't do the same. We looked at each other. I couldn't resist it: I made a face at it, and stuck my tongue out and wiggled my head.

Unfortunately, the groom looked back just at that moment to see what his charge was gazing at, and caught me in the act. I tried to transform my childish gesture into a detached scrutiny, but it was too late. The groom knew perfectly well that no officer and gentleman would sink so low as to stick his tongue out at a mere equine quadruped and that therefore my vulgarity must have been meant for him. The poor fellow, not knowing what else to do, tugged at his forelock again uncertainly, then hurried inside, probably to where he thought he belonged, among the manure. That unfortunate groom must have had his spirit broken at some time or another, I thought as I scuttled after the girl, making embarrassed faces at myself.

'What do you call that horse?' I mumbled as we went round to the front of the house.

'Hm? Oh – Marshall, he's called. We've had him for quite a long time,' the girl said in her shy, abrupt voice. 'They tried to requisition him at the beginning of the war but he kept falling on the trooper he was allocated to, and –'

'He kept what?'

'Whenever the trooper started to climb into the saddle,' she said seriously, 'Marshall would fall sideways on to him, he said. The trooper maintained the horse did it on purpose, but that was silly.'

I wasn't so sure of that.

'Anyway, the army seemed to agree and they finally accused him of malingering and sent him back. He's never given me any trouble. If that really was true about Marshall falling on the trooper all the time, I'm sure he was just having some fun, but of course the army hasn't got a sense of humour.'

'Hm,' I said.

The front door was opened by a servant with sloping shoulders and a black outfit that must have been just right for him during the Boer War. He seemed to accept it as a matter of course that the girl had gone out alone and come back with an intrepid airman in tow.

'I'm going upstairs to change,' the girl said. 'Would you show this gentleman the telephone please, Burgess.'

Burgess bowed perfunctorily and showed me the telephone. I stood admiring it; it was about five feet away.

I picked up the receiver and bellowed into it 'Hello, hello,' I said. It crackled alarmingly. Telephones always made me uneasy. 'Look, old chap,' I said to Burgess. (Lately I'd been finding myself speaking with an English accent whenever I was nervous.) 'Would you mind awfully getting on to my squadron for me? Thanks ever so much.' I gave him instructions, and while I was walking round the hall preparing myself for the ordeal he managed to get Major Brannon.

'Hello, hello,' I said, clenching the receiver tightly.

There was an exclamation at the other end; then a thick voice said, 'Good God, man, good God!' followed by heavy breathing.

'Who is it, what do you want?' I inquired, perhaps a trifle loudly. My normal volume can be heard the length and breadth of a
battleship. Then I remembered it was I who was calling, not he.
'This is Lieutenant Bandy,' I said. 'I've crash–'

'You've deafened me so much I can hardly hear,' the voice said.
'Who is it?' 'Bandy,' I shrieked.

There was a clatter at the other end followed by various unin-
telligible sounds.

'Hello, hello,' I said.

A new voice came on the line. 'Who is it calling?' the voice
inquired faintly, as if its owner was standing at the far end of the
squadron office.

'Is this Major Brannon?'

'No, he's – he's gone down to sick quarters. This is Captain
Thomas. Who are you?'

'It's Lieutenant Bandy. I –'

'Oh, yes. Bandy. I thought so. Why haven't you come back?
What have you done with our airplane?'

I told the adjutant what had happened.

'Where are you now?'

'A place called Burma Park,'

'Where the hell's that?'

'In Berkshire, I guess.'

'I know that, you idiot I mean where's it near?'

'I don't know,' I whined.

'Well, how the devil do you expect us to find you if you don't
know where you are?'

'Hold on a minute.' I held the receiver out to Burgess. 'Could
you –' He had his hands over his ears. I tapped him on the shoulder. He started. 'Could you tell them where I am, please?'

When Burgess had got it all sorted out and informed me that a
car would be along in a couple of hours, I was shown into a reception room to the right of the hall.

'Miss Katherine will be down in a minute, sir,' Burgess said. He
was gone before I could ask what her other name was.

I sat for a moment or two, then got up and strolled around. So far, the house, impressive enough from the outside, had not struck me as being particularly luxurious within. It had a worn look, as if the furnishings had been kicked by centuries of children. A patch of carpet near the hall door was almost threadbare; the ceiling badly needed repainting; the curtains were faded. But the place had a pleasing atmosphere such as you get in houses where families dwell in harmony. I relaxed in one of the chairs and smoked contentedly.

After a while there was a hesitant clack of heels in the hall and Katherine came in. She had changed into a white dress with short sleeves.

She was thinner than I'd thought, and had no bosom to speak of; not that I was in the habit of speaking even of full bosoms. The dress accentuated the dark beauty of her eyes which – yes, she had a slight squint. Was that why she was unwilling to meet my gaze?

'Would you like a cup of tea? Or perhaps you'd rather a drink?'

I said tea would be fine.

'My brother's in the Flying Corps,' she said abruptly.

'Oh, is he?'

'He'll be coming home on leave soon.' Her expression warmed when she mentioned her brother.

She was still not at ease, however. I had the impression from the reserve of her manner that she was much given to solitude, whether from choice or necessity I couldn't tell. Incidentally, the house was unusually silent. Surely she didn't live here alone?

She answered that question with her next abrupt words. 'Come and meet my father,' she said. 'He has a few days off; he's in the library.'

I followed her across the hall, through a long drawing room containing an enormous fireplace guarded by a massive brass fender with lions, through a double door into a room crammed with books, where a small slender man with a bald head and hazel eyes was wrapped in a leather armchair, reading. He hauled himself up when we came in and looked at us hesitantly.

'Daddy, this is ...' She looked at me. '...another pilot. His airplane came down at the wood pasture.'

'Oh, yes,' her father said quickly before I could introduce myself. He coughed; then, not knowing what else to say, held up the book in his hands. 'Just reading *The Castle of Otranto*,' he said. He spoke in the nervous, abrupt voice that he had obviously handed down to his daughter. 'Kind of – of forerunner of Edgar Allan Poe.'

'Oh,' I said, drawing on an interested expression.

'It's the first romantic novel, you know,' he said, holding the book up again jerkily. 'Quite macabre. Rather – rather hair-raising,' he added, running his hand over his bald head, which was beginning to gleam damply with nervousness. 'Walpole,' he said.

'Pardon?'

'Horace Walpole wrote it Or, as he preferred to be called, Horatio...' He looked suddenly vague.

I thought he was trying to remember the surname, so I said helpfully, 'Nelson?'

'Er, no, Lewis actually.'

'Horatio Lewis?'

'William,' he said abruptly.

'William Lewis wrote it?'

'No, no. Horace Walpole.'

'But he preferred to be called William Lewis, you mean?'

He twisted the book in his hands and glanced anxiously at his daughter, whose mouth was slightly open. 'Horatio,' he said.

'Where does William Lewis come in?' I began to say, when the girl interrupted quickly.

'I'm sorry. I should have introduced you properly. This is my father, William Lewis.'

'Perhaps we'd better sit down,' Mr Lewis said.

We had just finished arranging ourselves in the chairs when I said, 'And I'm Bartholomew Bandy,' so we all had to get up and shake hands all over again. Then we all sat and steadily avoided one another's gaze for a while; then all three of us started up at once.

'My mother is –'

'A remarkable collection of old tomes and –'

'Cold wind for this –'

We all stopped. 'After you, sir,' I said.

'No, after you.'

'No, go ahead, sir.'

'No, after you, Mr...'

'Well, all I was going to say was, you have a fine collection of books, sir.'

'Oh. Yes.'

We all nodded. There was another silence.

Then Lewis said, 'So you came down in the wood pasture, did you?'

'Yes.' Ah, I thought, now we're on firmer ground. He'll ask all the usual questions aviators are invariably asked. Everyone was interested in aviation.

'There is some very interesting Pteridophyta down there,' Mr Lewis said carefully, 'including examples of hart's-tongue which I've never found anywhere else, at least in this part of the country.' He hesitated, then looked at me with unexpectedly keen eyes in spite of his harassed manner. 'Or probably you know it better as *Phyllitis scolopendrium*.'

He spoke with the emphasis betokening a shy nature; and for no reason at all – for all I knew he might have been indulging in some kind of erudite japery – I was suddenly immensely fond of him. Yes, perhaps there was a reason. Throughout my adolescence I'd been surrounded by adults inflated with various ponderous varieties of self-importance, and to come across someone like Mr Lewis, so lacking in hot air as to be almost deflated, and, in the best sense, so simple as to take it for granted that my knowledge must be as profound as his – it was refreshing, if somewhat incomprehensible.

He was still talking, addressing his long, thin hands, which were having a wrestling match in his lap. 'Hymenophyllaceae, Cyatheaceae, and Polypodiaceae,' he was saying. He glanced at me apologetically. 'I've always been interested in the middle ground, so to speak, between the aquatic Thallophyta and terrestrial Spermatophyta.'

The conversation was beginning to sound not only incomprehensible but somewhat risqué, so I changed the subject 'I believe your son is in the R.F.C., sir,' I said. Lewis brightened. 'Yes. Oh, yes, of course, you're in the Flying Corps too, aren't you? Yes, Robert will be coming home soon. You must meet him.'

I said I'd be delighted. Just then Burgess brought in a tray loaded with afternoon tea, one of those light snacks the English regale themselves with between meals: sandwiches, bread, butter, and jam, biscuits, cake, cheese, crackers, and tea. We all tucked in, and I was touched by the warmth and ease with which they accepted me. All too soon Burgess came back to announce that a car from the squadron had arrived to take me back.

Mr Lewis said goodbye in the library, and said I must visit them again sometime. I'd been hoping for just such an offer, but unfortunately it was not couched in sufficiently concrete terms and I wasn't quick enough to pin him down to a definite invitation.

On the way out I asked Katherine what *Pteridophyta* was.

'Ferns.'

For a time in the library she had lost some of her self-consciousness but now it was back again.

'Ferns and mosses are his hobby,' she said in her soft but abrupt voice.

However, as we left the house she looked brighter. We walked over to the car, talking. The driver was smoking and chatting to the groom as we came up. The groom scuttled away tugging at his forelock when he saw me. He tugged at his forelock so assiduously it was a wonder he hadn't wrenched it out by the roots years ago.

The driver threw away his cigarette and held the door open for me. He had the motor running.

I was still hoping to get invited back to dinner sometime. I hinted delicately to this effect as we stood by the car.

'I guess you have dinner at about eight o'clock, or somewhere around there?' I asked.

As we had been talking about the problems of getting the Shorthorn out of the 'wood pasture', as they called it, the sudden change of subject surprised her.

'Yes,' she said hesitantly.

'I expect you mostly dine alone, you and your family, I expect,' I said, my voice heavy with innuendo.

'Yes,' she said. Behind me I heard the driver clicking the door handle impatiently.

'It was very good of you to invite me –' I paused subtly, then added, 'home,' then another delicate pause, 'to use your telephone.'

She smiled uneasily and rubbed her bare arms, which were developing goose pimples in the cold breeze. The car driver abandoned the door and got behind the wheel and bounced up and down on the seat a couple of times. He seemed in a hurry to be off.

'I suppose the submarine menace is causing a great shortage of food these days,' I said. 'I suppose that's why you don't entertain too often. I suppose.'

The driver revved the motor at this point and drowned out her reply.

'We occasionally have dinner in Reading,' I said, laughing lightly. 'It makes a pleasant change from the rigors of the squadron mess.'

'Does it?' she said, shivering and hugging herself.

'M'yes.' I raised my eyebrows expectantly.

She hesitated. I waited tensely. 'I expect so,' she said.

As her arms were starting to turn purple it occurred to me that I oughtn't to keep her standing in the open too much longer. The white dress she had on was quite thin and was flapping impatiently in the wind.

'Well, I'll be off,' I said, looking gloomy. 'Back,' I added, 'to the rigors of army cooking. For dinner,' I added.

'Goodbye, Mr Bandy.'

'Mm. Well, it's been very pleasant meeting you, Miss Lewis,' I said. 'Being invited to that beautiful house of yours for...'

As the girl's brachial muscles were now trembling with cold, and as the driver was clashing his gears and hinting at his impatience by starting to shudder the car down the driveway, I decided it was time to depart.

'Well,' I said, 'if I don't hurry I'll be late for dinner.' The automobile motor was roaring furiously by now. I clambered in, turned to wave once more, but the girl was already in the house, having a hot bath. By the time I got back to the squadron I was late even for the rigors of the squadron mess, the roast beef gravy having long since congealed. Also, I was roundly drubbed by the adjutant for landing the airplane in an almost inaccessible spot. I'd have been roundly drubbed by the C.O. too, but he was in hospital being examined by an E.N.T. specialist. Something was wrong with his eardrums, someone said.

The Man Who Went Abroad

I HAD EXPECTED to be sent to the Twenty-fifth Training Wing, at Castle Bromwich, for more advanced training but instead I was posted to a new airdrome in Surrey, and when I looked it up on the map found it was only thirty miles or so from Burma Park. Thirty miles by air, that is. By English roads it was 450 miles. But still, I felt obscurely delighted, for Burma Park was even then casting its strange spell over me.

In the meantime I was given a long weekend in London. I didn't particularly want the days off, being unwilling to miss any good flying weather. Not that I wasn't due for leave; I'd had none since leaving Beamington. However, Major Brannon seemed keen on my going, so off I went in a slow train for the capital with all my kit in the luggage racks and a copy of *The Times* clenched in my hands.

There wasn't much in it. A Turkish Bath attendant had massaged his wife to death with his bare feet; all was quiet in France; there'd been some kind of revolution in Petrograd, but this was a Good Thing as it meant that Democracy was at last coming to Mother Russia and President Wilson of the United States was said to be delighted with the turn of events and was urging a loan to the new leaders of Russia as soon as it was known who the new leaders were. And so on. It was all very insignificant So I put the paper aside and got talking to a charming person,

Lady Constance Chatterley, who was on her way to see her husband, Sir Clifford Chatterley, off to Flanders. They had only been married a month. I wished her all the best and hurried out of Victoria Station with a ton of kit and eleven pounds to spend.

I got a small room in the Spartan Hotel nearby, had a bath, then dined in the hotel restaurant, which contained just two other occupants, an elderly man and his wife, both of whom wore black moustaches and had strange accents that I took to be either Swahili or Scottish. In the evening I settled on a Spot of Entertainment.

It was a drama called *The Man Who Went Abroad* and had just begun when I stumbled into my seat in the stalls. Act II was almost over before I caught up with the plot. It concerned a fellow on an Atlantic liner called Kit Brent who was impersonating Lord Goring of the British Cabinet in order to draw off a pack of German spies led by one von Bernstorff. Kit is supposed to be taking some secret papers to Washington. To compromise the supposed Lord Goring, Bernstorff employs a beautiful Austrian dancer, Ani Kiraly, in the hopes that fears of a scandal will force 'Lord Goring' to hand over the secret papers. But Ani falls in love with Kit Brent, alias Lord Goring. Then it turns out that Ani is not an Austrian after all but a Dalmatian –

At this point I hurried to the bar and ordered a drink called 'gin'. For a moment I thought they'd made a mistake and given me a glass of perfume, *Nuit d'amour* or something. It tasted lascivious, but it was better than the play.

So I squelched back to the hotel, which was virtually un-heated, so that I couldn't get warm in bed until I'd togged myself out in a cardigan, scarf, a pair of socks, and a balaclava helmet. I made a mental note to buy pyjamas someday.

With peace and quiet in which to think, I tried to work it all out. What was it exactly that drew me to Burma Park? Was it because of Miss Lewis? But I had not experienced that quickening of the senses that is supposed to signify a sexual attraction. Perhaps it was snobbery. By making inquiries among the permanent members of the training squadron I'd found out that Mr Lewis was some kind of administrative civil servant and worked at the Foreign Office, that the Lewises were definitely County (I didn't quite know what this meant but it was obviously something impressive), and that their family had been living at Burma Park since Rockingham's Government (which practically made them upstarts, as this was a mere one and a half centuries ago).

Perhaps it was simply the place itself, with its welcoming atmosphere.

I sighed and turned over carefully, so as to admit the minimum volume of cold air, and found myself indulging in the absurd nostalgia of retracing in imagination the short journey from hall to library. And wishing ... I don't know what ... But there was something about the Lewises, something about Burma Park ... I fell asleep and dreamed of that horse Marshall, and woke with a fright to find spring sunlight pouring over London.

In the afternoon as I scuttled down Charing Cross Road looking at the bookshops, I found myself working out ways of regaining admittance to Burma Park. 'Why, hello, Mr Lewis, I just happened to be passing your house and I thought I might as well drop ...' No, that was no good: I could hardly happen to be passing the house when the nearest public road was three miles away. 'Good morning, Miss Lewis, I've just force-landed in your wood pasture again –'

'Now look here, Bandy,' she was saying, 'this is getting monotonous; it's the seventh time this month you've force-landed in our wood pasture. If you don't stop it I'll set Marshall on you.' I fled.

I found I'd been staring into a shop window for five minutes. It was filled with hymn books, tracts, garish biblical illustrations, and the face of the proprietor staring suspiciously at me from between two curtains. Being thus reminded, I went in for a new Bible.

The bookseller had a high, noble forehead, long tapering fingers, and a clerical suit. The atmosphere of the shop was purple with reverence. After he had satisfied himself that I wasn't contemplating a smash-and-grab, and seeing I was a Canadian and therefore grossly overpaid, he offered me a rare Italian gold-tooled Bible weighing forty pounds that had once belonged to the Duke of Radcliffe's mistress and was attractively stained with port wine. The bookseller assured me it had been the very best port wine available. Next I was offered a grey pigskin binding with blind tooling and painted line work with a dedicated flyleaf thick enough to deflect a .303 bullet. This cost a mere seventy guineas. Finally we settled on a small St James in bookbinding leather guaranteed free from harmful acids, for which I paid ten shillings. Later, on examining the rear cover, I found the correct price to be five and sixpence.

I had lunch at the Savoy, then went for another walk; but, getting tired of saluting senior officers along Whitehall, I turned on to the Victoria Embankment and watched the snowflakes extinguishing themselves in the river. Then back to the hotel, where I met a Canadian officer (I must say I thought he was English at first) called Renny Whiteoak. I also thought he was a bit squiffy, the way he kept bubbling on about someone called Jalna, no doubt some French girl he'd met on active service. To listen to him you'd have thought that Jalna was the most wonderful creation on earth; but I know these affairs – they never last.

That Damned Horse Again

I FORGOT ABOUT Burma Park, or pretended to. And then shortly after I began training in the Avro 504 (a delightful aircraft to fly, with a skid between the wheels to prevent one from turning it upside down whilst on the ground), I learned that one of my colleagues, Brian Penmane, not only lived in the neighbourhood of the Lewises but knew them fairly well.

I thought it was a coincidence at first until I learned that any landowner in the south of England usually knew every other landowner, provided each met certain minimum requirements of breeding, acreage, and eccentricity. (The first time I met Mrs Penmane she asked if I was one of the mad Bandys of Bedford.) The Penmane family was even better set up than the Lewises: they owned seven villages and half a river. I cultivated Brian's friendship shamelessly.

It wasn't too difficult. Brian Penmane was tall, graceful, and had that self-assurance that only the English public school boys seem to possess. He also had a permanent sun tan, though he'd never been out of England.

Initially I was astonished to find him behaving with what I at first thought was deference toward me; I later realized that it wasn't so much deference as incredulity, perhaps because of my background, which to him must have seemed exotic: log cabins, religion, and skunks. Of course, his experience of life was equally foreign to me (private tutor, cricket, fagging); consequently neither of us knew what the other was talking about half the time, so that we had very little in common except a love of flying. In spite of this he returned my friendship with only a modicum of reserve and listened to my opinions and experience with a bewilderment cleverly disguised as respect. During the weekend I spent at his father's house (fourteen bedrooms, one bathroom) he introduced me to everyone within five miles – bankers, fox hunters, coachmen, barristers, and gentlemen farmers, telling them with offhand earnestness that I was a gifted medical student, a nerveless fighter, an excellent flyer, a brilliant shot, a marvellous pianist, a superb tennis player, an indescribable horseman, and in general such a spiffing, ripping, jolly clever chap that everyone was immediately convinced I was a charlatan.

His house was grander than the Lewises', but although I was treated with unfailing politeness I didn't feel quite so comfortable there. Perhaps it was because the house was so impersonal. I never had the feeling that I could lounge in an armchair and feel completely secure, the way I could at Burma Park.

I found out that Brian knew the Lewises on a Sunday. We were strolling back after an early-morning walk, leaving a trail of green footprints in the silver dew.

'Gosh, I hope we get to the same squadron in France, Bandy,' Brian was saying. 'Don't suppose there'll be much chance, though.' He linked arms. 'You're bound to become an ace, the way you shoot so marvellously.'

'I'll be quite content if I survive intact,' I said cravenly.

'Oh, rot. You know you're simply dying to go after the Huns. You'll be an absolute wizard; everyone says so.'

A cuckoo sounded from a clump of trees. We stood and admired the view from a hill overlooking the tennis court. Far away a horse and rider appeared momentarily against the skyline, then slowly bobbed out of sight.

'That'll be Kath Lewis,' Brian murmured.

'Do you know her?' I asked. I thought he'd already introduced me to everyone in the entire county.

'Yes. Do you?'

'M'yes. How could you possibly tell that was her at this distance?'

'Oh, I couldn't see her; I just knew it was her. She's always out riding. Her place is about eight miles past that hill. She's ridden quite a long way. Funny girl.'

'How?' I asked, idly kicking an earthworm in the crotch.

'Oh – you know .... What do you think of her?'

'Sadly self-conscious about her squint. I don't know why; it suits her.'

'Do you really think so?' Brian thought for a moment. 'I say, I believe you're right. Makes her look more interesting.' He was silent for a moment, then: 'We used to tease her terribly about it when we were kids. Used to call her "cockeyes" and "skenny". Gosh, Bandy, I believe you're right.'

As we walked back to the house for breakfast, I asked if he knew the Lewises well.

'Mother knows Mrs Lewis. Marvellous old dragon, she is, Mrs Lewis. Her hobby is pressing charity on the undeserving poor. They think she's wonderful, even though she bullies them unmercifully. Mr Lewis doesn't seem to do much worth while – works in the Foreign Office or something. Robert's a bit queer, too. I believe he's on leave right now, but for all the visiting he's done he might as well be in France. He used to be mad about fox-hunting, but ... They're a solitary lot.'

As we walked through the high Roman arch of the front entrance, I asked if he knew them well enough to visit them in the afternoon.

Brian stopped and glanced at me curiously. 'Do you want to go over?' He thought for a moment. 'I don't see why not. It might be fun. I'll telephone and see.'

'Ripping,' I said.

Robert Lewis was riding morosely over the turf as we drove up in the Penmanes' Renault motorcar. He came forward as we got out. I recognized his horse right away.

'Hello, Lewis. This is Bart Bandy. Robert Lewis. '

'How d'you do.'

He got down and we shook hands and looked at each other like two surveyors examining difficult country. He had a dark, brooding face and an aura of dependability that I would have appreciated in a brother if I'd had one. He wore khaki slacks and a pullover that needed mending.

'Bandy? My sister was talking about a Lieutenant Bandy who force-landed over there.' He jerked his head in the direction of the 'wood pasture'.

'The same, 'm afraid.'

After a moment we smiled faintly at each other. Then he turned abruptly to Brian.

'Well, how are you getting on? How's flying?'

'Oh, not too bad, thank you, Lewis. We're going on to Pups soon. I believe you're transferring to scouts?'

As Brian and Lewis chatted, the horse came sidling up to me. I reached over to give him a preoccupied pat, but he moved away. A few seconds later he sidled up again. I glanced at him suspiciously. There was definitely something about that horse, its expression ... Then I saw what it was: the eyes weren't quite in the right place. They were slightly too high in the sockets so that the whites were showing not only at both ends of the iris but underneath as well. This, together with a slight droop to the eyelids, gave the beast a look of weary vindictiveness that I found distinctly disconcerting. I looked away.

I was about to join in the conversation when I became aware of another stealthy movement from the horse. Glancing sideways I saw Marshall cautiously raising his right foreleg. Fascinated, I watched as inch by inch the hoof came up. What on earth was he up to? Now he was moving the raised leg over. Now the leg was poised over my foot. The horse wasn't looking at me; in fact it seemed to be taking a decided interest in the discourse of the other two, which made its action seem philosophically detached.

Slowly its foot started to descend. Good Lord, I thought: it's about to shatter my instep. I was so absorbed that even when I felt the pressure of its hoof on my toes I could do nothing but stare stupidly. The next moment it started to put its weight behind the leg. The beast was still looking away in a disinterested manner.

Robert Lewis suddenly noticed what was going on. Perhaps it was because I let out a thinnish moan, more out of a sense of persecution than of injury.

'Marshall,' Lewis snapped at the horse, 'stop that!'

The horse leaned harder. 'Ouch,' I said, and shoved the beast. It didn't budge.

'Marshall!' Lewis put his hands on his hips and glared at the horse.

Marshall tossed his head and flapped his lips in a rather insulting fashion, I thought. So, apparently, did Lewis, for he flushed.

'That's enough of that, do you hear?'

There was silence for a few seconds broken only by the cursing of sparrows and a whining sound from me. There was a brief battle of wills between horse and master. At last, reluctantly, the horse removed its hoof and moved away. In so doing it buffetted me so casually that if I hadn't seen into those eyes of his I'd have thought it was an accident.

Marshall and I exchanged glances. His was triumphant. Mine – well, if Lewis hadn't been there I'd have given him a crack on the hindquarters.

'It's a bad habit he picked up as a foal,' Lewis said. 'He thinks it's funny.' He turned to Marshall. 'You'd better watch it,' he said sharply. The horse merely tossed its head in an uppity fashion.

In the long drawing room to the left of the main hall of Burma Park was a dusty piano. Being left alone for a few minutes later on in the afternoon, I sat at the instrument and tinkled out a dingy version of Mendelssohn's 'Spring Song'. The piano was out of tune, which didn't help, and the piano stool wobbled.

I'd chatted for a while with Mr Lewis. He was now busy in the library ironing ferns and placing them between the pages of a recent literary success story called *A Sense of Love, or Millie Doolie's Mistake*. Mrs Lewis was again out on an errand of mercy, pressing baskets of rotten apples, potato peel, and similar wholesome victuals on her tenants, and I had been temporarily abandoned.

I was attempting variations of a popular song to the effect that They Wouldn't Believe Me when I became aware that Katherine Lewis was standing in the doorway with a look of welcome on her face. I got up.

'Hello.'

'I heard you were here with Brian Penmane. I didn't know you knew him,' she said nervously. 'Don't let me interrupt your playing,' she added half-heartedly.

'I ought always to be interrupted when I'm playing,' I said.

'Oh, no,' she protested, rustling forward in a long grey skirt and virginal blouse. 'You have quite a feeling for the keyboard. Of course,' she added, 'you haven't much feeling for music, but you certainly do have a feeling for the – the keyboard,' she added lamely.

We fidgeted silently for a moment. 'Well, I – I was just going out for a walk,' she said. 'I expect Robert will be down in a minute, and Brian.' She started to go-

'Perhaps I could accompany you,' I said wittily.

'Well, all right.'

'May I call you Katherine?'

'Yes.'

'Katherine.'

'Yes?'

'Nothing. I was just tasting the name.'

She looked at me as if suspecting that I was making fun of her. That faint squint of hers affected me strongly. There was something almost erotic about it, which was peculiar. I barely stopped myself in time from smiling charmingly into her eyes; she was pale enough as it was.

Halfway across the park I held out my crooked arm invitingly, my heart thudding like a barrage. She hesitated, then linked arms. I was sure she would let go by the time we reached the path through the wood and was overjoyed when she didn't. It made me reckless.

'What an adorable girl you are, Katherine!' I said, perhaps too loudly, for a rabbit nearby shot up and streaked through the deadly nightshade. Before she could react to this I added, 'What do you do all day, Katherine?'

'Nothing.' She sounded a shade breathless. Perhaps we were walking too fast. I slowed. The path through the wood was so narrow that our hips brushed now and then. It was delicious.

'Nothing at all?'

'Well, I go out riding a lot, and...'

'Yes?'

'And read, and...'

'Do you ever go up to London?'

'Now and again I meet Father for lunch. He took me to see George Robey on New Year's Day. The comedian, you know.'

'Don't you have any friends?'

'Yes,' she said, and relinquished my arm and walked ahead. I guess it was because the path had become so narrow that we could no longer walk abreast, but I was disappointed all the same. However, it enabled me to watch her unobserved. Her walk was a little stiff and awkward.

There was a smooth branch overhanging the path. I jumped up and swung on it.

'What on earth are you doing?'

'Swinging from this smooth branch overhanging the path,' I said.

'Oh,' she said. Then: 'I worked in a hospital in 1914 and '15, scrubbing floors and fetching drinks of water for the troops, that sort of thing.'

I swung forward lithely, and landed gracefully beside her, twisting my ankle only slightly.

'Why did you give it up?' I asked through my teeth.

'I couldn't stand it.'

'The sight of the wounded, and so on?'

'No. I was surprised that I got used to that.' She glanced back, then stopped. 'What's the matter? Why are you hobbling?'

'I always walk like this,' I said. 'One of my legs is shorter than the other. When you come up to London with me I'll show you how I counteract it by always walking with one foot in the gutter.'

A look of great sympathy appeared on her face. I was about to reassure her when she said: 'No. What I couldn't stand was all the loving care they gave the soldiers, so they would get well; and then send them back to France. I thought it was awful. I thought they'd, well, suffered enough, and deserved a chance.' She sounded passionate; the abruptness of her speech had gone.

'I thought it was inhuman to send them back.'

She so far forgot herself as to look me straight in the eye. Then: 'You *have* hurt yourself.'

'Do you think you could give me a hand?' I suggested craftily.

'Of course,' she said. 'I'll go and get Marshall.'

'No, no!' The thought of being helped by that horse almost made me forget my injury. 'It's all right. I can manage.'

'Here.' She moved over. I put my arm over her shoulder and we started to stagger back. Her shoulders were unexpectedly soft.

'Would you?' I asked.

'Would I what?'

'Come up to London with me? I have some leave due.' I waited on tenterhooks.

'I couldn't do that.'

'Why not?'

'Well, I hardly know you.'

'I could leave some security or other with your parents, like a gold watch or a powdered wig or –'

'You're a heavy beast,' she said, and put her arm round my waist for better support, thus dissolving me into Bird's Custard. I glanced at her. She was smiling. The custard turned into a disgusting mess of English trifle.

We talked as we hobbled and lurched across the park. I don't know what came over me, but I told her almost everything there was to know about me up to my joining the army. She listened attentively until I started to describe my home life. It was then that she started spluttering. I thought my weight had become too much for her, but then saw she was laughing.

'It sounds simply awful.'

'Awful? What makes you say that?'

She stopped and looked equally astonished. 'Why, wasn't – wasn't it *supposed* to sound awful?'

'Certainly not,' I said, a little stiffly. 'I thought I was painting a picture of simple domestic bliss and harmony.'

'I'm so sorry. I thought you meant it to... I am sorry.'

We were silent until we reached the house. There I remembered the horse. During afternoon tea in the library I'd pinched some lumps of sugar for Marshall. I had decided to placate the animal.

I steered Katherine toward the stable. There were several stalls. Only two were occupied.

Marshall was in one of them, staring at the wall. He looked round when we came up to the door. He and I looked at each other. I fumbled for the sugar and held it out.

'He's tied up,' Katherine said. 'He can't reach it.' I didn't much like the idea of entering his stall, but there was nothing else for it, so I opened the lower door and edged in gingerly, smiling in a sycophantic manner, and held out the sugar.

Marshall glanced down at the sugar with those revolting eyes of his and jerked his head.

'If I were you –' Katherine began nervously.

But the horse bent its neck and I felt its velvet muzzle against the palm of my hand. Very gently it snuffled up the sugar and looked at me quite kindly. Smiling all over my face I felt in my other pocket and brought out another three lumps. I held them out, more confidently this time, and a warm feeling suffused my heart as Marshall, sweetly, gently, brushed my palm with his soft lips, and then stood crunching, regarding me fraternally. I beamed at Katherine proudly and gave my old friend Marshall a gentle, affectionate pat on the back. Whereupon Marshall shifted in his stall and pinned me to the wall.

'Help, I said. 'Help.'

He had my arms trapped so that I couldn't push him off. He was leaning his full weight against me. I believe he even had his legs crossed, leaning casually against the wall, using me as a horse blanket. I glared at him. 'You swine,' I said, my lips trembling with a sense of utter betrayal.

The beast wouldn't pay any attention to Katherine. She had to run for the groom.

As I walked away from the stable, brushing myself down furiously, I became aware that Katherine had stopped and was staring at me.

'What's the matter?' I asked, brushing the ticks – or whatever loathsome parasites that brute of a horse carried around with him – off my best uniform.

She was looking down at my feet 'What's happened to your limp?' she asked.

'Oh,' I said. I smiled. It was my smile that was lame now. 'It's – It's all right now.'

She frowned. It was half a minute before she spoke. I shuffled about uncomfortably, smirking.

'You sneaky beast,' she said at last, then strode angrily to the back door of the house. She'd have slammed it, too, if it hadn't been made of several tons of solid oak and wrought iron.

It was all that horse's fault. I went right back to the stable.

'This means war,' I said shrilly into the stall.

The bastard didn't even turn round, but calmly presented its loathsome hindquarters to my bitter gaze.

'Do you hear? You've asked for it. This means –'

The horse blew down its nose. Actually, it wasn't its nose it blew down. I hammered childishly on the top of the door with my fists in impotent rage. 'Shut up!'

The groom emerged from behind a pile of manure. He was wearing a hunted look. 'I didn't do nothing, sir,' he said pitifully. 'Honest, I haven't done nothing.'

I slunk back to the house. A dainty robin redbreast was tramping about on the front lawn. 'You shut up too,' I said.

Mrs Lewis

MY NEXT ENCOUNTER with the horse was in May. I'd got on quite well with Robert Lewis, and was delighted when he invited me back for his last weekend at home before leaving for France. Brian had been invited too, but was unable to come.

Robert was out when I arrived on the Thursday evening, but was due back any minute. I met his mother for the first time, being ushered into the presence by a diminutive housekeeper I hadn't met before.

Mrs Lewis was sitting straight-backed in a *chaise longue* in the room with the piano, knitting a pair of bullet-proof combinations, or perhaps it was a muffler. She had a long, aristocratic face and a voice that rattled the leaded windows.

'It's a gentleman, mum,' the housekeeper announced. 'He said he was expected, mum.'

'I did not expect him,' Mrs Lewis said severely. 'And for the last time will you cease addressing me as 'mum'? I am not your mum, and even if I were I could hardly be expected to acknowledge such an ugly offspring, especially one who conversed in a foreign tongue.'

'I keep telling you it's no a foreign tongue, mum; it's Scottish,' the little housekeeper said equably.

'Who is this uniformed person?' Mrs Lewis went on, unheeding. 'Surely you know by now that the gas meter is in the cellar.'

'He's no the gas man, mum; he's a military gentleman.'

'Bartholomew W. Bandy,' I said, bowing.

'Brandy? Never heard of him. Give him a cup of tea and six-pence, and send him away.'

'He says Master Robert invited him, mum.'

'Indeed? Then he had better sit down, I suppose.' Mrs Lewis looked at me, or rather, raked me fore and aft. Not a shade of expression crossed her long, lined, haughty face. 'My son,' she said, when the housekeeper had gone, 'is in the habit of bringing home some very odd company, Mr Brandy, but on this occasion I must say he seems to have excelled himself.'

'You mustn't flatter me, Mrs Lewis; it goes to my head.'

'There seems to be plenty of room for it there; indeed, you have the largest face I have ever come across.'

I nodded. 'It's sometimes a very time-consuming task washing it.'

'Let us hope that that does not deter you too often, Mr Brandy. However, I don't think we need go into your face any further this afternoon.'

'No, ma'am; I try to avoid it myself.'

'Very commendable, I am sure,' Mrs Lewis boomed. She examined me carefully for a moment longer, then patted the cushions at her side. 'Come and sit here.' I did. 'And now,' she said, 'would you care to paw me – ?'

'*Paw* you?'

'Paw me some port.'

We exchanged compliments until Katherine arrived. She wore the same simple white dress as at our first meeting, but had added a jade necklace. She smiled.

'I hope I'm not too late to save you,' she said. 'Oh. I see I am. I hope you didn't pay any attention to Mother, especially as she means everything she says.'

That was the effect Mrs Lewis always had on people: their dialogue took on a literary flavour.

'Your friend is a very argumentative fellow,' Mrs Lewis said crossly.

'Oh, is he? Then he must have been holding his own.'

'Holding his own what?' Mrs Lewis said, looking outraged.

'We've been having a very interesting discussion about my face,' I said hurriedly.

'It wasn't the least interesting,' Mrs Lewis said, starting to rise. I dashed over to help her. She bellowed. 'Mind my rheumatism, you fool.'

'She's offended,' Katherine said, giving her mother an affectionate hug, 'because it's usually her own face that comes up for discussion.'

'I can see that it would be a fascinating topic,' I said gallantly, 'with endless possibilities.'

'Your friend,' Mrs Lewis said, 'is argumentative, disrespectful, and impossible. Instead of looking suitably overawed in my presence he had the impudence to sit beside me with a casualness and lack of timidity that suggested he was interviewing me for political office, a bishopric, or some such disreputable position.' So saying, the old lady turned her redoubtable prow toward the door and started to sail out at half-speed, gasping angrily as her rheumatism twinged. I followed respectfully.

'I understand,' she said, turning at the door and glaring at me, 'that I'll be unable to avoid your face during the next three days.'

The old devil. She must have known all the time who I was.

'Fortunately,' she went on, 'I have been resigned to the inevitable ever since that hitherto squeamish person Lady Travellan cut her throat after poisoning her head gardener with his own weed killer.'

'She didn't cut her throat at all,' Katherine said. 'She fled to America.'

'Oh, did she? Well, it amounts to the same thing,' Mrs Lewis said, and, tapping me sharply on the head with her knitting needles, wallowed out of the room. Her angry gasps faded into the distance.

'She likes you,' Katherine said wonderingly.

English Plumbing

IF IT HADN'T been for the bathtub, I'd have had a most enjoyable weekend.

I was allocated a worn, creaking, but comfortable bedroom at the front of the house. Burgess also showed me where I could perform my ablutions, which room contained the most extraordinary contraption I'd ever come across. I thought at first it was some homework Mr Lewis had brought from the Foreign Office, a secret weapon of some sort. However, Burgess insisted it was a bathtub, so we left it at that temporarily.

After dinner Mr Lewis, back from a hard day's perfidy at the Foreign Office, suggested I play the piano for them. I thought this extraordinarily plucky of him as he couldn't have been in the best of spirits, having recently lost a near and dear one, as was evidenced by his wearing a black tie with his tweed suit. I was very tactful all evening, until I made some comment or other, whereupon he looked surprised, fingered the tie, and said: 'What this? Oh, no – nobody's dead that I know of. I'm wearing this because my other tie is being cleaned.'

Everyone was very polite about my playing. I began from that day to appreciate those qualities of fortitude, nay, cheerfulness in the face of adversity, that seemed to distinguish the British. All they needed now, it seemed to me, was the ability to remain equally cheerful and optimistic in the face of good fortune to make them completely civilized.

Mr Lewis even sang to my accompaniment. He had a voice so dreadful it made my playing seem superbly sensitive by comparison.

'I used to have a rotten voice,' he confided shyly.

When I went up to bed around midnight, I took a towel and soap to the bathroom but couldn't bring myself to face that tub. In fact I was scared even to turn my back on it. I decided to use the washbasin. Shivering in the icy air, which was a good thirty degrees colder than the outside atmosphere, I undressed, flinging my clothes in all directions. I realized with a moue of disgust that I hadn't changed my socks for two days when one of them happened to strike the wall with rather a thud. After sprinkling myself hastily, I began to wash them in the sink. I had the basin half filled with water when the flow ceased. It never did come on again that night. I was making do with what little water I had when Katherine came in.

'Oh.' She started to back out, flustered.

'It's all right. I'm nearly finished.' Fortunately I had my new pyjamas on.

'I'm sorry. I should have warned you; the bathroom door doesn't lock properly. We usually push this in front of it.' She indicated a small table with a marble top.

She was clutching a hideous quilted dressing gown to her. She looked adorable in it. In bed, all sorts of immoral reveries began to swirl in my head. It was I who had come in while she was having a bath. 'I'm sorry,' she was saying, 'I should have warned you – the bathroom door doesn't lock properly.' I was chockfull of wit and sophistication. 'It's quite all right,' I riposted. However, when I began to imagine myself soaping her back I decided it was high time I thought of something else, so I thought of the horse. That brought me down to earth all right. But I made up my mind to let bygones be bygones and to make one more effort to win the beast over. After all, I was not one to hold a grudge.

Friday morning found me down at the stables. In case there were any more misunderstandings, I made sure the groom was not nearby. He was mowing the grass a quarter mile away.

Marshall was lying in his stall. He didn't even have the decency to rise as I peered cautiously over the door, but I overlooked that. The Lewises' only other mount was watching intently from the next stall.

'M'now look here, Marshall,' I began in carefully modulated tones calculated to put the animal at its ease, 'you've nothing to fear from me. It's conceivable that you suffered some trauma during your sojourn in the army, but I assure you most sincerely I have no designs on you. I have no intention of requisitioning or conscripting you, or forcing you to re-enlist. You're entirely safe with me; you have nothing to fear whatsoever.' There was some fresh hay outside the stall. I drew a tuft and held it out, smiling winningly. The horse remained sprawled near its trough. It made no move to come forward. I held the hay out invitingly. 'Come on, Marshall.' The animal didn't budge. I made pleasant, enticing sounds with my lips. The horse glanced up and gave me a contemptuous look.

'All right, go to hell then,' I said, really annoyed, and started to stump out. It was absurd, anyway. What the devil did I care what that horse thought? On a spiteful afterthought I turned back and made a great fuss of the other horse and fed it the fresh hay and patted and stroked it fondly, casting malicious glances at Marshall as I did so. But the beast didn't seem to give a damn.

I was still feeding the other horse when Robert came in briskly, in corduroy riding breeches and the inevitable pullover with the holes in it.

'Morning,' he said abruptly.

'Good morning.'

'Feel like riding?'

'All right. '

'Which horse d'you want?'

I looked at Marshall defiantly. 'I'll take him,' I said.

If Marshall was displeased he gave no sign, and after trotting a mile from the house was proving so tractable I started to forgive him his idiosyncrasies or whatever was wrong with him. It was a glorious day. We jingled westward for two or three miles, silent but not uncompanionable, over the lovely rolling countryside.

At one point, without warning, Robert spurred his horse into a gallop and soared gracefully over a low gate. I didn't know whether Marshall was a jumper or not. Fortunately he was, and we sped wildly across fields, through a stream, down a steep slope, and at top speed along a narrow twisting path. Marshall was gasping when Robert finally reigned in. Snorting and spitting, Marshall was extremely cross. I smirked triumphantly. Robert became much more friendly, because I'd managed to keep up with him, I think.

We talked about flying in a clipped, brisk fashion. In the middle of this he changed the subject abruptly.

'What d'you think of Katherine?'

He was very fond of Katherine, as she was of him, and I think he was trying to find out if I was merely toying with her affections or something.

'Oh – very fond of her,' I said, finding myself adopting the other's clipped way of speaking. 'She's self-conscious about her squint, what?'

'Yes.'

'H'm.'

'Very.'

'Thought so.'

'H'm.'

'Rather,' I said. He glanced at me sharply. I added hastily, 'Doesn't she have any male friends?'

'Used to be keen on a chap. Fizzled out.'

'Hard luck.'

'H'm.'

Five minutes later he said, 'Doesn't know what to make of you.'

'Pardon?'

'Katherine.'

'Oh.'

'Nice day,' Lewis said, looking disapprovingly at the sky.

'M'm,' I said.

When we took the horses back to the stable, I gave Marshall a genuinely affectionate slap on the rump; and what did that horse do but swish me with its polluted tail. I don't know how many others have been lashed by a horse's polluted tail but I can testify that it stings, quite apart from the – the pollution.

'I'll get you for that,' I muttered savagely. 'You just wait.'

The groom's abject head popped up over the horse's backside. He was unable to say anything, his chin was quivering so. That poor fellow really must have been cowed in his youth. I would have given him a friendly pat on the shoulder but he had already locked himself in the hayloft. So I hurried after Robert, trying to decide whether to sneak out after dark that night and kick Marshall on the shins when he wasn't looking, run back to the airdrome and strafe the daylights out of the bastard, or to rise above the whole sordid business.

No, really, this horse business was becoming an obsession. I just had to pull myself together and try to look on it all in proper perspective. It reminded me of that dog back in Beamington, Ontario, who had known me practically all its life and still barked furiously whenever I approached and who once bit my leg after I'd gone to considerable trouble digging him from a hole he had got himself into under a house and – how do I get *involved* this way? That horse Marshall was a war criminal, but still, to feel this way about a horse, to let a horse get me down this way, it was – and that dog back in Beamington, Ontario, was once having a bath and it saw me and rushed at me and chased me halfway to Ottawa. It knew damn well I'd think it had rabies with all that foam all over it and – however, it was the horse I was talking about. I couldn't help mentioning it at lunch. Fortunately by then I'd recovered my poise and equanimity and was able to discuss the matter calmly, with a lofty and whimsical amusement.

'That horse hates me for some reason,' I was saying, laughing lightly. 'And it's out to get me. You wait and see, it'll get me in the end; it's its only aim in life, it ... I tell you that horse won't be satisfied until it's done me some grave injustice; it's not as if I haven't tried to make friends. Whatever happened to it when it was in the army – of course, I know the army's a bit of a shock even to the most hardened criminal and to a sensitive horse it must – but I tell you it's the way it looks at me, right from the beginning the way it's looked at me –' and I went on and on in calm, measured tones, and the others were all looking at me, their mouths open a little; and then I became aware that I was putting stewed prunes in my cup instead of sugar and stirring the tea with the mustard spoon, so I thought we'd better discuss something else. 'Nice day,' I said in clipped tones. Then I saw that rain was beating at the windows, so I thought I'd better give someone else a chance to talk, but nobody did for some time.

Then when I went up to bed after a merry evening of gin and charades, I just had to have a bath, I felt so hot and bothered. I piled my clothes neatly on the table with the marble top in the bathroom, then turned to the tub. It was an ominous sight, that thing. It was about seven and a half feet long and so deep I tickled myself climbing over the side into it. Giggling, I cautiously lowered myself to the bottom and took stock of the situation.

One end of the bathtub was enclosed by means of a large metal canopy over seven feet high. Arranged vertically at one side of this canopy were numerous large steel taps, each with a description of its function etched below in Old English, to wit: *Douche*, *Spray*, *Wave*, *Plunge*, *Hot*, *Cold*, *Shower*, *Fountain*, *Plug*, *Waterfall*, and *Sprinkler*. On the cracked enamel interior of the canopy were a dismaying variety of wounds, presumably entrance holes for the water. For example, there was a dirty yellow hole two feet above the bottom of the bath. Above this there was a disgusting-looking slit. Above the slit was another hole almost blocked with muck. There were holes of various shapes and sizes punctured in a semi-circle at chest level and in several ranks. High above, at the top of the canopy, were more holes arranged concentrically to one enormous ragged orifice through which I thought I could see daylight, or to be exact, the night sky. There were numerous other stained gashes in the canopy, and as I stood gaping at the bottom of the bath I tried to match them up with the taps. 'Wave', for example, probably referred to the long slit at knee level, as the water was bound to emerge from it in a wave. 'Shower.' Well that could only be the circular arrangement of holes in the roof of the canopy. 'Hot' and 'Cold' were explicit enough. But there I got stuck. What on earth, for instance, was 'Plunge'?

However, I was beginning to shiver, so I thought I'd better make a start, and what better method than by activating the control called 'Hot'? I tried it, and as I'd suspected hot water began to pour out of the dirty yellow hole. Or rather it trickled out regretfully. And immediately emptied itself down one of the two plug holes in the sloping gritty floor of the bath.

The usual rubber plug was nowhere to be seen. However, with lightning decision I turned on 'Plug'. Nothing happened for a moment; then slowly this obscene-looking object rose inch by inch out of one of the holes in the floor. It was coated with moss, scum, and old hairs. I backed away, licking my lips, staring as it slowly erected itself out of its lair. Finally it stopped and just stood there.

I cleaned it with a piece of toilet paper, with my eyes averted.

But I was beginning to get quite cold. I tried the 'Hot' tap again. Again the water merely trickled in; but the awful plug seemed to work because the water remained in the bathtub. Except that the water was a rusty colour and contained a spider desperately swimming after two embalmed bluebottles.

I should have given up there and then. But I really needed a bath, so after I'd emptied out the water once again I got the 'Hot' tap going. But it was soon evident that I would have to find some other way of filling the tub because the flow was so meagre; and there being no shortage of means, I next selected the control marked 'Waterfall'. It was extremely stiff, and I had to use both hands to turn it

At once there was a rumbling and boiling sound from behind the canopy. It got frighteningly loud and the whole bath began to vibrate so that my teeth started to click together, and my feet slid down the curved slope of the bath. Breathing faster, I seized the control to shut it off, but not quite in time, for a large dollop of filth shot out of the hole above the slit and smacked resoundingly against the far side of the tub. The bath rang under the concussion. Slowly the muck slithered lifelessly to the floor.

By now I was sweating so much with alarm that I needed a bath more than ever. I just had to go on. I stood waiting for the tub to fill, but the rate of flow was impossible, and after ten minutes I turned chilly and had to climb out to cover my nakedness with my best tunic. It wasn't easy getting out, because of the sloping sides, but I managed it. Then, standing once again in the rapidly cooling, rusty water, I reviewed the situation. I'd tried the Hot, Cold, Waterfall, and Plug controls. That left the Douche, Spray, Wave, Plunge, Shower, Fountain, and Sprinkler. Selecting the one marked 'Wave' as likely to be the least dangerous, I turned it on; but I misread the legend, and instead of turning on the tap above the word 'Wave', I turned the one below. This was the Plunge, and, naturally, it worked splendidly. A deluge of water bucketed down from the top of the canopy before I could get out of the way.

As I crouched at the other end of the tub, wringing out my best tunic, I found myself starting to laugh a little hysterically. However, after a time I pulled myself together and, flinging my tunic high over the top of the bath, I got under the Plunge or Shower or whatever it was – just as the flow ceased. Tremulous gasps halfway between giggles and despairing wails keened through my lips, but once again I controlled myself and in an almost carefree fashion turned on 'Wave'. A rapid clatter was immediately heard, so terrifying that I was halfway up the side of the bath before courage reasserted itself and I went back and shut it off. I then tried the one marked 'Spray', and at once a gout of scalding water shot out of the second hole in the floor of the bath like a geyser and caught me roundly between the legs. I gave an involuntary shriek and jumped so high my head clanged against the top of the canopy. The geyser continued to pour upward, but that obscene-looking plug undid all the good work by starting to retract into its loathsome hidey-hole, letting all the water out. I was starting to gibber now, and with wild eyes and clutching hands and emitting blood-chilling cries scrabbled at all the controls and turned on everything in sight. My crazed laughter bounced and echoed appallingly in the canopy as with rust-soaked hair and scalded scrotum I leaped and cavorted like some frenzied Hottentot among the streams of water pouring from thousands of gashes, punctures, wounds, slits, and holes, and also amid cascades of rust, enamel, spiders, and everything except old boots, the geyser spouting from the hole in the floor, dollops of filth flinging themselves out of the knee-high orifice and that appalling plug continuously erecting and retracting out of the floor – the whole bathroom, no, surely the whole house was clattering, boiling, gargling, and shaking, but I wasn't one to lose my head in an emergency; after all, I now had all the water I needed, in fact a good deal more than I wanted, and I grabbed the soap and soaped myself at frantic speed. I'd forgotten to shove that marble-topped table against the door to prevent anyone getting in, but even with my exaggerated sense of modesty that was a very minor worry, as I did the St Vitus dance at the far end of the tub, soaping myself and leaping up and down to keep my feet out of the boiling water. Just as I finished lathering myself, all the water stopped.

The water supply stopped, just like that, without warning, without so much as a dying gasp, hydraulically speaking. I was thickly covered in soap.

And that's when the real terror of it began. I'd no water to wash off the soap, and it was starting to itch. I thought of the washbasin and started to climb out of the bath, but I was so soapy I couldn't get hold, and kept sliding back to the bottom of the bath, and by the time I'd thought of lying down in the bottom of the bath all the water had drained out, and again and again I scratched and scrabbled frantically at the sides. Once I managed to get a grip at the top, but my legs were so soapy I couldn't haul myself over, and that's where Katherine found me at about two in the morning, crouched naked at the bottom of the bath, covered in dried soap and caked foam.

'That's another thing I forgot to tell you,' she said. 'We haven't used this bath for over ten years. It's not very reliable. We use the one along the hall.'

My New Squadron

AT LAST THE heat, dust, and tedium of Pilots' Pool were behind us, and Brian and I (we had, remarkably, been posted to the same squadron) were bumping down a rutted, hedge-bordered lane in a springless Crossley on the Flanders Front, nineteen miles behind Ypres.

The tender squealed to a halt in the farmyard of a large, off-white, L-shaped farm smelling of dung and army cooking. We dumped our kit in the officers' mess, which was a long, whitewashed room with a well-worn bar, and were directed to the squadron office. It was at the edge of the flying field, a pleasant three-minute walk through a tattered apple orchard of dust-drenched leaves. The apples were just starting to glow.

The C.O. seemed pleasant enough. It was his hands I noticed first. They were white, plump, carefully manicured, and they fluttered. Major Ashworth was a foot shorter than I and in his middle thirties, and even though his belt was secured at the last hole it looked too tight for him. He seemed fussy, but apart from his hands this did not extend to his appearance, for his uniform was a disgrace, grubby and threadbare, with the shirt pockets distended, pregnant with tobacco pouch, pipe, matches, diary, logbook, testy messages from Wing, flasks of whisky, filthy postcards, contraband cameras, maps, garters, bullets, fluff, dust and old bent nails. He wore wings and had earned the M.C. as long ago as 1915. He didn't fly unless he couldn't avoid it.

He informed us that we had joined a fine squadron that had ably maintained the traditions of the R.F.C. while flying Sopwith Pups, and now that it had just finished converting to the new Sopwith Camels even greater things were expected of us. He questioned us pleasantly and informally about our experience, shook his head sadly and hoped we would settle down all right. It seemed to me he didn't really expect us to.

The adjutant, nicknamed Bango, then took over. He was tall, skinny, and had a yellow front tooth and a loud, jolly voice; spray flew from the seaside of his lips as he allocated Brian to C Flight and me to B Flight. After talking non-stop for about five minutes he abruptly ceased and went back to his paperwork, playing a melody by clicking his upper and lower canines together and varying the width of his mouth. I even recognized the percussive tune that emerged: it was 'Alexander's Ragtime Band'. It looked as if we had joined a talented outfit.

Before taking a look at our new sleeping quarters, Brian and I strolled over the grass to inspect our first operational squadron. It wasn't at all what I'd expected. Could this collection of shaky huts, crude hangars, dilapidated tenders, scruffy Ack-Emmas, and burned grass really represent an active-service squadron? There wasn't even an aircraft in sight, either in the air or on the ground. In the training squadrons in England on a day as fine as this, the place would have been vibrating with activity, with aircraft taking off and landing every minute, new pilots chattering, clustered in nervous or bored groups, waiting their turn to fly, instructors bawling, motors revving, mechanics scurrying from machine to machine or lifting injured pilots from wreckage; and the air filled with the rattle of Avros or Pups or Nieuports or visiting B.E.S or Tin Whistles; and on Sunday afternoons the local inhabitants chirping excitedly along the boundary, gaping at every Scout that staggered overhead at dizzy speeds of fifty miles an hour....

But here? A mechanic picking his nose and one bird chittering like a piccolo.

The officers were accommodated in Nissen huts that were lined up untidily to one side, sheltered by trees. My kit had already arrived from the mess. It was dinnertime and the hut was empty. There were two windows at each end and a pregnant stove in the middle. There were four beds. As I was bouncing on mine and wondering how many flyers had slept in it and for how long, the batman came in, introduced himself, and bustled about, packing away my gear and chatting happily to the effect that this was a good squadron to belong to, as the average life of its pilots was a good seven weeks. Then Brian tramped in and together we strolled up to the mess. It was stiflingly hot and dusty.

There was a lot of noise in the mess. We took our places and ate in modest silence, listening attentively to the shop talk. It was evident that the pilots liked the new Camel in spite of its bad reputation. The Huns had already developed a healthy respect for it (except for von Richthofen's crowd) and tended to melt away magically at the sight of the little humped killer with the dihedral on the lower wing.

I had no difficulty in identifying my flight commander. He had that afternoon gained his twenty-fourth victory and was describing the fight with obvious relish.

I met him officially after dinner, being introduced by the adjutant. Beckett was stocky and broad with a square face and a hard, western accent. We both wore the badges of the V.L.I. Regiment. He wondered aloud how I had managed to transfer to the R.F.C. so soon after coming to France. His own application had taken eight months to go through.

'I had influence,' I said.

He grunted. 'Well, I hope you got influence over Camels. Last two fellows we had, cracked up and killed themselves before they even got over the lines. And we're goldarn short of planes. You'll have to borrow a machine for a day or two, until we can get one ferried from Candas for you. If we don't lose any more men, it'll be about three weeks before you go on active service. Try to get as many hours' flying as you can in that time. And go easy.'

'Have no fear,' I said. 'I intend to look after myself as if I were made of rolled gold.'

'Yeah,' Beckett said, eying me unlovingly.

This remark of mine proved to have been a more than ordinarily stupid one.

The three others were in the hut when I got back. We introduced ourselves. I was called Bandy; they were Lieutenant Richard Milestone, English, with a round, pleasant face, dressed in a disgracefully soiled regimental tunic with infantry badges; Brashman, very stable and quiet, with a dark, cynical face; and Second Lieutenant Ted Robinson, wearing the double-breasted garb of the R.F.C. Robinson had rosy cheeks and bright blue eager eyes and had been on active service only a week. Dick Milestone had been out for about one and a half months, as had his friend Brashman.

We yarned away, and I told them a little bit about myself – number of hours, types of aircraft flown, and where I'd trained. Milestone, it turned out, had had nearly two years of front-line duty before joining the Flying Corps, and had one and a half German planes to his credit, made up of quarters and halves where he had shared victories with other pilots. All three of us were in B Flight. I kept pestering Milestone with questions, and he was marvellously patient.

'I nearly got sent out here in April,' I said. 'They cleaned out the squadron for replacements for the heavy casualties. But I had only thirteen hours, so they passed me over. Even so, I had my training cut short quite a bit.'

'Even so, you were lucky.' Milestone yawned. 'We got three pilots in June with only about fourteen hours.'

'How did they make out?'

'One of them went west on his third patrol. The second lasted quite a few days longer.'

'And the third?'

'The third? Oh, he set out with the intention of not giving him-self for King and Country if he could possibly avoid it. He's still alive.'

'I suppose that was you?'

'Yes,' Milestone said, trying to look ashamed of himself.

'What about the anti-aircraft fire?'

'Archie?' Milestone said, sitting up. 'Oh, not bad when you get used to it. How do you like Camels?'

'I nearly cracked up on my first flight.'

'Who hasn't? I've been flying them now for about thirty hours, and still get terrified every time I have to turn round. I'd keep fly-ing straight forever if it wasn't for the thought of running into all those Huns ahead.'

'They certainly can get you out of trouble fast, though,' Robin-son said, 'the way they turn with that rotary engine.'

'They're Clergets, and not very reliable,' Milestone said. 'Don't be surprised if they cut out just after you take off, when you've no height to turn back.'

'I've got out of worse scrapes than that. I once spun from 450 feet,' I bragged.

'Good God!' Milestone said. 'Are you sure you're not dead?'

'No, it's only the way I look.'

Next day the weather was perfect, but there was no machine for me. Even the sole remaining Pup was unavailable, the C.O. having taken it to do some smuggling in. Then, the day after that, I was made orderly officer, and when I came off duty at eight the following morning it was raining. What with one thing and an-other several days passed before I was able to do any real flying, shooting at the ground target, and making trips with experienced men to learn the geography of the surrounding countryside so that I wouldn't get lost every time I took off.

As I said, we were about twenty miles behind the front, and it was surprising how different the French countryside looked from the air when it was compared with England. England was marzi-pan green and milk chocolate; France, yellow and mud. On my first familiarization trip I went down too low and nearly knocked one of the Chinese labourers off the telegraph pole he was repairing. I decided not to hedgehop in a Camel until I was more sure of my flying ability.

Meanwhile Brian and I were settling down in the squadron and were both very pleased with it. It was not one of the famous ones, like 56, but it was certainly not one of the worst, and it was a friendly place.

There was, however, the inevitable reserve of the veterans toward newcomers such as us. It was not a snobbish reserve, but rather a wait-and-see attitude. So many new pilots came, flew for a few days or weeks, then went west, that it was hardly worth while getting to know them. I felt this most markedly in the hut I lived in. Milestone and his close friend Douglas Brashman were consistently polite and friendly, always willing to answer questions on performance and tactics; but the petals of their personalities opened fully only in the warmth of their own company or in the company of other established pilots and veterans. A veteran, by the way, did not necessarily have to be an 'ace' but should preferably be on the credit side, with at least one victory.

It was actually a three-ringed reserve. At the centre were the 'aces' (flyers with five or more victories, according to the French system; the term and concept of the ace was not recognized by the Royal Flying Corps) or those who had a good many weeks of fighting behind them. In this group were the three flight commanders, Beckett, Don Parker of A Flight, a tall, angular Englishman of nineteen with hair so blond it was nearly white; and Robert Wordsworth, in command of C Flight (with no hair at all, owing to a scalp disease suffered in childhood); and the deputy leaders, Bob Handiman and Peter Scadding.

Around these circled the second ring, those who had settled down as useful fighters. Milestone and Brashman were among them, although Brashman was rapidly moving into the centre; he was so promising that he had already been made deputy leader of A Flight. And on the outside, looking enviously in, were the new boys like Robinson, Brian, and me, about whom not much was known.

There were a few other subtle classifications. It raised one slightly in the hierarchy, for example, to be entitled to wear wings on a regimental tunic, signifying trench experience. In this I had a slight edge over Brian, who, of course, had joined the corps straight from school and therefore wore the standard R.F.C. uniform.

It was easy to qualify for the elite, however. One had only to live through the next eight weeks.

All in all, the squadron was so full of peculiar people I felt quite comfortable – for a time. There was Rolls-Revell, for example, who had a lordly voice, a monocle, and a habit of looking cool in the most trying situations. Rolly, as he was called, had been with the squadron for a little over a month. Half the pilots considered him crazy; the other half were beginning to think him well worth cultivating. He was a superb flyer. During my second week he looped on take-off, and instead of being burned to death, gained a good 20 feet. No one had ever dared do that before on a Camel, probably not in any aircraft. Unfortunately his aim was not very good and he had already won a measure of fame by using up two complete belts of ammunition against an Albatros at point-blank range without even scarring it, a remarkable performance.

And in my flight there was Peter Scadding, who was affable, twenty-nine, and had prominent navy-blue eyes. Milestone said he was 'sex-crazy', that when he wasn't talking about women he was sleeping with them. He had been employed by the British-owned Argentine railways until 1914 when, well, to put it bluntly (as Scadding did), he was sacked for committing adultery with his boss's wife. The company had presented him with a third-class ticket home. He had promptly cashed it in, and when the money gave out continued to live in Argentina by his wits. Round about Christmas 1915 his *affaires* had grown too complicated to unravel; he had snipped himself free by borrowing money for his passage from the British consul on the understanding that he join up the day he arrived home. To everyone's surprise, including his own, he had done just that. It took him seven hours to solo, and he had nearly been washed out. He now had ten victories.

The weather was excellent during my third week of training and I was able to add a further twenty-five hours to the logbook.

Apart from ferrying duty, most of this was taken up in continued practice against the target and in more flights, alone and in company with veterans, over the surrounding countryside for the purpose of learning landmarks which, until I developed a homing instinct, would enable me to navigate back to the airdrome from any part of the front in our sector. I also cadged a trip in an S.E. 5. We shared the field with an S.E. squadron; they were billeted on the opposite long side of the airdrome.

The S.E. 5, I found, was a delightful aircraft to fly, stable as a bedstead compared with the Sopwith, and it flew higher and faster. But I still preferred the Camel. The Camel was a death trap in inexperienced hands; it was rigged tail heavy, and the torque was tremendous and constantly twisted the nose of the aircraft to the right so you were never quite going in the direction in which you were pointing. (This must have driven the enemy pilots crazy.) But it could reverse direction fast enough to get buffeted in its own slipstream and it could outturn any other aircraft flying; the visibility was superior and the armament deadly: two fixed Vickers machine guns firing forward. The S.E. 5 had only one synchronized gun. True, it had a Lewis gun in a Foster mounting on the top wing firing forward – or vertically if you felt like shooting up into the belly of an enemy two-seater – but I preferred the more concentrated fire of the Camel's Vickers.

It was during the third week that I got my first look at the front from the air. I sneaked along it alone one morning at 7,000 feet and gazed down blankly at the gashes and ruts of the trench system where they were visible through the tremendous barrage that was going on. For some reason the trenches, which snaked all over the countryside to within not much more than a mile of Ypres, were outlined in light grey. It was almost impossible to

172

make out which were the front lines, so illiterate was the calligraphy of the trench war, and only after flying up and down from Boesinghe round to Hooge was I able to deduce, from the absence of connecting trenches, which were the opposing firing lines. The entire landscape in the salient was ragged with overlapping mine and shell craters, and the roads, where they were discernible in the chaos of mangled earth, were slashed and frayed by near misses, and the trees were stripped and forlorn even at the height of this brooding, frenzied summer.

I flew up and down twice from Hooge to Boesinghe, and even at 7,000 feet was baffled and pushed about by the shell-shocked air. I was fascinated by the sight of this racked landscape containing tens of thousands of men and not one above-ground; by the clouds of dense yellow, grey, or black smoke that, snatched by the breeze, drifted, coiling and shredding to the east. It had been obvious for many days that a major attack was coming. Even from twenty miles off, the booming of the preparatory barrage had warned us. Below was the evidence. Down there it must have been hell for the Germans, the way the shells were sparking over their positions continuously. To the east the air was grey with smoke. A particularly violent explosion on the right caught my eye, toward Saint-Julien. Black earth heaved raggedly into the sky, then fell back slowly. Probably a mine. I continued to stare at the ground as I droned northward.

I was just banking west of Pilckem when it occurred to me that not once had I been fired on by enemy Archie, although I'd been within reasonable range. And simultaneously it occurred to me that if there had been enemy aircraft diving on me I would not have noticed them until it was too late.

Fortunately for me the enemy generally kept within their own lines except for the high-flying DFWs or Rumplers on photographic missions, or the occasional balloon raider. All the same...

I turned back toward Ypres again, this time keeping a careful watch on the sky around me. As the wrecked city came in sight through the smoke, I throttled back and went into a glide, keeping the fat nose of the plane in line with the Canal de l'Yser. When I got down to 1,400 feet, I distinctly heard the barrage; and shivered, and opened the throttle again to drown it out.

As I passed over the northwest outskirts, the Cloth Hall of Ypres appeared on the right. Even as I looked down on the historic, battered building a shell burst on a house about a hundred yards from it.

Going home, somehow I missed Vlamertinghe, although it was only 5,000 yards from the centre of Ypres. I kept straight on, however, hoping to pick up Poperinghe; but after flying for about ten minutes at seventy miles an hour without sighting it I had to study the map to pick out some other landmark. But the ground was singularly featureless. I could make out neither a recognizable railway line nor a main road. I turned back toward the lines to navigate from there. A few minutes later a village appeared on the right and I turned toward it, comparing it with the map. With some surprise I recognized the Etang de Dickebusch just beyond it. I had strayed surprisingly far south. Again displeased with my performance, I set a careful course of 175 degrees and was soon over the airdrome. For forced-landing practice I S-turned in, downwind. The machine bounced six feet, but fortunately the undercarriage stood it.

In the afternoon I went up with Milestone and another new pilot. I had difficulty keeping formation with them.

'You'll have to do better than that, Bandy, my boy,' Milestone said when we got back, 'or you'll be going out as a biplane and coming back a monoplane.'

'It's not so easy watching you and the sky as well.'

'So you were watching the sky. What did you see when we were flying along the front line?'

'I saw a stray S.E. coming back.'

'What else?'

'Nothing else.'

'You didn't see any other planes?'

'No.'

174

'For your information, the S.E. squadron across the field there overtook us 2,000 feet overhead going out. We passed a flight of Camels by only a quarter mile. They were at our altitude. There were two Harry Tales photographing the lines two miles east of where we turned away. Above them were five Camels, and about five thousand feet above the Camels were six Albatros or Pfalz.'

'Oh.'

'And that was just in the few minutes we flew along the lines. You say it's not so easy watching me and the sky as well, but you have to learn to do that as well as a dozen other things, all simultaneously. You'll be going across in two or three days, so it's best you get it clear now. Flying a plane is only a small part of the job, old boy. You have to learn to see what's going on everywhere. You think you know what a Camel looks like, for example, but when you see it from six different angles in the sky or against the earth it'll look like six different planes. The same with the Albatros. And your life may depend on recognizing an Albatros quickly. Learn to watch every foot of sky, especially round the sun. They love the sun.'

'How on earth do I watch the sun?'

'Obscure it with your thumb, like this, see? And listen, Bandy, take my earnest advice and don't try to be a hero right off. You'll need all your energy sometimes just keeping yourself alive.'

That was the day before the British and French attacked along a twenty-five-mile front in the average direction of Bruges, in Belgium. For days the hut had been trembling under the artillery barrage. Late that night Brian and I walked down to the field to view the continuous flash and flicker of the guns on the horizon, and we were soon joined by two or three others, including Milestone and Brashman. We watched in silence, our bones rattling under the dull concussions. Brian, who had never seen a barrage before, was impressed and excited. I could think only of Karley and the others, and I was hoping that they were not still on that front.

'Maybe it's the end of the war we're watching,' Brian said.

Nobody answered, and we slipped off silently to bed.

The next day Brashman barged into the hut at six-thirty, having just returned from the dawn patrol. His dark cynical face was alive with awe as he shook a complaining Milestone awake to describe the battle going on at the front. A Flight had not seen a single enemy aircraft but the sky had been crowded with British observation and scout planes, strafing and wheeling above the holocaust. Brashman had not seen one infantryman going forward; there had been plenty of them crouched in shell holes, though.

'By God,' he said fervently, 'I'm glad I'm not in that little affair.'

Late the same afternoon Brian came rushing in, full of excitement. 'I'm on the seven-thirty show!' he shouted.

'What,' I said, 'tonight?'

'Yes. Isn't it ripping? Wordsworth's just told me.'

He went on and on about it, hardly able to sit still for excitement. Brashman, who was lying in bed reading *Old Father Goriot*, looked at him soberly.

'You'd better calm down, my son,' he said.

'Yes, you're quite right, Brashman. I must remember to be cool, calm, and collected. You have to be terribly cold-blooded in the air, haven't you? I must remember that.' But then he bubbled over again, slapped me on the back, and looked sympathetic. 'Never mind, Bart, you'll probably be on a show tomorrow.'

'I shall try to possess my soul in patience,' I said civilly, but looking somewhat anxiously at Brian. I didn't want to have to write one of those letters to his parents describing his painless end. Really, he was only a boy; he ought to have been in his first year at university. What a waste of youth! and similar platitudes.

Still, I was a little envious, and restless. I strolled along to strip and check my guns once more, went back, changed, and took off to practice a few manoeuvres that might get me out of a jam, such as deft sideslips out of a theoretical line of fire. There was a little too much play in the joystick. I landed and got the rigger busy on it, then watched B Flight returning, four strong, with Beckett leading, his streamers fluttering gaily as he made a neat three-point landing. One plane was missing.

I followed the pilots into the office and stood in the background to listen to their reports. They had chased a two-seater without catching it. Most of their information was in map references to advise G.H.Q. as to the whereabouts of the new front line. Ted Robinson had become separated from the rest of the flight during the low flying over the lines. He came in a few minutes later. His bus was full of holes and he looked pale.

'I got caught by a machine gun and couldn't get away from it,' he said. 'I have holes in both my flying boots. Look.'

We inspected them, tchking and tutting sympathetically.

Beckett saw me. 'Oh, Bandy,' he said. 'You'll be on the early-morning show tomorrow.'

'Right,' I said smartly, and gave a scream of ecstasy, danced wildly on the major's hat, kissed the adjutant, fired six bullets into the ceiling, or in other words nodded faintly and turned almost as pale as Robinson.

Three weeks' mail caught up with me that day: one letter. I sat beside the empty fireplace in the anteroom of the mess and sipped the words slowly.

'My Dear Bartholomew: We were quite interested to get your letter from London. You seem to be having an interesting time over there, seeing Westminster Abbey and the Tower of London and all the other historic places so steeped in tradition. We were talking about you only the other week and still can't quite get used to the idea of you being an Aviator. Your father is still a little puzzled, but now I think he has accepted the idea, although he does not really approve of Aviation. Your Aunt Meg was saying that her son, your cousin Henry, was in the Flying Corps and was hurt in an accident at Camp Borden and is still in hospital, but we know you will be all right. Remember to do your duty toward God and those who have been set above you, your father says.

'Your former friend Mabel House is engaged to a Dr Proddle, who is Dr House's new partner. He has only been staying with the Houses a short time. He seems a pleasant young man although sometimes looks a little bewildered, perhaps at the speed with

177

which everything has happened. Mrs House is very pleased. Mabel still inquires after you from time to time. Your father is quite well, though his digestion is not what it was.'

The letter ended with more pious exhortations, reminders that I had promised not to smoke, swear, drink, or go with women, and to do my duty.

I wrote back, then began a letter to Katherine, and had difficulty deciding on its style. Should I write in the Affectionate style or in the Brotherly? In the Bold or Platonic or Intimate; or Tragical or Comical, or Pastoral or Historical, or Pastoral-Historical or Historical-Pastoral-Tragical, or the Stiff-Upper-Lip-in-Adversity style? As I pondered, staring into the empty fireplace that contained 111 cigarette ends, a rubber heel, some dried spittle, and a piece of purple fluff, this led me to a re-examination of my feelings for her.

I was still by no means certain that my affection for the girl was not the result of, or at least confused with, my romantic attachment, if that's what it was, for Burma Park itself. Assuming that my feelings for her were distinct, was I really in love with her? I had still no means of knowing, except that whenever I visualized those long black eyelashes and that lovably self-conscious walk of hers, I experienced an unruly sensation in my intestines. But this was hardly a reliable proof of love. It was a pity there was no objective chemical test for the condition known as being in love. Love was annoyingly subjective. Its symptoms – sleeplessness, lack of appetite, heavy sighs, filmy eyes, and loose bowels – could as easily be the signs of a nervous breakdown or an overdose of cascara.

Then I began thinking dreamily of Burma Park... and that's where it tended to become illogical and all the more complicated, because I had no doubt on that score: I loved Burma Park.

While I was thus preoccupied, Wordsworth came in with his flight and Brian came over to talk excitedly about his first patrol, flushed, excited, and full of confidence.

Peering Timidly
from a Camel

THE GREAT DAY arrived. I was already awake when the batman crept into the hut. It was still dark. I felt cold.

'I'll wake Robinson and Mr Milestone,' I whispered.

'Thank you, sir. You'll make sure Mr Milestone gets up, won't you, sir?'

'Absolutely.'

Robinson arose after groaning steadily for five minutes, and although I shook Milestone half out of bed Robinson and I were both washed, shaved, and dressed before he abruptly and irritably emerged from the blankets. We had already eaten the boiled egg before he staggered up, his eyes gummed with sleep. He refused to look at us, let alone speak.

Beckett gave us our instructions.

'We'll be on Offensive Patrol after we've had a look-see at the ground. Probably won't be any Huns about – they hate fighting before breakfast – but watch out anyway. Has everyone got his map?' We had. 'We have to find out where the front line is exactly. Keep close to me when we go down. We don't want any stragglers.'

B Flight was up to strength. Five of us were on this show: Beckett, Peter Scadding, Milestone, Robinson, and I. The remaining members of the flight, Millington and Fuller, had the morning off. Millington, by the way, was the squadron beanpole, six foot four and thin as a hat rack. Fuller, a poetic-looking chap, was the squadron pianist, with an inexplicable fondness for dissonant modern composers like Debussy and Ravel.

My Camel was already wheeled out and chocked. I climbed in, fastening the safety belt round my thighs with numb fingers, feeling distinctly apprehensive. I could tell I was feeling apprehensive because I got the safety belt fastened round the joystick, too. I was going over the lines for the first time. I ought to be blazing with eager aggressiveness, bellicose chin out-thrust, keen, cold eyes narrow-suited with martial determination, a Cavalryman of the Clouds, an Intrepid Birdman, a Knight of the Air, the personification of ruthless efficiency. Instead I had the control column entangled in my sidcot, my foot stuck in the rudder, and I was quaking like a mouse that had forgotten the way out of a hunk of Stilton with the cat approaching.

However, I managed to sort myself out after a time, and as I crouched in the cockpit, checking over the controls and pulling up the CC gear handle of the Vickers, I had a sudden vision of myself bravely, boldly, and intrepidly taking off straight into a sewage farm, or worse, into G.H.Q ....

But this was no time for glum reveries. Alertness, quick thinking, action. I was getting behind. Beckett's engine was already roaring. I hastened the business of getting airborne.

'Switch off, petrol on.'

'Switch off, petrol on.'

I pumped up pressure. The mechanic turned the rotary engine back, sucking in fuel. My goggles had steamed over. I couldn't see a thing. The others were already moving off toward the cinder runway.

'Contact.'

I switched on. I had nothing to rub my goggles with. Oh, blast, why hadn't I brought a handkerchief? Now there was a drip on the end of my nose. I pushed up the goggles with a quaking thumb, almost gouging my eye out

'Contact.'

The mechanic swung, the engine spluttered. He swung again. The Clerget started with a roar. I grabbed hastily for the throttle and hauled back. The engine went on roaring. The mechanic was staring at me. What the devil was he staring at? Didn't he know it was rude to stare?

Fool! Fine adjustment, full fine adjustment, full, full, full, fool! The other airplanes were already far down the field. What the devil was wrong with me? I eased back the adjustment lever until the engine was ticking like a cheap alarm clock. That was what I needed, waking up. The mechanic was now peering fearfully at me through the bracing wires. What now? Oh, yes: he was waiting for my signal. I ought to have run up the engine; I should have checked the rev counter, I should have had a handkerchief to wipe the drip off the end of my nose. It would be better to end it all now instead of waiting until I spun into that sewage farm through sheer incompetence.

I waved unhappily. The mechanic pulled away the chocks, then got out of the way fast. He was probably afraid I'd run him down. Now he was clinging to a strut to help me turn. He helped me turn too far, unfortunately, and the next thing I knew I was slowly trundling back into the hangar. The mechanic followed me into the hangar, gaping. 'Don't stand there like a fool,' I shouted over the din of the engine, which was reverberating mightily in the confined space. 'Get me out of here!' He had to call for help in hauling the airplane out backwards.

The others had already taken off. I inched forward the throttle, and guided by the mechanic, the plane turned and bumped off down the field. I went too fast, and the long-suffering mechanic was almost jerked off his feet. He let go and slowly faded into the distance, standing with his hands on his hips, shaking his head in wonderment.

A glance at the revs and at the windsock. I'd no time to run up. I opened up, flicking the rudder from side to side. The Camel rumbled and swung, the tail came up, and speed built quickly. I held the nose down until she was doing ninety. Then zoom. In not much more than six minutes I was at over 4,000, the Camel straining and shuddering.

But where were the others? I looked all around, easing the fine adjustment back a touch. I searched every inch of sky. Not a sign of them. It was impossible, but it was a fact. They had vanished. I dropped a wing and looked down. Surely they couldn't all have crashed? My eyes stung in the wind. I pushed down the goggles. The mist had cleared from them but there was a touch of grease on them now. A thing like that, grease on one's goggles and no hand-kerchief to wipe it off, sometimes spelled the difference between life and death in the air. Well, it was too late now.

I circled the airdrome, feeling lonely and neglected.

Suddenly three Camels appeared, to the right and above. I did a climbing turn and got up to them just as the fifth machine joined up. It was astounding the way they'd appeared from nowhere.

It was also a warning. If that could happen with *friendly* machines... At this rate I wouldn't last two days.

We climbed steadily. There wasn't much cloud. The air grew cold. Beckett levelled off at 10,000 just as we crossed the lines. The sun was low over Hunland. I remembered to keep my eye on it. I kept my eye on it. I suddenly found myself 500 above the rest of the flight. I dived, throttling back so as not to overshoot. The result was that I found myself a quarter mile behind. It took me two minutes to catch up. I wasted a lot of fuel trying to get back into my proper station at the rear.

You'd have thought I'd never flown before. I could see Milestone on Beckett's left twisting round to look back at me. I concentrat-ed hard on keeping steady and exactly twenty yards behind and twenty yards above the flanking aircraft. Consequently, I failed to keep a watch on the enemy. It was lucky for me there were no Albatroses about. The summer air was ice-cold. I was sweating.

Beckett banked suddenly to the left and the others followed neatly, with Scadding opening up to keep position and Milestone throttling back to compensate for his shorter arc. Me? I found myself five hundred yards behind again, and had to go full out to catch up once more. Just as I did so there was a deafening clang, and I felt my bus pushed high into the air, tail up; then I was diving vertically, engine full on, almost hanging outside the plane. By the time I'd pulled myself back in and got the Camel under control again, the rest of the flight had disappeared.

What on earth had happened? That noise? My engine was running all right. A moment later I was given the answer. There was a harsh cough, then another, and two black clouds blossomed no more than a hundred feet ahead. Archie. I was being shot at. Oh, the swine! The smoke whipped through the wires. I dodged to port instinctively and started to climb back to 10,000 feet, my heart beating frantically. I had heard plenty about Archie, but the other pilots had treated him as a joke, picturing him as some kind of entertainment put up by the Huns to break the monotony. I'd no idea he was so accurate. That first burst had been horribly accurate. A thought struck me. I looked back, expecting to find my tail in tatters, but there was no damage at all.

The black puffs continued to chase me upward, and what with the twisting and turning the compass was spinning so that now I didn't know which direction I was going in or where the rest of the flight was. The sky looked empty. I gazed down. The countryside looked unmarked. That meant I was far from the lines. But which side of the lines? Good Lord, I was lost.

I fumbled for the map but it was difficult to read, flapping; and the sun, like a tarnished bed-warmer, was shining full in my face. I managed to get the map under control but recognized no landmarks. The sun? The sun, of course. The sun, let me see, rose in the east. The Germans were in the east. Ergo, I was going in the wrong direction.

I turned upside down and pulled back the joystick, and in two seconds was travelling the other way. Woof, woof. Archie burst underneath and bumped the plane about.

I looked around. There was another plane flying in the same direction not far away. Strange I hadn't noticed it before. I flew toward it cautiously, hoping it was a member of my flight, but it was a DH 4. The observer waved. I followed, huddling close in spite of the Archie, and soon we came to the lines.

I wondered if it was time to go home. I looked at my watch and thought it had stopped. Surely I'd been out for more than half an hour? My legs felt weak. One of them was trembling like a clarinet reed. I gave it a kick with my more courageous foot.

However, I was beginning to calm down, almost enjoying the solitude after the strain of keeping formation. I took two or three deep breaths that made my teeth ache, but it helped me to relax, and it stilled the trembling of my leg. Then I remembered what I was out here for. I looked around for the enemy anxiously, almost dislocating my neck, but could see nothing but bursts of Archie streaming far behind me. I noticed that the DH 4 had gone; and I hadn't seen it go. I was getting steadily more incompetent every minute.

A little later I caught sight of a ragged line of Archie far to the left, and turned toward it. A couple of minutes later I made out four Camels. It was B Flight I joined up happily and waved. Nobody waved back.

It rained steadily for the next two days and there was almost no flying, in spite of the desperate requests from the front for tactical support and observation. A great victory at Pilckem Ridge had been claimed, but what we heard later from an infantry officer of a Lancashire division suggested no great triumph. He said the rain had turned the battlefield to deep mud and they had lost seven out of ten men, not a few from drowning in flooded crump holes. In other words the Huns, as usual, had turned on the bad weather just as the attack started. It was a well-known fact that the weather was under Hindenburg's orders.

Then we had a few days of low work, machine-gunning the enemy in his trenches, and if I had considered my first day in action upsetting it was paradise compared to flying at 500 feet above massed Parabellums. Hunland was crowded with machine guns.

Pilots tended to suffer from constipation; low work was the perfect laxative. But it was essential, I suppose.

It was during one of these strafing attacks that I saw my first plane go down, and it was one from our flight. We had dived on to a trench and were shooting it up when the plane to the right of me and only a few yards ahead did a lazy roll, lurched, then went down almost casually and flew to pieces. There was no fire. As I zoomed almost vertically, looking back, a shell landed smack in the wreckage, and when the smoke cleared there was nothing left. Second Lieutenant Fuller, it was; he'd been quite a good pianist; it seemed it wasn't always the best men who survived, either morally or musically. I nearly had a drink in the mess that afternoon. I'd have had plenty of company; the strafing was getting everyone down, and fraying already tattered nerves. No one commented on the silent piano. The next day Wordsworth announced that Brian had gone west. Ground machine-gun fire had got him, and he'd spun from 50 feet.

Splitarsing

AFTER ABOUT FIFTEEN trips over the line I was beginning to settle down, to fly with minimum reference to the map, to observe more accurately what was going on on the ground, and to see more clearly what the air had in store. During my first two or three trips I saw little except what was under my nose. Now I was starting to distinguish planes from miles away, and sometimes even to sense by their attitude what type they were.

But many days had gone by without my coming anywhere near an enemy plane, and I had almost forgotten they existed when, after half an hour of patrolling up and down the line one day, Beckett suddenly waggled his wings. It took me a couple of seconds to remember what this meant. Beckett started climbing and I peered up anxiously. There was a cluster of dots far away, about 1,000 feet higher. As we came closer I saw it was a flight of Albatroses.

I hummed a popular song or two, remembered to warm up the guns, and crept closer to the others. I was still in the tail position, the most dangerous of all. The rear man nearly always went first, there being nobody to protect him from behind. The Huns had a habit of diving, picking off the Charlie in the rear, then retreating upstairs again.

But I was determined not to suffer this fate. I had just one ambition: to become a flight commander with up to five machines guarding my back. That was all I wanted out of life: life.

The Albatroses saw us and started to make off eastward. Beckett followed. For once there was no Archie. We were hidden between cloud layers. The Albatroses were slightly slower than our Clerget Camels, but they had the advantage of height and so were able to keep a healthy distance between us. There were four of them and six of us, so it was unlikely they would stand and fight.

I saw Milestone draw abreast of Beckett, waggle his wings and point upward. There was another collection of Albatroses above, flying the same course as us and trying to hide behind the intermittent cloud 500 or so feet higher up. What beautiful-looking planes they were, with their curved top planes and tapering fuselages! Admiring them, I still kept one eye on Beckett, and it was as well I did, for he suddenly went into a dive. The rest of us tumbled after him raggedly. The Hun flight we had been chasing had flown under us, hoping to lure us down and make us cold meat for their pals above.

Sure enough, the top Albatroses dived after us. Only, they all seemed to be going after *me*, which struck me as very unfair. I felt exposed and shivery, and I splitarsed so much I nearly collided with Robinson. I was too anxious to see what the rest of my friends were doing. I heard a funny popping noise behind. Tracer was feathering overhead. I hauled back hard on the stick, looping. The rattle of machine guns grew louder, then faded. I was too scared to look back. I was diving now. A Hun passed somewhere in front. I fired an unnecessarily long burst, more for morale purposes than anything else, missed by at least a hundred feet, and twisted and danced around in case there was anyone still on my tail. I caught a glimpse of a plane spinning down, then another.

And then the sky was empty. I looked around, anxious and jittery. Not a sign of a plane anywhere. There was a faint streak of smoke where one of the planes had gone into the clouds below, but this was the only evidence that I had not been alone all along. It was uncanny. I was shivering with excitement. The whole affair had lasted only thirty seconds.

I seemed to have got lost again, and wasn't too happy about that, what with concealing cloud only a few feet above. I dived closer to the lower cloud level. A Camel appeared, then another, and I recognized Beckett by his streamers, and Milestone. Soon another Camel materialized and we flew around for a few minutes, probing the clouds, but saw no more enemy scouts. Beckett went home early. It turned out that he and Millington had each got a Hun. It was Millington's first full victory, and he exuded false nonchalance as he received our congratulations.

When I walked into the mess with Milestone and Millington, I asked what had happened.

'The Huns tried their trick of flying in layers,' Milestone explained patiently. 'Beckett pretended to go after the bottom layer, then turned to face the second as they came down. It's a dangerous thing to do, but it worked out right this time. It was lucky their top flight didn't see us.'

'What top flight? I didn't see them.'

'They were there all the same.'

'I'll never get the hang of this business,' I said peevishly. 'I wouldn't have seen the middle layer if you hadn't pointed it out.'

'You got back and that's the main thing. Did you see Millington pick off the one that was on your tail?'

'What? No. I thought I'd dodged out of his way.'

'Like hell,' Millington said. 'Incidentally, you don't want to try that trick of looping in a dogfight, either. You were very nearly picked off as you staggered over the top.'

'I didn't stagger over the top,' I said, offended. 'I executed a very beautiful manoeuvre.'

'Well,' Milestone said, 'if Millington hadn't executed *his* very beautiful manoeuvre, you'd be picking lead out of your arse right now. You'd better start forgetting that training-school stuff, Bandy, and concentrate on some ugly splitarsing if you want to go back to yelling "Timber" as the log cabins start to fall, or whatever you people do for amusement in that country of yours.'

Me and a Buxom Wench

I WAS FOND of strolling about the countryside, either alone or with company, but most of the tracks in the vicinity of the airdrome were rutted and dusty in dry weather, muddy in wet. The only really satisfactory lane led to a dilapidated farm, so it was in that direction I invariably went. Several times I had to circumnavigate a chubby but not unprepossessing and experienced-looking female of about twenty. She seemed to do most of the cleaning and cooking for the numerous farm workers, mostly elderly women and men, who flocked every morning at five into the surrounding fields, often not returning, except for a light lunch that took them three hours, until the sun went down. We conversed on one never-to-be-forgotten morning.

'Good day, sir,' she said.

'Good day, Miss,' I smirked.

Then I plodded on and she went back to her soup cauldron.

Each time we passed in the lane or converged in the courtyard we added a little extra fillip to our social intercourse.

'Good day, Lieutenant.'

'Good day, Miss.'

'You are from the Field Latrines, no?'

'No,' I said.

'Good morning, my lieutenant.'

'Good day, Louise.'

'You have perhaps killed a filthy Boche to death today, yes?'

'No,' I said.

She was rapidly becoming convinced that I was the strong, silent type.

'Good day, my lieutenant.'

'Morning, Louise.' Since we had first met she appeared to have abandoned most of her underclothes, perhaps because of the heat. All the same, it was becoming an effort not to stare at the unrestrained convexity of her abdomen. This forced me to meet her gaze, which was even more unrestrained.

'By blue,' she exclaimed. (I translate literally.) 'But it is hot, hein?'

'By blue, that is so.'

'Good day, Mr Bandy. It is still hot, hein?' she began, sticking her bare feet apart and fluttering her lips to indicate the extreme heat. It was about sixty degrees.

'There is no doubt of that, Louise.'

'You would perhaps like to swim, then?' she asked, gesturing presumably toward the only bathing spot within miles, a water-filled and somewhat malodorous quarry.

But I declined, partly because of the malodorousness but mostly because I suspected that her intentions weren't strictly ablutionary. After that I stopped going to the farm. For a few days.

She was one of the fifty or so villagers who congregated every Sunday afternoon at the southern boundary of the field to watch the take-offs and landings. I would have to be walking in that direction with Milestone, and she waved at me, her bust bouncing merrily.

'Good day, Mr Bandy,' she called out 'When are you visiting me again, hein?'

'Aha,' Milestone said, 'so that's what – or should I say, who – you've been up to during those perambulations of yours.'

190

'M'certainly not,' I said defensively. 'The only good walk in the neighbourhood happens to lead to her.'

That was just the trouble. Nowhere else to walk. Or was I rationalizing? Surely... surely sex wasn't rearing its ugly head, was it? I dismissed the thought as absurd; but how complicated life was, I mused philosophically, lashing the bocage with a bent switch and trying not to notice Milestone's ribald grin.

'Contact.'

'Contact,' I agreed, and the prop swung. The engine caught and roared healthily. I opened the fine adjustment. Throttle forward. The plane began to rumble over the grass.

I opened up, listened carefully to the engine note, then throttled down and waited for the others to start off; then followed close behind Robinson. The tail came up, the grass blurred, the wheels lifted gently, and with exquisite judgement I just missed the trees.

Recovering from the fright, I made a climbing turn so steep that the little aircraft shuddered and protested.

It was a fine day, with wisps of cirrocumulus powdering the sky. We all met at 3,000 and climbed the twenty or so miles to the front, crossing at 8,000. Archie opened up immediately and managed some fine shooting; but by now dodging came naturally.

The air seemed crowded with other planes. There must have been at least half a dozen observation types buzzing up and down the lines, with Camels frisking round them among the black Archie puffs. A complete squadron of Bristol Fighters was going out nearly 10,000 feet above. I recognized Sopwith, Bristol, and de Havilland types. There was no sign of the enemy, not even the familiar cluster of dots far in Hunland. It seemed to be R.F.C. gala day over Flanders.

We turned north toward the scar of Ypres. Even Archie seemed to become cowed by the display of Allied strength, for his shooting became half-hearted. After the disastrous spring, we seemed to have regained command of the air with a vengeance. I danced

191

from side to side at the rear of the little formation and rolled four times without altering direction by more than a few degrees, which was excellent flying, especially as I say so myself.

It was then I realized that I had graduated at last. I could fly. I had mastered the most treacherous of all aircraft, the Sopwith Camel; and every movement of stick and twitch of rudder bar was not only instinctive; it was exactly right. The plane and I were one, for richer or poorer, until ... something or other did us part.

It was a delectable feeling. For the first time the aircraft seemed not a separate thing of wood, wire and pistons but an extension of myself, the ailerons my muscles, the engine powered by my will.

This harmony of me and the flimsiness of metal and canvas was a slightly uncanny sensation. It was soon gone; but it had been there, and it had been pure exhilaration. Of course, this might have been caused by the rarefied atmosphere at 16,000 feet, but even so ...

Then we sighted a flock of Albatroses sneaking southward. We were in a perfect position to attack from the eye of the sun, but just then my engine started acting up again. I followed the others in a dive, and saw that they were going to catch up with the Huns. I kept on going, but the Clerget rapidly got worse. It sounded like two cylinders shirking. So much for the extension of my will. I fell far behind and had to turn back.

When the others returned an hour later, I learned that Robinson had been shot down. He had gone straight in from a great height and had had no chance.

Beckett listened to my report in stony silence, and when he'd finished with the bumf I saw him stride down to B Flight hangar. I had a good idea why.

I went back to the hut. When after ten minutes Brashman barged in, my heart skipped a beat, thinking it was Beckett come to tell me he'd found nothing wrong with my engine and that I was to be shot at dawn without a blindfold.

'I hear Robinson got it.'

'Yes.'

There was a silence. Milestone came in slowly.

'I hear Robinson got it,' Brashman said.

'Yes. He was too busy shooting to watch his tail, the bloody fool! You'd think he'd have learned by now,' Milestone said. He sat on his bed and kicked off his boots, then stared at the floor.

'Come up to the mess for a drink,' Brashman said.

Milestone got up and looked at Robinson's bed. 'Another load of kit to pack and letters to burn,' he said. 'Suppose we'll have to drop a note to his wife, too.'

'Later. Come on,' Brashman said. He started for the door, glancing at me as he passed. 'I saw you coming home early. Dud engine, was it?'

'Yes.'

I'd had several dud engines lately, and it was beginning to look suspicious even to me. Maybe Bandy had the wind up and was trying to blame his engine for his cowardice.

After a couple of hours I went up to the mess. As usual, half the squadron was drunk.

'What are you drinking, Bandy?' Peter Scadding asked, his face twisted into a lopsided expression and his sexy, dark-blue eyes bulging dangerously. 'What the devil, lemonade? Waiter, a whisky over here for our friend Bartolomeo Bandy.'

'No thanks,' I said. 'But I'll play the piano for you, you lucky devil.'

'You play the piano? Is there no end,' Scadding said, gesturing widely and tripping over a second lieutenant, 'to the talents of this lad?' He put his arm around me and helped me over to the battered piano that nobody had played since Fuller had gone west.

I played a spirited rendition of Schubert's 'Marche Militaire', and Parker led a march round the mess. I had to hammer the keys to be heard above the din. Several others tramped behind Parker, staggering and laughing, and those items of furniture that hadn't the sense to get out of the way were crushed. George Ginty, C Flight's Irishman, and Trimbull, the armament officer who had eyebrows like privet hedges bordering the neglected garden of his face, started a fencing match with two broken chair legs.

The marchers were now trying to circumnavigate the mess on one leg, so I changed from march to waltz time, belabouring the keys until my fingertips tingled.

Getting tired of this, several of the less inebriated gathered round the piano and attempted a singsong, a much superior method, it seemed to me, of getting rid of surplus energy. At ten-thirty the party started to break up as there were early jobs for two of the flights, and Brashman, who drank as much as his friend Milestone but usually managed to remain upright, helped me cart Dick back to the hut.

That night there was a raid, and a bomb landed on the other side of the airfield, just missing a hangar full of S.E.s. Brashman and Milestone slept through the din. Perhaps there was something to be said for booze, after all ....

'Six o'clock. Time to get up, sir,' the batman murmured, and I was half out of bed and reaching for my pants before I realized it was Milestone he was shaking, not me.

Milestone went grumbling to the latrine; Brashman snored on. I lay back again, but couldn't sleep, so I dressed and joined B Flight in the mess. Everyone was, as usual at breakfast, morose and silent, the communal headache thudding like a tom-tom.

I watched them waver off the runway, their wheels trailing in the ground mist, then went for a walk, dreaming about Burma Park and wishing I was there more than ever. Whenever I thought about Burma Park I felt wistful, and this irritated me. I'd never felt that way about any place before, except perhaps Karley's dugout. But there it was: I was already looking forward to November or December, to accept the Lewises' invitation to spend my leave with them. I was sure now it wasn't just my not inconsiderable affection for Katherine that drew me to the calm Georgian residence. Even supposing I did love her, it still didn't explain why I'd developed such an attachment for that harmonious dwelling with its worn, chipped, scarred, peeling, abused interior. I didn't even have that feeling for my own home, which proved how basically unwistful I really was.

I was so preoccupied with this mystery that I was in the farmyard before I realized it. I turned hastily to go back. Too late. Louise had emerged from the kitchen, wearing a thin black dress torn at a well-padded clavicle. It was doubly evident that she enjoyed no visible means of support.

This morning her eyes were so frankly bold as she chatted that I would have been terrified for my honour if I hadn't been so bemused by those reveries of Burma Park. But even through that fog of sentiment her look penetrated until I started to feel as if I was wearing only a short regimental tie and a pair of socks.

This should have warned me; but no. When she invited me inside for a glass of their coarse red wine, after checking my watch – I had a patrol at eleven-thirty – I accepted.

After all, *pourquoi que non*, I said to myself in my impeccable French that everyone except the stupid French could understand perfectly; and adopting a lord-of-the-manor expression to obscure my uneasiness, I followed her into the kitchen, which was a dark and smelly place and contained a grandmother, knitting and daydreaming. We continued on through to the dining room, where Louise belaboured the cushions in the best chair into submission. As I sipped my wine she studied my every movement, incredulously when she thought I wasn't looking, smiling broadly when she saw I was. Those eyes: they were like orgiastic coal tar and gave one a sinking sensation. Those lips, red as the apples that gleamed in the squadron orchard. Those – I had to take several deep breaths; they were aimed at me. Hands up, they were saying. They looked dangerous. The safety catches were off. They –

'The grandmother,' Louise was saying, 'is in the kitchen, and does not hear well.'

This was, of course, interesting, though a somewhat abrupt change of subject, for we had been discussing the harvest. I didn't see the point until she added, 'The others are at work and won't be back for a long time.'

'I have –' I lowered my voice to a manly squeak, and began again: 'I have to be back at the airdrome in an hour.'

She must have taken this as assent, because the next moment she had taken my hand with a smile that showed off a fine set of voracious teeth, and started to drag me off. Halfway up the stairs I murmured deprecatingly and drew back. As we were still clammily holding hands, this unbalanced her, and she teetered against me. I had to grab hold to prevent us both from pitching downstairs in a heap; and since she was one stair higher than I, my face was suddenly buried deep in her primeval mammaries. Taking this as a sign of uncontrollable passion, she clutched her arms round my head, burying my face even deeper in her bosom until my nose was bent almost double against her sternum and her nipples were stuck in my ear-holes like a stethoscope. 'Darling,' she murmured, 'my little, my aviator.'

We were still swaying about on the stairs, my head firmly wedged between those uncorsetted accessories. 'Let go, for God's sake,' I said, but my voice was so muffled it must have come out as something indescribably erotic, for she clutched all the tighter. For several seconds we undulated back and forth, until with the strength of suffocation I managed to wrench loose, gasping for breath. But it had been too violent a movement; for a moment I clutched wildly at nothing, then just before I tottered backward I got a grip on her dress. Unfortunately it was, as I think I've already mentioned, already torn, so that I found myself overbalancing with most of the dress in my hands. For a moment my wild gaze held an image of long blue-grey cotton knickers and a great bulging vest before I landed on my back at the bottom of the stairs, flailing and winded.

She bounced – it is the only word – hastily down the stairs after me. 'My God,' she murmured, cradling my head and stroking my cheek, 'but you are the impetuous one, no?'

'No,' I said, 'no, no.'

She put her arms around me, and for a terror-stricken second I thought she was going to pick me up and carry me struggling and screaming into her frowsy boudoir; but it turned out she was only helping me to my feet.

The ancient grandmother tottered in and surveyed the appalling scene through rheumy eyes and a great wide toothless smirk.

'So,' she chunnered, looking around, 'I see the lunch, it isn't ready yet,' and turning away, went back to her knitting and daydreaming.

When at length Louise realized that for some unfathomable reason I had no intention of following through, she started to make quite a scene, and to placate her I promised her a new dress.

Back in the hut I had to hurry into my sidcot, and was damned if I could find my gloves. I was at ten thousand feet before my face cooled sufficiently for me to risk lowering my goggles. They might otherwise have melted from the heat.

Fortune Smirking at Me

THE ENGINE SOUNDED fine again, but I wasn't fooled by that, even though the mechanics had worked on it far into the night. Beckett had the day off, and Scadding led a patrol of three. Our job that day was to protect some B.E. 2Cs while they photographed the lines: tedious work only slightly relieved by the threat posed by Huns hanging sunward.

But they made no effort to intervene. Huns were funny birds. Sometimes they were eager to attack; at other times they looked the other way like little old ladies trying not to notice a drunk peeing against their picket fence.

It was a cloudless day with little activity on the ground. The British Army had been fighting all year in rain and mud. Now that the sun was shining, their attack had stopped. Even the crump holes, which in August had been filled to the brim with glittering, stinking water, now looked as dry as stale bread. It made you wonder if it wasn't British policy to attack only when the going was hardest.

After a while the B.E.s waved goodbye and went home, and Scadding climbed after the Huns, who, however, flew away. After an hour of Archie dodging we too went home.

The engine was running smoothly. I hadn't disgraced myself.

My morale did a climbing turn, and I went so far as to play a Chopin etude on the rum-soaked piano. Everyone very politely pretended not to notice.

That afternoon one of the new pilots stalled on take-off and was carted from the wreckage snoring blood.

The engine still seemed to be running well when B Flight took off at six. As we would be late for dinner, I took a package of chocolate aloft. The chocolate was limp as I climbed into the plane but soon hardened in the colder air as we crossed the lines at 7,000. Archie was evidently glad to see us, for he gave us an ovation.

Soon we were ten miles over, and I sensed we were in for a fight. After many trips you began to get this kind of intuition, and it was often reliable. There were a fair number of enemy aircraft up.

But although we bored after them repeatedly, they kept sheering off. Once a bunch of them came quite close, overhead, and seemed about to dive but then suddenly hurried home as a squadron of S.E.s appeared.

The S.E.s didn't notice them, however, and soon vanished eastward, and the Albatroses came back and again hung overhead, wagging their wings indecisively. There were only three of us, but perhaps they suspected a trap.

Abruptly Scadding waggled his wings and dived on full engine. Milestone and I followed.

There was a flight of Albatroses below, making for their own lines, four of them. Scadding went down so steeply we were soon doing over 170. I wondered how we were going to pull out without losing a wing or two. I felt excitedly alert. We were catching up with the Albatroses below, easily. They were speeding along with nothing on their minds except the danger of being late for dinner. My stomach started to coil into a reef knot, and I was praying for the engine not to fail, not now, not this time. We were in the sun, coming down at a great speed. And my Camel kept up – in fact I was almost level with the leader, a hundred feet higher.

I got a plane in the Aldis. He grew larger every second, flying level. Now all it needed was for my guns to jam. I should have warmed them up. It was too late now. I was only forty feet behind him. I pressed the lever and prayed the guns would fire. They did.

The aim wasn't at all bad, but I was going so fast that I had time for only a short burst before I was forced to zoom to avoid colliding with him. I missed his tail by the width of a hair.

I had time to see the astonishing sight of three of the enemy spinning down simultaneously and almost abreast of each other.

You'd have thought they were doing it deliberately, those three planes going down side by side. I shall never forget that sight.

Just as I remembered the Albatroses that had been hanging over us, they arrived.

One of them flashed in front. Behind was a dull popping sound. But I had plenty of speed, even after the steep zoom, and by hacking at the rudder bar and flicking the tail over I was able to shake off the one behind, and by accident found myself on the tail of another of the new arrivals. I wrenched my head around to make sure I wasn't being followed. The Hun in front jerked about rather sloppily and only succeeded in slowing himself up. The twin Vickers rattled. He went into a spin almost at once.

I looked around hurriedly again, but the sky seemed clear, so I watched my German go. But then I saw his engine was off, and went after him, but it was too late. He pulled out and streaked for home. I ought to have remembered that trick of spinning out of a tight situation. I'd heard about it often enough. Generally it was a dangerous thing to do, because the moment one pulled out of the spin one was at the mercy of any opponent who had the speed or the quick wit to follow one down. In this case the opponent had the speed but not the wit. Another lesson learned. I waved him goodbye.

Still, I'd got one. My first victory. I was in the middle of nodding smugly to myself when it occurred to me that the other Hun might have used the same trick, pulled out and gone home. After all, I'd fired barely twenty rounds into him. Well, never mind. He must have had a nasty scare at least.

I looked around for the other pair of Camels, but they weren't in sight. I didn't think I'd ever get used to the way planes vanished so abruptly. It was uncanny.

There weren't even any Archie bursts for company.

I was in the act of popping a square of chocolate into my mouth by way of celebration when it occurred to me that this absence of Archie was a mite suspicious. A moment later I saw the reason: there were about a dozen Albatroses coming at me from above the sun.

It was too late to dive away; they'd built up too much speed. I banked and turned toward them instinctively. Tracer spat around, curls and wisps of grey smoke, some of it horribly close. I ruddered the leading machine into the Aldis. His Spandaus were alight, firing continuously, but I took time to aim carefully before pressing the lever, managed a short burst, and saw my tracer clearly hitting him square in the propeller boss. And I wondered in a calm, detached way who would be the first to give way. Me. I slammed the stick forward and we passed only feet apart, which gave me a shock. Then I was through the lot of them, and diving for home. I stared back over the rudder. Their leading machine seemed to have got away with it – no, by God! He was smoking. I kept on and was nearly a mile away when he started to go down, smoking heavily. His smoke left an erratic line in the sky, which was curious because he seemed to be descending in a straight line, flat out – if he had any engine left to go flat out down with.

So I had one after all.

The other Albatroses followed me a little way, but without enthusiasm, and turned back even before I sped across the lines. I flew in flat circles over Broodseinde, I think it was, eating chocolate. It was still too early to go home. I flew across, but kept to within a mile or so of the front, and looked the plane over for damage, but there didn't seem to be any, which was surprising considering the amount of shooting that had been done at me. In that head-on charge, the moment I dived away I should have got raked.

There was no sign of the other Camels, though I didn't search too diligently, for it was pleasant being alone. A single machine sometimes drew more than its fair share of Archie, but without formation to keep, it could manoeuvre more effectively around the bursts. One manoeuvre that always seemed to work was to make a shallow dive for a few seconds, then zoom up; it made you laugh to see the Archie bursting below, where you should have been. Another was to fly through the bursts ahead, then alter direction slightly. Simple evasive tactics, but they worked. The trick was to lose as little headway as possible while executing the maximum changes in height or direction.

This was not to say that Archie was not a dangerous beast. If you flew for more than a few seconds in a straight line you were soon bracketed, but a shell had to burst very close before it did any real damage.

Having heard rumours that the Canadian Corps was once again in the lines in the Passchendaele sector, I flew north to see if I could give them a little moral support. Somewhere down in that chaotic network of burrows, gouges, and blue barbed wire was Karley. Really, it was too bad there wasn't a bus service to the Front so one could visit other units on one's day off. As it was, it sometimes took as many days to cover a mere eighty miles of Front as it did to go by train from say Toronto to Winnipeg. A car was the thing to have. The major had a car but he hardly ever used it, except to go on leave.

I thought I saw something, a reflection, a flash. I peered over the left side of the plane, dipping the wing, and saw what it was – the remains of an Allied observation balloon flaming down about two miles behind the lines. A hit-and-run job. I scanned the earth between the balloon and the lines, circling, tilted over vertically so that the ground turned slowly like a wheel with trench lines as spokes; and I saw the Hun who'd done the dirty deed. He was silvery against the darkening ground, making off fast for safety. No doubt the pilot was congratulating himself on a useful piece of work and looking forward to some sausage and an Iron Cross, second class.

I was between him and the lines too, poor devil. I went into a vertical dive at two-thirds throttle, estimating that I would catch him at the lines. My bus was glowing in the rosy sun, so he could hardly fail to see me; he did, and changed course, going down to daisy level, hoping to obtain, probably, the protection of his anti-aircraft guns. But I caught up with him just as he crossed what was probably the Canadian front line, and he had no room to manoeuvre, being too low. I'd throttled back 500 feet above him, so as not to overshoot, and opened up at seventy yards, aiming for the pilot; and saw my tracer going into his fuselage well behind his head, which was not very good shooting.

But it upset him. He banked jerkily to get out of the way; his left wing dropped, struck the ground, and he flew to pieces just about exactly in the middle of no man's land, scattering shreds of canvas and himself into a hundred shell holes. He never had a chance. It was just his bad luck that there had happened to be a stray Camel exactly in the right position to nail him. I was almost sorry in an insincere sort of way, for he had deserved to get away after his valiant effort in firing that balloon. Balloons were extremely well protected, surrounded by a dreaded Archie called 'flaming onions'.

I was forced to fly for several seconds with my belly toward the enemy gunners, but, surprisingly, they didn't fire. Perhaps it had all been too sudden. I think someone waved as I whizzed over the British front line.

It was dusk when I landed, and Milestone, Scadding and the major and the adjutant were waiting for me at the office, looking at me cheerfully for a change. Scadding slapped me on the back.

'Well, you opened your bag with a vengeance, old boy,' he said.

'Two Huns. Very nice, Bandy, sah, very nice,' Bango said, exhibiting his large front tooth in a wide grin.

'Oh. You heard about the other?'

'What other?' Scadding said.

'Which ones are you talking about?'

There was a silence for a moment. Then: 'The one you got in a spin and your flamer.'

'Oh, the first one went down then, did it?'

'Yes. I followed mine down to make sure he wasn't up to any monkey business,' Scadding said. 'All three of them crashed. One each. Then Milestone here saw you turn on those others and get one down in flames.'

'Then I got three.'

'What?'

'I got a Hannoveraner, too.'

'By gad.'

'Give us the map reference and we'll get on to the batteries and see if we can get any witnesses,' the major said.

'I'd say there'd be quite a few witnesses, Major,' I said, giving a dreadful simper. 'I shot him down in front of about a thousand Canadians.' Which was a shocking exaggeration, as only one company's sentries could possibly have seen the Hannoveraner hit the crumps.

Beckett came pushing through. 'What's going on?' he asked.

'Bandy here just got three Huns,' Scadding said. 'All confirmed, or sure to be.'

'Yeah?'

'It was nothing,' I said modestly.

Sex and Death

THE EVENING WE went down for dinner at the local village was the first time I had been away from the squadron in about a month and a half, not counting my strolls in the neighbourhood. Since my narrow escape from being raped I had kept completely clear of Louise and the farm.

There were four of us: Wordsworth, Scadding, Darwin, and myself. We walked the two miles, talking shop and other dirt. I had a reason to celebrate, as I had just scored another triple victory over two two-seaters and an Albatros that tried to intervene, an achievement that automatically made me one of the squadron's elite. I was also considered ripe for the loony bin, for to attack even one two-seater was considered the height of stupidity; but nobody had told me this beforehand.

The village was a drab huddle of cottages without even a church. However, one of the more enterprising inhabitants had converted the ground floor of her house into a cafe which served quite good meals for only two or three francs. We had a bottle of wine each – I'd given up drinking but saw no harm in *vin rouge*, it didn't really count as intoxicating liquor – and everyone became quite jolly.

The proprietress, a Madame Malfait, was plainly fascinated by Wordsworth's baldness but even more by Scadding's unique leer. She spoke no English. She told us her husband had been killed in 1914, following this information with several heavy sighs.

'I wonder if that's an invitation for one of us to take his place,' Scadding said in English.

We looked at her. She wasn't unattractive. Her hips were perhaps a shade motherly.

'How about it, Wordy?' Scadding said. 'She's interested in you. If you like, we'll keep your wine hot if you want to pop upstairs.'

'I leave that kind of thing to you unmarried chaps,' Wordsworth answered. He had recently acquired a pipe. He blew down it, creating a spine-chilling gurgle.

'Didn't know you were married, old boy.'

'On my last leave, to the ugliest girl in the world,' Wordsworth said, gargling complacently.

Madame Malfait nodded and beamed at her aviators as if she understood every word.

'How about it, Madame?' Scadding smiled up at her, his eyes bright with lust. 'By gad, I wouldn't mind having two handfuls of those jolly old buttocks.' He continued to smile charmingly. Madame smiled back and looked at me inquiringly.

'The monsieur said he wouldn't mind having two pounds of butter if you had any to spare,' I translated.

She smiled, shrugged, and went into a voluble explanation to the effect that butter was hard to come by.

'What did you tell her?' Scadding asked.

'I told her that you wanted to sleep with her. She replied that, alas, she suffers from insomnia.'

'Tell her that what I have in mind is the best soporific in the world.'

'The monsieur said he has enjoyed your meal so much that as a mark of gratitude he would like to help you wash the dishes.'

She replied, shocked, that an officer couldn't do a thing like that.

'She said she always does that kind of thing in the kitchen and that she couldn't expect an officer to make love among the pots and pans. It wouldn't be delicate.'

'Tell her I'm ready to make love in the sink, breadbox, kitchen table, anywhere,' Scadding said.

'The monsieur insists. In civilian life he was a professional dishwasher and he wants to keep his hand in.'

No, no, she couldn't permit it. An officer of the gallant English Army washing dishes? Certainly not. Madame was getting flustered. She looked at Scadding with indignation mixed with a little concern.

'She said her favourite place was in the sink, for her husband always made love to her at the sink after drying the dishes.'

'Tell her it sounds awkward but I'm game.'

'He says, Madame, that it's part of English military training to wash dishes. It's the first thing they learn in the army before they go on to advanced training in peeling potatoes, ironing, sewing, knitting, and gunnery.'

Madame replied that she had long since ceased to be surprised at anything the English did and that if the monsieur really insisted ...

'She said,' I told Scadding, 'all right, provided you wait for her signal.'

'What signal?' Scadding asked.

'I'll find out.' I turned back to Madame Malfait. 'The monsieur does insist. You can see plainly how the thought of dishwashing excites him. But one should warn you that washing dishes gives him another kind of excitement, how would one say, the excitement sexual, and the more dishes he washes, the greater is the erotic effect.'

She blushed crimson and her eyes sparkled with offended dignity. She said it was disgraceful. I interrupted.

'If you want your honour to remain intact,' I told her, 'do not on any account smooth your dress in a seductive fashion, for this is the signal that will turn him into an animal with uncontrollable and raging desires.'

'I shall be very careful,' she said agitatedly, then went on to wonder what the British Army was coming to. Still, if the English officer was adamant, well, it was her duty to maintain the *entente cordiale*; but assuredly she would exercise great caution.

'The signal,' I told Scadding, 'will come when she smoothes down her dress in a seductive fashion.'

He jumped up. Madame bowed to him stiffly, turned, and went out. Scadding followed with an armful of dishes. Darwin and Wordsworth, both of whom spoke some French, looked at me. Darwin half rose to call Scadding back, then slowly sank back into his seat. We had to wait a long time for Scadding. Finally he sauntered in from the kitchen smoothing *his* dress.

He looked only moderately relaxed.

'What happened?' Darwin asked at last.

'What do you think? It was excellent, too. Only, she certainly made me work for it, the devil.'

'How?'

'Well, I thought she'd never get through washing up. Took simply ages. I don't mind telling you I started to get a bit impatient when she began taking down *clean* dishes from the cupboard and washing them, too.'

As Madame didn't come back, we placed a few francs on the table and left thoughtfully. All the way back I kept saying, 'Sex, sex, sex. What on earth,' I mused aloud, 'is France coming to?' which made everyone look at me rather queerly.

My hours of work stripping, cleaning, and sighting the guns and constant target practice began to pay off in earnest with a modest one here and a half there. It was obvious that I was becoming more than competent in air fighting – clearheaded, alert, daring, dashing, and deadly. It was only when I had my feet planted firmly on the ground that I tended to fall to pieces.

There was the day the Menin Road battles began, for example.

The battlefield presented a fantastic sight, with swarms of troops wandering toward the enemy position as casually as if they were picking poppies. The moans, shrieks, yells, hissing, and sighs of shrapnel shells, trench mortars, 75s, 5.9s, the whizz of 77s, and the great bash of howitzers sounded a gibbering chorus even above the roar of the Clerget motors. We were flying unpleasantly low, working over dose boxes and isolated crumps full of Heinies; and I actually saw one of our shells. It tumbled slowly through the air above my head, end over end, and I watched it fall behind the enemy lines. We were being tumbled about ourselves with the turbulence caused by the passage of shells, and I was still gaping at this visible missile when another must have passed only inches below my tail. The resulting buffet made me bite my tongue painfully as well as nearly sending me into the ground. This trench strafing was brutal work.

That day A and B flights were operating together, and we were so wrapped up in our work we didn't see the Albatroses until someone waggled his wings frantically and started to climb. The next moment the same pilot was dead in the wreckage of his plane, and the air was filled with Albatroses. Tracer whizzed and crossed, it seemed, over every cubic foot of air around us. It was a perfect surprise attack. I saw one Camel try to gain height. He was attacked by at least five Huns at the top of his zoom and fell to bits. He carried two streamers. Flight Commander. I didn't see who it was. I was busy.

I couldn't get out of Hunland. I zigzagged crazily all over the landscape. I had an Albatros hardly sixty feet behind, firing continuously. This Hun was no great marksman, but even he was bound to get me sooner or later. I was down to 10 feet. I didn't dare climb. I wasn't nervous. I felt I was going to be dead in a few seconds, but fortunately this had the effect of stimulating me to rapid, clear thought. I knew I couldn't dodge my opponent laterally. There was no room to dive. So without working it out consciously I tried it vertically. I soared up and the sky rushed under the nose. I kept the stick right back in my stomach. The earth swept into view from above, blurred, the centrifugal force cramming me hard into the seat. A tiny handful of seconds passed. It worked. The Albatros was unable to follow, didn't dare follow. I came right out on its tail and had a perfect no-deflection shot.

The Vickers rattled briefly; the Albatros smashed into the ground upside down.

I had stumbled on a brand-new – if somewhat risky – method of dealing with Huns at ground level. With his heavier Mercedes engine he hadn't dared to follow the lightweight Camel in a loop, which is what I had done, a loop from only about 10 feet up, for he would certainly have gone in head first.

His dilemma was that if he *didn't* follow he was a dead pigeon anyway, the distance lost in the tight loop bringing me directly behind him, a perfect target that even Rolly could hardly miss.

I was so impressed I forgot the other Huns until another of them tied himself to my tail by two smoky lines of tracer.

Well, it had worked the first time, why not again? I let him get me in his sights. My back tingled unpleasantly, as if it had a target painted on it. I hauled back on the stick. The Camel soared, whipped on its back, rushed to earth, flattened. He was in front of me. It took less than four seconds. I was firing the guns as I straightened. He was surprised. He could do nothing but gape over his shoulder. A long burst. He cart-wheeled over the ground. One of his wheels bounced and rolled over the battlefield and vanished into the yellow smoke.

Still keeping just above crump-hole level I skidded back over the lines and kept right on going until I had regained some composure. Fright hadn't set in yet. I looked at my watch: I was astonished that only twenty minutes had elapsed since take-off. I couldn't go home yet. I spiralled up to 5,000, then crossed over again, looking for other members of B Flight or A Flight. Not a sign. I tried to make out who had been shot down, but could find no wreckage in the raging battlefield below. Someone with a flamethrower was working over a dose box, its flame a hideous dull crimson among the smoke of high explosive and perhaps mustard gas.

There was a lot of cloud about. It was sure to be full of Huns. I sneaked into it. When I came out to look around I almost ran into another Camel, which dodged frantically until it saw I was friendly. We waved at each other. It was marked W: Millington. His fuselage was riddled, but he seemed to be flying all right. I was about to slip in behind his wing when he slipped in behind mine. I had been elected leader, it seemed. I turned cautiously eastward, keeping just above the clouds, scanning the sky. There were some Huns several thousand feet above. They saw us and started to work toward us, trying to cut us off; so I turned back and dived through the clouds. We spotted two more Camels and raced over to them. Brashman and Milestone. Together we flew up and down, pursued spitefully by Archie until, although we'd been out less than ninety minutes, we followed Brashman's streamer home. And very glad to do so.

We gathered on the ground and discussed the fight unhappily, trying to work out who had been lost. As Brashman had been leading A Flight, it must have been Beckett who'd gone in. If so, it was a heavy blow to the squadron, especially as only three Huns had been picked off.

The major listened to our reports. As I had witnessed Beckett's end, I had to describe it. 'He tried to gain height. In the circumstances I guess it was the worst thing he could have done,' I concluded.

'Did anyone see Bandy's two go down?' the major asked.

'Yes, I did,' Brashman said. 'Incidentally, how the hell did you do it?'

I described the manoeuvre. 'It was as much a surprise to me as it must have been to the poor Hun,' I said.

'Hardly,' Brashman murmured.

The mess was gloomy that night. Besides Beckett, two others had been shot down, Lieutenants Webster and Christey, and Rolls-Revell had crash-landed. They were all from A Flight which reduced its effective strength to just two, Brashman and Sanford. It was the worst blow the squadron had suffered in more than eight months of active service.

Beckett's loss was felt keenly, not so much because he had been popular – his large score had brought him respect rather than affection – but as an example and inspiration to the newer pilots. The unspoken question was, if someone with the skill and experience of Beckett, with his rear so well protected by veteran fighters, could get shot down so easily, what chance had anyone of surviving?

Rolly had been seen to crash on our side of the lines, but it was some hours before we got definite news of him. He had been knocked unconscious and was being treated at an advanced dressing station. He turned up late the next morning, still rather dazed from a crack on the head. The wing doctor washed him out for two or three days.

So a new flight commander was posted to us, a Captain Swiss. Wordsworth was transferred to the command of B Flight. When Captain Swiss was killed shortly afterward, I succeeded him.

Chock-full of Aplomb

I WAS WALKING back after breakfast one day with Rolls-Revell when the major stopped us.

'You're off for the day, aren't you, Bandy? You too, Rolly? I'm going to Boulogne. Would you like to come? Well, hurry up,' he said, gesturing fussily, 'the car's waiting.'

It took most of the morning to make the sixty-odd miles to the Channel. Rolls-Revell, imperiously surveying the usual military chaos through his monocle from the back seat, looked so lordly and contemptuous that several officers mistook him for a staff officer and had flung themselves into a ditch to avoid having to salute before realizing their mistake.

After a leisurely lunch in the town during which Ashworth became expansive and showed us pictures of his wife and nineteen children (he happened to have his photograph album with him), he confided that I had been recommended for the Military Cross for my exploit in shooting down the two two-seaters single-handed.

After the meal he went to visit some staff friends, and, pleasantly primed with wine and champagne, Rolly and I strolled about Boulogne. Compared with the local village it seemed a bustling metropolis. Passing a dusty-looking millinery shop, I suddenly remembered that I owed Louise a dress.

I'd never bought any women's clothes before and I felt a bit nervous about it. I stared into the shop window for quite some time before plucking up courage to enter. The window contained just one dress, a long spotted frock with frills at the bottom, or rather at the ankle.

The interior was dark and smelled of dust and old corsets. A woman with a fantastically long body came up. It was the longest trunk I'd ever seen in my life. She seemed to have a habit of rubbing her left thumb and forefinger together as if testing material or hinting that she was open to bribery; in fact, I started to reach for my wallet out of pure reflex. Rolly was looking around and caught the eye of a girl of about nineteen behind the counter, who had been looking bored until he came in. She was now looking vaguely taken aback at the sight of a painfully contrasted pair of aviators, one tall and looking like a bland horse, the other short and looking like an effete fox.

I cleared my throat. 'I wish a dress, Madame,' I said baldly.

The proprietress looked disapproving. However, business was business. 'Certainly, sir,' she said discreetly. 'And what size does the monsieur take?'

It was obviously going to be one of those days. I drew myself up. 'It is for a young woman,' I said coldly.

'Ah. Of course. And what size is the young woman, sir?'

'Eh?'

'What size is the bosom of the young woman,' the proprietress said patiently.

'Er . . . oh,' I said, and raised my hands and started to illustrate, then quickly put them behind my back again. 'Large,' I said. 'Quite large.' *(Tout a fait grand.)*

'That must be Louise,' Rolls-Revell said.

I looked at him sharply, but before I could say anything Madame had started to prompt me by quoting various measurements in what seemed to me excessive numbers of centimetres.

'Oh, no,' I said, sweating a little, 'not as large as all that.'

Madame indicated the girl behind the counter. 'Is it as large, perhaps, as that of my assistant?'

The assistant drew herself up and took a deep breath. I went over and studied her. So did Rolly. His monocle fell out.

'Yes,' I said. 'That's ... that's about it. Perhaps –' I cleared my throat. 'Perhaps, incredible though it may seem, even somewhat larger.'

The assistant looked depressed and expelled her breath, which blew a pair of lacy nether garments off a wire rack.

'Larger?' Rolly said, studying the assistant. 'Oh, I don't know ...'

The assistant smiled gratefully at him and started to take another deep breath.

I was beginning to get flustered by what appeared to me to be an unseemly curiosity on the part of the Madame.

'A commodious robe, that is all I wish,' I said with dignity, and started mopping my brow, until I realized I was doing so with the pair of lacy nether garments I had retrieved, and hastily put them down and looked quickly at the ceiling, where my eyes fell on several pairs of houseflies copulating in a veritable entomological orgy.

The proprietress just couldn't let the subject drop. 'But it is necessary,' she was saying, rubbing her thumb and forefinger together in a manner that now seemed slightly obscene, 'that I know the size of the young woman, sir.'

'Quick,' Rolly said at the window. 'There's a woman going past who's about the right size.' The rest of us rushed to the window and peered through the curtains. 'Hurry,' Rolly was saying, 'half of her is already out of sight.'

We strained over each other to peer down the street. An elderly shopper who had stopped to look in the window recoiled and hurried on. Too late to examine the one Rolly had meant, we all looked this way and that for a facsimile of Louise.

'How about that one?'

'No,' I said.

'That one, Monsieur?'

'Too – too pendulous,' I said uneasily, following the woman down the street with my eyes.

'There,' the assistant shouted in my ear. 'How's that one?'

'Too close together,' Rolly said, warming to the problem.

'There.' There's a fine bosom –'

'No.' Rolly shook his head.

'Ah. Here is a fine prominent citizen.'

'Too wide apart,' Rolly said.

'Look here,' I said, turning to Rolly, 'I'm supposed to be buying this dress, not you. Whose bosom is this, anyway?'

'Regard, sir, ' Madame said eagerly. 'There is an example magnificent.'

'Yes,' I said, and followed the girl down the street interestedly. When I got back to the shop, I said, 'No. But it was close.'

However, I thought it was about time to put a stop to all this. 'Perhaps,' I said pointedly, 'it would be easier if you showed me a robe or two.'

This struck the proprietress as an inspiration, and she came back with an armful of dresses. 'Come here, Cecile,' she said. The assistant came forward, smiling at Rolly, and had a dress fitted to her.

'Too fussy,' I said.

Cecile modelled another. 'Too plain,' I said.

This went on for some time. I finally purchased the polka-dotted dress in the window with the frills at the bottom, or to be exact, at the ankle; then we all went out for a cup of coffee to celebrate, and the next thing I knew Rolly had disappeared with the assistant, leaving me holding the bag, or to be exact, the proprietress, who had, as I say, the longest trunk I'd ever seen.

I soon made some feeble excuse and went shopping by myself and bought some notepaper, a silk scarf, and a parcel of rotten pears. Of course I didn't know the pears were rotten until I opened the parcel, when it was too late to return them. Rolly, when he turned up later at the agreed rendezvous, had also bought notepaper as well as a stick of sealing wax and a family heirloom the assistant had given him, a pornographic book called *The Dialogues of Luisa Sigea.* He read one page, the blood drained from his face, and his monocle steamed over.

On the way back I had a look at it too, and discovered there was a lot more to sex than I had thought. In fact the book made it seem like a branch of mechanical engineering. I had to take cold showers for several days.

Tripehounds

By September 29th I had brought my score up to sixteen and a quarter. That was the day we saw the new triplanes for the first time. We had been warned weeks before that the Germans were putting a new Fokker into service. The squadron on the other side of the field, who flew S.E. 5s, and who therefore penetrated much further into Hunland than we did, had reported their presence several times but had not made contact, and so were unable to assess their performance. It was believed that they were exceptionally good. This was not surprising, as Fokkers had been highly respected craft since 1915 (it was a Fokker that first appeared with the modern synchronized machine gun). So we were anxious to take the measure of this latest design, to find out how it compared with our own aircraft. If the triplane was greatly superior, we were in for it, as we ourselves had no new designs forthcoming. With its three wings, its climbing powers were likely to be exceptional, and ability to gain height over your opponent often made all the difference.

We were able to assess it the next day.

There was a squadron show before dinner led by Robert Wordsworth, and as we crossed the lines north of Warneton we were savaged by the fiercest barrage I'd yet experienced. Hundreds and hundreds of shells burst and drifted over the sky until our twelve machines were bobbing about like water bugs. Gilden, a new pilot who had inherited the unenviable rear position in B

Flight, was skidding about all over the sky some distance back and drawing a few score rounds entirely to himself. I knew how he was feeling, and waved to him when he finally caught up.

Just as I saw the Fokkers, Wordsworth waggled his wings and turned toward them, climbing. Four, eight... fifteen... twenty of them – and a handful of Albatroses! Twenty Tripes: they had arrived with a vengeance. My heart thumped faster. They were several thousand feet above us in the clear air, but climbed even higher as we mushed upward.

Then a squadron of Bristol fighters appeared even higher up and the Triplanes buzzed off east. However, the Bristol merchants continued on far to the rear, and the Tripes came back cautiously and hung overhead.

At 17,000 they were still above us. This was a slushy height for Camels, and the squadron was beginning to get badly scattered. It was maddening the way the Hun maintained superior altitude.

Wordsworth circled slowly and the Fokkers circled with us and began to drop lower. Soon only 500 feet separated us. They were a colourful bunch. The leading machine was pure white from propeller to elevator except for the black crosses. I slewed outward from the flight and pressed the trigger. The guns fired only single shots. I worked the loading handles, and after a while the Vickers burst properly into song. The sound gave me confidence.

Still the Fokkers drifted about upstairs without attacking. It went on like that for several minutes, with the Fokkers now planted firmly between us and home. Maybe they wouldn't attack after all. The average Hun usually kept away from the larger British formations.

Then three of them dived. Three others followed. They were down on us in seconds. I shoved over the stick. The plane banked erratically in the thin air and almost fell sideways. There was a distant rattle. The vivid Tripes zoomed up again. God, they could climb! It was marvellous to see them.

One of them was in a spin. No, it was a Camel. They'd got a Camel. That was quick.

As if this were a signal, about three quarters of them came down. In a few seconds the sky was a madhouse of three dozen twisting machines and the air became laced with curving tracer. It was exhilarating. I splitarsed about crazily, unable to sight on a plane for more than a second before another was snapping at me from behind. A gorgeous bird with black and yellow diamonds splashed over its red hide reared up only yards in front. Jesus, I'd not time to – there was a jarring crash. I started to tumble. I caught a glimpse of the Tripe. He'd lost his entire top plane, was falling into small pieces even before he began to go down. Tracer cut around me, zipped between the wires. I kicked the rudder and sank so fast it felt as if my guts were on the end of a kite. A Tripe levelled out in front. Instinctively I fired. Too far left. I was too excited. But he banked right into my tracer. I held him, this time not caring who was behind, and held him in the Aldis with rudder easy. The tracer was going in all round the pilot. He flopped into a spin. Oh, no, my boy, not again. I dived after him on full throttle, but the Tripe fell faster. A red and green job. He fell faster and faster, getting away. No, his wings started to fold like hands praying. Next moment there were three of him, fluttering down. I hauled back on the throttle and started to ease out and turn, looking back to make sure I wasn't being followed.

Then my engine spluttered and died. Christ. Miles over, too. I'd had it this time.

No, it was only the pressure gauge. It had blown on the dive. I was ashamed for having sworn. But perhaps it had helped? I switched over to the gravity tank. The engine stayed dead, then caught its breath and spluttered. The prop windmilled. Then flashed round evenly. The engine roared and I hurried toward the lines, diving gently now on two-thirds throttle, about 1,000 r.p.m., watching my tail very carefully.

The plane felt different. It seemed very light and frisky, as if it enjoyed fighting. Marvellous what the Camel could stand up to. Those new Tripes seemed to fall to pieces very easily.

Suddenly I remembered the one with the diamond pattern. I'd hit it I'd actually survived a mid-air collision. I'd never heard of that before.

Or had I collided? Had I dreamed it? I seemed to recall a crash. Yes, there *had* been a crash. It had pushed me into a dive. What had I done then? Yes, I'd pulled out on to the tail of another Tripe. It was extraordinary. I ought to be dead. It must have been a hell of a crash to tear the Hun to pieces. I wondered if I could claim him as a victory. I would certainly put in for it. Serve him right, getting in the way like that.

Archie burst dead ahead. I flew through the smoke, then waltzed around. I noticed a bullet hole in the side of the cockpit an inch from my arm. The bullet seemed to have been fired from the side, and I looked on the other side of the cockpit opposite, but there was no exit hole. I shrugged. Another of those peculiar things. The bullet ought logically to be rattling around somewhere inside me. I forgot about it.

As there was not enough fuel to get home anyway, I opened up to get away from Archie, who was becoming annoying.

The lines at last wavered into view and passed under the tail, and the infuriating bombardment ceased. I dived down and flew low and fast, lifting gently over the faint rises of the ground, the contours laughably called hills in this desecrated countryside of Belgium or France or wherever it was. Marching men swept underneath. They looked up, open-mouthed, and the front ranks stopped, and the ones behind bumped into them, until the column looked like a disorganized caterpillar.

Concentrating on the low flying cheered me up. Chasing only a few feet over the land, lifting up and down over telegraph poles, swishing past trees, dancing over batteries, the dull green grass blurring, ruined houses hurtling past – it was the only time you really appreciated the marvellous speed of the Sopwith Camel. Nearly two miles a minute of drab carpet unrolling under you, the slightest nudge of rudder or twitch of joystick carrying you round the gentle curve of a railway track or over the faintest contour of a ridge. This was the most enjoyable part of flying; you really felt you were going somewhere.

I hauled back on the stick until the plane was going almost vertically, then shoved it forward and dived happily on a line of transport creeping painfully over an apology of a road, guns, limbers, wagons, lorries crawling and jerking, jammed, grinding. Drivers and officers with plainly creased brows looked up as I blazed down the road, my wings wavering in the bumpy air. A group of Tommies gesticulated wildly. As I roared away, the shadow of my bus crossed a field, leaped a fence, skidded sideways as the ground dropped away and then disappeared.

The shadow had looked oddly unfamiliar.

I started to go down again to study the shadow, then shrugged. It had probably been the effect of the sun, which was slanting its beams almost horizontally. Anyway, evening shadows were always grossly distorted.

I was an idiot to have gone contour-chasing. I ought to have been at altitude, searching for an airdrome. I couldn't possibly have more than five minutes' fuel left

I climbed economically. This part of the front was crowded with airfields. I couldn't see a single one.

I sensed rather than saw a plane behind, and kicked hurriedly at the rudder, heart pounding in sudden funk. It was a couple of Camels. The pilots were both waving.

I waved back, but they kept on waving, which was very comradely of them, but after a minute or two it became a little tiresome. Or were they pointing?'

One of the Camels began to edge closer, and the pilot pushed up his goggles. It was Brashman. He went on pointing, jerkily, pointing down then at – what? My wheels? Undercart. It must be my undercart

I dipped down to look at that shadow again, an unpleasant suspicion forming.

Even with the shadow smeared over a hundred feet of field there was no mistaking its information. I had no wheels. In fact I didn't even have wheel struts.

Now what the hell was I going to do?

The two Camels came down with me. I turned back to the field that had contained my shadow. It would be a tricky but not especially dangerous landing if I was careful. And it could have been worse; by rights half the bottom of the fuselage should also have been torn off in that collision. It could have been a lot worse.

I circled, studying the field, and the other two came round with me. I couldn't risk travelling any further. The field looked all right. I climbed gently to 600 feet, aimed the aircraft with care, then throttled back. Nose down for the glide. The breeze hissed through the wires and sounded reassuring. The field had a slope. All the better.

The engine spluttered and I shut off quickly. There wasn't too much wind but at least I was into it. The slope seemed pleasantly flat. Too fast. Back an inch on the stick. The grass came up fast and spread out on all sides. Damn it, too fast, too fast. I was running out of slope. What lay on the other side? Maybe a hedge, or a bivouac, or a field kitchen.

The Camel, still not reaching stalling speed, soared gracefully over the top of the rise. Then I found out what was on the other side: a senior officer on horseback, slowly trotting across the field. I could see his red tabs clearly.

Just beyond the field was a chateau, probably his headquarters. I saw his mouth open. He had moved right to the spot where the Camel was bound to land on him. The bus was now shooting downhill, still not stalling. I waved frantically with my free hand. 'Get away, you idiot!' The fool was just sitting there high up on his horse, paralyzed. Then as the airplane hurtled downhill toward him he almost visibly pulled himself together; and he did just what I'd have probably done myself, something indescribably stupid: instead of spurring his horse onward in the direction he'd been riding, the idiot turned tail and went careering down the slope ahead, and naturally found himself being hotly pursued by the airplane. He was lashing his horse madly, standing in the stirrups, staring round, showing his great bulging eyes, thudding across the grass at reckless speed, but still along the axis of the plane.

It was impossible for me to turn aside. All I could do was streak after him helplessly, gazing at his behind, which was stuck in the air and growing larger and larger in the ring-sight. Any second now I was going to be embedding the propeller boss deep into his sphincter, and the Camel's propeller boss is rather a sharp thing, all edges and so on; it was going to make quite a mess.

I hauled the stick back into my stomach. The propeller shattered, there was a series of violent shocks, and grass and earth showered forward over the officer; he must have been certain his last moment had come, especially as I was thrown forward and must have pushed the levers inadvertently, because the machine guns exploded into life, sounding hellishly loud with no engine to muffle their momentary chattering. Tracer whistled and smoked low, just past the rider, who convulsively threw himself off sideways – and was promptly scooped up by the lower plane of my machine like a shovel picking up a heap of fluff, motes, and cat fur.

Then there was silence, with only a restful humming. A bird twittered stupidly and the thud of horse's hoofs faded into the distance.

When I opened my eyes, the officer – he was a colonel – was hopelessly entangled in the bracing wires and thrashing feebly and cursing in the most shocking fashion I'd ever heard. It was simply disgraceful. Although I guess it was a good sign really.

'Surely there's no excuse for language like that, sir,' I observed reprovingly.

Whereupon the officer started violently, lay stock still for a moment, then slowly, with what seemed an enormous effort and stiffening of the sinews, summoning up the blood and so on, started to turn his head to look at me as I climbed out. Even before his large face was right round I recognized him. It was my old battalion commander.

Just before completing the turning of his head, he closed his eyes and took a deep breath. Then he opened his eyes, closed them again, and a faint moan escaped his cracked lips.

After a while he opened them again. He tried to kick free of the bracing wires, but without much conviction.

I cleared my throat nervously. He gave a little shudder. Then we just looked at each other. I smiled weakly.

'You've ...' I stopped, then started again. 'I see you've shaved off your little moustache, sir,' I said. It was true. He had shaved off his little moustache.

He began to breathe faster, and peculiar sounds emerged from his lips, which were dry and cracked, as I think I've already mentioned. Finally, however, he seemed to get a fresh lease on life, and the whimpering sounds gradually died down.

'You,' he said at last. 'Of course. How, how could I have doubted it for a single moment? As soon as I saw that flying machine careering down the slope after me, out of control, I said to myself, That's Bandy, I said; it's bound to be. He's after me again. Wasn't – wasn't that a coincidence? Yours was the very first name that flashed through my mind, or what was left of it. And by God,' the colonel said, his lower lip trembling, 'not content with running me down in his airplane he – no, not content with that, he has to open fire, too, just in case there's anything left of. me; and then...' The colonel again began to thrash about in the wires, but not with any real hope of ever getting free. He started to moan again.

'Steady, sir,' I murmured.

For a puzzled moment I thought I'd already said this; then remembered that it was at least eight months since I'd spoken those same words to him in the hospital.

Under the circumstances it was difficult to know what to say to the poor fellow. I cast about for some topic that would take his mind off his troubles.

'It's remarkable,' I said, gesturing at what was left of the aircraft. 'It's quite a crash, yet I'm not in the least hurt. Not a scratch,' I added, laughing lightly.

But this didn't seem to help much, because he lay back, trying to stifle an unmilitary display of emotion; or rather tried to lie back, but the bracing wires prevented him. I reached forward to unwind a piano wire from around his neck because his face was turning a little purple. 'Here, let me help you, sir,' I said; but the poor fellow became violent. Shock, no doubt.

'No, no,' he shouted. 'Don't – don't touch me. Just – just leave the wire round my throat where it belongs. I... you ...' But he couldn't go on. Fortunately a major or two came running across the field just then and managed to get him untangled, and he was helped slowly off the field. He'd recovered more or less by then, but he didn't say goodbye. Perhaps he felt we were bound to meet again sometime. I expect that was the reason he went off so rudely without even saying *au revoir*, so I wasn't too offended.

Me, Still Virgo Intacta

THREE DAYS LATER the weather was too bad for flying, and by six it was obvious there was going to be a first-class binge in the mess. M.C.s had arrived for Darwin, deputy leader of C Flight, and myself.

After dinner and the toast to the King, Wordsworth, who presided, got up to congratulate the winners, his skull gleaming, his eyes bloodshot, twirling a glass of champagne slowly and thoughtfully between his fingers.

'Gentlemen,' he said in his calm, unhurried voice, 'we are here to do honour to two of our stoutest pilots, Lieutenant Charles Darwin, and Captain Bartholomew Bandy.' There were cheers. 'I had the privilege of joining this squadron at least two months after Darwin's arrival, so I have no personal knowledge of what he was up to before I came; however, I can certainly vouch for the fact that on at least one occasion during the last three months this bold, tenacious, and gallant officer has more than earned his decoration. I refer particularly to this fearless fighter's exploit in going into battle against the unsuspecting Albatri with his safety belt unfastened.'

This reference brought forth a good deal of merriment, and Darwin grinned sheepishly.

'Fortunately for the war effort, the Huns were not in a playful mood that day. Fortunately for them, that is, for it is doubtful if even the toughest opponent could have stood the sight of a large, red-faced flyer cursing and hurtling through the air, swearing as only a large, red-faced hurtling Cornishman can.

'This of course is not Darwin's only feat. He has two others to his credit, and I had the misfortune to be present in his hut that never-to-be-forgotten day in August when he removed his socks from those two feats for the first time since his Aunt Cecily knitted them on the occasion of the first battle of Ypres, for as is well known –' The rest was drowned in the uproar. There was an element of truth in this nonsense. Darwin was always complaining about how copiously his feet sweated; and so were his hut mates. 'Darwin is also, of course, the author of *The Origin of Species*, and the continued existence of the gentlemen who share his Nissen bear ample witness to his theory of the survival of the fittest.'

After some more conventional stuff, Wordsworth looked slowly round the mess and fixed his eyes on me.

'We now come to Bartholomew W. Bandy,' he said, and paused, and everyone laughed. I looked blankly round, wondering why they were laughing, and they laughed even harder.

Wordsworth seemed to be searching for words. 'The point is,' he said, 'is he or is he not genuine? Sometimes, when I'm feeling a little the worse for wear, such as at this moment, I get the peculiar sensation that he is nothing but a figment of my overheated imagination. When I first saw him – I won't say met him, one doesn't meet Bandy, one experiences him – the first time he spoke I had to call for the medical officer, I was so overcome by the sheer horror of it all. And then the fact that he spoke approximately in the accents of a Canadian but could neither swear nor play poker – well, here was a case of out-and-out fraud. Or worse, a case of hallucination. Or better still, a case of whisky.

'However, hallucination or not, his accomplishments are real enough, as witness his exploit of three days ago when, growing tired of the civilized restraint of Vickers guns, he took to ramming as a new tactic of war, and instead of being killed as would be only natural and, indeed, proper, he not only comes back minus his undercart; he doesn't even know he's lost it. I won't go into subsequent events as being far too unseemly for an assembly such as this.

'The nature of this strange creature *Bandinius canadensis* is difficult to define. Is it fish, flesh, fowl, or merely farfetched? Take for example last Sunday, when his Vickers jammed. *Bandinius canadensis* was seen to draw a hammer from the depths of its cockpit, stand up and commence to beat its guns in an indescribable fit of fury –' There was quite a din at this, and I looked down, sheepishly pushing the remains of my Brussels sprouts around the plate. It wasn't at all the way he was making it sound. True, I carried a hammer because I'd found that hitting the guns in a certain spot was an efficacious method of clearing stoppages, and it was also true that on the occasion he was referring to I *had* lost my temper when the guns still wouldn't fire, but as for standing up in the cockpit that was absurd.

'The sight,' Wordsworth was saying, 'of Bandy standing up at ten thousand feet over enemy lines, furiously belabouring his Vickers, was a never-to-be-forgotten –' the rest was drowned in the uproar. When it had abated somewhat: 'Where was I? Oh, yes, in spite of moments like these,' Wordsworth went on in a serious voice, 'generally speaking – and it's the only way one can speak of Bandy – he's otherwise unspeakable – this aviator has proved himself to be a not undedicated air fighter whose deadly aim has in a remarkably short time brought him to the forefront, even among his skilled compatriots. When he has his head in the clouds he is, in fact, not ineffective. But on the ground... Well, it seems to me that when he gets down to earth he becomes truly of the earth, earthy; all hell, it seems to me, breaks loose when Bandy reaches *terra firma*, or is it *terra incognita*? Anyway, the wing colonel himself, who I understand has just had a complaint from some battalion commander or other, was asking if there was any way in which the squadron could keep Bandy aloft all the time, providing nourishment by lowering loaves and fishes, sausages and hard-boiled eggs at the end of a string into his cockpit, and...'

There was a lot more of this slanderous talk. Afterward I tried to restore some sanity to the proceedings by replying in a cool and dignified fashion as befitted the occasion, but I hardly got a word out, partly because I was shamefully inebriated, but mostly because the moment I started to whine a reply the mess broke down completely. It was often a great nuisance having a face and voice like mine.

Wordsworth left almost nothing out of his speech, not even the polka-dot dress. Rolly had told everyone about it. I still had the thing in my hut, not yet having screwed up the courage to take it along to Louise. I tried to get that snitch Rolly to deliver it, but he had told me it was my duty to do so myself. Then I tried Milestone, but he said much the same thing, though in somewhat more vulgar terms. By now everyone in the squadron was getting interested in that damned dotted dress. I thought of dropping it into the farmyard from the air, and did actually carry it down to the hangar. But then my offensive spirit reasserted itself. I was damned, I thought to myself, if I was going to let a chit of a girl overawe me in this fashion. Of course, she was no chit of a girl but a great spanking animal of a woman; but still. So I spent days summoning up courage; then, having made up my mind, started to parcel it as a present for Katherine, until someone said it was hopeless trying to get parcels out of the war zone. Besides, Katherine would think it strange, receiving a dress half a foot too long and with a forty-inch bust (101.6 centimetres) when even I must have been aware that her own could hardly have measured much more than 86.6 centimetres (34 inches). So I was stuck with it, and either had to deliver it, give it to some undeserving peasant, or wear it myself. Finally I set off for the farm with the blasted thing under my arm. Half the squadron turned out to see me off and cheered lustily, or was it lustfully as I strode unconcernedly into the sunset, tossing my head in a defiant manner. Actually I was tossing my head to get rid of the beads of perspiration dotting my brow.

And yet I felt full of a curious anticipation.

But after all that, all Louise said was, 'Thank you a thousand times, sir,' although her eyes undeniably shone with pleasure as she caressed the polka-dotted dress with the frills at the bottom, or rather –

I had been so certain that I was to lose my virginity that afternoon...

Perhaps the reason she wasn't more demonstrative was that there was a great, hulking *Poilu* hanging possessively around her and glaring at me suspiciously; but all the same it was rather an anticlimax. But I accepted the situation philosophically, especially as the great hulking *Poilu* kept fingering this sharp-looking bayonet stuck in his belt and asking questions, such as how had his fiancée's robe come to need replacing? and things like that.

So I hurried back to the squadron, whistling happily, intensely relieved that it had all come out so well; except that on the way, for no reason at all, I kicked viciously at a large rock which had the temerity to get in my way.

When the medical orderly had finished bandaging my toe, I went up and shot off two hundred rounds without hitting a thing. It was no good being irritable in aerial warfare; it just spoiled one's aim. Though what I had to be annoyed about I don't know.

Anyway, by the time I came in to land I'd convinced myself that it *had* all been for the good. Suppose I'd delivered that spotted dress just before the great hulking *Poilu* came on the scene... And so once again I had remained true to the moral principles inculcated in me by my parents, and if I did have a few drinks that evening, it seemed to me to be the least I should be allowed after missing a marvellous opportunity like that – I mean after a narrow shave like that.

Me, from Bad to Worse

THE DAYS WERE drawing in now, and each morning the batman found it harder to get us out of bed to face the cold and damp of the hut. Bert Playall – it seems a little late to mention him, but he had replaced Robinson in the hut – had just been wounded on a trench-strafing jaunt and was in hospital, so once again there was an empty bed in the Nissen.

There was a combined celebration for Captain Parker and the major, and the new C.O. attended, a Major Fitzsimmons. He had pale, prominent eyes, and we didn't like the look of him much. He looked too smart and military.

The day Ashworth left, October 13, Fitzsimmons took a Camel up to show how good he was. Several of us watched, huddled against the wall of the squadron office as he gyrated, spun, Immelmanned, looped, and rolled.

'My goodness,' Brashman said dryly, 'isn't he simply wonderful?'

As the new C.O. started a pretty S-turn on to the field, I clutched Rolly by the sleeve.

'Say, Rolly, go and get your bus and do a few turns.'

R. R. looked at me coolly for a moment, nodded, and set off for A hangar. There was a chitter of anticipation from the others.

The C.O. parked near the office and strolled up, looking carefully nonchalant. Just then Rolls-Revell took off with a roar.

Fitzsimmons turned with raised eyebrows just in time to see Rolly go straight into a loop from the ground. We were all watching the major out of the corners of our eyes. He stood with his glossy boots apart and his lips compressed as tight as the turns R. R. was making in rapid succession. The turns grew tighter and tighter and the Camel lost height until the right wingtip was hardly a foot from the grass. Then he chandelled, then spun, then pulled out 50 feet above us, then flew round the field and did eight spectacular rolls, and barrelled and climbed vertically, and dived vertically from 250 feet, and did a wide, slow circuit of the field, upside down.

Fitzsimmons watched all these manoeuvres. As R. R. went into another tight turn at 0 feet, the C.O. turned sharply, glared at us, then pushed through and into the office. His face was a picture. He slammed the door. I wore a carefully sympathetic expression but somebody sniggered loudly.

Fitzsimmons wrenched the door open again.

'What are you all hanging round here for?' he barked. 'If you've nothing better to do, I'll soon find jobs for you. Clear off.'

We scattered. When Rolly came into the mess, his monocle firmly in place, he was offered numerous free drinks. But half an hour later Fitzsimmons made him orderly dog for the following day; then picked on me by dispatching A Flight after an observation balloon. Luckily, it had been hauled down by the time we got there, but I killed the pilot of a two-seater with about ten bullets from each gun and shared in the destruction of a second, so we came back feeling smug and pleased with ourselves.

I went up alone late in the afternoon, and after spending almost ninety minutes creeping up on him, shot down an L.V.G., again with only about twenty rounds. It was confirmed by artillery and made me the squadron's champion Hun-getter.

By the time leave came due, things were becoming a bit hazy, with dogfight merging into dogfight and binge into binge. As I went about my flight commander's duties, making up returns, sending in reports, chivvying mechanics, being smooth, bland, and maddening with riggers and Fitzsimmons, I kept remembering how I'd promised them at home to be a virtuous, clean-living lad. And look at me now. But by the end of a day's fighting and paperwork and being nonchalant, brave, and invincible, and setting a bad example to the new pilots, making sure they got sufficient flying and target practice, I really needed that pick-me-up at the end of the day. Except that the pick-me-ups invariably floored me.

The wildest binge I ever took part in was two days before my leave commenced. I was half sozzled even before dinner ended. I remember somebody showing me a copy of the *London Gazette*:

Awarded The Distinguished Service Order
Lieut. (Temp. Capt.) Bartholomew Wolfe Bandy, M.C.,
Canadian Infantry and Royal Flying Corps.
For conspicuous gallantry and devotion to duty.
    On 18th September 1917 during a lone patrol he attacked a hostile two-seater and drove it down.
    On 20th September whilst machine-gunning the enemy lines he was attacked by numerous enemy machines but, although at a grave disadvantage owing to lack of height, drove down two of his attackers.
    On 1st October he engaged several hostile scouts and shot down one and rammed another, tearing off its top plane. The latter machine was seen to crash.
    During the twelve days ending 1st October 1917, this officer destroyed a total of ten enemy aircraft.

Smirking modestly, I cut out the paragraph and stuffed it drunkenly in my bosom beside the sweat-stained citation in French for the War Cross, an award I'd gained for shooting down a Gotha bomber bound for Amiens. I was tight at the time; you had to be well primed to attack one of those huge planes. They even had machine guns firing downward, which struck me as being very unfair.

At one point during the evening I staggered queasily out of the mess and fell over the padre, who was tying his shoelace.

'I'm disappointed in you, Bartholomew. You started out so well, and now –' But he laughed good-naturedly, to show what a decent chap he really was.

I smiled hideously, too drunk even to feel ashamed. Immediately the padre vanished in a pinch of pixie dust and I grabbed hold of an apple tree to prevent it falling, leaning my forehead against the trunk. It was the longest trunk I'd ever seen except for the manageress of the dress shop, and it was damp. I turned my face to catch the raindrops on a swollen tongue, legs braced against the earth, which was swaying because of the barrage from the Front twenty miles away. The gun flashes silhouetted the spidery trees.

Someone came up, his feet swishing in the wet grass. He handed me a cigarette. We smoked in the rain, two red glows wavering.

'You know, Dick – it is Dick, isn't it?' I said.

'I think so.'

'Listen, Dick, are you going to tell me ...' I thought deeply for a moment, wondering what it was I thought Dick was going to tell me.

'No,' Milestone said with emphasis. 'I am not.'

I nodded agreement – what an understanding chap Milestone was! – and stared with concentration toward the Front, which flickered like a dying fire. There was a pregnant silence. 'Not what?' I asked.

It was his turn to think for a moment 'Not going to tell you anything.'

'Quite right,' I said. Then: 'I'm going to tell *you* something, Dick. You won't tell anyone else, will you?'

'On m'honour,' Dick said, drawing a limp finger in a ragged cross over his heart.

'am, am a virgin,' I said thickly.

'Oh dear, oh dear,' Milestone said.

'Isn't it disgusting? I'm – I'm twenty-four, maybe even twenty-five for all I know, an'... an'...' I hiccupped and sneezed, then dug the earth with my heel morosely.

'Well, well,' Milestone said dimly, attempting to raise his eyebrows in simulated or perhaps genuine surprise; but the effort was too much and his face collapsed again.

'Why?' I said. 'Why, why, you ask?' Milestone hadn't asked, but I was going to tell him anyway. 'Because it – Dick: it's a precious thing. Not to be squandered.'

'Church stuff,' he said, prodding me with his forefinger. The forefinger buckled. 'Family 'n' honour, and all that. But tell me this. Go on, tell me.'

'What?'

'Tell me this.'

'What?'

He was silent a moment, then nodded wisely. 'Exactly,' he said, then had to cling to my lapel, his freshly-complexioned face dripping with rain and sincerity. 'By supporting this war,' he said with marvellous clarity, 'they have destroyed their own essentially romantic morality. They can't have their ... their ... and eat it too, can they?'

'Yes,' I said. 'I mean, no.' We seemed to have strayed off the subject, whatever the subject was. I had something very important to say, but the thought was too drunk to stand upright. Something about home. 'Dick?'

'Yes, Bart, old thing?'

'When – when I was in England I was invited to a ... er ... several times. Two or three times anyway, a place called Burma Park.'

'Were there lots of wild deer roaming about?' he asked.

'No,' I said. 'There was a dear girl, though.' We giggled for fifteen minutes or so at this marvellous pun. 'Kathering,' I said. 'I loved it, Dick,' meaning Burma Park.

'Loved what?'

'Kattering.'

'You loved kattering?'

'Er ... yes.'

'I've never done any kattering myself,' Dick said. 'How do you do it?'

'Do what?'

'Kattering. How do you play it? Something like croquet, is it?'

I was darned if I could remember how it was played. 'I've forgotten,' I said.

'Forgotten what?'

Then I was darned if I could remember what I'd forgotten. But I was feeling very sad at the thought of never seeing Burma Park again; then brightened when I remembered that I was going there in a few days.

'Let's go inside,' Dick said. 'You seem to be getting all wet.'

We tottered back into the mess, arms around each other's shoulders. There was a hell of a row going on.

'Waiter!' we shouted together.

Trimbull, the president of the mess committee, strode over purposefully. 'You've had quite enough to drink,' he said sternly. He glared ferociously. 'Cease this drunken debauchery. Act like men. Go back to your huts, you disgusting, inebriated swine,' he said. 'Stop drinking all the booze; there'll be none left for the rest of us. Don't be so beastly shellfish.' Whereupon his eyes vanished into the roof of his head and he stiffened and fell on his back with a crash.

We stepped over him and shoved rudely toward the fireplace. Hyams Wraught, our new American, grabbed my arm. 'Why aren't you drinking?' he asked, shoving a glass in my hand. His eyeballs bulged from his handsome, sensitive face. 'Jesus Christ, Bandy,' he said, looking at me closely. 'You look cockeyed.' He laughed heartily, then fell against a wall and began to slide down it. We watched fascinated as inch by inch gravity overcame him and drew him on to his buckling knees. Nearly everyone had been buying him drinks, celebrating his remarkable achievement in bringing down a Hun on his second trip over the lines. He was gloriously happy.

Dick and I sat by the fire, which was hot and cozy and was guarded by a mess waiter in case anyone fell into it, and resumed our cozy chat. Except that now we had to scream above the din. George Ginty was dancing, Scadding was reciting a

237

dirty poem, furniture was being fractured, glass was breaking, the gramophone was making a high-pitched plaint unheard.

It got even worse. There was a shriek. Dick and I looked round, blinking and trying to focus on the merry scene. Someone was trying to cram Scadding into the piano, and Hyams Wraught, miraculously recovered, was pounding on the keys to see what kind of a tune he could get out of him, with Scadding laughing hysterically and trying to catch hold of the felt hammers as they drummed on his ribs. Ginty was waving a sword dangerously.

'Ginty,' Fitzsimmons thundered.

Ginty stopped, lowered the sword, and turned unsteadily toward the major, who had just come in.

'Put down that sword. At once, do you hear?'

Ginty blinked several times, trying to recognize the C.O. Then he whooped loudly. 'I'm King Arthur,' he announced, 'and I'm going to be after cutting off your balls, Fitzy old thing,' and he charged the major.

Fortunately, at least one person had the presence of mind to kick a chair in front of him, and Ginty went sprawling, cursing horribly in Gaelic. Fitzsimmons fled. The P.M.C. laughed so much his lower dental plate fell out, and I think it was Ginty again who seized a poker. 'A scorpion, a scorpion, bejaze,' he said, and promptly beat the false teeth to death.

The surprising thing was that when I woke up at seven I felt fine. We couldn't find Milestone anywhere, and had to organize a search party, and finally discovered him snoring in the depths of the orchard.

It was in the afternoon that I got killed.

Between the morning dogfight and the afternoon patrol I had taken up two new men to visit the lines. My flight should have left at four-thirty, but we had to wait for my aircraft to be refuelled, so I was in a hurry. I took off without running up, as the engine was still warm. Just as I cleared the trees at the north end of the field, there was a crash, the windscreen cracked, and oil and smoke blew back in my face.

I was to go west this time all right. The windscreen was opaque with cracks and oil, and the bus was shaking with palsy. It was so unexpected and sudden I hadn't even time to get wind up. I pushed the stick forward. The smoke cleared but there was a stink of petrol. I shut off. I had to lean over the side to see where I was going. The ground was rushing up. Shaken now, soaked in sweat and breathless, I pulled back too hard with shaking fingers. The sight was twisted, the guns cross-eyed, the engine cowling in shreds, and part of the top plane seemed to have gone. The canvas rattled like a machine gun. The controls still worked, though. No time to turn into wind.

The ground blurred up, the wheels struck the top of a hill. The Camel was careering drunkenly down the other side at ninety miles an hour. I wrestled to keep the bus level. The prop was still spinning, grinding, shaking the plane in a rage. A hedge rushed up, and in spite of the speed we couldn't get over it. There was a smash, an angry crackling. The entire lower plane seemed to have been stripped off. The remainder of us catapulted into a lane.

I guess I must have been shot through what was left of the top plane, because when I came to, a minute later, I was about thirty feet farther on, in some kind of a pond with grey slime over it, and a startled duck protesting.

The Camel, what was left of it, began to blaze. I felt the heat even from thirty feet. I crawled farther away and leaned up against a pig trough, very shaken and weak in the knees and awed at my luck. If the safety belt had held I'd have been cooked. Even the duck had fallen into a stunned silence.

I was staring at the smouldering trees, still wondering how it was that I was alive, when the Crossley tender, crammed with pilots and mechanics and riggers, raced up the lane, followed by the major's car, which contained Fitzsimmons, Wordsworth, Bango, and a new Canadian flight commander, Jeff Hoyden.

They all leaped out, ran up, stopped. Then they moved forward more slowly, stopped again, and stood in silence.

I hauled myself up and walked up behind them, shivering and stinking. Part of the hedge flamed briefly, hissing, and dirty white smoke puffed out. I was feeling myself over to see if I had any broken ribs when Wordsworth spoke.

'Well... least we'll have some peace now, from that awful piano playing of his.'

'Yes,' Bango said.

The wind blew smoke and embers over them and they moved farther away. Somebody coughed.

'Bloody rotary engines,' Milestone said.

The mechanics muttered faintly among themselves. One of them kicked at a charred *longeron*.

'Don't suppose we'll see another quite like him,' Wordy said. 'He was an infuriating bastard sometimes. Just looking at that blank face of his – when my nerves were bad it made me, you know, feel like climbing the wall, and... But... I don't know.'

I shivered, feeling sad.

'He certainly was quite a shot,' Brashman said. I think he said 'shot'.

There was silence. I coughed, but nobody heard, and I began to wonder if perhaps I might not be dead after all.

The major said gruffly, 'Thought he was a bit shell-shocked at first ... He was certainly the most disrespectful devil I'd ever come across, but ...'

I glared at the C.O.'s back. Disrespectful? I was the only respectful person in the entire squadron. I liked that.

'I didn't know him well personally, of course,' Hoyden said. 'Not like you fellows. But we knew all about him at my old squadron. Was it true about him running down a general in his airplane?'

'Oh, no,' someone said. 'It was only a colonel.'

'Oh,' Hoyden said faintly.

There was another pause.

'Didn't give a damn about anything,' someone else said. I looked around, offended, to see if I could identify this speaker.

'Poor devil,' Milestone said.

I looked down and sniffed.

Wordsworth sighed. 'Well,' he said.

'Jesus Christ,' Ginty said. I looked up. He was staring at me. 'He's come back to haunt us.' He crossed himself hurriedly.

They all turned. Milestone looked pale. He tottered over and touched me. 'He's cold and clammy right enough,' he said, and drew back.

'I got thrown in a duck pond,' I said. 'That one over there.'

Later the wing doctor came and pummelled me.

'Take a few days off,' he said. 'Nothing wrong a rest won't cure.'

'Now you tell me, when I'm going on leave anyway.'

I left at nine next morning to catch the cross-Channel steamer. Fitzsimmons was good enough to lend me his car. He wasn't too bad when you got to know him, in spite of that uncalled-for remark about my being disrespectful.

Brashman and Milestone caught up a few miles from the field and strafed the car like madmen, then waved and flew off side by side, their wings almost touching; but I hardly noticed them, because I was thinking about Burma Park.

Part Three

Me, in Buckingham Palace

AMONG MY OTHER excesses I went up to Buckingham Palace in my best service uniform, badges glowing, stick swinging, received a magnificent salute from the guards, followed several other officers into the building, checked my hat, gloves, and stick as instructed, and went down an icy corridor and sat around for the damnedest time with about forty others in a vast, drafty chamber, up to the ankles in brilliant royal blue carpeting. It was not long before I needed to go to the bathroom.

We sat around fidgeting. Finally I got up. Everyone looked at me.

'Anyone know where the latrine is?' I asked politely.

There was a startled silence. Nobody answered. I looked around, waiting. 'Bathroom,' I amended.

Someone snorted and muttered something. The officers – generals, lieutenants, colonels, and captains – were all sitting bolt upright in high, stiff-backed red plush chairs, their knees carefully together, lips pursed. I looked at my neighbour, a major with red tabs.

'Well, come on,' I said kindly, 'speak up. I can't wait all day.'

The major's face turned mauve. 'Who the devil –' he started. Then stopped, looked around guiltily, and went on in quieter tones, 'Who the devil d'you think you're talking to, sir?'

I said impatiently, 'Do you or do you not know where the bathroom is? At least give me the courtesy of an answer. Any of you.' My voice ricocheted among the marble pillars.

They were all glaring now. I swung round impatiently, turned and walked out of the room and started off down the corridor, feet clacking. If I'd had my stick I'd have been lashing my thigh.

The corridor was endless. I caught sight of my reflection in black marble, stopped, studied the reflection with some interest, concluded that dissipation had added a new dimension to it, and was in the act of twisting its eyebrows into sundry haughty expressions when another face appeared in the marble. Turning, I saw that a footman in breeches and velvet was staring at me. I hurried on, humming.

It took two or three minutes of travel through half a dozen beautiful icy rooms covered in Dutch-style pictures before I found the bathroom. There was a bearded admiral there, washing his hands.

'Morning, Admiral,' I said conversationally.

He was still thinking this over when I returned to the washbasin and waited for him to finish. He blinked at me.

'Good morning, er ... Captain.'

'You here to get decorated too?'

'Not exactly.'

I shivered. 'Lord,' I said, 'imagine living in a place like this.'

The admiral looked at me sharply, then began washing his hands all over again. 'What's wrong with it?' he demanded. He had a rather harsh, barking voice.

'It's not exactly the kind of place you pad around in, in bare feet, is it, sir?'

'Don't quite understand you, Captain.'

'Goldarned chilly, I mean. No wonder the English take to the trenches so well. The dugouts must seem quite cozy after the rigors of civilian life. Excuse me.' I moved respectfully round him and started to wash. The water was cold. 'If I were the King I'd install

246

central heating, or at least put in a few stoves or something. What's the sense in living in a luxurious place like this if you have to go about wrapped in blankets?'

'Blankets?' the admiral said. He was beginning to look alarmed. His beard vibrated. 'It's good for you,' he said.

'What is?'

'What?'

'I said, what's good for you?'

'What?' He thought. 'The cold,' he said. 'Good for you. Do you hear?' There was another lengthy pause. He coughed. 'Was always warm and comfortable – 'til I joined the Navy. *Britannia*. Training ship.'

'Oh, yes?' I said, combing my locks.

'Fiendishly cold it was.'

'The *Britannia*, sir?'

'Fiendishly.'

There was another long silence. He was standing stock-still, barely moving. I was about to leave when he laughed, abruptly and harshly. 'Har har.' I turned inquiringly. A minute later he said, 'Dashed tough place it was.'

'The *Britannia*? '

'Hm?'

'The *Britannia* was a tough ship?'

'Oh, was it?' he asked, looking interested. 'Yes, I was in the *Britannia*, too. Specially for me. Miserable, you know.' He nodded to himself, smiling beneath his whiskers. 'Just a cadet. When was that?' He thought hard. I was edging out when he said harshly, 'Used to get a hiding twice a week. Didn't matter who you were. Just about broke my nose once. When was it? Some time last century. 1877. That's right. I was only twelve,' The admiral looked a little sad.

'Well,' I said, 'I'd better not keep the old chap waiting.'

'What old chap?'

'The King,' I said.

'Oh, yes,' the admiral said, nodding faintly.

When I got back to the chamber the others were all standing at attention, being addressed by a general. He stopped when I entered. Everyone turned. I waved a hand languidly, in a good temper now. 'Carry on,' I said.

The general gazed at me for a long time with eyes as blue as the carpet but not as soft. 'Thank you very much indeed,' he said at last.

'As I was saying. The Sovereign will be sitting on the left as you enter the room. You will march exactly ten paces forward, halt, turn smartly to the left, bow slowly to an angle of thirty degrees, then stand to attention. Your citation will then be read out. When it is ended you will take precisely eight paces forward and again stand at attention, whereupon His Majesty will hook the medal to your tunic. You will not look him in the eye. You will, of course, not address him unless spoken to first, and then only with extreme brevity.

'When he offers his hand, you will smartly transfer your glove from your right hand to your gloved left hand, bring your right hand up smartly, and –'

Christ, gloves! I'd left mine with my stick and hat. I started to leave hurriedly.

'Where do you think you're going?' the general called out. Once again, everyone turned to look at me.

'Left my gloves behind,' I called back. 'Won't be two 'ticks. Don't go off without me, now.'

But when I got back I found the bastards *had* gone off without me, the bastards. There was nobody in sight, not even a fairy godmother.

After searching about for a few minutes I found them just as my name was being called. There were only a few others in my group, recipients of D.S.O.s, mostly senior officers, and as I hurried into the Throne Room they looked at me as if I were a lump of regurgitated cat fur.

I forgot all about the instructions. Catching sight of the King on his throne, I just scampered across as if meeting someone at

Number 2 platform, Huston Station. But then I stopped dead. It was the admiral again.

I suppose I should have recognized the King. I'd seen his picture often enough.

I stood uncertainly, slack-jawed. The Chamberlain, after an incredulous look in my direction, stepped forward and began to read the citations. I wasn't listening. I stood there, approximately at attention, and looked at the admiral.

His Majesty had his head turned to one side and seemed to be listening carefully to the rigmarole. The citation gave me time to get a grip of myself.

At last the medals were brought forward on a fancy cushion, and the King arose and picked them up, I trotted forward and he hooked them on to my uniform.

Then he stood back a foot or two and looked at me in silence. Didn't offer to shake hands or anything.

'I, er ...' I began.

There was a sudden indrawing of breath at this scandalous fracture of protocol. I stopped, then began again.

'Actually,' I said, 'it's a very nice palace when you get used to it. Quite comfy when – when you get right down to it.'

I looked at the King. He stared back.

I cleared my throat.

He continued to stare at me. Then suddenly he smiled and nodded several times.

I smiled back with relief.

He offered his hand. I shook it vigorously.

'It *is* a damned cold place,' he said.

Orgy at the Conservative Club

I DIDN'T TELEPHONE the Lewises immediately on getting to London, partly because telephones upset me and partly because I wanted to give myself two days of boredom and inactivity so that the pleasures of Burma Park would be all the keener.

So I mooned around London for two days following the investiture, purposely doing nothing interesting, keeping myself unexcited. The subdued mood of the capital was a help, for it was obvious now, even to the loudest bawlers of patriotic songs, that the Flanders campaign had been a failure.

Finally the longed-for moment arrived. I paced up and down the lobby of the Spartan Hotel, bracing myself for the ordeal of telephoning. Then it occurred to me that I didn't have to. All I had to do was walk round to the Foreign Office.

Mr Lewis was at a conference, so I had to wait for half an hour in his office, which served only to increase the pleasurable anticipation. It was a spacious room with a fine thick carpet, but looked as if it hadn't been redecorated since the Charge of the Light Brigade. The panelling was almost black with the grime of countless fogs, and brittle leaves of paint had separated from the ceiling and were hanging down in a manner that gave one an urge to swipe them off. I did in fact get hold of the long, hooked window pole and tried to dislodge a patch or two, but the ceiling was too high.

I got behind the desk, the carpet crackling underneath, with the intention of standing on the desk, but then thought better of it. Even Mr Lewis would probably find it rather strange if he came in and found me standing in his Out basket thumping paint off his ceiling.

So I put the pole back, and then wondered why the carpet had crackled. I went back behind the desk. There it was again. I tramped round the room, but the only part of the carpet that crackled was on the side of the room where the desk was. It was peculiar. Perhaps it was the underfelt. I hesitated, and listened. There was silence except for the distant scratch of a quill pen, or perhaps it was rats in the wainscoting. Probably Mr Lewis would also find it strange if he came in and found me sneaking a look at his underfelt, but it was so intriguing that I just had to investigate, so I lifted back a corner of the carpet. There were a good many documents underneath, some of them yellow with age.

Well, that explained that, so I replaced the carpet and looked out the window. But then I fell to wondering what the papers were doing under the carpet. And I was on the point of hauling the carpet back again when I heard someone talking in the next office, so I moved away, whistling and looking innocent

Mr Lewis came in.

'Bart, my boy.' We shook hands warmly. 'I'm sorry I had to keep you waiting.' He looked as harassed as ever, and somewhat older. 'Sit down, my boy, sit down.'

I expected him to barricade himself behind his desk, but he drew a straight-backed chair close to mine and beamed at me. 'I read a paragraph about you only yesterday and was hoping you'd call.' He looked at me keenly, and I thought he was going to congratulate me on my polished appearance. 'You look terrible,' he said.

He chatted for a while, scrupulously avoiding such vulgarities as politics and the war, but made no reference to my invitation to Burma Park. After ten minutes, when the conversation started to become desultory, I saw I'd have to bring the subject up myself, which I did with my well-known tact.

'M'and how are things at Burma Park, sir?' I said with a hearty air.

'Oh, fine, fine.' He stopped, and looked at me in a stricken fashion. 'Oh, yes. We were going to have you along, weren't we?'

I relaxed happily.

'What a shame!' he said.

I blinked, then smiled bravely. 'I promise,' I whined, 'not to be in the way, you know; I'll be so circumspect you'll hardly know I'm there....'

'What a hope,' Lewis said, smiling. 'No. I meant, what a shame, because there's nobody there.'

'Oh.'

'Mrs Lewis and Katherine are up in Scotland staying with the McIntocks, some friends of ours, and as it's not worth my while going up to Berkshire every evening. I'm staying at my club. We didn't know you were coming. Katherine didn't say anything –'

'No, she didn't know,' I said. 'The investiture messed up my leave dates.'

'Yes, I see. It is a pity, though. You see, they're not due back for two weeks or so.' Lewis hunched over, drummed with his fingers on the side of the chair, thinking, then invited me to his club for dinner.

As I was going out, I said, 'By the way, what's the idea of all those papers under the carpet?'

He was in the act of opening the door. His male secretary, who was doing *The Times* crossword puzzle, looked up and started to rise. Mr Lewis closed the door again.

'What?' he said.

'The papers under the carpet,' I said.

'The papers under the carpet?'

'I noticed them because they crackled. '

'Oh, you –' He laughed. 'You mean the – the *papers* under the carpet. Oh, *those* ...' He laughed again. 'What papers?' he asked.

I went over and showed him. He stared goggle-eyed.

'My goodness,' he said. 'How on earth did those get there?' He looked utterly shocked, and his bald dome began to steam.

I set off for the door. 'I'll ask your secretary,' I said. He rushed after me, and just as the secretary was getting to his feet again, closed the door and stood with his back to it. 'No, no, he's terribly busy at the moment,' Lewis said. 'I don't like to disturb him when he's terribly busy. Well, I must say,' he went on, 'that's most extraordinary. I've often wondered what that crackling was under the – the carpet. I kept saying to myself, William – that's my name, William; I often address myself as William when I'm in an informal mood – William, I said, one day you really must, you know, look under that carpet and find out what all that crackling is about. And now we know.' He laughed again. Thanks to you,' he added in a grateful tone of voice, mopping his dome and not looking the least grateful. He opened the door again, and the secretary started to rise but then thought better of it and went back to his crossword instead.

'Well, I'll see you at six o'clock at the club,' Mr Lewis said.

It was a dark, damp place so hushed and withdrawn from the world that for a minute I thought I'd strayed into a mausoleum or a crypt. Perhaps it was the terra-cotta-coloured and friezed walls that gave this impression, or the fossilized remains of former members sunk in the armchairs. But no; some of the bodies were in fairly modern dress, and now and again one of them would breathe, but only when nobody was looking.

The dining room was equally lugubrious, and Mr Lewis and I champed our way as quietly as we could through the boiled beef and cabbage, and afterwards sat in the lounge with Sherry at our elbows. Sherry was an aged parson who had attached himself to us at dinner. He had wobbly cheeks and, like everyone else, whispered; but so sibilantly that spray fountained from his lips at every plosive consonant. In order to be heard, he had to bring his mouth close to one's ear. This was rather hard on Mr Lewis, who had to keep swabbing the side of his neck surreptitiously with his handkerchief.

Moreover, whenever the Reverend Mr Sherry had finished several whispered sentences addressed to Lewis he would turn to nod and smile at me as if it were *my* ear he had just filled with saliva and information, an unsettling habit, as one inevitably begins to feel somewhat foolish, nodding and smiling without knowing what one is nodding and smiling about.

So I wasn't feeling very comfortable even before the bony-looking gentleman in black coat and striped trousers came up. After a whispered introduction of which I didn't catch a word, he started to jerk his chin high in the air repeatedly, as if trying to free his Adam's apple from the confines of his wing collar. I didn't mind this mannerism so much, but *his* whisper was something else again: because of a slight gap in his front teeth it contained a nerve-jangling whistle, and after a few hushed murmurs to Lewis he insisted on giving me the full benefit of his hissing conversation; and the shrillness, borne on his cold breath pouring into my left earhole, made me twitch and convulse almost uncontrollably. The effect was similar to that caused by the sound of a fingernail rasping across a blackboard or a razor blade screeching over glass. If the other members of the club had been sufficiently alert, I imagine we would have presented a rather frightening sight, with the Reverend Mr Sherry smiling and nodding with increasing uncertainty at me as I made excruciating faces in reply and squirming and shuddering in my chair, Wing Collar alternately raising and lowering his chin and whistling into my ear, and Mr Lewis desperately trying to keep his neck dry with a sopping handkerchief.

Finally neither of us could stand it any longer, and Lewis and I heaved ourselves up and with many an agonized expression, meant to convey reluctance to abandon such fascinating company, made simultaneous excuses for leaving. Unfortunately our excuses clashed somewhat, Mr Lewis announcing in a high-pitched voice that we had some work to do at the British Museum (forgetting it was ten o'clock at night) and I equally loudly stating that we both had a train to catch. At the bedlam of sound from our two hushed voices every single occupant of the lounge started, and with a creaking of badly oiled leather jerked round and glared as we stood there, all uneasy smiles and shuffling feet

'Sh-hh,' a badly wrinkled member ejaculated, but cautiously, as his dentures appeared to be loose. Then silence once again descended over the clubroom, broken only by the sound of Mr Lewis nervously shredding his handkerchief in his clenched fists as we backed out, sweating and smiling in a sycophantic manner.

Later, however, Lewis got a little of his own back. He confessed afterward that he had been wanting to do it for twenty-two years. We had retreated in disorder to the library, which fortunately was empty, and had become maudlin after a few stiff drinks to calm our nerves. When the time came for me to leave, Lewis was all ready to join the Royal Flying Corps and I was talking about vegetating at Burma Park to study the local Pteridophyta.

As we were crossing the hall he tiptoed over and, stifling his giggles, looked into the lounge. None of the members appeared to have moved a muscle since we had left them six brandies ago. Lewis swayed very slightly; then he looked at me with one eye dramatically half closed and raised a wavering forefinger, and stuck his gleaming head into the room, put two fingers to his mouth, and emitted a piercing blast. It was such a tremendous whistle it must have sent the Piccadilly warriors scuttling for cover two miles away.

The badly wrinkled member who was near the door jerked so violently his false teeth shot out on to his egg-stained vest, and there was a communal convulsion that put my earlier shudders to shame, but before everyone could wrench themselves round in their armchairs Lewis was already outside the main entrance, laughing and holding on to an imitation Doric column.

'That was a marvellous whistle,' I said admiringly.

'Wasn't it?' he said proudly. 'I haven't done that for years, for years and years.' We laughed and held on to each other.

The doorman came up and touched his cap. 'Can I call you a cab, sir?' he inquired.

Mr Lewis drew himself up. 'I'll get one,' he said, and, putting his fingers to his mouth again, blew another piercing blast, and a taxi drew up, shuddering and backfiring. 'What was the name of the hotel?' Lewis asked.

'The Spartan,' I said.

The Spartan, my good man,' Lewis said to the taxi driver in his most precise voice, and got in, and the taxi clashed off down the street. I was just going back into my club when it occurred to me that there was something wrong somewhere. A short time later the taxi came back and Mr Lewis got out apologetically and I got in and we waved to each other, the street echoing with our hiccups and protestations of eternal friendship.

Pride and Prejudice

IT WAS JUST like Mr Lewis not to have said anything.

> 'Dear Bart: Daddy has just telephoned to say you have escaped and are running around loose in London. You fool, you should have let me know the exact day you were coming on leave. However, you've given me a good excuse to get away from here. It's been raining so much I've hardly been able to leave the house since we arrived. Anyway, it's all right with everyone here if I come up to London for two or three days. I'll be arriving at Euston Station this Wednesday at 4:10 p.m., if you can be bothered to meet me, and I'll be staying with my aunt in Kensington. Mother sends her love – K.'

She was smiling all over her face when she got off the train, and she looked so lovely, in a dark-blue cape over a light-blue velvet dress, that I couldn't resist giving her a hug. Well, I could have resisted it easily, because I'd been preparing myself for half an hour for this moment, trying to decide whether to embrace her, kiss her on the cheek or on the lips, shake hands, or merely salute. I'd decided on the lips, but at the last moment my nerve failed and, as I said, I just gave her a warm embrace. But even that made her blush, and she pretended to be preoccupied with her luggage, which wasn't very convincing as she had brought only one suitcase.

Her aunt in Kensington was a dainty old lady, so sweet, white-haired, and apple-cheeked that she looked just a trifle unconvincing; one expected her to remove her wig and makeup at any moment and start swearing dreadfully.

'Well, well, well,' she said, beaming at me and fussing around. 'Katherine has told me all about you, Bartholomew.'

'Well, now you can get my side of the story,' I said, repressing an urge to give her rosy cheeks a friendly pinch, and speaking in a tone so arch and charming it sickened even me.

'How nice,' she said vaguely. 'And are you sleeping here too, Lieutenant?'

'He's a captain now, Aunt Clo, and he's certainly not sleeping here. There's only one bedroom apart from yours.'

'Is there? Oh, yes, so there is. Well, well, well, so you're a captain now, are you? My goodness, promotion seems to be very easy these days, doesn't it? You must certainly stay for supper, anyway. We're having pork chops.'

'Pork chops give me indigestion,' I said apologetically. But she didn't hear, or pretended not to, probably because of the meat shortage; so I didn't press the matter.

Her house was small and cozy and crammed to the bulwarks with knickknacks, ornaments, a fantastic number of ornate clocks none of which was accurate, and a scruffy-looking parrot, inevitably named Polly. As soon as it saw me it started to screech and rock back and forth from one claw to the other, its tattered overcoat ruffling in a hostile fashion.

'Get fell in!' it shrieked.

'Polly used to belong to a sergeant major,' Aunt Clo explained. 'He seems to have picked up some dreadful language from somewhere, I don't know ...'

Loyally, the parrot shrieked at the top of its voice, 'Dozy bastards. *Get fell in!*'

'Tchk, tchk, tchk, tchk, Polly,' Aunt Clo said reprovingly, but giving it a biscuit all the same. The bird closed one eye and shuffled. I didn't make the mistake of currying favour with the brute. I knew instinctively I'd get badly bitten if I tried. I'd learned my lesson. It had taken me a quarter century, but I'd finally learned it.

All the same, I was relieved when Aunt Clo covered the cage after dinner.

We stayed in all evening as it was a damp, cold night, and Aunt Clo obligingly went to bed at nine, leaving Katherine and me on a chintzy sofa before a fire banked high enough to last until 1918. We talked and talked, and by eleven I still hadn't summoned up the courage to put my arm around her, although our shoulders were touching.

And then the air-raid siren went, and she looked at me wide-eyed; and giving three hearty, un-British cheers for the Gotha bombers I put my arm around her protectively; and by Jove, as the expression is, if she didn't lay her head on my shoulder.

It was simply... My heart splitarsed as I felt the slight weight of her breast over my wrist. I felt...

What exactly *were* my feelings as I sat there in the firelight on a chintzy sofa with my arm around this slender creature with the exciting squint? I felt ... There was difficulty in putting it in words. I felt so childishly and absurdly... It was not merely the sensation of pride in holding my very own woman, it – it was not merely the sensual thrill at the contact with her right breast, or the fragrance of her hair, or the moistness of her parted lips, or the gleam of her flawless skin. It was more than that. It was an overwhelming – *je ne sais quoi*; not reverence exactly, nor was it exactly ecstasy, it – it was bigger than both of us. It was – indigestion. It was those damn pork chops we'd had for dinner; there'd been far too much fat on them, and too much fat always gave me a touch of indigestion.

Still, it was very pleasant there in the firelight with the bombs dropping all over the place. One of the bombs landed quite close, in fact. Katherine told me next morning that when her aunt came down she said, 'You were *very* noisy last night, Katherine. What on earth were you and your friend doing on the sofa, to make all that noise?' and had looked at Katherine very disapprovingly.

She told me this in the taxi on the way back from a show. 'You have a bad influence on people,' she said, snuggling against me. 'I don't know what you and Father were up to at the club, but he says none of the other members will speak to him now. He's very fond of you for some strange reason,' she added, then said something else, but I didn't catch it because she had her face hidden in my coat. Then: 'Have you ever been in love, Bart?'

I gazed out of the taxi at a passing coffee stall, in front of which cloth-capped men in mufflers were sipping coffee, presumably. Actually, it wasn't the coffee stall that was passing, it was we who were passing the coffee stall. The coffee stall was stationary.

'No,' I said. 'It's a ghastly experience.'

'How do you know if you've never been in love?'

'Well, I read all about it in *Pride and Prejudice*.'

She was silent the rest of the way home; or perhaps speechless would be a better word.

The Last of the Colonel

I HADN'T MISSED much; the weather had been atrocious while I was on leave, and at the beginning of December it was still bad, with mist and cloud at only 500 feet; so everyone was feeling very rested and jolly. I was touched on my return to the squadron by the warmth of my reception. It seemed I wasn't so bad when they got to know me.

'Well, he's back, God help us.'

'Hello, Bandy.'

'Hello, Bart.'

I sat round the fire with Brashman, Wordsworth, and George Ginty. In spite of a lengthy rest they all looked exhausted.

'Well,' I said, 'who's dead, wounded, missing, or got V.D.?'

We yarned for hours. Before I went on leave I was sick of shop talk. Now I revelled in it.

'And how's old London Town?' Wraught said, coming up.

'Great,' I said.

'Did yis have any saxual adventures?' Ginty asked.

On December 6 there was yellow sunlight and the earth steamed. My plane fairly leaped off and climbed steeply at eighty miles an hour. The mechanics had done wonders with the engine; it sounded sweet and strong and gave more than its revs. It was good to be aloft again. I felt relaxed, my grasp on the spade grip light and precise. The wires sang up and down the scale.

Archie greeted us with a joyous barrage, its first targets for days, and I was delighted to make his acquaintance again and pretended to dive, then zoomed, and snickered as his smudges appeared far below, and splitarsed about happily until I caught sight of numerous dots far in the distance. I sobered up, testing the guns. They jammed, and wrenching at the handles did no good. But I had my hammer with me, and knew just where to hit them, which I did, and the stoppage was cleared and they rattled healthily.

I had two experienced men with me, Sanford on the right, his deputy leader's streamer fluttering gaily from his rudder, and Armstrong on the left. Sim Case, a new Canadian – the R.F.C. was filling up rapidly with Canucks – was behind and held this position steadily. It was his second trip over. He had been so promising and the Flight's need of him so pressing that he had become active after only ten days' training with the squadron. He was a tough, hard, unsentimental devil, and I had a feeling he was going to do well.

The R.F.C. was out in strength that day. Squadron after squadron of Camels, S.E.s, Brisfits, and a flight of DH 9s were going out, most of them much higher than we, and lumbering Harry Tales were busy exposing plates surrounded by clouds of Archie. The Huns, too, were up in strength, but stayed well inside their own lines.

Far northward – visibility was exceptional – I saw two groups of planes come together, like bunches of gnats. Two planes spun down. But we had no luck. We tried to catch five Albatri, and for a moment it looked as if they were prepared to fight, but then a pack of S.E.s appeared and they sheered off, so we went back to our own sector and patrolled ineffectively. Richthofen's Tripes had moved down to Cambrai, and we had an Albatros Staffel opposite us now.

We had to be content with emptying our guns into a second-line trench.

The same quartet set off in the afternoon but was reduced to three when Armstrong gave the dud-engine signal and went home. We were carrying four bombs apiece, and I made an earnest effort to do some relative good with them. The front was inactive, Archie had quieted down after his morning spree, and there didn't seem to be any targets at all. We bombed a second-line trench, and as I pulled out of the dive, banked to see where my bombs went. They went nowhere. I was lousy at bombing.

Tut-tutting, I headed toward the clouds, making barely sixty miles an hour in the wind and thus presenting a tempting target for Archie.

He didn't fire. Thoroughly alert, I looked around quickly. Nothing. I was just sticking a thumb in the sun when there was a dry rattle, distant but getting louder very quickly. Cursing, I lashed out at the rudder bar and flicked the stick as the Albatroses appeared out of the sun. One of them flashed past only a few feet away and I chased after him, but he was going too fast. Another came from the side. I could see his Spandaus alight. A dive and then a climbing turn, feeling calm and precise, and I got behind him with no difficulty, though at long range. He was no veteran. What a beautiful plane the D.V. was! I fired confidently, glancing back once to make sure I was clear behind.

But the long holiday had spoiled my marksmanship. The tracer was 'way off. Then I had to dive away when someone else got on my tail. Someone flashed past, close, plummeting straight down, friend or foe I couldn't tell. We had really been jumped on this time.

I pranced about ineffectively for a few seconds, trying to size up the situation. There was a Camel circling with two Huns. I hastened over. It was Sanford. The Huns were both bright green except for their curving top planes glittering silver in the sun. I envied the Huns their freedom to paint their buses any colour they liked. We had to be content with dun colours by official order.

I dived in and fired a long burst at one of the green birds. Startled, both Albatroses hesitated, and in a flash Sanford was firing into one of them. The Hun rolled sluggishly and started to dive upside down.

I looked around again. The rest of the attackers had disappeared. Sanford's victim was spinning now, seeming to go slower as it neared the earth. Then it vanished. Dead for a ducat, as they say.

Sanford joined up, waving joyfully and looking pleased, and we patrolled up and down looking for Sim Case. When we got home we found him morosely examining his Camel. It had thirty-five bullet holes in it and a *longeron* had been split.

Sanford slapped him on the back. 'That's what it's always like when you go out with Bandy,' he said. Case just grunted.

I spent the rest of the afternoon having a long discussion with Trimbull, and we trestled my bus in front of the ground target and adjusted the Vickers until they made a single group at thirty yards' range.

The next day I had no job until one-thirty and was getting ready to set off on a lone patrol when Hyams Wraught sauntered up and asked if he could come.

I looked at him, hesitating. He was a handsome, hard-drinking, and modest man of about my age, already the most popular man in the squadron. Also, he didn't have too much experience.

'I can watch your tail while you ferret out a little something for both of us,' he persisted.

'When's your next job?'

'It's my day off, Captain.'

'M'well,' I said doubtfully.

I marvelled again at the transformation the mechanics had worked on my bus. It was rigged perfectly with just the right amount of tail heaviness, and climbed to 2,000 in hardly more than three minutes. I was about to circle to wait for Wraught when, glancing back, I saw him only twenty feet behind and on my right and above. I was startled at the speed with which he'd caught up. I found out later that he had taken off with me.

Taking off in formation! Nobody had ever thought of that before. Wraught, evidently, was a man of some originality.

We dodged over the lines south of Ypres at 10,000. The sun was shining, but there was a lot of haze, which probably put Archie off, for he came nowhere near us. There was little wind, so I flew straight on into Hunland. There were plenty of aircraft up but none near us except for a solitary Harry Tate stooging up and down, taking photographs and being shot at.

There didn't seem to be much game. I turned up to look at Passchendaele, which the Canadian Corps had finally taken on November 6. But the so-called heights with its blood-filled craters was mercifully veiled in fog; so I turned east again, carefully checking the map. It would be only too easy to get lost on a day like this.

The mist made the air soft and pink. My lower plane looked transparent. It gave me a strange feeling, being able to see through the wings, to realize that that rosy flimsiness was all that suspended me above the earth.

Wraught drew alongside and waggled his wings and pointed down. I couldn't see anything though I tilted to get the wings out of the way. Just streamers of mist, and here and there patches of ground in musty yellow and dirty brown. I looked at Wraught questioningly. He gestured insistently. I looked again, then saw them, about nine Albatroses, skimming the mist a mile below, like dragonflies. I waved back, grinning. I looked around and up and behind. Nobody else in sight. The Huns were dancing about, travelling obliquely, almost under us now, going in the general direction of home. We had the sun on our side.

I throttled back and pushed the bus into a shallow dive. The Pitot rose to 130 and stayed there; the wires sang happily in the foam bath of the sky. With luck we would pay back the Huns for that surprise attack yesterday.

They were still carrying straight on, probably not expecting to see us so far over, about fifteen miles. I had that familiar, disturbed feeling in the bowels, and my ears crackled with the changing pressure. I sensed rather than saw Wraught slewing outward to take the Huns from the right. I hoped he knew enough to get out fast once the surprise was lost. If we did surprise them. It looked as if we would. Already I had one of the Albatroses in the Aldis. He enlarged rapidly. There was a crackle of guns on the right. I opened fire and immediately hit. A slight correction on rudder and the tracer splashed in all around the pilot.

The Albatros jerked, flipped over, and went into a spin, end over end. I caught a glimpse of Wraught's victim going down ahead of it.

Then the man twenty yards in front and to the left of the one I'd hit banked sharply and raggedly right in front. The Vickers rattled; he put his pointed nose into the tracer.

There was a fire on my right. An Albatros fell, burning into the ground mist, and disappeared, and a few seconds later there was a diffused flash. I saw my Hun. Also on fire, a nasty sight. He rose straight up, black oily smoke and flames licking between the centre sections, hung for a second, then slipped sideways, flaming. God, what a slaughter! Four of them in about thirty seconds.

I manoeuvred violently in case there was anyone behind. A Hun streaked past, its wheels almost touching my top plane, its guns still firing. A touch of rudder, a slight but exact pressure forward, and there he was. I was jittering with excitement now. The tracer started to eat along his fuselage. However, his great-er speed took him quickly out of range. I turned away, diving to pick up speed, made sure there was nobody following, and looked around, weaving jerkily. Wraught was already well away. Good for him. I flew after him. The remainder of the Huns had disappeared.

Just for the hell of it we went home at 50 feet, laughing and waving at each other like idiots. Wraught was delirious with pleas-ure when we landed, and kept pummelling me on the back. At eleven that night he was still describing the fight. We had a binge to celebrate his success and my thirtieth victory. But I went to bed almost sober.

I was on fire two days later, after a day off, and led the flight an unheard-of twenty-two miles over. I was feeling reckless.

We set out five strong, but Milestone and Case both turned back with engine trouble. When Sanford, Armstrong, and I turned back twenty-two miles out we hadn't encountered a single enemy aircraft, and it was starting to rain. The cloud ceiling began to close in, forcing us lower and lower. It looked too dense to climb through.

Then, looking around at the untouched countryside, something caught my eye, a dull glint from below. Tilting over, I saw a two-seater just coming in to land at a Hun airdrome. It was too good an opportunity to miss. I waggled the wings, half rolled, and dived. The two-seater, an L.V.G., never saw me. It spun in and fell to pieces on the airfield, just as Armstrong drew level. I saw Sanford bank vertically and turn back, followed by Armstrong, and wondered what they were after when both began firing. It was another two-seater, painted dark green. It fell into a wood and caught fire, sending up a column of white smoke.

Machine-gun fire began to come up from the airdrome, and we veered off and flew wide, looking for other targets. The rain had already stopped, but the air felt wet and icy. We hung around too long.

I should have realized that other fields would have been alerted. The Huns didn't even have to waste time climbing, for we were at only 1,000 feet. The first thing we knew we were being dived on by at least a dozen multicoloured Tripe-hounds. Armstrong went down at once and smashed to pieces not far from the wreckage of my L.V.G. I saw Sanford twisting and turning, surrounded by Fokkers. As for me, I was in a net of tracer, struggling to claw free. I shot up one chequered brute but had no time to watch him go, if he did go. We were only a few hundred feet up.

A nasty situation, to put it mildly.

I flew in narrow defensive circles, just managing to keep out of the way of the two following Huns but constantly harried by snapshots from others. I felt calm enough, but had a good idea

I wasn't going to get away with it this time. I kept licking my lips, and disconnected rhymes ran through my head. Luckily, we were doing right-hand turns, which was best for the Camel with its powerful torque. I caught up with one of my hunters and gave him two short bursts, but there were holes appearing in my own wings and there were grey lines of tracer feathering overhead. I had to let my friend go and concentrate on jiggling, side-slipping, skidding, twisting, and banking. I didn't see what happened to Sanford, but as I seemed to have all the Tripes to myself – about twenty of them now – he must already have caught it.

I was forced to keep turning. But getting nowhere. The Tripes with their three wings were able to gain height with each circuit, and I was having trouble maintaining what height I had, which wasn't much. I had to break out soon or run out of fuel – and when I did I'd be a goner. I was still calm and thinking clearly, glad I hadn't binged the night before, but afraid I might panic.

Now I had only 400 feet beneath the wings. The air seemed filled with Tripes diving and zooming, loosing off short bursts, trying to kick me out of the charmed circle: 350 feet. The tracer was horribly close. So was the wood beneath. Less than 300 now, it was impossible to get higher; the Camel was almost completely on its side as it was, banking almost vertically. Goodbye, Karley; goodbye Katherine, I thought to myself, goodbye, Mr and Mrs Lewis; goodbye. There was a flash – one of the Vickers had been struck. Even above the din of the engine, I thought I heard the *bzzz-t* of a bullet. It must have been close, very close. All I hoped now was that I wouldn't go down in flames.

I nearly ran into a line of trees. It was a horrible shock. I was right down at ground level. I just managed to stagger over the treetops and got raked as I did, but nothing vital was hit.

Well, there was some hope. Now I'd managed to get down, I'd stay down. Fokkers were roaring over the trees. There must have been twenty of them at the very least, which struck me as being most unsporting. Two of them came at me from the side.

I glimpsed the face of one of the pilots; he was wearing a white collar. He'd probably been interrupted in the middle of a formal celebration. The castor oil from his engine would soon foul that pretty collar, I thought.

I took a chance and banked vertically and turned in between two of the trees. The trunk of one hurtled past barely a foot above my head. That was funny, having a tree horizontally above you. A real scream.

But it had gained me a respite, taken the Huns by surprise; the way was clear. I straightened and roared along at about 5 feet, the straight line of trees, Lombardy poplars, slashing past on the left, *whip-whip-whip-whip-whip*. Tracer suddenly appeared above and tried to feather down to my level. A Hun right behind. A tremor of the stick, a twitch of the rudder and I managed to skid back through another gap. Branches clutched at the undercart. Then I was through just as the rest of the pack jumped over in the opposite direction. It was like a game. Of course, I'd have nightmares after it was over – if I was ever in the position to have nightmares again – but that would be a small price to pay.

The Pitot showed over 115 m.p.h. That was marvellous, and I blessed the mechanics feverishly; they had really done wonders with the Clerget; over 115 was marvellous for a Camel. I might even have gained on the Tripehounds if I hadn't had to do so much dodging. The trees ended.

The compass was spinning. I was in the open. At once the Tripes came down, and I was so low I thought I saw dollops of earth being kicked up by the enemy bullets. I was no longer cool, but drenched in sweat. There was no room even to sideslip in that inimitable Camelish way.

A town. I was over it. Grey stone. A church steeple dead ahead. I kept going, rooftops unrolling below. Whoops – up and over a tenement. Woman on balcony. I eased over to the left with rudder, church tower 100 feet, 40 feet, 10 feet, at the last moment flicked the old bus over vertically. I imagined I felt the air bounce back from the spire.

I should have been dead a dozen times over. Incredible I was still alive, still flying. Canvas was flapping noisily. Tear in the lower plane.

I flew down the centre of a dingy-looking park, risked a glance back. The Fokkers still following, soaring over the spire, falling back very, very slightly, surely? Diving again. One of them firing in spite of the houses below. No, a railway station – then sidings, then fields, holes appearing in the wings. I skidded and relaxed my hold on the stick by a couple of pounds per square inch. Back over the town again, strange, should have passed it, God, maybe I was going in circles! The compass still spinning. Pressed the stick forward as a street lined up with the nose, and dropped into the street. I was below rooftop level, the wheels almost touching the cobbles at maybe 118 miles an hour. Ahead, a man crossing the street flung himself flat at the last moment. Then the street curved and I had to jump up. The Fokkers weren't firing.

But which way was I going? I had a crazy idea I ought to go back to those crossroads I'd just passed, to study the signposts.

A long convoy appeared ahead, motor vehicles and horse-drawn carts, and swept underneath, a few men in field grey and spiked helmets. I twisted around. The Tripes were still there, but there seemed to be fewer of them.

I was going in the same direction as the convoy, but was it returning to the front or leaving it? The sun wasn't visible, and the compass, though it was at last settling down, was still unreadable. Anyway, I'd no option but to keep on going.

When I next looked back there were only four Tripehounds after me, and I was sure of it now: they were falling behind. Should I risk climbing? No, they'd catch up in seconds because they climbed better. I did risk a zoom up to 50 feet. At that height I wouldn't lose so much headway jumping over telegraph wires and slag heaps and soaring up rising ground. Between frequent backward glances I had a chance to look over the plane. Two bracing wires had gone and the left top plane was sagging slightly. The wings were riddled with bullet holes. The sight was bent. There was a chip out of the strut holding the little pressure-pumping propeller. An inch lower and I'd have been done for. Some shredded canvas was flapping noisily. All the same, considering what I'd been through, I was practically unscathed.

Some wide-awake gunner fired from the ground, so I dropped a little lower, looking back. The same four Tripes. They must have been almost blind with fury, seeing me getting away. And it looked as if I *was* getting away.

Even as I watched, one of the Fokkers gained height, pointed its nose at me, and fired a long burst. But he was just out of range.

The ground below changed. It became steadily more normal: that is, devastated. And then, wonder of wonders, support lines started to snake over it and quickly became more tangled. I caught a glimpse of machine gunners in a double gun pit.

Then the engine quit.

I soared, managing to get to 600 feet before losing flying speed, lost a hundred feet on the stall, then glided, waiting for the gravity tank to feed in. But the engine failed to pick up. Now it was raining and there was mist swirling. As speed dropped I looked back anxiously. The Fokkers had gone.

They'd given up just a few seconds too soon.

A huge water-filled crater sailed by underneath, its surface spattered with raindrops. Surprisingly, nobody fired from the ground. Now front-line trenches and dose boxes were passing lazily by. Then barbed wire. I had about 90 feet of air under the wings to get me across no man's land.

And then I was over our front line, just managing to stagger over the top of a ridge. And my luck held, because beyond the ridge the ground sloped and I was able to stay in the air another four or five seconds before the wheels smashed into the ground and the bus slithered wildly downhill with a tearing, squelching noise. Then silence.

It was only a two-foot drop to the ground. I stood goggling stupidly at the wrecked bus. But I soon recovered my aplomb after searching around a bit – it had fallen in the mud – and began to stock-take. After I'd counted fifty bullet holes I lost interest and examined myself but couldn't find any punctures except where the buckle of the yoke had dug into my shoulder. I wondered light-headedly if I could claim another wound stripe for that. It seemed to me that I'd had a miraculous escape and that God was saving me for something much worse, such as the guillotine, delirium tremens, or marriage.

When I started to walk away, my legs gave under me and I had to cling to the fuselage. I'd have hated to fall into the slime I was standing in; it was already halfway up my boots. Perhaps that's what I was being saved for: the filth underfoot that sucked disgustingly with every movement

'Hello, there. You all right?'

It was a lieutenant. There was a sergeant behind him.

'Yes. Where am I?'

'That's Passchendaele over there.' The Canadian pointed, then let his arm fall with a wet slap against the ground sheet he was huddled in. 'Better come in before they start shelling your plane.'

To underline his words the first shell whistled over the ridge and burst fifty yards away. When I'd finished staggering and slithering into the trench it occurred to me that Karley might be in the general area.

'I don't suppose there's any Victorian Light Infantry people hereabouts, is there?'

'What? Yes. The Second Battalion's holding the line that way.'

'Is it? Is Captain Karley still O.C. B Company, do you know?'

'I don't know. But if his company's in the line it should be only two or three sectors over, I should think. Do you want to go there?'

'Yes.'

'I'll get the sergeant to show you the way.'

'Thanks very much,' I said, and tripped over a telephone wire and fell flat on my face in the mud. My language, which had deteriorated disgracefully over the past two months, was so vile that even the sergeant looked a trifle shocked.

He led the way, twisting and stumbling along the zigzagging, duck-boarded, trickling channels. The trenches were so deep one could see only narrow strips and tatters of wet sky overhead. The few soldiers we passed stared in frank and natural curiosity at the sight of a dishevelled and slightly wobbly aviator in full flying regalia except for the helmet, which I seemed to have lost somewhere.

B Company was in the firing line, and I was handed over to its sergeant major. He wasn't the one I'd known – Winterbottom... Ramsbottom... Blackbottom, what the hell was the name? – Higginbottom, yes. I inquired after him, but the C.S.M. had never heard of a Sergeant Major Higginbottom. This seemed a bad omen; but the first officer I met –

'Bandy! By God! Thought you were dead months ago.'

'My dear Spanner.' We shook hands, grinning at each other. He hadn't changed. The same look of utter indifference, the same sardonic twist to the mouth.

'We've never heard a word from you,' he went on in answer to my query about letters to Karley. 'Come on, he's in the dugout. We'll shake him out of his drunken stupor.'

Karley was reading a tatty copy of the B.E.F. *Times* as we lurched into the bowels of the earth.

'Jesus Christ, Bandy!' We shook hands and laughed like idiots. 'Where the hell have you sprung from?'

'I crashed over that way. How are you, Karley? You look terrible.'

'Thanks a million. Yours is the first relatively clean face I've seen for weeks.'

We exchanged unwholesome badinage while Spanner watched with a faint smile. Karley did look terrible. He'd lost a lot of weight and some of his old bounce; the skin under his eyes looked like opera-house curtains, and his dark hair was grey at the temples.

'Look, take off your – whatever you call that thing. We've often wondered how you were getting on. No, I never got any letters. Billings,' he screamed into the adjoining dugout, 'bring the whisky.' He turned back to me. 'I trust you haven't slipped back into any bad temperance habits,' he began, then stopped and his eyes bulged.

'Good God.' They were both staring at my filthy regimental tunic. Karley slumped slowly on to a padded crate. It squealed painfully under his weight. 'Spanner,' he said faintly, 'do you see what I see? The bugger's a captain.' Spanner was covering his eyes. 'D.S.O., M.C. – and is that the Croix de Guerre?'

'Pretty, isn't it?'

'Good God!'

'Where did you manage to buy all that?' Spanner said.

I sniggered. 'Do you mean to say,' I said, 'you haven't heard of me? I thought my fame was resounding from Nieuport to Armentières. You certainly are out of touch, aren't you? You grubby bastards.'

'How did you do it so quickly?' Karley asked.

'Christ, Karley, don't look so goddam impressed; it doesn't become you. I was just lucky and shot down a few planes.'

'How many, for Chrissake? You only joined the Air Corps the beginning of the year. How could you have done all that training and – how many?'

I couldn't resist telling them. 'Thirty or thereabouts,' I said, simpering.

'Thirty. Jesus,' Karley said. He gripped his mug and took a swig. 'You must be ... Jesus.'

'No, not Jesus,' I said modestly. 'How about another drink?'

'Look at him knock the stuff back,' Karley said. 'And swearing, and I don't know what all. Maybe even women. Oh, no, not that,' he said, pretending to swoon. 'Anything but that. For God's sake, Bart, put your flying things on again; you're blinding me with all that glory.'

'God,' he went on, shaking his head, 'I can't get over it.' He looked at Spanner. 'Our Bandy. That silly son of a bitch who turned up one evening in the middle of a battle looking like the answer to a maiden's nightmare.'

'It's a ghastly war, right enough,' Spanner said dolefully. 'Shells, gas, bombs, flame-throwers, tanks, and now Captain Bandy.'

We yarned for two hours, and I forgot all about lunch. By afternoon I was stinking, figuratively as well as literally.

'Swonnerful to be here again, dear old Karley,' I babbled in a blubbery tone after six neat whiskies in rapid succession.

'Oh, sure. You'd much rather be here than in your nice clean hut with real sheets on the bed.'

'Strue, Karley, I swear...'

'And you certainly can swear.'

'I know,' I said mournfully. 'And – and – and I drink, too.'

'You don't say.'

'Yes,' I said. 'And – and … but it's true, Karley, dear old Karley. It is wonnerful to be back with you, I don't …' I leaned my face against the wet wall of the dugout, staring with great concentration into the mug as I sloshed the whisky around; and for a lucid moment I had the answer. But by the time I'd opened my mouth to communicate it, it was gone.

At last Karley got up and put his arm round my shoulders. 'Look,' he said, 'we'd better get you out of here before the colonel sees you, you drunken aviator.'

'Oh no, not that,' I said dimly. 'Anything but –'

'You know his habit of venturing into the front lines to make sure we don't have any women around.'

He and Spanner started to haul me up the dugout steps. 'You'd better get out quick,' Karley went on, grunting with the effort. 'He still hasn't forgotten you.'

'He turns white whenever your name is mentioned,' Spanner said.

'I never meant him any harm,' I mumbled, stumbling.

'We know. He just kept getting in your way.'

'And it's obviously fatal to get in Bandy's way,' Spanner said.

I was being pushed and shoved into the open air. 'What's all the hurry, men?' I was mumbling. 'Stop pushing; I'm not a goddam wheelbarrow.'

There were a group of soldiers in the trench, grinning. I waved at them.

'Hello, boys.'

'Jesus, it's Bandy,' said a voice, and a blue face surmounting a disgusting bundle of old rags pushed through. I forced my eyes wide open to study him, creating a face that even these warriors hardened to the horrors of war blanched at.

'Poole! By all that's holy,' I said, and embraced him. 'God, Poole, you stink.'

'Better than you, Captain; you smell of castor oil.'

'Glad you're still alive, Poole,' I said, and patted him on the back.

It took Karley and Spanner several minutes to get me into my sidcot. I kept telling Karley how glad I was to see him again; and then I began insisting on staying with the company and maybe trying one little surprise attack, just Karley and me, for old times' sake. But they kept pushing me along until we arrived at the communications trench.

'Spanner had better take you back and put you on a lorry going toward your squadron,' Karley said.

'It's so God-damned good to see you alive, Karley, old fellow,' I said emotionally. ' 'S always the best men who go west.'

'Thanks very much,' Karley said.

'Thanks very much for your hospitality,' I said, shaking every hand within reach and some of them twice over.

'Christ, the colonel,' someone said, and everybody stiffened to a semblance of attention. It took a couple of seconds for the words to penetrate, by which time my old friend the colonel was only a few yards off, having just rounded a bend. He had a cowed-looking lieutenant in tow.

He saw me and stopped dead. The lieutenant ran into him and started to apologize abjectly until he noticed the colonel's expression.

I stiffened to attention too, and threw a magnificent salute. Karley and Spanner somehow kept me upright.

'Good morning, sir,' I said; then looked doubtful as I tried to work out whether it was morning or afternoon. 'Or, or good afternoon,' I said. 'Shtrike out whichever is inapplicable.' I was so proud at being able to pronounce 'inapplicable' I beamed round at everybody, including my old friend the colonel.

Some trick of vision made it look as if he was receding. I forced my eyes wide-open again and focused on him with an effort. Then I saw it wasn't a hallucination. The colonel was slowly moving backward, feeling his way blindly along the wall and trampling on the cowed lieutenant's feet, who didn't seem to mind too much.

'I ... I've just remembered, I have an appointment,' the colonel began. But then seemed to pull himself together, and to recollect his dignity as a senior officer. He stopped moving backward, although he didn't come any closer.

'Captain Karley,' he said in a strangled sort of way, 'get that man out of here. At once.'

'Yes, sir,' Karley said, and took my arm and started to lead me down the trench.

'No, no,' the colonel said in a high voice. 'Not this way, not past me.'

'But it's the only way back, sir.'

'I don't care. Help,' the colonel said. 'Help.' Then he swallowed and said, 'Help him up the side of the trench. He'll have to go that way, out in the open.'

'But he'll be in full view of the enemy, sir, and –'

'I don't care.' The colonel's voice rose another octave. 'He's not coming past me. Something dreadful will happen. I know it.'

'Well, you'll have to go back yourself then, sir,' Karley said.

The colonel regained his dignity. He drew himself up. 'Are you seriously suggesting,' he said, 'that I go back along this trench for over a mile, merely to avoid this – this lieutenant?' Fortunately I had my sidcot on so he couldn't see my badges. The shock would probably have killed him.

'Well ...'

'Though I admit the temptation to go back not merely a mile but all the way back to Paris is – is quite strong, but…. But no, not even for Lieutenant Bandy will I – though I admit the temptation to go back not merely to Paris but to Flin Flon, Manitoba, there to end my days in senility and safety is… ' Then the colonel realized he was beginning to lose control of the situation. He drew himself up again and said coldly: 'Karley, you have my orders. Get that man out of here.'

'He could go down into a dugout until the colonel's past,' Spanner suggested.

'No,' the colonel said, his voice rising again. 'No. That's where I'm going, I'm inspecting the – No, definitely not.'

'I don't mind,' I said with dignity, gesturing up the side of the trench, and feeling very hurt about the whole thing.

'It's too dangerous,' Karley said, ignoring the colonel's face, which had lighted up. 'Besides, you'd never get up the side of the trench.' It was nine feet to the top.

'You could give me a leg up,' I said.

'Yes, you could give him a leg up,' the colonel agreed eagerly. He looked round, then added, 'There aren't too many snipers around here.'

Karley started to say something. The colonel glared. 'All I know is,' he shouted, 'he's not staying anywhere in this sector while I'm here.'

'He hates me,' I said to Karley.

'I don't hate you,' the colonel said. 'I simply –'

'You do. You hate me.'

'I don't,' the colonel said, looking hateful.

'It wasn't my fault about the airplane,' I said sulkily.

Karley didn't quite catch this. 'What?' he asked.

'He ran over me with his airplane,' the colonel said.

Karley and Spanner looked at each other. Even the cowed-looking lieutenant blinked.

'He ran over you with his airplane?' Karley said faintly.

'I did not,' I said.

'You did,' the colonel said, raising his voice. Then caught Karley's eye. 'He did too,' he repeated, and sniffed, and his lower lip began to tremble.

Karley and Spanner were beginning to look worried.

'I did nothing of the kind,' I said. 'Ran over you with my airplane? What kind of nonsense is that?'

I began to explain that I'd had no earthly idea the colonel was riding in the field, but he was shouting too loudly.

'You dare accuse me of talking nonsense – you? I'll have you court-martialled if you're not careful. You know very well you ran over me with your airplane, and don't try to deny it.' The colonel looked around wildly. I have witnesses,' he said.

The cowed-looking lieutenant looked intensely relieved at this. 'You have a witness that Bandy ran you down in his airplane, sir?' he said. 'They actually saw this?'

'Well, not exactly saw it,' the colonel said. 'But ...' He caught the other officers exchanging glances, and flew into a rage again. 'I tell you he ran right into me with his airplane, and take that look off your faces or I'll have you all court-martialled. I'll have every one of you court-martialled if you're not careful.' He was getting hysterical.

'Did you ever hear anything so absurd?' I murmured.

The colonel turned blue, presumably from lack of oxygen, but before he could say anything Spanner asked helpfully, 'What altitude was this, sir?'

'How the devil would I know?' the colonel said. 'Three hundred feet,' he added, looking suddenly distraught and disoriented. He drew palsied fingers across his forehead. I think he meant either the height of the hill I'd crashed on or the elevation above sea level of the countryside in that particular part of France. Being a senior officer concerned with planning and so on, elevation and such would naturally be much on his mind.

'I see,' Spanner said. 'You were flying, were you, sir?'

'Of course I wasn't flying, you fool,' the colonel said, beginning to emerge from his momentary trance. 'I was riding my horse.'

The cowed lieutenant was beginning to look genuinely concerned. 'He means he was riding his horse on Bandy's airdrome,' he said. 'That must be the explanation.' He looked hopefully at his commander.

'I wasn't,' the colonel bellowed. 'It was at battalion headquarters.'

'He ran over you with his horse in battalion headquarters?' Karley asked, obviously trying his best to get it straight.

'What was Mr Bandy doing riding a horse around battalion headquarters?' Private Poole said.

Sweat was beginning to pour down the colonel's face, which was now a gorgeous magenta. 'Bandy wasn't riding the horse in battalion headquarters,' he screamed. 'It was me.'

'So that's the kind of thing goes on at battalion headquarters,' Spanner murmured. 'No wonder we're always getting horse manure from battalion head –'

I wasn't following the conversation too well, but I thought I'd better try and bring some sanity into the proceedings. 'Well,' I said, 'I can un-un-unnerstan' someone riding around battalion headquarters on a horse all right, but how do you get an airplane into battalion headquarters as well? It seems rather peculiar to me.'

'Me too,' Poole said.

'You keep out of this, Poole,' Spanner said.

'What pool?' the lieutenant asked. 'I thought it was battalion headquarters we were talking about.'

'That's a good point, sir,' Karley said to the colonel. 'How *do* you get an airplane into battalion headquarters?'

''S impossible,' I said. 'Unless you dismantled it first.'

'Rubbish. How could a dismantled airplane run over the colonel?' Spanner asked.

'It wasn't dismantled. It was flying,' the colonel bellowed, and began to beat his fists against the trench walls. The lieutenant touched his arm.

'Perhaps you'd better come back to battalion headquarters for a lie-down, sir,' he suggested timidly.

The colonel's eyes were quite wild. 'You think I'm crazy?' he asked. 'You all think I'm crazy, but I'm not, I tell you. Bandy...' He began to gasp for breath. 'I tell you Bandy ... he did, he ran over me –'

'With his airplane,' Karley said. 'Yes, sir.' He turned. 'Run and get the M.O.,' he whispered out of the corner of his mouth.

'I heard that,' the colonel cried. He stared around wildly, then grabbed hold of me and began to sob uncontrollably. 'Tell them, Bandy, tell them! You did run over me with your airplane, didn't you? Tell them, admit it, tell them!' But he kept shaking me so much, his large magenta-coloured face all crumpled, that I couldn't get a word out. At a signal from Karley the other three officers seized the colonel and tried to pinion his arms, but he fought like a madman, swearing terribly and saying over and over that I had run him down with my airplane while he was having a peaceful ride around battalion headquarters, saying it over and over until finally the cowed-looking lieutenant sapped him with an entrenching tool.

We all gazed at the colonel's limp body.

'You'd better get him to the clearing station,' Karley said to a couple of Red Cross men who'd been summoned.

'The strain was too much, I guess,' Spanner said.

'Yes,' Poole said. 'I guess it must be a strain, being in charge of a whole battalion. You know, giving orders, arranging for the rum ration, things like that. The responsibility,' he added wisely. 'Yes.'

We all nodded.

'You won't tell anyone it was I who subdued him, will you?' the lieutenant asked anxiously.

'He'll probably think it was me, anyway,' I said sadly.

Finally the Red Cross men took the colonel back to a casualty clearing station where he apparently became violent again and insisted he had been run over by an airplane while riding round battalion headquarters on his horse at an altitude of three hundred feet, minding his own business, and was so insistent that they had to put him in a strait jacket. However, I believe he calmed down once he got back to Canada, and the last I heard of him he was in charge of recruiting, with a nice office in Toronto and a kind but wary staff of convalescent shell-shock victims, amputees, and similar cases. I think it was not long after this that the Canadian Government introduced conscription; but I may be wrong. It may have been before this.

Another View
of Burma Park

THE DAY FOLLOWING the drunken orgy of Christmas, I was told I
was to be an instructor at a special school of flying at Gosport. I
looked up Gosport and found it was only about fifty miles from
Burma Park, and although I had some doubts about my abilities
as an instructor, I accepted joyfully. Fifty miles. Images of myself
strolling arm in arm with Katherine about its velvet lawns, col-
lecting ferns with Mr Lewis, riding with Robert, and swapping
insults with Mrs Lewis unrolled before my dreamy gaze. Burma
Park ... For the hundredth time I wondered what it was that drew
me to that place, that oasis of sanity in a world gone crackers ...
I sighed pleasurably and picked up a letter. As usual the mail
had been held up and several missives from Canada had arrived
together.

The first was from a farmer's wife in Beamington. She had been
at my farewell party. It was the first letter she had written.

I couldn't make head or tail of it. After a protracted essay about
barley, feed, and peas she hoped I hadn't taken it too badly. Everyone had, of course, been terribly shocked and was still talking
about it. There was a new minister, but he wasn't half as good,
in her opinion, as the Reverend Mr Bandy had been. But that
others –

Perplexed, I put the letter aside and picked up the next. It was
from a Mrs Henry Proddle, and it took me several seconds to work

out that this was my old girlfriend Mabel. It was the first time she had written as well. 'My Dear Bartholomew: I just wanted to drop you a note to let you know how sincerely we sympathize with you in your misfortune, and that despite everything we are still your friends. I am speaking for myself and Father and Mother, but I am sure Henry feels the same way. If we can be of any assistance, do not hesitate to call on us. We shall not be found wanting, within reason. We want to assure you that none of the unpleasant things that are being said –'

What unpleasant things? What on earth were they all talking about?

I read the next two pages. There was no clue.

'I am not, of course, trying to excuse or condone, but as Daddy says, we are all human, and –'

I looked through the remaining letters. There was one from my Aunt Barbara. She was my great-aunt really, and old enough to speak her mind.

'Dear Bartholomew, I have just learned from your foolish mother that she has not yet told you about your father, so I am writing to do so before the other busybodies of Beamington get to you with their spurious sympathy. I hope you will not feel too hurt and shocked over the sorry business, Bartholomew. Remember that God in his wisdom –' I skipped this bit. 'Your father was discovered in the cornfields late one night with Denise Webster, who, I gather, has morals as loose as Beamington's tongues, in circumstances making it rather difficult to credit the Reverend Bandy's somewhat pathetic protestations that the girl had fainted and he had been engaged in loosening her apparel in order to revive her. Apparently this had been going on since the middle of 1916.'

Middle of 1916? Good God, that was before I left!

'They had gone so far as to rent a room in Ottawa. Your father apparently had been supporting her financially since late this fall. I won't go into any further details except that in the circumstances it was impossible to hush it up.

'Apparently your mother had known about it for some time but had failed to assert herself sufficiently to have the liaison ended. Of course, as soon as the affair became public she was forced to act. She is living at home still, the object of a nauseating country-wide curiosity, and she is putting up with it with remarkable calm and dignity. Your father, naturally, has resigned his position and is living, alone, as far as we know, in Montreal, from where he writes numerous letters to your mother. However, she refuses to read any of them –'

I dropped the letter and stared at the wall. In the light of the candle two earwigs were making passes at each other. The hut trembled under some distant concussion.

My father and Denise? Caught in the act with Denise? Denise? My father?

I pictured my father, his noble silvery hair, his aesthetic hands, his long, haughty, condescending face.

I pictured Denise as I had last seen her – dark, pretty, scornful eyes... I tried to put them together but they wouldn't conjoin. I struggled, but they remained immiscible.

How humiliating.

A thought occurred to me. He must actually have had a modicum of sex appeal. Denise, loose though she was, had not been in the habit of sleeping with just anyone.

How extraordinary. Come to think of it, how hilarious!

I started to snort and convulse. Two or three others also reading their mail around the mess fire looked up.

'What's the joke?'

After a moment they began to get irritated.

'What the hell are you laughing at?'

'Just some – news from home,' I gurgled.

Then remembering I hadn't finished Great-Aunt Barbara's letter, I took it up again, avid.

'It will be a long time before she ceases to be an object of pity in Beamington. Your mother, I mean. While I personally could tolerate any amount of curiosity, I doubt if I could stand what went

285

with it, the pity, or perhaps scorn would be more appropriate. However, she seems to be bearing up quite well.

'I'm sorry to have to break this news to you, Bartholomew, but obviously someone has to do it. I know it is useless to commiserate with you in your natural distress, but I hope you will not take it too badly, and try to understand –'

I put the letter aside and read the last one, which was a semi-illiterate scrawl advising me not to come back to Beamington if I knew what was good for me, signed, a Churchgoer.

I went to bed early and brooded about it. My mother and I had been about as far apart as it was possible for kin to be, not out of animosity or conflict: it was just the way we were. She had raised me out of a sense of duty but not, so far as I'd ever been able to tell, out of anything else. I had long faced this fact with my usual phlegmaticism, just as I now faced the fact that I could bring no sympathy to her now, even if I'd felt any. It was heartless of me; but there it was.

I had no home now. Oh, well.

Then I thought about Burma Park, and realized at last what it meant to me. It was the only house in which I'd ever felt at ease.

At home, in fact.

This was quite a revelation (everyone should have at least one revelation to break the monotony of his life), and I fumbled around in the dark for a cigarette, and lighted it with clumsy fingers.

Of course. That was it. My mother had by nature always been cold and withdrawn; I suppose she lacked that one quality, that highest virtue that woman can possess: tenderness. And my father had always been fundamentally – indifferent? I guess so.

I remembered my feelings when I left home to go to the University of Toronto. I hadn't understood them any more than I'd understood the sensation that swept over me when I started out for Europe. I knew now. It was unutterable relief at getting away from it all.

Yes, of course. It also explained my feelings for Captain Karley and my old company dugout. They had cared about me there. They had been my family.

Karley had done his best to look after all his officers and men, but he had been especially solicitous – concerned, anyway – about me. He had, in a way, been ... tender.

Logically, I should have felt the same way about the squadron; but I didn't, partly because in the R.F.C. it was not done to get closely involved with others. On the contrary, there was a not quite deliberate effort to keep friendships superficial. 'Old Swiss's gone west. Hard luck, but the silly bugger should have watched his tail. Waiter, two whiskies.' The squadron, like purgatory, was only a way station. Whereas, although one's demise was no further away in the front-line company dugout, you were one of a close unit. Yes ...

But even then I didn't fully realize that my feeling for Burma Park was really rooted in a warmth and affection for its inhabitants, that reserved, civilized, slightly dotty family, the first people I'd ever met who had discerned the hunger for something or other behind the curious facade of my face and personality.

Two days before 1918 the decline and fall of Bart Brandy began to draw to a close. That morning, following the inevitable binge, everyone came to see me off in the C.O.'s car. The major said he was sorry to see me go, but he looked pretty cheerful all the same. As the squadron's apple orchard, naked, wet and dripping, faded from sight I had a lump in my throat. But this was caused by a hazelnut from a packet somebody had received in a food parcel rather than by any feelings of sentiment. Most pilots professed to regret their departure from the dear old squadron but, quite apart from my joy at the prospect of seeing Burma Park again, I was not sorry to go. The air war had dwindled to a drab silence broken only by the spasmodic coughing of Archie. Bad weather had closed in; and what was there to do when one wasn't flying except make one's liver stone hard with booze? Milestone had been posted to Home Establishment. There was nobody left I could really talk to.

And anyway, I wasn't one to look back; except when Tripes, Pfalz, and Albatroses were around.

Two days later, carried away by my elation at being back at Burma Park, I proposed to Katherine and was accepted. That's when my troubles *really* began.

One of My Pupils

MICHAEL MANSERGH STARTED yelling again, over Southsea.

'Yes?' I inquired. 'Is there something you wanted to say?'

'The airplane's in a spin,' he shouted. 'What should I be doing about it?'

'The thing to do,' I replied, 'is to get it out of the spin – and fairly soon, as you have only half a minute left before you crash onto Southsea Pier.'

It was true. There was only half a minute left before the aircraft we were chatting in crashed headlong on to Southsea Pier.

'Yes, but how?'

'Well,' I said, noting that under stress his Irish accent became more pronounced, 'they say the simplest method is to centralize the controls with the stick forward.'

The dual controls in front of me wiggled about somewhat ineffectually. We were now only seconds away from destroying the pier. As this was bound to irritate Southsea Corporation – they had recently spent a lot of money on restoration work, including the installation of a brand-new telescope for watching girls undressing on the beach with – I thought I had better take a hand. Abandoning the telephone, or Gosport tube as it was called – a useful, one-way instrument that allowed the instructor to taunt his student but prevented the student from employing the same means for his reply (though of course there was nothing to stop him from turning and hollering over his shoulder or making rude gestures with his gauntlets) – I attempted to take my own advice; but Michael was gripping the controls too tightly. We fought a brief battle for ascendancy in the cockpits. It was not an easy struggle, as Michael was a big fellow with a determined grip, rendered even firmer by his alarm at the sight of the pier hurtling up to meet us.

'Leggo,' I shrieked into the howling wind, keeping my thumb pressed on the button switch and hauling back on the stick as if attempting to lever out one of your typical Ottawa Valley stumps.

With only a few feet to spare, the Mono-Avro pulled out of the dive and shot over the upturned faces of two elderly fishermen in sou'westers who were gripping the pier rail with manifestly whitening knuckles. The wings groaned and flexed dangerously as the biplane clawed again at the sky. But even now our tribulations were not at an end. When I removed my thumb to restore power to the Gnome Monosoupape engine, nothing happened. My pupil was also pressing the engine button and was refusing to let go.

Having survived a spin, we were now in danger of stalling into the drink.

Fortunately, just as the nose started to drop for the last time, he remembered to remove his thumb. The rotary engine underwent a fit of coughing, then began to roar again, and to spray castor oil all over the place. The two-seater staggered over the beach, where a bunch of children were jumping up and down and waving excitedly, presumably under the impression that we had been practicing some clever Gosport manoeuvre.

They became positively ecstatic as Michael seized the controls again by brute force and attempted to climb sideways. At the same time, I became aware that he was shouting indignantly over the noise of the engine, 'Chroist, Bandy, what kind of trick is that to play on a fellow? Some instructor you are, putting the fear of death into one of your pupils.'

How did he think I was feeling? I'd never had a student like Michael before. He had already done eight hours dual, which was well over the average; but he still used the controls as if he were fighting off clouds of fruit flies.

When at last we were flying more or less straight and level, I stuck my head over the side, partly to make sure we weren't headed in the wrong direction, say toward the Bay of Biscay, but mostly to dry the perspiration that was dotting my face; a face, incidentally, that was rapidly taking on a look of utter determination.

This time I *would* wash him out, I thought, and no arguments about it. I would be firm but tactful. 'You're an utter washout,' I would tell him, as soon as we got back to Fort Grange, if we ever did. 'You're an abominable pilot, Mansergh, who will never master the art of flight in a thousand years. You'll kill yourself if you go on this way.

'My gosh,' I'd say, 'even the thought of your being let loose as an instructor' – Gosport was a school for instructors –'is enough to make me consider going over to the enemy. When you're not wrestling the stick as if it were a python, you're letting the plane fly itself. Take the last time we landed. You distinctly gave me the impression *you* were handling the controls. How was I to know you were clinging to the sides with your eyes shut, reciting litanies and things.'

No, that wouldn't do. It might reflect, somehow, on my abilities as an instructor. 'Michael,' I would say, 'you've survived three years of war; why give up now?' I would say.

Captured at Mons in 1914, Michael had been one of the soldiers whom the Irish traitor Sir Roger Casement had attempted to woo from his allegiance to the Crown. He had answered Casement's call for volunteers for the German-sponsored Irish Brigade by booting Sir Roger smartly in the rear, an action that had earned the patriotic Irishman a week in solitary confinement, and the sympathy of the German guards, who had been shocked to the core by Casement's activities.

Subsequently Michael had broken out of the prisoner-of-war camp, made his way through the wilds of Mecklenburg to the Baltic, stolen a boat, and rowed all the way to Denmark, arriving home in the middle of 1916 to receive a Military Medal, a commission, and a month's leave in Tipperary, or some such place that it was a long way to go to.

'Michael,' I would say, finally, 'go back to that stores depot of yours and resume your former career of seducing the Liverpool colleens and flogging army blankets on the black market. Be sensible, man.'

On returning from leave, Michael had been put in charge of a small army clothes depot (or, to be precise, a small depot of *large* army clothes). But, for some reason, he had not been happy in Liverpool, and had spent most of 1917 trying to get out of this cushy job and into the R.F.C., where the average life expectancy in combat was now approximately three weeks.

Satisfied with my forthcoming efforts to dissuade him from breaking his neck, I took out a bar of chocolate and nibbled at it contentedly.

The Mono-Avro continued to drone along the south coast of England, flapping its wings slightly as it collided with a cloud. I looked over the side again, to make sure we were headed in the right direction. Portsmouth docks were directly below. A narrow warship was steaming slowly out of harbour, followed by a confetti of gulls.

Now the city was passing underneath. In the wandering gaps between the buildings, laughably called streets, the populace could be seen scurrying about their business of shopping for Brussels sprouts, pinching cobs from the coal depots, or taking their Christmas presents to the pawnbrokers.

Michael also turned and looked over the side, presenting his left profile, the good one; though in fact he was a handsome fellow even face on, with a dimpled chin and the kind of hazel eyes and long eyelashes that made women oxyacetylene workers come all over queer.

Catching my eye, he flashed me a carefree grin. But I wasn't to be put off by his old blarney, and I began again to rehearse what I would say when we landed. It would be difficult, but after that last lark I had no alternative. It really was an achievement, upsetting a Mono-Avro that way. Nobody would believe it back at base.

Perhaps I'd better not mention it, then. The commandant would be bound to ask what I was doing while Michael was busy working out a method of spinning an Avro 504J. The commandant, who glowered a lot, was an unpredictable sort of fellow ...

A scout plane suddenly appeared ahead on a collision course. Automatically I snatched for the controls, but the other plane turned and drifted past, above us. The adjutant waved lazily over the side.

I could tell it was the adjutant because of the hideous paint scheme of his Sopwith Camel. At Gosport we instructors were allowed to decorate our personal mounts as we pleased. The one that had just gone past was a particularly vile specimen. The adj. had done it up in bile green and canary yellow.

But then, few of the instructors showed much aesthetic sensibility when it came to aircraft *décor*. Captain Potter's personal Camel, for instance, was painted in – I can hardly bring myself to describe it – Burgundy and pea soup, for heaven's sake. I guess my fellow instructors were reacting against the colour bar at the front, where only the regulation chocolate and dope colours were permitted. Still, there was no excuse for colour schemes like that. Red and green, and green and yellow indeed. Why couldn't they emulate *my* tasteful colours – *pink* and green.

I was recalled unpleasantly to duty again as Michael suddenly put the trainer into a steep dive. The engine note rose to a howl.

Here we go again, I thought, and tightened the seat belt another notch.

The sound of the engine must have carried all the way to the airdrome, for as we porpoised downwind, pupils and instructors began to trickle from the huts to see what Michael had in store for them today.

But they were in for a disappointment. I had decided not to let him attempt another landing. Instructors were personally responsible for their training aircraft, and I was already in trouble because

Michael had broken my propeller a few days before. Incidentally, I still hadn't quite worked out how he'd managed that, as Mono-Avros wore skids between the wheels that made it *impossible* to damage the propeller.

So I called him up on the Gosport tube and said, 'After that little episode over the sea I don't suppose you'll want to try a landing today, will you, Michael, I don't suppose?'

'Course I want to,' he shouted. He sounded confident enough, I must admit. But, then, he had sounded just as confident the day he attempted a forced landing on a ploughed field, *across* the furrows.

'No, you don't,' I wheedled.

'Yes, I do!'

'Tchk,' I said, my lips compressed in a mean line. Then: 'Well… well, if you *have* to, this time would you mind holding off from two feet? Try to remember that it's not good for the undercarriage or my liver to have the machine drop like a stone from thirty feet.'

'And don't I always?' he sang out, not making it entirely clear which method of landing he was referring to. Whereupon he canted the left wing suicidally low toward the ground to turn cross-wind, simultaneously jamming his thumb on the button.

The noise of the engine died away, to be replaced by the whistle of the wind in my larynx. He had taken off power prematurely again.

But I was so fed up complaining about this sort of mistake that I sat back, tightened the safety harness still farther, and waited for the worst. He continued to glide across the wet, January wind, allowing it to push him farther and farther from the airdrome.

Surely, *surely* it was obvious to him that if he didn't restore power fairly soon we'd be ending up in the sewage farm near the Members' Bridge?

Apparently not. The Avro continued to whistle fearfully toward the frosty earth. I reached for the tube, but then sat back again with a mulish expression. The devil with him, I thought. If he wants to disgrace himself again, then let him. It would teach him a lesson.

So, mouth set in a thin red line, I waited for the worst.

But just after he had turned, far too low, on to final, an updraft caught the plane and flung it skyward, restoring it to its proper altitude. My hands and feet poised themselves millimetres from the controls in case he did anything to cancel out this sheer good luck, but he sailed serenely on, as if the use of updrafts was an integral part of his landing technique. The grass, still speckled with the New Year's snow, rose into focus. He jerked the stick back roughly. The Avro settled neatly on to the grass for a perfect landing. I was furious.

'First-class landing, that,' the commandant said. 'Put him down for solo tomorrow morning, Bandy. He's obviously ready.'

Earning Another Wound Stripe

MY ENGAGEMENT TO Katharine Lewis had excited some interest among her family's circle of acquaintances – except that, being well bred, they weren't in the habit of looking either excited or interested. So when I was invited to spend the weekend at the residence of the Rackinghams, some posh London friends of the Lewises, I reckoned I'd been included out of curiosity rather than hospitality; to give Lord Rackingham and his missus a chance to inspect Katherine's brand-new fiancé, and wonder what on earth she saw in him.

'Lord Rackingham ... The name's vaguely familiar,' I said to Mr Lewis.

'It should be,' he said. 'He's your boss.'

Ah, yes, of course. The Royal Flying Corps and the Royal Naval Air Service were in process of combining to form the Royal Air Force, and Rackingham had recently been appointed Air Minister.

Bland House was in Mayfair, opposite a small public gardens with wrought-iron gates kept securely locked, to protect the vegetation. It was a grey, classical pile with a semicircular driveway and a stone balustrade running the length of the façade. The steps to the front door were guarded by a couple of fancy pedestals. There were puddles of rainwater in the flower beds. The shrubbery dripped disconsolately.

I was shown into a grey marble hall by a grey marble butler. A fair number of guests had already arrived, judging by the whinnying and braying noises coming from the drawing room. The lady of the house herself came out to greet me.

'My husband will be down in a few minutes, Mr Bandy,' she said, gesturing limply at a bunch of scrofulous cupids on the ceiling. She was wearing a gown that seemed to be made up of panels from a box kite. A small hand emerged from between two of the panels. I shook it cautiously, as it didn't seem too firmly attached anywhere.

'So you're Katherine's fiancé,' she said vaguely. I admitted it straight out, and an animated silence ensued.

Lady Rackingham proceeded to gaze around the hall as if she'd seen this place before, somewhere. A typical English draft fluttered her panels, increasing her resemblance to a kite. I couldn't help wondering how she'd look at the end of a piece of string.

'The Lewises were supposed to be here at two o'clock, but they haven't turned up yet,' she said, starting slightly as she caught sight of her butler. He was waiting patiently beside my cheap, colonial valise. He had placed it in the darkest part of the hall.

Anticipating an imminent ascent, the butler picked up the valise, but put it down again when his mistress went on in her vague tones, 'They're motoring up to town, aren't they?'

'I believe so, Lady Rackingham.'

'Hubert's here, though. I expect you know him. He's in the Army, too.'

'Hubert? Uh... ?'

'Hubert Ferris. He's Commander-in-Chief in Ireland now, I believe.'

At this, a shriek of fear rang through the house. For a moment I thought it was me. Generals often had that effect. But it turned out to have been caused by a small girl, who came running along the corridor into the hall, pursued by an undersized knight.

Seeing Lady Rackingham, the little girl ran and hid behind her, clutching her skirts fearfully. The knight, wearing a helmet and carrying a rusty but dangerous-looking sword, skidded to a halt.

'Don't clutch, Sybil,' Lady Rackingham said. 'Claud wouldn't hurt you, would you, dear?'

The knight raised his visor. A sullen twelve-year-old face appeared.

'This is my daughter Sybil,' Lady Rackingham said as the girl peeked at me mistrustfully.

I murmured something, and beamed at the child. She promptly disappeared again behind her mother's skirts.

'And that's Claud,' Lady Rackingham said. 'He's visiting us from Chester.'

'Well, well, so your name's Claud, is it?' I said, pulling on one of those sickly smiles with which one was supposed to favour children. 'Having lots of fun with your little friend, eh?' I didn't like the look of him at all.

Claud looked down at his sword, then dug the tip into the marble floor and started to lever up one of the blocks.

'He was going to cut off my pigtails,' Sybil said tearfully.

'Now, that isn't a very nice thing to do, is it?' I said to Claud, but smiling to show I wasn't really being too censorious. I reached out to chuck him under the chin in avuncular fashion. Claud promptly snapped down the visor, almost amputating two of my fingers.

'He's mean,' Sybil shouted.

Claud shouted back, 'And I *am* going to cut off your rotten pigtails!' He raised the sword. The little girl shrieked again, and ran into a grandfather clock and slammed the door.

'Leave Sybil alone, Claud,' Lady Rackingham said. 'Remember, you're a guest here.'

'I didn't want to come,' Claud said.

'All the same, dear, you must remember to behave like a –'

Claud cut her off. 'You a pilot?' he asked, raising the visor again.

'Yes,' I said, still feeling a bit faint.

'I bet you're a rotten one.'

'I probably am now,' I said, holding my fingers under my arm and wincing pointedly.

'You talk strangely, in my opinion,' Claud said in a lofty sort of voice.

'Claud.'

'Horse face.'

I untucked my crushed fingers. Claud retreated toward the corridor. 'Horse face!' he shouted again, then turned and strolled off, dragging the rusty sword across the marble.

Lady Rackingham gave me a long-suffering look, perhaps not noticing that I already had one. As she fluttered limply over to the grandfather clock to extricate her daughter, the butler picked up my valise and started for the stairs, but was foiled again, this time by a sudden thump and a crash from the front of the house.

'That'll be the Lewises,' I said.

It was. They had just arrived at the front entrance in their Ford Tourer.

Robert Lewis was in the front passenger seat, Katherine and her father were in the rear. They were all glaring at Mrs Lewis. She was perched behind the steering wheel, looking flushed and slightly dishevelled after the trip from the depths of Berkshire; and also because she had crashed into not just one but both of the pedestals that guarded the front steps of the house.

We inspected the damage in silence. One of the stone balls that had been sitting on top of its pedestal had been knocked off, and the other pedestal was standing askew. Even as we watched, its ornament, too, slowly rolled off. It fell on to the hood of the car with a crash. Mrs Lewis started slightly.

We all gazed at the stone ball as it sat there, half embedded in the hood. Katherine glanced at me, then looked away quickly. Mr Lewis stared expressionlessly in front of him as if he weren't really there but was attending an interesting Foreign Office conference on South American bauxite. As for Robert, he was looking positively matricidal. It was his car. He had purchased it only a couple of weeks before from a brother officer who had wanted to settle his affairs, having had a premonition that he was not much longer for this life, as indeed proved to be the case, for a few days later he was posted to Taliaferro Field, Texas.

Mrs Lewis' large hat had tipped forward on to her nose. She thrust it back grandly before turning to Robert.

'Well, I warned you not to buy a car,' she said severely. 'I told you they weren't safe.'

By then, several other guests had emerged from the house and were standing about at the top of the steps, gaping at the scene of carnage. Among them was a bulky man in an untidy suit and a wing collar. He had a large, bull-like face with heavy-lidded eyes, and hefty moustaches above a pair of fleshy lips. These were now decidedly compressed.

He stepped forward to study the disarranged pedestals. His expression suggested that he not only owned them, but had been rather proud of his balls.

'That's all right,' he said quickly, thinking he was forestalling an embarrassed apology. 'Don't worry about it, it's all right.' He forced a laugh.

'All right?' Mrs Lewis said, gazing up at him in haughty astonishment. 'All right? It's not all right, at all. Look at our car. It's *dented*.'

Lord Rackingham swallowed as best he could inside his tight wing collar. 'Most unfortunate, most unfortunate,' he said. 'I suppose they were rather in the way, those ... those pedestals.' The pedestals were a good ten feet from the driveway.

'Of course they're in the way, Harry. You know perfectly well it's an absurd place to put those pedestals,' Mrs Lewis thundered, flinging aside a dozen yards of veil. 'Not to mention that oversized cannon ball.'

'Yes, it is, rather ... rather ...' her host said, staring blindly at the stone ball that was nestling on the car hood.

'Be so good as to remove it this instant,' Mrs Lewis said. 'We cannot possibly drive home with a cannon ball buried in our motorcar. It could cause panic throughout the country, or at the very least considerable apprehension among the more impressionable of the widows and agricultural workers.'

'Yes of course,' Lord Rackingham said, and started to hurry down the steps; but then slowed, and after a moment, said, 'Yes, I'll get one of the maids to remove it ...'

'Do so,' Mrs Lewis said, and gave him a curt but approving nod, as if after some initial incompetence he was now proceeding more or less on the right lines. Then, clasping her hands imperiously in her lap, she waited.

I hurried forward to open the car door for her.

'Ah, Bartholomew, you have arrived before us,' she said.

'Yes, Mrs Lewis,' I said, as I helped her down into the nearest flower bed. I turned to assist Katherine, and nodded in a friendly way at Robert; but he was still glaring through the windscreen.

There was a hum of conversation from the guests assembled at the top of the steps. Among them was a general. He was a man with a mottled complexion and almost no chin, which somehow drew the attention to his worst feature, a pair of bulbous and faded eyes that looked as if they had been boiled in urine. For some reason he was looking triumphantly at Mr Lewis, as if he'd just scored a subtle point against the Foreign Office.

In the background, the London traffic hooted and grumbled, and moisture dripped from the rhododendrons. I became aware that Lady Rackingham was performing introductions. Hearing my name mentioned I hurried forward to bob and smile and shake every hand in sight. Unfortunately I got out of synchronization at one point, and found myself murmuring replies to one of the ladies while being introduced to the next guest. 'How d'you do, Major Auchinflint,' I said to one old dowager, beaming straight into her angry-looking eyes. But generally I acquitted myself not too badly; until I reached the general.

'Maud, can't we finish the introductions inside?' Lord Rackingham said, a bit snappily. 'It's freezing out here.'

Obediently, several of the guests began to shiver, and two or three of them edged back into the house.

'Captain Bandy,' his wife said vaguely. 'General Sir Hubert Ferris.'

Determined to make the best possible impression, I ploughed eagerly through the rhododendrons and offered my hand with as sycophantic a smile as I could muster. As the stone balustrade was in the way, and as I couldn't reach over it, I had to thrust my hand between two of the little stone pillars.

I suppose I should have gone round the balustrade, past Robert's car, and up the steps, but this seemed an unnecessary amount of activity for such a minor salutation, so, as I say, I reached up through the balustrade. My hand emerged on the far side, and wiggled about a bit.

The general regarded the hand stuck through the stonework with such supercilious disdain that the hand seemed to wither and curl up like a spent lucifer. As it disappeared shame-fingeredly into the stonework again, the general turned and walked off with a *Pshaw*.

It didn't help in the least when a moment later I caught sight of Claud smiling spitefully at my humiliated countenance from the front door.

It was a good job he wasn't within reach, or I'd have taken it out on him with a vengeance.

At a Posh Dinner

By THEN THE butler had tired of waiting for me and had gone off to look through the nearest keyhole. Accordingly a maidservant was deputized to carry my valise upstairs.

She was still grumbling as she manhandled the spare bed into my room. 'One of these days I'll just pack up and leave,' she panted, as she dumped a half-ton mattress on to it with a reverberating crash.

It appeared that apart from the cook, the butler, the valet, the odd-job man, and the chauffeur, she was the only servant remaining in Lord Rackingham's employ, the others having given up domestic service for the comparatively idle life of the heavy munitions worker.

When she had gone I unpacked a few things, then strolled round reading the walls. The room had once been a nursery, judging by the graffiti *(Nanny is a sod)*. Then I went over to the window and stared down into the lowering garden, thinking of the uncouth impression I must have made on the particular guests in general, and the general in particular.

It was too bad, it really was. One of my most determined New Year resolutions had been to curb my disorderly proclivities. I had resolved that from now on I would treat my superior officers with the respect they deserved. And now look: I had done it again. I had made another Exhibition of Myself.

The maddening thing was that until this afternoon the resolution had been triumphantly successful. I had not had a single run-in with a brass hat all year. Mind you, it was still only January; but still. Why, only last week I had made an unforgettable impression on none other than the Chief of the Air Staff himself.

He had come to visit us at Gosport on Friday afternoon, and after a tour of inspection had come stumping into the mess bar with the commandant for a couple of quick snifters before dinner. During the general conversation that followed, my respectful submissions on such matters as wing organization, formation take-offs, and egg timers had made a remarkable impression on him. 'I feel, sir,' I'd said, pattering toward him over the gleaming brown linoleum and looking at him with a sincere look, 'that under the present system a lot of unnecessary time is lost in assembling the various flights in the air. Sometimes after he's taken off, a new pilot can't even find the other old beans in his flight and has to buzz about all over the place, searching high and low for them, looking under clouds and so forth – wasting time. With formation take-offs, or takes-off if you prefer, we should be able to obviate this delay.' Obviate – that was a new word I'd learned. For a while I'd used it on every possible occasion, and occasionally some impossible ones.

The great man nodded and turned to say something to the commandant, who was glaring at me ferociously, for some reason.

'Then there's the problem of egg timers,' I went on.

The general turned sharply. 'Egg timers?' he asked.

'Yes, sir. You know – for timing eggs. To obviate guesswork. And that's the root of the problem,' I went on, treading on his heels as he began to edge farther along the bar counter. 'The Dawn Patrol hard-boiled egg, for instance, is – would you mind not kicking me, Potter – invariably hard-boiled. The squadron cooks obviously haven't been supplied with egg timers, obviously. Now, it's to obviate this lack of egg timers –'

'Yes, I understand,' the Chief of the Air Staff said, turning the corner of the bar counter and thumping slightly against the wainscoting at the end.

' – that I'm proposing some rethinking in the supply department, re eggs. I happen to like my eggs soft-boiled,' I explained, sidling close to him. 'And I think if you took a survey, sir, you'd find that as many as, oh 79 per cent of the pilots prefer their eggs soft-boiled.'

'Indeed. Yes, well –'

'I mean, hard-boiled eggs are all right for salads and things like that, but –'

'Quite, quite. Salads,' he said, as the commandant's face began to turn an unusual shade of burgundy.

'I mean, all the cooks have to do, to obviate this state of affairs, is to *time* the things properly,' I said.

'Yes, yes,' the general agreed as he slid along the wall.

'And that's why I thought, sir, if you could distribute a few more egg timers to the front-line squadrons –'

But the Chief of the Air Staff had to hurry off to London at that point, even though the place of honour had been set for him at the dining table. He must have been pretty peckish by the time he got home. Still, I'd obviously made quite an impression on him. I was sure that he would obviate the situation as soon as possible.

By now it was almost dark in the ex-nursery. There was a low growl of traffic from the street beyond the public gardens. By doubling my nose against the window pane I could just make out the open tops of the double-decker buses through the stark tracery of the trees. In the distance a searchlight fingered the sky thoughtfully.

I had just drawn the curtain and switched on the light when there was a tap at the door, and Katherine came in. She had changed into a long white gown, and looked pale, delicate, and extremely beautiful in spite of, or perhaps even because of, the slight squint in her dark eyes.

'Well, you've made your usual impression, Bartholomew,' she said, offering her lips for a kiss. 'I overheard two of the guests talking about you in hushed tones.'

'Please don't tell me what they said. Things are bad enough as it is.'

'You mean the general snubbing you? You don't want to worry about that, darling. You know what they say: *Nil carborundum illegitimus.*'

'What does that mean?'

'Don't let the bastards grind you down,' she said, and looked pleased when I stared at her in a shocked way.

'Papa's not much taken with him either,' she went on, pirouetting to see if her dress would flare. 'That's the main reason Papa's here, by the way.'

'Because he isn't very taken with Ferris?'

'*No.* Because he has to talk to him.' She tiptoed over to the door, and closed it softly. 'Papa's been trying to track him down for weeks,' she whispered. 'Sir Hubert's in charge of Ireland, I suppose you know, and the Foreign Office isn't too happy at the way he's running things there. They're worried about American opinion or something. But Sir Hubert refuses to go along to the F.O., to listen to reason – or even to Papa. Every time Pa tries to get in touch with him, Sir Hubert hides in his club, or pretends he's ill, or sometimes even goes to Dublin.'

'What does your father want to talk to him about?'

'Well, the trouble is, Sir Hubert's a strong Unionist.'

'I never knew generals had a union.'

'A Northern Ireland Unionist, silly. They're against giving Home Rule to Catholic Ireland. Sir Hubert detests the southern Irish, and the F.O.'s afraid he's going to stir up trouble in Dublin again, just when they've started to calm down after the Easter Rebellion. Papa's supposed to speak firmly to him about it.'

'So that's why he's here,' she ended. 'Lord Rack arranged it for him.'

'Your father has Irish affairs on his plate now, does he?'

'Yes. It's getting him down terribly.'

She came close, and put her arms around me, and leaned her face against my chest 'Oh, Bart,' she said tremulously.

'Wot?'

'Kiss me, you great, blank-faced colonial upstart.'

At the dinner table I managed to keep well clear of the general. The fact that Lady Rackingham had placed me at the foot of the table was, of course, a considerable help. I found myself between Katherine and another young woman, who talked as if her mouth was filled with an inferior brand of wartime toffee. I think she said her name was Lucrezia Borgia, but I may be wrong about that.

Halfway down on the opposite side sat Major Auchinflint. Throughout the meal he addressed most of his remarks to the head of the table, and taking his cue from Sir Hubert, he behaved as if I were a tailor's dummy that had been placed at the dining table to fill an unexpected gap.

But I forgave him. After all, he couldn't help it, being a major. I'd never met a major who wasn't thoroughly thick and awkward. Captains were all right – after all, I was one – and lieutenant-colonels could sometimes be relied upon, but majors were invariably pesky, insecure creatures, occupying as they did the no man's land between the settled brass hat and the jolly decent junior officer.

Beside Auchinflint sat his wife, who had a mass of black hair, sharp brown eyes, and a moral expression. She looked like one of those stringy, sarcastic Englishwomen, and I might have taken an instant dislike to her had she not behaved so warmly toward Katherine between the soup and the fish.

'Katherine tells me you're a horse,' she said across the table.

I looked offendedly at my fiancée; but apparently Mrs Auchinflint (pronounced Afflunt) hadn't quite finished her sentence because of a frog in her throat 'Horseman,' she amended.

'Yes,' I said.

That was the extent of our social intercourse that weekend.

Seated on her right hand was Robert Lewis, who was wearing his brooding look again; though what he had to be unhappy about

I don't know, as he had just been posted to Home Defence, at an airdrome near Ilford, in Essex: a well-deserved rest, for he had been flying at the front since 1916, first in observation machines, then as a scout pilot. He had, I noticed, a bar to his M.C.

As Katherine and I whispered seditiously at one end of the table, a subdued altercation was developing at the other. The general, still in a bad temper after his conference with Mr Lewis, had become irritated enough to break the rule that politics, like sex and the lower classes, should not be discussed in the presence of the ladies.

He had started on the government the moment Lord Rackingham had been called from the table to take a telephone call from Downing Street.

'I was talkin' to Robbie last week,' he said, looking down the table at Auchinflint.

The major jerked his head attentively. He really did look extraordinarily like an ostrich. I could quite easily picture him with his rump in the air and his head in the Sahara.

'Know how many men Lloyd George is keeping in the country doing sweet nothing? D'you know how many? One and a half million!'

The general nodded his head triumphantly. Auchinflint looked suitably appalled.

'There's Dougie in France, desperately short, crying out for more men. And that, that frock is holdin' back one and a half million of them! In spite of the Russians being out of the fight' – he glared at Lewis as if the Russian Revolution were all his fault –'and the Eyeties done for, and the French just about ready to give up as well –'

'And the Yankees nowhere in sight,' Auchinflint put in.

'Exactly! What in God's name does the man think he's playin' at?' Sir Hubert blared, suppressing a belch and rapping the wall of his chest as if to silence a noisy neighbour.

Robert caught my eye and smiled sardonically. Mr Lewis continued to gaze silently into his wineglass, his face flushed.

Sir Hubert's lips slid aside, revealing half a dozen teeth of assorted sizes. He started to shake his head in a palsied sort of way, as if trying to dislodge a stubborn wad of wax from his earhole.

He was obviously preparing to say something highly amusing. Everybody waited with varying degrees of expectancy.

Two or three times he opened his mouth to speak, but each time snickered loudly instead. Finally he shouted, 'Heard an interestin' story about the P.M. the other day!'

Auchinflint laughed in anticipation and said, 'Did you, sir?'

The general twitched again. 'During one of those Hun Gotha raids, you know.'

'Oh, yes?'

'Lloyd George came into the, oh, some blasted ministry or other. What ministry was it? Anyway, there were a couple of typists there – typin', I suppose. During one of the Gotha raids on London, it was.' Sir Hubert's eyes were alight with pleasure. 'And our prime minister, our prime minister, mind you, was so pale – they fainted! The typists fainted! Because he was shivering in sheer funk!'

The general spluttered and gasped, his mottled face growing scarlet. Finally he burst out with, 'Typists thought some calamitous news had just come in, don't you know! That's why they fainted!'

He heaved with laughter. Then, in case we hadn't got the point: 'The rotten little Welsh frock was terrified – terrified of the Gothas!'

There was a sycophantic chortle from Auchinflint. Sir Hubert stared triumphantly at Lewis. Lady Rackingham looked vaguely displeased.

Twisting a napkin ring round his finger, Mr Lewis said somewhat agitatedly, 'The P.M.'s a highly strung man of extraordinary imagination, Sir Hubert. Anyway, the point is, he carries on in spite of his fears, doesn't he?'

Sir Hubert glared at Lewis, then grunted with such disdain that Katherine and Robert flushed simultaneously. Mrs Lewis' face, as usual, remained haughtily expressionless.

Robert sat up straight and started to drag in a slow, deep breath, his burning eyes fixed on the general. Lewis looked at him imploringly; Robert was a career officer.

'I saw a most interesting play in London,' I said.

Everybody jumped. I found myself at the intersection of two dozen pairs of wide-open eyes.

'Did you?' somebody said faintly.

'Yes. In London it was,' I said. Realizing I'd already said that, I added, 'Last year. Or was it 1916?'

Nobody seemed to know.

'*The Man Who Went Abroad*, it was called. Very interesting plot, it was. The hero was taking some secret papers to Washington, you see, and a fellow called von Bernstorff was trying to foil him.'

'Count von Bernstorff? The former German Ambassador to Washington?' Lewis asked, looking very grave and attentive.

'Why yes. Did you see the play?'

'No, but von Bernstorff was German Ambassador there from 1908 until last year.'

'You mean there's a real von Bernstorff?' I asked.

'Yes.'

'What was he doing in this play then?' I asked.

'How should *we* know,' Mrs Lewis thundered, '*You're* the one who saw it.'

'Yes, that's right.' I cleared my throat a couple of times, then: 'Actually the play was really about the hero. Kit Brent, who was pretending to be Lord Goring, you see, and –'

'Lord Goring? Of the British Cabinet?' Mrs Lewis boomed.

'Uh … yes,' I said uncertainly, wondering if she was trying to make things difficult for me. I was pretty sure that Lord Goring in the play was entirely fictitious.

'I know him well,' Mrs Lewis said. 'A charming man. Charming.'

'Are you sure we're discussing the same Lord Goring?' I asked. 'The one I mean was in this interesting play called –'

'That's the one,' she said. 'There's not likely to be two Lord Gorings in the cabinet, are there? I hardly think that even Mr Lloyd

George would go to such extremes as to have two Lord Gorings in one cabinet. Things are confused enough, heaven knows.'

Sir Hubert, perhaps feeling that the conversational initiative was being wrested from him, jumped in at this point. 'Exactly,' he said, glaring. Though confused is a charitable description.' He turned to Auchinflint. 'That Welshman –'

'I didn't think Lord Goring was all that confused,' I said to Katherine.

'It's nothing to do with Lord Goring!' Sir Hubert bellowed, refusing to take his eyes off Auchinflint.

'What I don't understand,' Katherine said, 'is why Lloyd George keeps even one Lord Goring in a cabinet. I mean, surely he'd suffocate.'

'It was a liquor cabinet,' Mrs Lewis said. 'After all, you know what Goring's like.'

'But it's Kit Brent we're talking about,' I said. 'He was masquerading as Lord Goring, you see, in order to take these secret papers to –'

'I wasn't talking about Kit Brent, either,' shouted the general, just as our host, looking puzzled at the turn the conversation had taken, slipped unobtrusively into his seat at the head of the table.

'What I also don't understand is where von Bernstorff comes in,' Katherine said.

'Well, he doesn't actually come in at all,' I said. 'He employs this beautiful spy, played by Miss Mabel Hagworth, who is an Austrian spy –'

'Mabel Hagworth doesn't sound like an Austrian name to me,' Mrs Lewis said, her voice rattling the prisms in the chandelier.

'Actually it turned out she wasn't an Austrian spy, but a Dalmatian,' I explained. 'She admitted as much on the promenade deck.'

'I didn't think they allowed dogs on the promenade deck,' Mr Lewis said.

'Well, it wasn't a very high-class ship,' I said. 'In fact it was quite jerry-built, because halfway through Act Two, one of the ventilators fell over. Fortunately it was just made of cardboard, so it wasn't too much of a distraction when it fell ov–'

'What the devil has all this to do with Lloyd Goring?!' Sir Hubert shouted, clutching at his collar.

'Well, sir, it was Lloyd Goring who picked it up,' I said. 'Or Lord Goring. Or to be exact, Kit Brent.'

'Make up your mind,' Robert said.

'It was all three of them,' Katherine said.

'Surely it doesn't take three men to pick up one cardboard ventilator?' Mrs Lewis said severely. 'Really, I don't know what this generation is coming to. When it takes three full-grown Englishmen to pick up one cardboard ventilator, then I should say it is the end of the world as we know it.'

The general's collar was turning sodden. 'What the devil,' he shouted, 'have cardboard ventilators to do with it?!'

'It wasn't the cardboard ventilators, it was that Dalmatian dog that was at the bottom of it,' Mr Lewis murmured. 'Cherchez la dog,' he added significantly. 'Being allowed to run loose and do what it wanted on the promenade deck, it probably weakened the supports of the ventilator. You know what dogs are,' he added.

'Exactly,' Mrs Lewis thundered. 'That's what you get for allowing Dalmatians to run loose on the ship. I shall certainly make a point of not travelling on *that* ship. Whichever one it was.'

Sir Hubert said in a strangled voice, 'I wasn't talkin' about dogs, ventilators, or ships! I was talkin' about Lloyd Goring!'

'Sorry, sir,' I said. 'What was it you were saying about Lloyd Goring?'

'He's an upstart,' he shouted. He took a deep breath, but then slowly let the air out into the silence. 'Bertie was telling me that he... he...' He faltered to a halt, and stared into his congealed dinner, looking a bit disoriented.

After a moment Katherine turned and said, 'Anyway, what happened?'

'What happened when?'

'The play. How did it end?'

'Oh. Well, I'm not too sure, really. I left at the end of Act Two.'

For the first time since we had been introduced, General Sir Hubert Ferris condescended to look directly at me. His mottled face was working and twisting about in a very queer fashion above his vermilion-coloured gullet, under which his thyroid cartilage was bobbing about like a misshapen crab apple, and his plump, ginger-haired knuckles were whitening. Also, wisps of steam seemed to be rising from his collar.

I couldn't quite put my finger on it, but it seemed to me he was in something of a snit.

Deep in Politics

AFTER THE LADIES had withdrawn, there was a strained and stilted conversation that ranged from the dearth of taxicabs to the disgraceful behaviour of Lieutenant Siegfried Sassoon, M.C. According to Sir Reginald Niles, an Air Council member, Sassoon was an infantry officer and war poet ('Not my sort of poems, of course') who had publicly denounced the war the previous July as being evil and unjust. As a result, he had been put away in a neurasthenic hospital in Scotland.

'I didn't hear about that one,' one of the civil servants said.

'It was played down,' Niles grunted. 'The national newspapers have *some* sense of responsibility, after all. Refused to print his letters.'

He glanced toward the head of the table. Lord Rackingham tapped the ash off his cigar and nodded in a bored way. Sir Hubert, who had been glaring and sulking ever since the cardboard ventilator, revived momentarily at this point and said the fellow ought to have been shot instead of being mollycoddled in a madhouse.

As for me, I had the good sense to take no part in this discussion, even though I had nothing to say.

But it didn't save me. As we were on our way to the drawing room to rejoin the ladies, an imposing bulk appeared at my elbow, and Lord Rackingham's voice sounded harshly in my ear. 'I want a word with you,' he said.

Major Auchinflint smirked. He was obviously convinced that I was being taken to our host's study for six of the best.

I shared his opinion, aware that the minister had been regarding me doubtfully throughout the postprandial chinfest, as if he'd been trying to work out who could have invited me, if indeed anyone had.

But it turned out that he merely wanted a private chat before his wife collared him for a round of bridge.

'Loathe the blasted game,' he muttered, as he poured brandy from a cut-glass decanter with a chipped lip. 'Sit down, sit down,' he said impatiently, pointing to a huge leather armchair. I sat down. The cushion wheezed as I sank slowly toward the floor.

Lord R. took the armchair's twin brother, cupping his glass in large, plump hands as he rounded up his thoughts. They must have been widely scattered, for a lengthy pause ensued.

I filled the time by gazing around the library, which was lined with *The Anatomy of Melancholy*. On a leather-topped side table was a photograph of his son in uniform, arranged so that Lord R. could look at it whenever he was seated at his desk. The boy had a long, horsey sort of face that I liked the look of, somehow. It had real personality, I thought.

I was about to make some flattering comment to this effect when I remembered just in time that his fine-looking son had gone west not so long before.

'Tell me about your experiences in France,' he said suddenly.

'Well,' I said nervously, 'I didn't really have many experiences – but there was this Madame Malfait, I remember, who –'

'I mean your war experiences, man.'

'Oh,' I said. 'Well ...'

He went on to explain that he had called me in because he liked to keep in touch with his men, to find out what the average pilot thought about the air war in general and the Flying Corps organization in particular. But he spent so much time telling me how anxious he was to hear what the average pilot had to say that I could hardly get a word in edgeways.

However, by persevering, I managed a brief account of my achievements before he changed the subject abruptly and asked if I enjoyed being an instructor.

That was an easy one. 'No, sir,' I said.

'Why not?'

'I don't think I'm cut out for it,' I said, thinking about the way the commandant at Gosport had taken to regarding me out of the corner of his eye.

He mulled over this reply for a good two minutes before fixing his heavily-lidded eyes on me again and asking what I thought of the C.A.S.

'Ah. C.A.S.,' I said, sinking deeper into the man-eating arm-chair and wondering what C.A.S. stood for. 'M'yes,' I said. 'I've given a good deal of thought to that, sir,' I said judiciously. Somebody's initials, was it? Or was he spelling out a rude word? 'You're on good terms with the C.A.S., I understand?' Chief of the Air Staff, that was it. The general I'd got on so well with at Gosport 'Oh, yes,' I said. 'We get on quite well, smaller of fact, sir.'

'He's been talking about you ever since he got back to the Ministry.'

'Has he? How nice.'

'Hardly stopped,' Lord Rackingham said, pinching his leather armchair spitefully. 'Got you in mind for some job, has he?'

'I wouldn't be surprised,' I said, crossing my legs complacently. In fact I *had* overheard the general saying something to the commandant about seeing what could be done about this fellow Bandy.

The minister was silent for a moment; then, eyeing me closely, said, 'I take it, Bandy, that you subscribe wholeheartedly to the etiquette that governs the services?'

'Etiquette, sir?'

'Protocol. Proper procedure. Going through channels, and so forth.'

He seemed to be encouraging me to confirm that I was a thoroughly right-minded officer, inflexibly orthodox in my opinions and in my conception of the military hierarchy, and I got ready to affirm this, in as loyal and sincere a manner as I could simulate.

But then I suddenly recollected some confidential tittle-tattle that Mr Lewis had passed on to me in an unguarded moment: that Lord Rackingham and his Chief of Air Staff were on such rotten terms that they had hardly spoken to each other since 1917.

It was a result, Mr Lewis said, of the minister's unconventional methods. As soon as he had taken up his appointment, Rackingham had started to seek out the views of some quite junior members of the Flying Corps, colonels and such, instead of relying on the services of his senior military and naval advisers.

Circumventing the proper channels was an approach Lord R. had become used to during his years with one of the country's great newspapers. It may have worked all right with his journalists, Lewis said, but apparently it wasn't going down at all well with the military.

The question was, could I depend on Mr Lewis' tittle-tattle? I had considerable respect for him as a person, but he was so wrapped up in his ferns that I wasn't at all sure his Whitehall-type gossip was entirely trustworthy. He had his ear to the ground, all right; but was it the right area of ground?

I decided to chance it 'I... wouldn't say that,' I said cautiously.

Lord R. started to pat his armchair affectionately.

'No, I wouldn't say I subscribe overmuch to service etiquette,' I said, injecting a ruggedly independent note into my voice but eying him warily, and preparing to beat a conventional retreat at the slightest sign of disapprobation.

He nodded. 'And what about the C.A.S.? You don't feel towards him any particular...? How shall I put it? What's the word?' he said, gesturing with his hands. Whatever the word was, it was in the shape of a medium-sized breadfruit.

'Not in the least, sir,' I said, by now not having the faintest idea what I was talking about. 'Not in the least.'

Lord R. grunted, and changed the subject, leaving me still uncertain as to whether I had earned his approval or otherwise.

A few minutes later we rejoined the others in the drawing room. It was a handsome, high-ceilinged place decorated in Regency style, with pearl-grey broadloom and several high windows covered with blue and gold curtains. On the opposite wall was a huge painting of a Noble Stag at Bay. ('Looks more like a Clydesdale horse,' Mrs Lewis whispered loudly, 'in rather tasteless disguise.')

Most of the guests were heaped up at the other end of the room near the green baize tables, squabbling over who was to sit with whom. As usual, Robert was standing aloof from the crowd.

'You seem very pally with our host,' he muttered – a bit jealously, I thought.

'Oh, you know,' I said, smiling in what I thought was a modest fashion. Only, my expression seemed to revolt Robert quite a bit. Even Katherine found it a bit hard to take, especially when I started to titter and tee-hee behind my hand.

I tried to explain that I was still savouring Auchinflint's reaction when he saw Lord R. patting me on the back a few minutes ago. The major had looked quite disturbed, as if he'd taken me for an inconsequential toad only to discover that I was really a handsome prince in disguise.

'If only Mother could see me now,' I said to Katherine, expanding my redoubtable chest 'How ashamed she'd be of all the times she told me I'd never amount to a row of beans.'

'Don't be so smug,' Katherine said. 'It makes you look like a Tibetan yak.'

However, I was proof against her insults. As she moved off with her brother I followed contentedly, avoiding the plump doctor with the sandy hair and the pipe who had been questioning me before dinner as to what Canada was like. He had looked quite disappointed to learn that my family had not once been attacked by Redskins.

In avoiding him, though, I came too close to a bleak-looking gentleman who was posing between a pair of busts on marble pedestals. (Plato and Socrates? Victoria and Albert?) He was pursing and unpursing his lips as if in disapproval of his own thoughts.

This was Claud's father. He had been introduced as the headmaster of Fallow, apparently a well-known public (i.e., private) school in Chester.

As I was squeezing past, he caught sight of my ribbons. He looked at them suspiciously with his small, sharp eyes and said abruptly, 'What did you say your name was?'

'Me, sir? Bandy, sir,' I piped.

'Ah,' the headmaster said. 'You're the one.' He pursed his lips a couple of times, started to move away, then turned back again. 'Ever spoken in public?' he asked sharply.

'Just the occasional word,' I said. ''By Jove, it's chilly' and 'Get a move on, you chaps' – things like that.'

'No,' he said crossly. 'I mean addressed people. A public gathering.'

'Well,' I said, 'I once stood in a mess. '

'Stood in a mess?' He looked uneasily at my boots.

'Squadron mess,' I said 'To make a speech.'

'Ah. Splendid.'

'It wasn't all that splendid,' I said, and started to explain that I'd been too squiffy to utter a syllable.

But he must have thought I was merely being modest, for he interrupted with, 'We often have officers along to address the school towards the end of term.'

'Oh, yes?'

'Old boys of Fallow who have distinguished themselves in the war.'

'Oh, good.'

'Unfortunately, war heroes are in rather short supply just now. So I thought that you... We were going to have a naval commander along this term, but he's let us down.'

'Who was that?' the doctor asked, joining us.

'Chivers-Jamm,' the headmaster said. 'Stood in front of a fifteen-inch gun. Got himself killed.' He looked me over carefully for symptoms of mortality. 'You're not likely to be... sent to the front, are you?'

'Not for a while yet,' I said uneasily.

'Would you be interested?'

'In going to the front?'

The headmaster's nostrils quivered a bit. 'In giving,' he said patiently, 'a short talk at *Fallow* at the end of *term*.'

'But I'm not an old Fallowite, sir,' I said, in my whining North American drawl.

The doctor winced. After a moment the headmaster said, 'I have just explained, Captain, that we've run out of heroes who were once *Fallovians*. We'd been discussing the possibility of putting you down for a speech.'

'That's very flattering, sir, very flattering. But –'

'It's quite an honour, you know,' the doctor said.

'Yes, I'm quite sure it is. But –'

'Well, we'll put you down, then,' the headmaster said, taking out a black book and making a note in it. Then he looked searchingly into my face for a moment before turning away and massaging his eyes. 'We can get in touch with you through Lewis, I expect,' he muttered.

I was a bit anxious for a while. However, a few minutes later I thought that sanity had prevailed when I overheard him asking Mr Lewis if he was quite sure that this fellow Bandy was a genuine hero. The headmaster said he didn't want a repetition of the last occasion, when an old Fallovian wearing a V.C. had turned out to be a megalomaniac wine waiter from a Lyons Corner House. He didn't want a repetition of that sort of thing, Lewis ought to understand. It put the school in an unfavourable light, and wasn't much of an inspiration for the boys either.

Naturally I assumed that Lewis, with his diplomatic training, would vouch for my authenticity, while at the same time subtly conveying the impression that no good was likely to come of any ceremony in which I was involved.

I forgot that, under his shy and hesitant exterior, Mr Lewis could be pretty malicious sometimes. In fact, now I come to think of it, it was probably he who put the headmaster up to it in the first place.

'I'm certainly not giving any speech at any school,' I mumbled, as I rejoined Katherine and her brother. 'I mean, what on earth could I tell them?'

Robert said, 'You could tell the boys how you got that wound in your behind. Bet that would interest them.'

A hefty woman in the uniform of the Army Auxiliary Corps turned and looked at Robert. She outranked him and looked as if she were ready to take advantage of the fact.

'Good morning,' Robert said to her. He always said good morning, regardless of the time of day. This had confused the infantry no end when he was in the trenches. Once he'd wished some sentries good morning when it was ten at night, and they had gone back to their dugout for a game of ludo, thinking it was after midnight and were off duty. As a result we'd lost the Battle of Arras.

'What's that about a wound?' the Army Woman said loudly. She had a patent-leather face and a bosom like an old bolster. She had been pawing Katherine rather a lot, I thought.

Katherine must have thought so too, for as the Army Woman came closer, Katherine moved away. Unfortunately this brought her into a conversation between the sandy doctor and Lady Rackingham. The doctor was busy telling Lady R. about a post-mortem he'd done recently on a subject so long deceased that he'd had to lay aside his knife in favour of a spoon.

As she listened to the doctor, Lady Rackingham started to wave her left hand around, palm downward, as if calling to the wood-wind section for *diminuendo*; or possibly she was feeling around for something to hold onto.

Robert caught Katherine's eye. Her face was scarlet. She turned away once more and tried to distract herself by listening intently to the Honourable Hyphenated and his wife, who were seated at adjoining tables. But that didn't help much either, for the young man, an assistant censor with Military Intelligence, had a habit of whinnying when he couldn't think of anything to say, while his wife, an unnecessarily healthy-looking girl, had no topic of conversation other than the acute shortages that were now preoccupying the civilians. 'Did you hear that marvellous poem the Minister of Agriculture wrote?' she called out.

> 'My Tuesdays are meatless;
> My Wednesdays are wheatless;
> I'm growing more eatless each day.
> My home is heatless;
> My bed it is sheetless –
> All are gone to the Y.M.C.A.'

'Isn't it beautiful? And so true, too!'

'I want to hear more about this wound,' the Army Woman said loudly. A terrible expression crept over her face, soon identified as coyness. 'I see you have two wound stripes, Captain,' she said looking at my sleeve.

'Yes, Ma'am.'

'Tell me about 'em,' she said, nudging Robert and sniggering girlishly.

'Well,' I said, 'they're little stripes about, oh, two or three inches in length, and they're usually worn on the –'

'No, no, I mean, where did you get them?'

'I got one at the front,' I began.

'And one at the back, I gather,' the Army Woman said, and started to chortle heartily.

Lady R. approached, looking a trifle fed up with her guests. They did seem rather a disorganized bunch, the way they were milling around the card tables, trampling on each other's feet. She had succeeded in getting only one game started so far and had had to wrench quite sharply at her husband's tail before she could even get him to sit down. He was now at a nearby table, listening sulkily to Mr Carlton, a civil servant.

'Come along, Katherine,' Lady R. said wearily, 'and you, too, Robert. Or it'll be too late to play at all.'

Katherine and Robert obediently took their places at the green baize.

Lady R. looked at me uncertainly. 'I'm afraid,' she began.

I'd already noticed there were going to be two spare bodies, so I said, 'I'll watch, if that's all right.'

She smiled, looking relieved. As she moved away I caught sight of Claud. He was standing in the doorway, clenching the sides of his short trousers as he peered in, perhaps hoping for an invitation to join the grownups.

For a moment I felt sorry for him, and when I caught his eye, gave him a friendly wink, to show there were no hard feelings. But the undersized swine merely treated me to a snotty, upper-class sort of look, obviously thinking I was trying to curry favour.

I was so annoyed I started to make a face at him, to expose my fangs and lower my eyebrows until they were resting neatly on either side of my nose; but then I hurriedly reassembled my features, in case anyone else was looking. People tended to recoil even from my normal expression.

Luckily only Claud was witness to this physiognomical lapse. He gazed back at me from the hall with an expression of the profoundest contempt, and turned away. And from that moment was born the feud that was to have some very upsetting consequences indeed.

As the only non-combatants, Mr Lewis and I chatted for a few minutes at the other end of the drawing room. As soon as we had run out of interesting things to say about ferns, we moved over to watch the play.

We found ourselves inexorably drawn to the battle going on at Lord Rackingham's table. He and the important-looking civil servant, Mr Carlton, were partnering the Army Woman and the Honourable Hyphenated's wife, respectively, and though the talk was necessary desultory because of the demands of the game, what there was of it was apparently of considerable significance.

Gosh, I thought to myself, who would have thought two years ago that the Reverend Mr Bandy's underestimated son would soon be hobnobbing with aristocrats, lordships, high Army officers, and the real rulers of the nation, the administrative civil servants? Who would ever have expected him to have the privilege to listen to their polished wit and banter, and the civilized cut and thrust of high political debate?

'Feedle, fidle, fodle, fum,' the civil servant was murmuring, looking contemplatively at his partner. 'I smell the blood of an English mum ... no bid.'

'H'm, rub-a-dub-dub, three men in a tub,' the Army Woman said. 'And what do you think they've ... Let me see, now ..., One spuh, spuh ... puh, puh, puh ... spade, I trow.'

'One spade, eh? One spadey-wadey, eh?' the Honourable Hyphenated's wife said brightly. 'One spadey-wadey is biddey-widdey, she trowey-woweys. Yessssss. Two hearts, one bids. Or does one mean one heart two bids, ha, ha, ha. No, two hearts, two hearts in springtime, as they say.'

'H'm,' Lord Rackingham said, looking irritably at the civil servant. 'Tricky ...'

Mr Lewis explained in whispers that Lord R. was referring to Curzon, the Lord Privy Seal in the coalition government, who had recently come out in favour of female suffrage.

'I see,' I whispered, wide-eyed.

The game proceeded. The Army Woman suddenly broke into a labial canter. 'Putt-putt, putt-putt, putt-putt, putt-putt,' she putted; then, with a highly significant look at Lord R. as he trumped her queen: '*Quite.*'

She meant, Lewis murmured, that it was not the first time Curzon had spurned a cherished principle for the sake of political expediency.

'Carlton?' The Honourable Hyphenated's wife said, looking fixedly at the civil servant. She meant that Lloyd George, though not finding Lord Curzon's talents particularly useful, nevertheless continued to employ him in his predominantly Liberal cabinet because he believed that Curzon still had the backing and support of the Carlton Club establishment; though, in fact (Lewis murmured), the Privy Seal's prestige and influence in that Conservative stronghold was highly debatable.

I nodded, twisting my lips about cynically.

Lord R. and his partner lost yet another game. As bidding began anew he growled angrily, 'Two clubs!' Evidently he meant that in spite of the P.M.'s most solemn promises that Churchill would never be admitted to the Coalition, Lloyd George had utterly damned his reputation by sending Churchill to the Admiralty.

'Mine, I think,' Mr Carlton said smoothly, retrieving a trick that Lord R. had just added to his own pile. Lewis looked at Carlton with a new respect, appreciating this subtle allusion to the apology Bonar Law had been forced to make to Churchill after he had lost his temper and castigated the Admiralty chief for his unwarranted interference in the conduct of the war at sea.

(Outside, the wind was cold against the cheek, the trees by the river stood stolidly against the slushy sky. Inside, Mr Carlton glanced knowingly at Lewis, and played another card. It was – the eight of diamonds.)

'Talking about Lord Curzon,' I said.

Everybody jumped, and the Army Woman dropped her propelling pencil.

'He visited us behind the lines once,' I said, chuckling and slavering slightly. 'He was watching some Tommies performing their ablutions in a beer vat. Which of course was filled with water. They'd just come out of the line, you see ...'

The entire bridge party had come to a dead stop by then. Everybody was sitting in a tense sort of way, staring in front of them with queer, fixed looks in their eyes.

'And Curzon,' I went on, 'said, "By Jove," he said, "I'd no idea that lower classes had such white skins".'

After that, the political discussion, or in fact any kind of discussion, lapsed for quite a while.

Spats

THE REST OF the evening passed off without further difficulty – until I reached my bedroom.

'Mrs Auchinflint likes you, though,' Katherine was saying as we climbed past a cracked Etruscan vase at the head of the main staircase.

'She does?'

'She said she was sure you had a future.'

'Well, I should hope so.'

'She wondered if you'd like to come hunting some weekend.'

'Hunting?'

'Yes. Auchinflint is our local M.F.H.'

'M.F.H.? Manager of – Feminine Hygiene?'

'No!' Katherine said, looking revolted. 'Master of Fox Hounds!'

As we reached the head of the staircase, I caught sight of Master Claud tiptoeing along the corridor in his flannel pyjamas. He hurried out of sight when he saw us.

'I don't know anything about fox hunting,' I mumbled.

'It's quite simple. You just gallop around, usually in the pouring rain, until it's time to go into hospital with pneumonia.'

'Sounds like Army manoeuvres.'

'All you have to remember is not to get in front of the hounds.'

'In case they tear you to bits?'

'In case you spoil the scent, darling. Major Auchinflint would shoot you in the back if you did that. He's very keen.'

'I shouldn't think he'd want me along.'

'I don't know. He seems to have suddenly got this utterly mad impression you're a person of influence.'

She paused as we reached my bedroom door. It was slightly ajar, though I was fairly sure I'd closed it before coming down to dinner.

'He'll put up with anyone if he thinks he might be able to give him a leg up some day,' she said, faltering as she gazed up at me with her lovely dark eyes.

I kissed her hand. I happened to be still holding it as I pushed the bedroom door gently. She drew back, wide-eyed.

'We shouldn't,' she whispered. 'Should we?'

'Shouldn't we what?' I asked, preoccupied.

She took back her hand. After a moment she said, 'Have you nothing better to do than stare up at the ceiling that way?'

I whispered, 'What does that look like up there?'

She frowned at the top of the door. 'It's just a bucket,' she said shortly.

'Yes, but what's the bucket doing on top of my door?'

'It's not doing anything. It's just standing there.'

We gazed up at it in silence.

'I expect,' she said at length, 'it's filled with vile, brackish water.' She sounded quite complacent about it.

'I expect so.'

'If you'd gone into your room you'd have got showered with it,' she said, patting her hair. 'Not to mention getting clonked on the head with the galvanized iron.'

'Luckily,' I said, 'I'd have let you go in first.'

'You're such a gentleman.'

'Breeding will out,' I smirked, taking a chair from the alcove behind us. I stood on it and gingerly brought down the bucket.

After that, I kissed Katherine good night and went to bed feeling very pleased with myself; though I didn't feel quite so smug next morning when the maid came in with a cup of tea and saw the brimming bucket beside my bed. She gave me rather an awed look.

I didn't have long to wait to get my own back, though. On my way down to breakfast next morning I met Lady Rackingham. We descended together, chatting vaguely but in a reasonably friendly way about the weather. She understood that it was pouring with rain outside. I agreed that it probably was. She also said her husband had enjoyed my story about Lord Curzon (after he had adjusted to the rather abrupt introduction of the topic). He detested Curzon, she said, and was always glad to listen to derogatory anecdotes about him.

As we were crossing the entrance hall, Claud came pelting along the corridor from the kitchen, shouting something over his shoulder at the cook, who was waddling after him tight-lipped, holding a bread saw.

Without thinking, I stuck out my foot. He went sprawling on the floor and lay there, gaping up at me, too surprised even to swear.

I snatched Lady R.'s arm – a presumptuous gesture, I know, but I was so agitated – and hurried with it to the nearest exit before Claud had a chance to fetch his rusty sword.

As we entered the breakfast room, where the Lewises and the headmaster were being served pease brose and marmalade (most of the other guests had had the foresight to leave the previous evening), I was trying to whistle nonchalantly; but the guilty thudding of my heart was modulating the sibilance so noticeably it sounded as if I were whistling in Morse.

Throughout breakfast, Lady R. kept glancing at me whenever she thought I wasn't looking. Reprovingly, I'm sure. She was quite right, of course. It had been a dastardly and unprovoked attack on an unsuspecting child, an action ill-befitting my role as an officer and gentleman.

Still, she must have forgiven me, because just after lunch, shortly before I was due to leave with the Lewises to catch the train back to Gosport, she heard me trying out a chord on the grand piano in the reception room. Confessing herself a keen music lover, she invited me to play for her.

Accordingly I sat down at the keyboard, and after shooting my cuffs and moving the piano stool back and forth the requisite number of times, I launched into a spirited rendition from my remarkably varied repertoire of patriotic tunes and classical masterpieces. But apparently Lady Rackingham wasn't in the mood for too much good music that day, for after listening for a while she got up and went for a walk in the rain.

Claud, however, came in to listen. He stood by the gleaming black piano, picking his nose and staring at me as, sacrificing precision to musical feeling, I pounded my way through some Schumann that happened to be on the rack – on the music rack, that is.

As I paused in the middle of a *fortissimo* passage to lick my thumb and turn a page, he said, 'Will you take me for a ride in your airplane sometime?'

'No,' I said. It wasn't allowed, anyway.

He listened some more to my playing, obviously impressed but determined not to show it. 'You're not much of a pianist, are you?' he said.

'You're not much of a practical joker, either.'

I tried to play on, but he stared at me so scornfully that the mistakes started to come thick and fast.

'Wasn't me who put that bucket on your door,' he muttered.

'How d'you happen to know about it then?' I asked, casting him a look of petty triumph.

'Well ... you tripped me up.'

'That was after. Anyway, you ruined my fingers.'

He listened to my performance for a few seconds. 'Yes,' he said. 'I can tell.'

I banged down the lid and got up. 'That bucket trick was pretty puerile, don't you think,' I said with restrained dignity.

'I'll think of something better next time.'

'You do, and I'll punch you on the earhole,' I said, just as his father came in.

Luckily Katherine broke the rather stony silence by peering in a few seconds later – cautiously, in case I was still playing. 'Time to go, Bart,' she called.

'Yes,' I said. 'You're right.'

The Lewises were giving me a lift to Paddington Station in their dented motorcar. As it had stopped raining by then, Lord R. was gracious enough to get out of bed to see us off. Lady R., of course, was already outside, wearing a large, damp hat pulled down over her ears.

Just as I was about to step into the car, Lord R. once again took me aside, this time to ask if I thought I was contributing effectively to the war effort at Gosport.

I looked at him suspiciously, wondering if he was thinking of posting me there and then to some ghastly theatre of war, like the Persian Gulf. Nevertheless I muttered that, no, I didn't think I was particularly cut out to be an instructor.

'What are you cut out to be?' he asked.

'A civilian,' I nearly answered. But he'd been so reasonable I just said, 'Oh, just a pilot, I guess.'

He grunted and nudged a rhododendron with his foot, dislodging a shower of water. He started to move away, but then turned and glared at me. 'I don't necessarily disapprove of a man who doesn't allow himself to be browbeaten,' he said, in a browbeating sort of way.

I was still trying to disentangle this as the car reached the front gate of Bland House. As it turned the corner I glanced back, half expecting to see him standing at the salute, or at least waving ta-ta; but he was merely balancing on one foot, moodily wringing out his saturated spats.

Had I known then what his plans were, I'd probably have flung myself from the shuddering Ford and rushed right back and begged him on bended patellas to send me instead to the nearest plague spot on Salisbury Plain. But, poor ignorant devil, I continued to chug blissfully into the future, quite unaware of the awful new significance he was to bring to the expression *War is Hell.*

End of Volume One of The Bandy Papers

Preview

Strangely horse-faced World War I flying ace Bart Bandy finds himself kicked upstairs – to everyone's appalled surprise – and made a Lieutenant-Colonel in the Royal Flying Corps.

But not for long. Persuaded to give a school speech on the many shortcomings of Field Marshal Haig, he finds Fortune's Wheel definitely on the turn and soon he is once more heading for the hell of the trenches – this time on a bicycle.

With the daredevil commander of the 13th Bicycle Brigade, Bob Craig, there follow a series of edge-of-the-seat adventures, always accompanied by what Craig later refers to fondly as "brilliant exchanges of utter nonsense".

The Bandy Papers, Volume Two

OUT NOW!

About The Bandy Papers

Donald Jack's blackly humorous Bandy Papers are classics of their kind. Opening with Bartholomew Bandy's life in Canada shortly before leaving for Europe and the First World War, the "memoirs" follow his adventures through the war as a flying ace and into the 1920s and 30s, with the last books carrying him into the Second World War. When not busy avoiding death, winning medals, or oscillating through ranks like a yo-yo, Bandy spends his time driving his superior officers into apoplectic fits.

The full series –

Three Cheers for Me

That's Me in the Middle

It's Me Again

Me Bandy, You Cissie

Me Too

This One's On Me

Me So Far

Hitler Versus Me

Stalin Versus Me

About the Author

Donald Lamont Jack was born in Radcliffe, England, on December 6, 1924. He attended Bury Grammar School in Lancashire, and later Marr College, Troon (from which he was briefly evicted after writing an injudicious letter to the editor).

From 1943 to 1947 he served in the Royal Air Force as an AC, or aircraftsman, working in radio communications. During his military service Jack was stationed in a variety of locales, though he concentrated on places beginning with the letter 'B': Belgium, Berlin, and Bahrain. After de-mobbing, he participated in amateur dramatics with The Ellis Players, and worked for several years in Britain, but he had by then grown weary of 'B'-countries and decided to move on to the 'C's. Thus, in 1951, Jack emigrated to Canada.

In 1962 he published his first novel, *Three Cheers for Me*, about fictional Canadian First World War air-ace Bartholomew Wolfe Bandy. *Three Cheers for Me* won the Leacock Medal for Humour in 1963, but additional volumes did not appear until a decade later when a revised version of the book was published, along with a second volume, *That's Me in the Middle*, which won Jack a second Leacock Medal in 1974. He received a third award in 1980 for *Me Bandy, You Cissie*.

On the strength of *Three Cheers for Me*, Donald Jack's original British publisher Heinemann considered him in 1963 to be "one of the few really major writers working in Canada today."

Jack returned to live in England in 1986, where he continued to work on additional volumes in the Bandy series. He died in 2003. His final novel, *Stalin vs. Me*, was first published posthumously in 2005.

Note from the Publisher

If you enjoyed this book, we are delighted to share also *Banner's Headline*, a short radio play by Donald Jack – in which Arthur Banner, a rocket scientist, gets passed over for promotion one too many times, and decides to resign to work on a project of his own . . .

To get your **free copy of *Banner's Headline***, as well as receive updates on further releases in the Bandy Papers series, sign up at http://farragobooks.com/bandy-papers-signup